HC
R

'Kath
Corn

'Like
is a th

'Auth
weavi
police
good

'Voice

'Brilli
Linda

'A fas
and s

'Fans
new c
believ

'Patric
morgu
marri
Independent

'Fox is stomach-churningly go

'[This] forensic thriller. . . has just the right balance of pathological detail and tight plotting. Think *ER* meets *CSI* . . . Gripping from its very first page, it carries you breathlessly through its deftly plotted twists and turns' *Vogue* (Australia)

'Forensically speaking, *Malicious Intent* is top-notch in its genre' *Sunday Telegraph* (Sydney)

'A finely crafted novel' *Sydney Morning Herald*

'Watch out Patricia Cornwell' *Gold Coast Bulletin*

'*Malicious Intent* is . . . much better than anything Cornwell has written lately, and much superior to anything Reichs has ever written. Fox may be a medical practitioner, but she knows how to write decent prose, create sympathetic characters and pace a thriller, and she keeps the reader turning the pages. It's all very unsettling and deeply satisfying' *Australian Book Review*

'If you're into grisly forensic detail, as in the gore-spattered novels of Patricia Cornwell and Kathy Reichs, you'll love this' *Saga*

'Highly recommended reading' *Daily Telegraph* (Australia)

'With a chill factor that is enhanced by the reality of recent scandals in the sporting world, this compelling page-turner puts a stunning new talent firmly on the thriller map' *Daily Record*

About the Author

Kathryn Fox is a medical practitioner with a special interest in forensic medicine. *Death Mask* is her fifth novel and her books have been translated into over a dozen languages.

Kathryn lives in Sydney and combines her passion for books and medicine by being the patron of a reading programme for remote and indigenous communities that promotes the links between literacy and health.

www.kathrynfox.com

Also by Kathryn Fox

Malicious Intent

Without Consent

Skin and Bone

Blood Born

kathryn
FOX
death
mask

HODDER

First published in Great Britain in 2011 by
Hodder & Stoughton
An Hachette UK company

First published in paperback in 2011

3

A CIP catalogue record for this title is available from the British Library.

ISBN 978 0 340 91908 8 (B format)
ISBN 978 1 444 70952 0 (A format)

Typeset in Plantin Light by Hewer Text UK Ltd, Edinburgh
Printed and bound in the UK by Clays Ltd, St Ives plc

Hodder & Stoughton policy is to use papers that are natural, renewable
and recyclable products and made from wood grown in sustainable
forests. The logging and manufacturing processes are expected to
conform to the environmental regulations of the country of origin.

Hodder & Stoughton Ltd
338 Euston Road
London NW1 3BH

www.hodder.co.uk

For Daniel, Sarah and Duncan, for being you

Acknowledgements

I'd like to thank a number of people who continue to believe in my passion. Cate Paterson, Louise Bourke, Isobel Akenhead, you are all champions. And to my wonderful agents, Fiona Inglis and Euan Thorneycroft, thanks for your integrity and faith.

My fantastic assistant Renee Lauer deserves a special mention. Thanks for your support, organisation and humour, even during the fifth rewrite!

PROLOGUE

Hannah spun around in her dress, still unable to believe this day had arrived. The ivory duchess satin felt luxurious against her skin. The strapless style seemed to widen her narrow shoulders and enhance her bust, particularly with the hand-sewn pearl detail. At the same time, the A-line skirt accentuated her waist and glossed over her hips. She'd never felt so attractive.

For once she wasn't self-conscious about her body. She looked womanly and was proud of it. Years of being teased about the size of her hips no longer mattered. They would bear the children she and Brett wanted so much.

Hannah looked in the mirror and checked her hair. Three hours at the hairdresser's; the highlights, hot curlers, the teasing and pulling, had been worth it. Wearing her hair up and off her face accentuated her cheekbones and lengthened her neck. The make-up was heavier than she was used to, but the beautician promised it would look natural in the photos.

She put her hand up to her face and caught the sparkle from her finger. The engagement ring she had worn so proudly for the last six months glistened in the mirror. The bright lights in the motel bathroom made it look blinding – well, almost.

There was a tap on the door.

'Hannah, the photographer's wanting a few more shots before we leave. Dad's meeting the car around the front. We don't have much time.'

She took a deep breath and opened the bathroom door. Her younger sister had tidied the room and thrown pink rose petals on the bed. The gesture brought tears to her eyes.

'Oh no you don't!' Dakota threatened. 'You look so beautiful. Don't go messing up your make-up now!'

The pair hugged tightly. Hannah felt like the luckiest woman in the world as her eighteen-year-old sister lifted the lace veil from the chair. The antique comb fitted snugly into the back of her bun.

'Now you look perfect. Brett will be so proud.'

A husky voice interrupted from the doorway.

'Remember, I got married at your age and it was the biggest mistake of my life.'

'So Dakota and I are mistakes? Thanks, Mum.' Hannah had hoped her mother would be happy for her, but that was too much to ask. The daughters had heard it all before and didn't need another lecture, especially not now.

The older woman stepped forward and straightened the gold and diamond cross Hannah wore around her neck. 'You girls are the best thing that ever happened to me. I just don't want you making the same mistakes. If you're having doubts or want to put it off for another couple of years, just say so. If that boy really loves you, he'll wait.'

'We already waited until the end of the football season so our friends could come.'

'You mean *his* friends. Your father was loyal like that, only to everyone but his family.'

Hannah was embarrassed that her mother would talk like this in front of the photographer. She hoped he was too busy snapping candid shots to listen.

Dakota handed her the bouquet and Hannah smiled for the camera. She glanced at the bed while the photographer worked away. A small part of her wondered if Brett would have waited much longer. Her purity pledge had strained their relationship, but he knew when they met how committed she was to her faith. Tonight they could make love for the first time, right here, only metres away from the beach they had camped on the night Brett proposed.

Her mother lifted the front section of veil over her face. 'Just remember, marriages can be made or ruined on the wedding night.'

'God, Mum, give it a rest. She's nervous enough without your doom and gloom. How about you go check on Dad?' Dakota saw their mother out before returning to collect her own bouquet. 'Don't worry, after another wine she'll be telling all the single women about the horrors of childbirth.'

Hannah laughed, but had to admit to being more than a little apprehensive about her first sexual experience. What if it hurt? What if there was blood? Suddenly it didn't seem so romantic. She felt the waves in her stomach tumble.

'Mum's talking complete rubbish,' Dakota winked. 'The secret is finding the right man. Which reminds me, I've got your present.'

She reached under the bed and removed a slim box tied with a satin ribbon. Inside was the softest silk camisole and panties, with a matching robe. Hannah felt her cheeks redden. She hadn't thought of lingerie; this was sexy but not too revealing. It was perfect.

'I've got a set just like it, and you should feel like a woman for your first time.'

Hannah locked eyes with her sister. 'Are you saying . . . ?'

A cheeky smile burst across Dakota's face. 'For months, and I can tell you it's worth waiting for.'

So that's what happened at university. Hannah was not shocked, but she was still surprised. The two of them were close, but there were many things she didn't know about her sister. She wondered if there was anything she didn't know about her husband-to-be.

3

'It's time,' Dakota almost whispered. 'After tonight, your life is never going to be the same again.'

Brett Dengate waited nervously on the sand. So far, so good. When Hannah's regular minister had cancelled first thing this morning with food poisoning, a mate from the footy club had come to the rescue and called in his uncle who was a celebrant. Uncle Lionel looked more like Uncle Fester, but there was no point upsetting the bride with details. Pity, Brett thought, that her bitch of a mother hadn't come down with poisoning too.

'Don't worry, son, the woman usually does turn up. I'm sure there's nothing to worry about.'

Brett's first instinct was to punch Uncle Lionel's face in, but he counted to ten and breathed. To be honest, he wasn't worried – until now. What if Hannah had second thoughts or, worse, what if she found out somehow? Loose lips, as they said. It only took one person to ruin everything. If anyone had let anything slip, he'd find out and sure as hell make them pay.

Hannah would make a loyal wife. She worshipped him and, unlike other women, she didn't ask too many questions. She understood he had obligations that didn't include her. She understood he was the boss. End of discussion.

His best man, Lurch, patted him on the back.

'Don't worry, it'll be over before you know it.'

Despite the cool change, Brett wiped the sweat from his hands on his cream linen trousers. The wind gusted. Women guests clutched at their skirts and the odd hat as dark clouds moved in overhead.

'Mate, you need to get this show on the road before it pisses down.' Lurch opened his jacket to reveal a hip flask. 'Want some Dutch courage?'

4

As tempting as it was, two morning beers were enough for the moment. 'Save it for later.'

'Everyone's looking forward to the reception, if you know what I mean.' He waved towards the road. 'The rest of the boys just arrived.'

Brett glanced up. The entire team was here, many with their wives and girlfriends. He thought back to everything they had gone through together. The best mates you could ever have.

From the first days at high school they had been like family, only better. You could always depend on them. When he broke a wrist during a game, his team mates finished the retaining wall for his boss so he still got paid. That's what mates did – they covered for you and watched your back. And you did the same for them.

The guests lined up and Uncle Lionel cleared his throat. Hannah's sister appeared over the sandhill first. Then he saw his bride escorted by her loser father.

Lurch leant closer. 'Mate, can you set me up with the sister? You never told me she was that well built.'

Brett had to admit Lurch was right. He could have gone for Dakota's looks, but she was wilder than Hannah. Dakota was girlfriend material all right, but he had chosen the sort a man could settle down with.

The harpist played the bridal waltz as the party approached. Errant drops threatened the arrival of the storm.

Hannah looked surprised at the celebrant, but didn't interrupt the ceremony to ask questions. The vows passed quickly and they only stuffed up a couple of lines.

'You may kiss the bride,' Uncle Lionel announced, and was followed by a crack of thunder. 'And then we all might head for shelter.'

The guests were already working their way to the resort's function centre as the couple's lips met. The photographer was stuffing around and missed it. Hannah wanted to do it again.

Someone volunteered an umbrella for shots the photographer thought would be atmospheric. More like bullshit, Brett thought. They fluffed around as the sky darkened, posing and repositioning hands, chins and dresses. All Brett could think of was how much he wanted to start celebrating inside with a drink – alcohol they were paying for. Hannah seemed more concerned about the umbrella being a lightning rod, and how her hair would be ruined.

His attempts to explain that, with the amount of gunk and pins in there, her hair would withstand a nuclear attack didn't help the situation. Lurch was ogling Dakota and made a remark about the weather helping her nipples come out to play, which Hannah overheard. For his trouble, he was on the receiving end of one of her ice-melting stares. Lurch didn't mean anything, it was just him paying Dakota a compliment. Besides, her nipples were pretty hard to miss, sticking out of that shiny gold dress.

Hannah's precise schedule for the day hadn't taken into account a storm. With droplets multiplying to a heavy downpour, they struggled to smile, pose and capture Hannah's fairytale image of married bliss. There was little time to mimic the photos she'd plucked from bridal magazines for the photographer's brief. A few more cracks of thunder and lightning out to sea had them rush for cover.

'They say rain on a wedding day is lucky. Then this couple must be very blessed,' Hannah's father declared as he announced Mr and Mrs Brett Dengate to the reception guests. The group of ninety applauded and whooped, all with glasses in hand.

'I'm not big on giving advice, not with my track record, but I will say one thing. Brett, if you ever hurt my little girl,

I'll bloody kill you.' The old man grinned through a missing tooth and raised his glass.

Everyone laughed, except Brett.

'Your make-up still looks good,' Dakota reassured Hannah. 'Don't worry about the photos. You can get some upstairs on the verandah at sunset, after the storm passes. They'll be perfect.'

Hannah kissed her sister's cheek. 'You're the best sister ever. Oh, and you might want to avoid Lurch. I don't like the way he was looking at you before, and he is kind of . . .'

'Sleazy? My slime detector went off the scale when I saw him. You don't have to worry, I can handle him.'

The groom approached with a glass of champagne for each of them but Hannah was too excited about seeing relatives and friends to drink it. Brett was pulled off in another direction by his mates and the pair didn't meet up again until the formal speeches. By that stage most of the buffet had disappeared and Hannah had forgotten to eat, more concerned that the guests were enjoying themselves. Brett seemed edgy and nervous by then, and she suspected his sugars were running low, although he did have a beer in his hand when it came time for him to speak.

'My wife and I want to thank you all for coming today. As many of you know, marriage is a tough sport and I'm rapt to have Hannah on my team. To my wife.' They all toasted the bride. He sat down again, but Hannah's reminder had him on his feet again. 'Oh yeah, and the bridesmaid looked pretty good too.'

The men cheered again, Lurch louder than anyone, and the women clapped. All except Hannah's mother, who polished off another glass of wine instead.

7

Hannah stood up. It wasn't traditional for the bride to make a speech, but Hannah had read that it was more common these days and she knew Brett wasn't one to say how he felt in public. 'I'd like to say something. I've always been the nerdy girl, unsporty and uncoordinated, who got teased for always having her head in a book. I thought all sportsmen were Neanderthals.'

Jeers and boos went out, along with some grunting noises. Hannah laughed and used both hands to quieten the response. 'That was, of course, before I met Brett. He accepts and loves me for who I am. I am so proud to be his wife. We are blessed to know and love you all. The support and loyalty you show is inspirational. Thank you all for coming, and have a wonderful night.'

'We love you too,' a drunken male voice called from the back. The crowd laughed.

The four hours passed in a blur and the weather turned to a balmy evening with a soothing sea breeze. The reception room emptied as many of the guests moved on. Hannah looked down at her dress, the hem muddied from the wet sand, and torn where someone had stood on it sometime after the speeches. It might as well have been the clock striking midnight on Cinderella's big night. She doubted the stains would come out, so dreams of passing it on to her unborn daughter disappeared. Gifts sat piled on a trestle table beside half-eaten cake. Her mother was asleep in a chair by the wall.

Dakota appeared by her side. 'Don't worry, I'll look after all this. A few garbage bags and some elbow grease, this place will be spotless in no time. And I'll make sure Mum gets to bed.'

Hannah was beyond feeling embarrassed by her mother. She thanked her sister again. 'Where's everyone going?'

'Some of Brett's mates are pretty tanked. They've been partying hard. I overheard one boasting how they have big plans later in one of the rooms. Just hope they don't keep us awake all night with the noise.'

Lurch appeared then with two glasses of wine in his hand. 'Here you are, ladies, a drink to say thanks for a great night.' He made a point of giving the one in his right hand to Dakota, despite her being closer to his left side. Hannah had never felt comfortable around Lurch, there was something about him that unnerved her. She felt guilty about thinking badly of him, today of all days, so she took the drink and the sisters toasted to wedded bliss.

Hannah's father came over to the girls to say his goodbyes.

'Don't worry about your mother, it won't be the first time I've put her to bed.' He seemed resigned. 'You have a good night,' he said, hugging them both. 'I couldn't be more proud.'

Brett came over and kissed his bride on the back of her neck. 'If you'll excuse us, we have some married business to attend to.' He lifted a startled Hannah, empty glass still in hand, and carried her out the glass doors, along the path and across the threshold of their suite door.

Brett opened a bottle of champagne and refilled his wife's glass while she locked the sliding door and closed the floral curtain. After a few sips she felt tired and struggled to stay awake. She must have underestimated the stress of organising the wedding day. She asked him for a diet cola from the bar, something with caffeine in it.

Brett ignored the request, unzipped the back of her dress and laid her face up on the bed. He kissed her cheeks and lips before lowering his mouth to her breasts. She tingled all over with the sensation, and the anticipation.

'We don't have much time,' he said, lowering himself on top of her.

Hannah felt him push between her legs then the force of him inside her. 'It's hurting,' she tried to say, but his mouth

9

was covering hers, his tongue sticking in and out as he thrusted. Suddenly he let out a moan and it was all over.

Brett rolled over, got up and kissed her forehead.

'Sleep well and you'll never know.'

His eyes ran all over her naked body. Her breasts looked smaller than they felt, but her skin was almost velvety against the white sheets. The tuft of hair was darker than the hair on her head. He felt himself aroused again and reached down to suck on her nipples. He'd waited so long. The sight of the clock by the bed stopped him. Shit! It was time and he'd be back soon enough.

He covered her bare flesh with the sheet and stroked her eyelids to make sure she wouldn't wake up.

He dressed and left via the sliding door. The wind gusted and buffeted the curtains in and out of the opening.

Hannah slipped deeper into unconsciousness . . .

I

'Your 10 am appointment rang to say they're running late trying to find somewhere to park,' the receptionist said through the intercom.

'Thanks.' Doctor Anya Crichton wasn't looking forward to this meeting but was trying to keep an open mind. Still, no wonder they were late – hospital parking was an oxymoron. Planners failed to consider that most people attending the sexual assault unit were not in a fit state to catch public transport, nor were they likely to be brought by ambulance.

She checked her watch and took the opportunity to glance over the file one more time.

Hannah Dengate, twenty-eight years old, had presented to her general practitioner in distress, three weeks after marrying her boyfriend of twelve months. Investigations and testing revealed two different sexually transmitted infections. Testing of the husband failed to detect either infection.

The GP had asked Anya to see the couple and attempt to determine how only one of the pair had become infected, after supposed monogamy. Anya's first reaction had been disbelief at the doctor's naïvety. Hannah had to have had sexual relations with another man or men. However, the GP knew the patient from church and believed that Hannah had not been unfaithful. Two gynaecologists had failed to share this view.

This sexual assault unit was set up to deal with forensic medicine, not infidelity, but Anya had given in to the pleas of the GP. She wasn't sure how the meeting would go; she just hoped it would be quick and straightforward. Faced with the evidence and two, possibly three expert opinions, Hannah would surely have to stop the charade and come clean.

When the couple finally arrived Anya greeted them in the foyer. Hannah extended one hand and held on to the arm of her husband with the other.

'Thank you so much for agreeing to see us, Doctor. We're really hoping you can help sort all this out.'

Slightly overweight, the woman was dressed in a plain shirt and tailored trousers. Her hair was pulled back off her make-up-free face into a tight bun, with slight darkening at the roots. It had probably been coloured for the wedding. On her feet were flat black ballet shoes, worn at the toes. This woman dressed for comfort, not to attract attention. She had an almost childlike innocence about her.

'This is my husband, Brett.'

The man wore jeans and a buttoned shirt with rolled-up sleeves; he stood with his hands in his pockets. The stale smell of tobacco leached from his clothes.

'Is this going to take long? We've already seen two special-ists who said the same thing.'

Hannah tightened the grip on his arm.

'Honey, we talked about this. Doctor Crichton might have seen something like this before, in her . . . particular field. I've been praying she can help us.'

The front door opened and one of the counsellors entered. Anya didn't want to have this discussion in a public area.

'Please come through. We can chat in private.'

The three walked along the corridor into a room with a double lounge facing two armchairs. In the middle was a coffee table, with a box of tissues in easy reach. The pair sat together, Hannah more forward, knees together, still clinging to her husband.

Anya sat opposite with the folder on her lap. She decided to start with something safe, like the woman's medical history.

'I see that your past health has been good. Have you had any operations?'

Hannah exhaled. 'No, I've rarely seen a doctor apart from the usual childhood coughs and colds. I've never had a filling, and I don't have wisdom teeth either. The dentist X-rayed me and apparently they're not even there.'

Brett squeezed her hand and she stopped speaking.

Anya smiled sympathetically. 'Any family history of medical problems?'

'Not that we know of.'

'Can I ask when you had your last pap smear?'

The infections could have been old and flared due to stress. A previous gynaecological exam may have picked something up.

Hannah flicked a glance at her husband. 'I was told I didn't need one.'

Anya raised her eyebrows.

'I was told I should have one a year after we had sex. We took a vow of purity and didn't have sex until our wedding night, six weeks ago now.'

'What about before you pledged purity?'

Hannah touched the crucifix around her neck. 'I've always wanted to save myself for the man I married. That probably sounds old-fashioned, but my parents divorced and I wanted to make sure that didn't happen to me.'

Brett began to shift in his seat. 'I had girlfriends, and got around a bit . . . you know . . . before we got together.'

Anya was beginning to wonder whether Hannah was a great liar or in total denial that she had been unfaithful. Something made her uncomfortable about the whole story. Two sexually transmitted infections within weeks of getting married, with no previous sexual contact?

13

Brett could have carried the infections from previous partners, but he had tested negative on two separate occasions.

One option was that Hannah had been assaulted and not told anyone. Anya needed to speak with her alone.

Brett didn't hesitate when she suggested he go for a cigarette whilst she talked to Hannah by herself.

'Please help me,' Hannah implored, tears rolling down her face. 'I'm going mad trying to understand how this happened. Brett's been amazing and says he knows I wouldn't have slept with anyone else. Did I get it from a public toilet seat? At someone else's house? On a bus? What other explanation could there be?'

This woman was pretty convincing. And there was little point sustaining an act without her husband present. Anya leant forward in her seat.

'What you tell me now is completely confidential. Nothing you say will go further than this room. Not to your GP, Brett, family. Anyone.'

'I just don't understand.' The tears flowed faster. 'This whole thing has been a nightmare. I haven't done anything wrong.'

'I'm not suggesting you have.' Anya locked her gaze. Figures showed that up to one in three women had been sexually assaulted but most incidents went unreported. The question had to be asked. 'Did someone have sex with you without your permission?'

The woman wiped her eyes with a tissue. 'You mean like rape? No! I'd think I'd know if that had happened.'

'Not necessarily,' Anya offered. There was a chance she could have been drugged and not remembered an assault. 'Did you have a hen's night, for example? Out somewhere?'

'Just dinner with my sister and a few girlfriends at a local pizza place. And no one got drunk, if that's what you're thinking.'

'Have there been any times in the last couple of months when something could have happened? Someone who gave you a drink? Maybe being unable to remember aspects of the night before, even though you hadn't drunk much?'

Hannah stared at the carpet, rolling the tissue in her hand. 'I went to the gym every day before the wedding. I lost sixteen kilos to get into my dress. We paid for everything; we didn't go out for about six months so we could save the money. Brett went down to the pub with his friends some nights, but I stayed home. I'm the one who budgets anyway – Brett would spend everything he earns if I left it to him.'

'What about work functions?'

'I don't mix much with people from the office. Most of them think a good night means getting blind drunk and sleeping with someone they'll never see again.'

Anya could appreciate why Hannah might prefer to stay at home.

'Tell me about your wedding.'

Hannah leant back in the lounge and her shoulders relaxed. 'It was everything I ever dreamt it would be, if you don't count the rain. My bouquet had deep purple irises and Brett looked so handsome. The only downside was that we didn't have time to eat much, by the time we'd got around to everyone and made sure they were all having a good time.'

'Did you at least get to have a glass of champagne?' Anya remembered her own, less than formal wedding, without family or friends present.

'Come to think of it, I did have one glass of wine at the reception, but because I hadn't eaten, it went right to my head.'

Anya glanced at the door. Brett wouldn't be much longer.

'What happened then?'

'I don't remember much, to be honest. I started out nervous, but Brett undressed me. I know we made love because the next morning there was blood on the sheets and I was sore,' she lowered her voice, 'down there.'

The comment alarmed Anya.

'Do you remember making love?'

'Brett told me I fell asleep with exhaustion from all the dieting and stress. But I feel a bit silly – what sort of bride can't remember her wedding night?'

Anya wondered the same thing. Tears refilled Hannah's eyes.

'We had breakfast in bed, and he didn't even try to make love again. I must have been disappointing. My mother always said that a marriage is made or ruined on the wedding night. Maybe that's why my mind blanked it out.' Her voice trailed off. 'But once Brett commits himself to something, there's no going back.'

It seemed an odd statement for a new bride to make.

'What else is Brett committed to?'

'The local football club. He's been playing with them since high school, and the team are all really close. I didn't understand it at first, but they have a real sense of belonging and he's never missed a practice or a game. Women get used to that closeness with girlfriends or sisters, but it's important for men to have it too.'

'What about the honeymoon. Noumea, wasn't it?'

'We were inseparable, and Brett wanted to make up for lost time. That's why I thought I'd become so sore again.'

Anya still believed Hannah. Nothing in her mannerisms or voice suggested she was lying at any stage of her story.

There was a rap on the door and Brett appeared. 'Are you OK in here? I was beginning to worry.'

'I'm fine,' Hannah answered. 'Doctor Crichton's exploring possibilities.'

'Is that so?' Brett answered, barely entering the room. 'Haven't got too much time on the meter, how much longer do you think you'll be?'

He transferred his weight from one foot to the other. It was evident he didn't want to be there and was keen to leave as soon as possible. For such an understanding and forgiving man, he seemed surprisingly anxious.

'I hoped we could have a quick chat,' Anya said. 'Is that all right with you, Hannah? There's a water cooler outside, if you'd like to help yourself.'

Hannah stood up, but her husband hesitated and checked his watch. 'I guess I can stay a few minutes, but I'm not the one who gave her the infections.'

'This situation must be pretty difficult for you,' Anya began when Hannah had left the room and Brett was sitting down again.

He shrugged his shoulders and looked distractedly towards the window. 'Hospitals creep me out.'

Anya watched him for a moment longer before speaking. 'Do you think Hannah is lying?'

'No way, she blames herself for things she didn't even do.'

'What happened on the wedding night?'

His eyes flicked back. 'What did she say about it?'

The hairs on the back of Anya's neck stood up. 'She told me she had a drink at the reception, went back to the room with you but she couldn't remember much after that.'

His jaw tensed and he wiped his mouth with his hand. 'Look, she's a one-pot screamer, always has been. With all that starving herself, it just went to her head quicker than usual. She looked pretty good, by the way; you should have seen her in the dress and veil.'

Anya decided to ask about his memory. 'Are you absolutely positive that was all she had to drink? Sometimes in the excitement it's possible to drink more than you realise.'

He twisted his mouth as if straining to remember. 'No, the hotel gave us a bottle of champers but she didn't like it.'

Anya felt uneasy. That night – the wedding night – was the only time Hannah couldn't remember. For someone who had waited so long to make love to her husband, one drink shouldn't have been enough for her to lose her memory. Yet Brett seemed to remember all about that night.

'What happened then?'

'After we had sex, she fell into a deep sleep. Guess it had been pretty stressful organising the wedding and all that. I went out on the motel verandah, off our room, drank some beer, had a few smokes and turned in. She hadn't even moved on the bed.'

Anya noted that Brett hadn't once raised the possibility that his wife had been unfaithful.

'Does Hannah use any recreational drugs?'

He laughed. 'No way. She's way too straight for that.'

That ruled out another reason for the amnesia. Anya tried another tack. 'Do you?'

He looked defiant.

'You wanna do a drug test on me now?'

Anya persisted with the questions. 'Did anyone visit your room after the reception?'

He ran his hand across his mouth again. 'What do you mean, anyone else? I just told you it was our wedding night, for chrissakes.' Tiny beads of perspiration appeared on his forehead.

Anya pushed further. 'Maybe someone wanted to wish you both luck for the honeymoon? It's not uncommon.'

He nodded. 'Now you mention it, some blokes from the footy team dropped by to give us their present, but then they left again when they saw Hannah was asleep.'

The hairs on the back of Anya's neck stiffened again.

'Brett, I'm sure you want to get to the bottom of this as much as Hannah does.'

He nodded slowly.

'Hannah has no memory of the wedding night. A spiked drink would explain that. If someone did add a drug to her glass that night, we can test a sample of her hair, and even pinpoint the period of time in which that substance was ingested. If you didn't give her the infections, someone else did. I think you know more than you're telling, and I'm wondering if the police need to be involved.'

'You're fucking kidding, right? You can't call the police!'

The colour drained from his face and he slumped back into the lounge.

Anya waited, silence closing in like a vice.

Brett Dengate's eyes darted from the door to the window as if seeking an escape route. A few moments later he buried his face in his hands.

'Shit! None of this was ever meant to happen. They were supposed to use condoms.'

2

'You can't repeat any of this 'cause of doctor confidentiality.' Brett Dengate chewed on a fingernail. 'I know my rights.'

Anya could barely believe what she was hearing. Brett Dengate had been a member of the local football team for over ten years and felt his mates were like family. They trained together, socialised, raised money for local charities. Only problem was, these men also shared the things they should have held most dear – their partners. It seemed 'the boys' had an initiation ritual whenever one got a new girlfriend.

The first time had been five or six years earlier.

'Lurch, he's like a brother, he got me out of a speeding fine that would have cost me my licence. He's that good a mate.'

One that would lie in court, or on a statutory declaration, Anya thought. Obviously laws were things to be bent or broken.

'And I guess you'd do the same for him.'

Brett paused but either missed the point of the comment or chose to ignore it.

'Anyway, after we won the grand final – it was our fourth time – we went back to his place for a boys' night. He had a couple of kegs, heaps of food and it was a great night. His new girlfriend turned up and drank and danced with some of us. We'd all had a few and were celebrating when Lurch disappeared into the bedroom with . . .'

21

He struggled to recall the woman's name.

'A few minutes later, the bedroom door's open and she's lying on the bed naked, and they're going for it. He saw me and waved me to come in. It was pretty obvious she was up for it, so I had sex with her too.'

Anya wondered what 'obvious' meant. 'Did she ask you to have sex with her?'

'Well, not in so many words, but I could tell she was into me watching. So when Lurch moved off and I climbed on, she didn't exactly refuse. After that, the other boys took turns.'

Anya could imagine the scene: alcohol, testosterone and one woman. It was possible that the woman was too intimidated or drunk to refuse the string of men. Inability to refuse sex never equalled consent. She made a mental note to check back on reports of assaults by groups of men against women in the region.

'Did you see her again?'

He shook his head. 'He moved on to someone else pretty quickly. Women go mad for our Lurch. And you've got to understand, I hadn't even met Hannah back then.'

'So after that, how many times would you all have . . . shared girlfriends?' She tried to remain impartial.

'Only eight or nine times. We all started to settle down.'

He talked as if it were a harmless adolescent phase.

'Did those other women all consent to having sex with the team?'

'Yeah, although a couple needed something to loosen them up.'

Brett spoke as if this were the most natural thing in the world. As perfunctory as eating breakfast or driving a car. Anya felt her jaw tighten.

'What loosened them up?'

'I had some Roeze from when I did my back in a game.'

'You mean Rohypnol?' The benzodiazepine was used in date-rape, with an amnesic effect. It was commonly used for sedation in medical procedures like colonoscopies, where patients could still be compliant with instructions but later have no memory of the procedure. She didn't expect to find many reports of assaults, if the women couldn't actually remember what had happened to them.

'Sure, they relax your muscles and make you chill. Hey, partner swapping isn't against the law.'

He was right. But partner swapping was not what he and his friends had done.

'It's called bunning and everybody does it.' Brett hastened to explain that they only ever 'initiated' each woman once. He vacillated between bravado and qualifying his actions.

Anya took a deep breath. 'Bunning' was a term bandied by elite athletes who participated in group sex. Except in these groups, there was only ever one woman.

She had no idea how to break the news to the poor woman outside; her world was about to be completely shattered. First, Anya needed to establish the facts. Hannah deserved the truth, but needed as much information as possible if she chose to make a police statement.

'What happened after you met Hannah?'

'Well,' he blew out through his mouth, 'she wanted to save herself for marriage, but men have needs, you know.'

'What happened when it was Hannah's turn for the initiation?'

'I copped a lot of shit for that. She doesn't drink much, and because of her purity pledge she was never going to be up for it on her own. Lurch kept telling me we were still a team. Hell, I knew that, we came runners-up the week before the wedding. It's why we waited till the season was over to get married.' He sat forward. 'Listen, Hannah knew the deal

23

and never complained. It's who I am in that team, and she knew that when we started going out.'

Anya had to remind herself that this was club sport – no salary, no sponsorships, no written contracts – and yet Brett spoke as if his life revolved around the game.

'Lurch came up to me before the wedding and said it was payback. We'd all scratched each other's backs and now it was my turn.

'I told him she wasn't like that and wouldn't agree to sleeping with the team. Only he said I'd slammed the ham with everyone else's women, so I owed them. He had a point.' He wiped the end of his nose with the back of his hand. 'Lurch was right. It was my turn.'

Anya took a couple of slow breaths, trying not to show how angry she was.

Brett explained that once the team had shared the spoils, they could all get on with their lives. He really loved Hannah, he said, and this was only a few hours, and she never even had to find out.

Anya listened to this man justify his actions, bile rising in her gullet. This was someone who had not only betrayed his wife, but subjected her to gang-rape on what was the night of her first sexual experience. He had also risked her contracting a life-threatening infection and becoming infertile. All for his football mates.

Face in his hands, he said, 'If the boys had worn condoms, none of this would have happened.' He looked up at Anya. 'What you do is tell Hannah she probably got the infections from a toilet seat, like on the plane. She doesn't need to know any different.'

Anya put her pen down. 'You're telling me to lie to your wife?' He stood up, car keys in hand. 'It's the best thing for her. The way I see it, telling her what happened will ruin her life. Why do that to her? Her infections are now clear and she doesn't remember anything. Why put her through this?'

Anya felt a rash forming below her neck and continued to try to contain her anger. 'Hannah came here because she wants – and deserves – the truth.'

'I think I know better than you what my wife wants. Besides, you can't say anything I don't want you to. Everything I said is confidential. You say one word to her and I'll sue you for everything you've got.'

Anya swallowed hard. 'I'm afraid that in some situations, where others are likely to come to harm, I'm legally bound to notify the authorities.'

He jabbed a finger in her direction. 'That's bullshit! I know my rights.'

The thing he hadn't considered was that other people had rights as well.

'The infections passed on to Hannah are what we call notifiable diseases. The information has to be forwarded to the health authorities. In fact, the pathology lab may have already passed on the results of Hannah's tests. What that means is that it's a legal obligation for doctors not only to notify but also to begin contact tracing, with or without your cooperation. We'd begin by asking Hannah for the names of the other players, which would be otherwise easily located in club records. It's then my job to phone every member of the team and warn them that they may have come into contact with these infections. It also means alerting their partners to the possibility they had been exposed to sexually acquired infections and the possible complications.'

Perspiration returned to Brett's face, this time above his top lip and forehead.

'Jesus, the shit will really hit the fan. Some of the blokes are married with kids.'

Anya chose to leave the room before she said something unprofessional and provided him with an opportunity to play victim in court. The possibility of police involvement was, of course, entirely up to Hannah.

She was sitting outside, flicking through an old magazine. Anya asked her into another room and offered her a coffee while she popped out to check some results. Mary Singer was in a nearby office. As one of the most experienced rape counsellors in the unit she was Anya's preferred choice to become involved with Hannah's case.

Anya tried to explain the situation as succinctly as possible. 'I've just found out from the husband that his wife was drugged and assaulted on her wedding night by him and a group of his friends.'

Mary's eyes widened over her half-glasses. 'I thought I'd been around long enough to hear everything.' She quickly downed the dregs of her own coffee. 'I'm guessing the bride doesn't know yet.'

'Nope,' said Anya, 'and I need your help to tell her, and to make sure things don't turn nasty with the husband.'

Anya made a piping hot cup for Hannah and took it in while Mary retrieved Brett Dengate.

3

Photographers and reporters hounded Anya and Hannah outside the court. Dakota tried in vain to protect her sister.

'We hear there was a settlement. Can you tell us how much you were paid?'

'Did your husband and the other men admit to raping you?'

'Why did you take a settlement? Did you think you were going to lose?'

'Can you tell us why you chose to sue for damages? The public deserves to know.'

'How do you feel now the trial's called off?'

'Why aren't you giving interviews? What do you have to hide?'

Hannah clutched Anya's hand and tried to escape all the attention. The large sunglasses did little to disguise her distress. Even so, Hannah had come a long way in the year since Anya had first met her. She had moved to the inner city, changed her surname and job, and bought a small apartment, which she was busy decorating. The decision to sue her husband and his friends for damages caused by sexually transmitted infections and the emotional stress they had caused had not been easy. Without physical evidence or a corroborating witness, no criminal charges could be laid. Instead, Hannah had wanted her former husband and his friends to answer for their crimes, albeit in a civil court.

It was the only way she could make any of them face up to what they had done. She wanted them to know the damage they had caused, and warn other women about their rapist behaviour. The case was sure to set a legal precedent and attract extraordinary media attention.

'Who'd rape you, you fat ugly bitch?' a male voice rasped from the crowd.

'You filthy slut! You seduced my husband then cried rape.' Anya turned to see the speaker this time, as something hard hit the side of Hannah's head. Hannah dropped to the ground, as if a bomb had gone off. Dakota shrieked.

Momentarily stunned, Anya looked at her jacket to see egg dripping from her cheek.

A dark-haired man in a sports jacket moved in front of them, shielding them all from further hits.

Mary Singer pushed through. 'We need the police. She's been assaulted.'

The cameras moved in even closer to record the incident and aftermath.

The man in the jacket was already phoning for assistance and copped an egg on his forehead for his trouble.

Realising the projectiles were harmless, Anya pulled Hannah to her feet. Mary and Detective Inspector Hayden Richards, head of the sexual assault unit, herded the three women towards an unmarked police car. Anya looked for the man who had tried to protect them, but he had disappeared into the crowd.

'Get your fucking hands off me,' a woman yelled behind the pack. Some of the cameras gave chase as uniformed police pushed her to the ground.

With the four women in the car, the detective screeched into the traffic, ensuring they weren't being followed before heading for a nearby suburb. He parked off a side-street, near a café. There was little chance of being harassed at the Green Fiddler, a popular spot for police at any time.

Anya removed her jacket and went to the bathroom, with Hannah and Dakota close behind. The two women dabbed at their stained clothes with paper towels and cold water. It was Anya's new jacket and it was supposed to last her for years.

'What just happened?' Hannah was still shaking. 'I didn't do anything wrong, but it's as though what Brett and his friends did to me is still all my fault.'

'Still?' Anya looked her in the eye. 'It was never your fault.' She sighed. 'To the media, this is another headlining story, and judging by the response on talkback radio, it's dividing more than your local town. Unfortunately the whole press machine thrives on anything involving sex, sportsmen and scandal.'

'You shouldn't have to defend yourself. You were the one who was drugged and gang-raped.' Dakota had clearly been deeply affected by her sister's ordeal and the subsequent legal proceedings.

Anya grabbed some more paper towels and dabbed her jacket again. 'Court cases, even civil ones, are rarely about justice. They're more about winning at any cost. Brett could have faced criminal charges if he admitted to what he did under oath. So he did everything possible to discredit you by saying you were unstable and seeing a counsellor. The last thing he wanted was to have a jury decide. That's why his lawyer chose to fight it out in the media, and get free advertising for himself in the process. It's the old adage, "The best form of defence is attack." '

'So I'm violated by my husband and his mates, then publicly called crazy because I needed professional help dealing with it? No amount of money will make up for that.' Hannah hurled her wad of wet towelling at the wall. 'It's just wrong.'

Anya couldn't argue. She moved to the wall and collected the wet towels, depositing them in the bin. She touched

Hannah on the arm and said gently, 'Look, I know it's been really hard on you but you've stood up against those men and let everyone know what they did to you. That has to count for something, doesn't it?'

Hannah washed her face with cold water while Anya picked up her jacket. 'Take your time, we'll see you outside when you're ready.'

Hayden Richards had already ordered the coffees.

'How's she doing?' Mary asked.

Anya rubbed her eyes with one hand. 'She needs a few minutes. Dakota too.'

Mary pushed back her chair. 'I'll go talk to her.'

Anya was relieved for the emotional break. This case had affected her more than she'd anticipated. It was the betrayal of trust that was so difficult to take, and the fact that Brett Dengate had stolen Hannah's innocence and optimism. Hannah had been wise to settle the matter before it got to court. Publicity had ensured the men were identified and any potential victims warned off. It was the best outcome under the sad circumstances.

Hayden poured some sugar into his cappuccino.

'I thought you'd given up.'

He grinned, some froth lingering in his moustache. 'GP now thinks I've lost too much weight. Wish he'd make up his mind.'

The detective looked pale, a stark contrast to the man who had been morbidly obese and perpetually ruddy-faced less than a year ago. Inflammatory bowel disease was obviously still taking its toll, not that Hayden would ever discuss it.

'You've got . . .' She waved a finger near his moustache, which he wiped with a serviette.

He lowered his voice. 'How are you doing?'

'Oh, fine. I think Hannah's decision to settle will help her to move forward. She's come so far already, I know she'll be fine.'

'Any chance of you taking a break?'

Anya appreciated the detective's concern. 'We're presenting that study we talked about to a senate committee in the morning. Believe it or not, the Federal Health Department wants me to work on a programme for the sports industry in order to teach male team players that women aren't sexual objects for vilification and humiliation. It could take months – that should keep me off the streets for a while.'

'Good luck with that,' Hayden said, touching her wrist. 'That culture's ingrained in team sports, has been for as long as I can remember.'

'Glad you're so supportive because I recommended you for the education programme.'

His mouth turned downward.

Hers did the opposite.

'Your years of experience in homicide and sexual assault are exactly what we need. I heard from one of the committee that you played state level rugby league.'

'Yeah, well, most of my old team mates are now crippled with knee damage and some are unemployable. A labourer isn't much good if he can't bend his knees.' He waved to a waiter. 'A turkey and cranberry sauce wrap with a plate of potato wedges, thanks. What about you, Anya?'

She shook her head. 'I'm fine for now.'

Just then Hannah, Dakota and Mary returned from the bathroom. Hannah looked brighter, but Anya could see the strain around her eyes.

'OK, I need an opinion,' Hannah announced. 'For curtains.' She pulled out two swatches of fabric. One was pale pink with pastel checks, the other mauve with lilac and turquoise flowers.

Just then her phone vibrated and she tentatively glanced at the screen. 'I need to change my number again. It's a text. From Brett.' She put the phone down and Dakota picked it up and said, 'If he's making threats, the police need to know.' After a few moments' silence, Dakota read out the text.

'He says he forgives you and wants you back.'

Hayden wiped his mouth again. 'I'll be happy to help the cause, Anya, however I can.'

Anya checked her watch. 'I'll let the health department people know. I'm sorry to leave you, but I have a plane to catch.'

Hannah stood and hugged Anya tightly. 'Thank you, Anya. Without you, I never would have found out and I'd still be with Brett and his friends.'

Anya placed her hands on the back of the woman's shoulders, unsure what to say. 'I was only doing my job. Without you, I wouldn't have begun researching the culture of men's sports and the government wouldn't be taking steps to address it.' Hannah broke away. 'And for what it's worth, I'd go with the floral material. It's fresh and the flowers are perennials.'

A nya wanted to be sick. This was even worse than testify-ing in court, more like oral exams at medical school. The equivalent of six examiners – the senate committee – were about to tear her down and humiliate her, only this would be far more public. The television crews confirmed that.

The paper she and Professor Nigel Everett had co-authored was still receiving international attention. Thanks to publica-tion in the *International Journal of Forensic Science*, psychology and sports magazines had run stories, along with newspa-pers all over the world. The US media had highlighted a number of alleged cases of gang-rape in elite sports teams, using sex, celebrities, money and scandal to sell stories and referring to the study for authority. It was not the response she had anticipated after questioning sports team culture since meeting Hannah.

The investigation into a code of conduct in sport wanted Anya to present her study results. Professor Everett had flown to Australia from his retirement villa in Florida to appear, but only on the condition that he then go fly-fishing with his friend, forensic pathologist Doctor Peter Latham, who was also Anya's mentor.

'Beautiful morning,' Nigel said, clapping his gloved hands together. He seemed pleased to be here, despite the cold – hardly Florida weather. The temperature was yet to hit two degrees Celsius in Canberra, despite the cloudless sky. Anya shared neither the professor's enthusiasm for the weather, nor his apparent delight at the attention of the television cameras set up to greet them outside Parliament House.

She slipped inside the glass doors and left Nigel to conduct a doorstep interview; he was an old hand at media grabs. Profiling some of America's most notorious killers had led to regular appearances in the news and interviews.

Anya had first met Nigel when she was a pathology registrar, and immediately understood the friendship between her then boss, Peter, and the flamboyant professor. Where Peter was serious and methodical, Nigel was witty and often went with his gut instinct. The yin and yang friendship had lasted for decades.

Anya had Peter to thank for the study in the first place. After seeing Hannah, and noticing there was an increase in the numbers of women attending sexual assault units who had been assaulted by groups of men belonging to sporting teams, Anya had decided to survey a number of professional male sports players and teams to establish their attitudes to sexual assault. Peter had discussed the idea with his old friend, and Professor Everett had been kind enough to co-author the study. His name had attracted government funding for their work and, subsequently, international attention.

Today he was wearing his favourite floral bow tie and a green jacket, and he had trimmed his short grey beard for the occasion. At five foot three, with a walking stick and an impish grin, he was the closest thing to a leprechaun Anya had seen.

Anya straightened her suit skirt and waited for her colleague. A committee member she did not recognise approached.

'Thanks for coming, Doctor Crichton. We're all looking forward to hearing what you have to say.'

She suspected the media attention made the politicians more responsive to the study's findings than they otherwise would have been. Rumour had it not all the committee members were pleased with the media attention.

Nigel gave her a self-satisfied grin as he came through the door. 'Gave them a three-second and a ten-second grab. Keep the message simple and they'll run with it every time.' He squeezed her hand and whispered, 'Just relax and don't forget to breathe, in *and* out. Remember, no one knows more about your work than you.' He offered Anya his arm. 'Shall we?'

They headed through security and into a room with tables set up in a U-shape facing two seats behind microphones. A stenographer sat to the side, and camera crews had already set up to record the proceedings. Most committees came and went without the public knowing, but this one had become more of an issue after a former star footballer had been named in a group sex incident. Despite pleas by the woman concerned and the game's administrators, he refused to implicate any of the others involved, maintaining the code of silence.

Public outcry had coincided with the release of the study and the senate investigation into sexual misconduct in sport. So far, social commentators, sports executives and coaches had appeared before the six-member committee.

They took their seats in front of the two female and four male senators. The chair, Senator Woodrow, spoke first.

'I would like to thank Professor Everett and Doctor Crichton, who have attended today at their own, considerable expense.'

The chair continued. 'We have all received and read your submission and are particularly interested in the results of your study. I, for one, am disturbed and alarmed by your findings. Would you care to describe how you came to your conclusions?'

Anya deferred to Nigel, who remained silent, his head down. For a moment she wondered if he had dozed off. Clearing her throat, she began.

'We showed a number of dramatised scenarios to five hundred professional male players coming from a number of sports including swimming, rugby union, rugby league, soccer, Australian Rules and tennis. We then presented the same scenarios to five hundred first year university students and compared the responses.'

A woman appeared from the side and pushed the microphone closer to Anya's mouth. The committee members flicked through the pages in front of them.

'To clarify,' the chair added, 'what did you find were the main differences in the two groups?'

Anya glanced at Nigel, whose head was still down. 'In the sports that were predominated by team involvement, the four forms of football, sixty-nine percent of players were unable to identify the situations in which sexual assault of a woman had taken place. That was in comparison with scores of two percent for the swimmers and four percent for the tennis players. The university students were unable to recognise sexual assault in fourteen percent of the scenarios. In contrast, ninety-eight percent of all participants correctly identified a man being sexually assaulted.'

'So what you're suggesting,' Senator Woodrow summarised, 'is that more than two-thirds of male footballers are incapable of determining what constitutes rape of a woman?'

'From our data, that appears to be the case.'

One of the male senators rubbed his forehead. 'Does this suggest that these men are potential rapists, who refuse to take "no" for an answer?'

Nigel lifted his head but remained quiet. The public gallery behind erupted into protestations.

'No,' Anya raised her voice to dispel the suggestion. 'We are not alleging that. All we can conclude is that a higher percentage of footballers, when compared with men from other sports, were unable to recognise when a sexual assault took place.'

An older, bald senator wearing small spectacles shifted in his seat. 'I'm sorry but I find that difficult to believe. Claiming sexual assault is easy, but there are always two sides to every story. By what standard could you unequivocally state that rape had occurred in these scenarios?'

'The woman in each dramatisation had not consented to the sexual act, was clearly distressed and immediately sought medical attention. When the scenarios were presented to a series of prosecutors, there was unanimous agreement that each woman had been sexually assaulted as defined by the law.'

The other female senator, a former champion swimmer, sat forward. 'Do you have any possible explanations for the significant differences in results from tennis and swimming participants? All were elite athletes at the top of their game, with, I assume, endorsements or salary packages that generously rewarded their level of skill.'

Nigel replied this time. He must have decided to put Anya out of her misery. 'I believe the results are telling in a number of ways. Tennis and swimming aren't really team sports. Medley and relay teams, and doubles in Davis Cup or the Olympics, are not comparable to a team of eleven or more males who bond, train, eat and play together. A totally different culture is created in that environment, one in which pack mentality becomes the norm.'

The bald man tugged on an earlobe. 'So, by implication, teams of men working closely together in a combative situation are more likely to abuse women. I find this insulting to our boys in the military who lay their lives on the line to defend this country. They are highly trained, eat, sleep and work together, and are dependent on every other man in their unit to survive. And yet we don't see these men raping women. I believe your analysis of men in teams and sexual abuse is absurd.'

Anya felt her stomach lurch. This was the part where she and Nigel were both publicly humiliated and their professional reputations tarnished by an ultraconservative who was merely looking to win political points. He would probably be given a private box at the next NRL Grand Final for his trouble.

Professor Everett nodded patiently. 'Perhaps I have not made myself clear enough. This is not merely about men in groups. It is about men with money, celebrity and physical strength who are enabled by the administrators and sponsors of the sports they represent. Men in the military do not enjoy any such privilege, at least not in my country.'

This comment amused the public gallery. Anya turned and suddenly caught a glimpse of the man who had tried to protect her and Hannah outside the court the previous day. Suddenly, she felt even more uncomfortable. What was he doing here?

Meanwhile, Nigel had everyone in the room hanging on his every word. 'To put it another way, Senator, this alarming trend is something you have perhaps witnessed in your chosen profession of public service. The issue is really abuse of power. Plainly and simply.'

'Doctor Crichton,' the chair asked, 'in your experience, why are women who are raped by footballers loath to report the matter to police?'

Anya began by citing a case of a young waitress who had reported being raped by four footballers at an after-game function. 'When I examined this woman, who had been brought into the sexual assault unit by police as per the protocol, she was in severe distress. She was crying, and seemed frightened of the players finding out she had told the police.' Anya spoke more confidently, remembering every detail about the case. 'The players were in a training camp, staying next door to where she worked. She was afraid they would be able to find her and assault her again, so she decided against giving a police statement. I had to respect her wishes and inform the police that she had changed her mind.'

The bald senator seemed unimpressed. 'Yes, well, it could also be that she had good reason to withdraw her complaint. Her distress could have been due to regret once she sobered up at participating in consensual sex with a number of men.'

Senator Woodrow spoke next. 'Doctor, was there any physical evidence to suggest the woman had been raped?'

'Yes. The pattern of bruising on her wrists and upper arms suggested she was held by large hands, and purpuric bruises between her upper thighs were fresh and fist-sized. There was also a significant amount of vaginal bleeding and she had a tear that required eight stitches. I believe the physical evidence was consistent with the story she gave of violent, nonconsensual intercourse with a number of men.'

'Why in heaven's name wouldn't she give a police statement?'

Anya let out a deep breath. 'The assault occurred not long after a woman who accused a rugby player of rape had been named on television and had had her past sexual history detailed in every media outlet. As it happened, the station that first named her owned broadcasting rights to that particular code of football.'

Two of the committee members shook their heads either in disbelief or surprise.

'In this case the woman was a single mother and she didn't want her daughter to find out what had happened, but somehow the press got hold of the story. She ended up losing her job and going into hiding. She knew the players would claim the intercourse was consensual, so it would essentially be her word against theirs. She didn't feel she could fight the four perpetrators, the rest of the team, the fans and the promoters.'

Anya's mouth and throat felt as dry as sandpaper. She took a sip of the water provided.

'To be sure we are all clear on this,' Nigel added. 'What we're all dealing with in these cases has absolutely nothing to do with sex. It is about abuse of power, a gross abuse. The only solution is to remove that power.'

The bald senator seemed to take offence at this. 'My concern is that you appear to be tainting entire sports on the basis of a few bad apples. Surely those apples can simply be identified and removed.'

Nigel rubbed the top of his stick again. 'Sir, with all due respect, it's not a few apples that are rotten here, it's the barrel itself.'

An assistant handed the chair a note, and she covered her microphone before conferring with her colleagues. 'I'd like to thank you, Doctor, Professor, for taking the time to meet with us today. We'll take a twenty-minute recess before we resume.'

Anya sat numbed by this dismissal. She had prepared so much more data on sexual assaults and had expected a deeper analysis of the issues. In addition, she had a presentation on the results of previous programmes designed to educate players in social skills, responsibility and behaviour. Being dismissed so quickly made her suspect the committee was not really interested in changing the current culture.

'I think that went rather well, don't you?'

Nigel gave her a cheeky grin, one that made his eyes twinkle like a boy with a mischievous plan. Anya wondered what he had to be so cheerful about.

Nigel stopped to speak with a member of the press as they headed for the door. Anya turned to tell him she would wait for him outside and almost bumped into someone behind her.

'I'm sorry —' she began.

The man looked down and smiled. Beneath the brown hair hanging over his forehead was a bruise, a few centimetres above deep blue eyes framed by long black lashes that any woman would die for. Anya was shaken – it was the man from the courthouse yesterday.

'I'm not sorry. It's a pleasure to finally meet you.'

He had an American accent. He was dressed in a navy shirt and tie, with a tan jacket and casual chinos.

'Is there a reason you're following me across states and getting bruised in the process?' Anya asked with a frown.

'I assumed . . . OK, I can see I was wrong. Prof hasn't told you, has he?'

Anya had no idea what this man was talking about. 'Told me what?' She clutched her papers to her chest, and stood aside for a group of people filing out of the room.

'I'm Ethan Rye. I work for the USA Professional Football Leagues.'

She put down her briefcase to shake his hand and dropped the papers in the process. He immediately bent down to help.

'Thanks,' she said, embarrassed at her clumsiness. 'Are you involved in the plans for a US component of our study?'

'No.' He handed over her notes, which she placed safely in her briefcase.

'I've been out here checking out potential recruits for our teams. Your Aussie Rules kickers are of particular interest.'

'You're a talent scout?'

They moved out into the corridor, which was full of people hurrying in each direction. There must have been a number of committee hearings that morning.

'Not exactly. I'm a private investigator and I've been asked to check out which players are most suitable, from a personal point of view.'

He was doing background checks – but that still didn't explain why he had been at the courthouse.

'Thank you for trying to shield us from the eggs, and I'm sorry about the bruise on your forehead. You'll have to excuse me.'

She turned and Nigel, finished with the journalist, waved to Ethan Rye behind her.

Anya didn't like being kept in the dark. What was the old fox planning?

'Nigel, why is a private investigator – from America – here?' she demanded.

Nigel clutched his walking stick. 'For the moment, he's examining possible candidates for transition to American football. Ethan here is a man of many talents. He is also involved with a new education programme involving around three hundred football players, of which I'm certain you will approve. There's a summit next week as part of a pre-season training camp and I have been invited to participate. It's a real honour, and will attract a lot of attention from the media and other sports.'

Anya had assumed Nigel would be fishing with his old friend next week. Peter would be disappointed.

'When do you leave?'

Nigel glanced at Ethan Rye. 'Next month.'

Anya could not read his expression. 'You just said the seminar is next week.'

'Correct. I was invited to participate. Unfortunately, due to personal reasons, I am now unable to attend.'

Ethan took a step forward. 'The Prof here suggested someone who could present to the players instead. He tells me you would be perfect for the job.'

Anya glanced at Nigel to see if this was a joke. From the grin on his face, he was feeling pretty pleased with himself. The fox had planned to pull out at the last minute so she could be offered the job. Ethan Rye must have been checking her out at the courthouse. Anya didn't know whether to be pleased or annoyed.

'Tell her the deal,' Nigel enthused.

Ethan nodded. 'You'll be provided with first-class return tickets to New York and five-star accommodation, with all meals and expenses covered. In addition, you will be paid an appearance fee of $30,000, excluding your regular consulting fees for any other contributions you make. This will be paid in American dollars. If you are willing and available, I know that individual teams may also request your expertise and advice on educating players. Some may wish to discuss individual cases with you, if you agree. I'll be on hand during your stay to assist with anything you need.'

Anya could not believe it. This man was offering to pay her to present to players, which she would have done for free if it meant increasing awareness of sexual assault. She had never flown first class to anywhere, and had always wanted to visit New York. There had to be a catch.

The investigator reached into his jacket pocket, removed an airline envelope and handed it to Anya.

Nigel rubbed the white hair on his chin. 'It's the perfect

opportunity for you to spread your wings. It's the big time, Anya, and this experience will only benefit your career.'

Inside the envelope was an electronic ticket in her name and one thousand US dollars in cash. Nigel Everett had handed her his pot of gold.

'Why me, though? You have plenty of experts closer to home. They'd work out a lot cheaper.'

Ethan Rye countered. 'Your qualifications are unique. Either forensic nurses or emergency doctors perform rape examinations back home. Our pathologists give opinions, but Australia and England lead the world in forensic physicians. You've developed the specialty of sexual assault medicine, and you have the qualifications and forensic experience to back that. No one can question your credentials. Whether or not you know it, you're highly regarded in the US. In fact, a New York assistant district attorney highly recommended you and suggested you might give a talk on sexually transmitted infections before a session with her on sexual assaults. That way the players get the medical and legal ramifications of their actions.'

He had done his research. The assistant district attorney who recommended her had to be Linda Gatby.

'If I agree, when do I have to leave?' She thought of her lecturing duties, and her son, Ben.

'You've got time to get back to Sydney, say goodbye to your son and pack. We leave the day after tomorrow.'

6

Anya's taxi pulled up at Sydney International Airport.
'Thanks, Doctor Crichton.' The smiling attendant checked her passport. 'I'm afraid there isn't an earlier flight I can put you on.'

Anya felt her face redden. 'Force of habit. I'm always early for plane trips.' Obviously, first-class passengers arrived later than their economy counterparts.

She had never been so far away from Ben before. Although her five-year-old son lived with his father, she always took comfort in the fact that he was only a short drive away. Martin had left nursing and was supposedly looking for part-time work while he stayed at home with their child. At the time of their separation he had been unemployed. Anya's demanding work hours and frequent nights on call meant Ben would have to be cared for by a nanny a lot of the time if custody were shared. For that reason, the judge had awarded Martin custody. Anya had been devastated by the decision, and by the fact she only had access visits on weekends. Having to pay child support and maintenance meant she was locked into long working hours and could not cut back to spend more time with Ben or reapply for custody.

Instead of being sad when she had told him she was going overseas for a few weeks, Ben had bombarded her with excited questions. Was she going to Disneyland? Could he come too? Would she meet anyone famous?

Martin had been more concerned about her safety. Since Anya had been attacked in her home Martin had been more solicitous towards her and they were on better terms, much to Ben's delight. Despite Martin being immature and selfish at times, he was a good father, and whilst Anya may not have accepted the custodial arrangement, she was learning to live with it.

It had been all she could do to stop breaking into tears when she had dropped Ben back home. It was difficult to accept that her son didn't miss her as much as she missed him. His life pretty much revolved around the moment, whereas her focus was the next access weekend. In between, she focused on her work and building her reputation as a forensic consultant.

The whole airport process was seamless. She'd never been fast-tracked through customs like that, avoiding any semblance of a queue. She almost felt guilty. Almost. She passed through the multitude of duty-free offerings and headed upstairs to the first-class lounge. Beyond the frosted doors she was greeted by a beaming man in a suit, who checked her boarding pass.

'Good morning, Doctor Crichton. If there's anything I can help you with, order a car for you in New York, or perhaps make a restaurant booking, please let me know.'

Anya thanked the concierge and wheeled her carry-on luggage inside, allowing a grin to unfold on her face. She felt like a child let free inside a lolly shop for the first time. With ample time before the flight, she chose a restaurant table and was immediately met with a waiter and menu. Even the bread rolls looked inviting; they were warm and she didn't hesitate to slather them with the organic butter provided on her table.

'I thought you would have booked in for a spa treatment.'

Ethan Rye, in an open-collared shirt, jacket and dress trousers, appeared as she was midway through her third mouthful of crusty bread.

'Mind if I join you?'

'Please.' She wiped her mouth with the napkin, hoping no crumbs clung to her lips. 'I looked this place up on the net. The spa doesn't open until nine.'

'Finally, someone else who has an eye for detail,' he grinned, sitting opposite. 'Thought you should have this sooner rather than later. It's background on all the players slated to attend the education summit. It should give you added insight into what you're dealing with.

'There's a lot of information there. Over three hundred players will attend the workshops, press and meetings. August is still pre-season but there's a celebrity game against last season's champions, the New Jersey Bombers. You'll get the chance to catch it.'

Anya remained quiet. She would prefer to visit a museum than watch sport.

Ethan seemed to suppress a grin. 'It's a professional camp for players. These boys eat, sleep, breathe and exercise with their team mates. No wives, kids or girlfriends allowed. Even if they have apartments in New York City, they still have to stay in the hotel. League rules.'

Anya couldn't imagine anything more claustrophobic. She enjoyed solitude, quiet and privacy. Something the players seemed to be denied in their world.

Ethan took a seat and pulled out a thick file from a travel case and placed it on the table. Anya's heart sank. It would take all of the twenty-odd hours en route to get through it.

'I can summarise a lot of what's in the reports if it helps. That way you can still watch a movie or two.'

Anya never slept the night before a trip, making sure she had packed everything, going over her list of things to be organised while she was away. She had hoped to make up for her sleepless night by taking a sedating antihistamine that would make her sleepy and would have the added bonus of diminishing her anxiety about take-offs and landings. By the size of the file, even with Ethan's briefing she'd be working the entire journey. The antihistamines would have to wait.

The waiter arrived with scrambled eggs, smoked salmon and a thick slice of toasted sourdough. Another delivered a pot of Irish breakfast tea. It looked and smelt appetising.

'May I have a black coffee, and I might try some of your Vegemite on toast, thanks.' Ethan turned to Anya and saw her raised eyebrow. 'Hey, when in Rome . . . Please start, don't let yours go cold.'

Anya hadn't eaten much the night before, clearing out her fridge contents of mouldy vegetables, expired juice and milk. She was starving. She tried not to show it, though, aware of Ethan's scrutiny as she ate.

After a leisurely breakfast they boarded the plane. Rye seemed right at home in first class. His jacket and carry-on were fully stowed before Anya had even peeled off her coat. With only a single window seat, there would be no banal chatter with a stranger. The attendant offered her a drink from a tray. She chose a glass of spring water and sat down, quickly slipping on the seatbelt. Opening the file, she began to read, distracted only by the offers of nuts, canapés and more drinks.

When the plane reversed, she closed her fingers around the file. Images of plane-crash victims on whom she'd performed post-mortems came to mind. A crop-duster who was decapitated; passengers with barely recognisable internal organs; numerous corpses ravaged by fire after impact. The only safe position in a plane was where the staff sat, facing backwards with a four-point harness.

After take-off, flying held no concerns for her. Until the landing. Anya concentrated on positive thinking and blocking out images of crashes as the plane taxied for endless minutes and finally lifted off. It was only when she heard the wheels clunk safely back into their housing that she realised her fingers were clamped around the file.

Breathing slowly and deeply, she sifted through the papers Ethan had given her. Typical college-style portraits accompanied detailed biographical information.

She chose one at random. A twenty-three-year-old born in Harlem. His hair was cropped short, highlighting steely eyes and an almost muscular jaw. Even in the photo he appeared determined. Mention of two deceased brothers caught her attention. Cause of death was described as unnatural. That left homicide, suicide or accident.

With the extent of the man's police record, Anya had to remind herself that this was a professional footballer, not a suspect in a criminal investigation.

His offences ranged from break and enter to possession of illegal narcotics. Four years earlier, he had been shot in the back of his shoulder by police at the scene of an armed robbery. There was no mention of a conviction in that instance, or of any jail time served for the litany of other offences.

A number of statistics was listed, including weight, height and records pertaining to his football career. Medical history described an early knee injury, and the gunshot wound appeared to have grazed his shoulder without causing structural damage or long-term disability.

The next portrait featured a fresh-faced sandy-haired player who looked like a poster boy for good dentition. He played quarterback and had won an array of awards, including player of the year, sportsman of the year and most valuable player at high school and two separate colleges. There was no criminal record. On paper, the contrast between the two players could not have been greater, although this man's medical history was also peppered with injuries, including rupture of the anterior cruciate ligament and multiple arthroscopies on both knees. Despite these he still maintained a high fitness assessment.

After a while, names, places and injuries began to blur. What took her by surprise was the number of players with criminal records. Drugs, robbery and assault on women predominated.

Anya looked up from the file. Most of the other passengers were either lying flat and asleep or engrossed in their video screens.

Anya decided to stretch her legs and found her way to the first-class bar. Ethan Rye sat reading at one of the stools. He saw her before she could retreat.

'Please. Join me. I can't tell if it's supposed to be night or day.'

Anya slid onto the stool and asked the attendant for a champagne cocktail. Suddenly she felt as though the stress of the last two weeks had caught up with her.

'You should probably try and get some rest. We'll hit the ground running when we get there.'

Anya knew she looked drawn. Hannah's case had been emotionally demanding, and was compounded by preparing for the senate committee.

Ethan made a circle on the condensation on his glass. Those lashes were even longer when his gaze was downward.

'How's the reading?'

'Interesting. The number of criminal records is surprising. I can understand the occasional player getting into a scrape with the law, but that many?'

Ethan sipped his beer. 'One stat often quoted is that twenty-five percent of players are felons. You've seen the sheets. Violence is the theme in most of them. Against partners, overzealous fans and each other. You have to look at those figures in context. A lot of players come from pretty rough backgrounds, often where the only life options involve joining a gang, going to prison or getting killed.

'Football is their way out, which is why I'm such a fan of the game and the whole ethos of giving disadvantaged guys a chance to make it big.' He took a couple of cashews from the bowl on the bar and popped them into his mouth. 'Only trouble is, sometimes it's taken too far. As soon as their skills are discovered, they get preferential treatment. Schools, colleges, university, and someone's always covering their back. They're constantly told they're better than everyone else, and not just at throwing a piece of leather around. Guess sometimes the machine turns them into monsters.'

Anya wondered whether it was the machine or the choice of the players? Not every player had a criminal record.

The attendant delivered Anya's cocktail. 'Is there anything else I can get you?' he asked in an English accent.

Ethan let him know they were fine and turned to Anya. 'Of course, soccer players in England,' he gestured to the steward, 'have the same reputation as footballers in Australia and America. You pick a bunch of teenagers with ball skills, pay them outrageous amounts of money, treat them like gods and wonder why they go off the rails. No code or sport that behaves like that is exempt. A lot of people are wondering why it took so long for Tiger Woods to get caught out by his wife. They don't know how protected and enabled these guys are, for whatever wrong activities they get involved in.'

Anya considered Woods's situation very different from players who committed violent acts. It wasn't a crime to have a number of mistresses and, as far as she'd heard, there was no violence involved in his alleged infidelities.

'Wrong and illegal are vastly different things.'

'Your job,' Ethan grabbed another handful of nuts, 'is to teach them the difference.'

7

Kirsten Byrne climbed from the taxi and pulled down the hem of her dress to obscure the chunkiest parts of her thighs.

The outfit was tighter than anything she would have chosen for herself. Representing Cheree Jordan Fashions meant she had to look the part. 'Sophisticated Sassy', the designer described her clothing. Cheree had reassured Kirsten that the dress was what people would see tonight, not the girl in it.

The crowd groaned when they saw Kirsten. They were obviously expecting a celebrity or a star player. Reporters and fans had lined the street outside the hotel. She breathed in the excitement. Here she was on 42nd Street, and for a moment she allowed herself to live the fantasy. This is what being rich and famous felt like. If only everyone back in Louisville could see her now.

She slowed and fidgeted with her handbag. What was she thinking? How did she ever believe she could fit in with these people? The girl at high school voted most likely to breed cats.

But that was before she had become an intern for a New York fashion designer and was given the task of signing Pete Janson, one of football's biggest stars and most lucrative players. A line of clothing in his name would be a coup for her boss. He was just so difficult to get to, with all of his managers, minders and hangers-on. A function like this was the best chance to meet him and make an informal approach.

She teetered her way past lines of fans holding posters and photos of their favourite team members. Boys as young as five jostled with men of all ages, wanting a glimpse of their idol, each adorned in purple, gold and green, the colours of the New Jersey Bombers. A small boy clutching a home-made scrapbook caught her attention.

'Who are you waiting for?' she asked.

'Pistol Pete Janson,' the boy announced excitedly.

'Good luck,' she said. 'I'm hoping to meet him too.'

Catching a glimpse of her reflection in the glass doors of the hotel, Kirsten did a double take. Thanks to the hair-dresser, gone was the mop of messy brown hair; in its place was a smooth, flat style highlighted by a sophisticated clip-on ponytail. An eyebrow wax, professional make-up and a sequinned halterneck dress completely erased the girl from last year.

Clutching the invitation, she headed through the revolving doors into the quiet of the foyer. A fountain trickled water and she felt goosebumps over her arms. As she rode up the escalator, she could already feel burning where the shoes dug into her toes and rubbed the balls of her feet.

Further along, tourists milled with more fans in team jerseys. Heading past the elevators and through double doors was a steady stream of tall, glamorous women.

Kirsten stretched the dress hem as low as it would go.

A sign saying *Private Function* told the world this was an exclusive party. Invitation only.

Handing across her entry ticket, she held her breath. This really could be the best night of her life; it could make her career in New York.

Inside she stood by the wall, taking in the scene. Revellers in one group cheered and laughed in unison; women in revealing dresses stood in groups, constantly looking around to see who else was in the room. For a moment, Kirsten felt her outfit was the most modest here.

The glass of champagne tickled her nose and she wished she hadn't been too nervous to eat lunch. Music pounded as she squeezed her way to the bar for a drink of water.

Suddenly a hand was on her bottom, creeping under her dress. Horrified, she spun around. A group of men laughed.

'Look, fellas, it's new blood.'

Another meowed and they laughed again.

'Manners, boys,' a booming voice commanded. Kirsten stood back, amazed at the size of the man. He must have been at least six foot six of solid muscle.

'That's no way to treat a lady,' he said and moved forward. The others parted without a word. He put his arm around her shoulder and led her to a table where four people were engrossed in conversation. When they arrived, the occupants made room for them and the men exchanged high-fives.

Blond wavy hair, a dimpled chin. This had to be Peter Janson. Only he was far better looking than his pictures. He asked Kirsten her name but didn't introduce himself. This man knew he was important and assumed everyone else knew too. She just hoped she wouldn't say the wrong thing.

A number of drinks arrived at the table, and she stirred her pink concoction with the straw.

The others drank and laughed at Pete Janson's jokes. He began to tell them about a recent game, the details of which went over her head. She didn't know what a quarterback did specifically, apart from throw balls and set up touchdowns. He didn't hesitate to mention how crazy the fans went every time he got hold of the ball.

Kirsten tried to join in the conversation. 'Did you see all the people out the front lined up for autographs?'

'Hell no,' the big man said, sliding his arm along the chair behind her. 'We always come in the back. That way the paparazzi and fans who check into the hotel so they can camp in the foyer don't see us. This is our time.'

'They looked like they'd been waiting for ages; some kids have travelled a long way.'

He touched her shoulder. 'Kirsten, right? We work our butts off all week training and giving everything for the fans, so now's the only time we get to unwind. Tomorrow we go into lockdown for a camp. Besides, most of those are professional memorabilia collectors. Within an hour, anything we sign will be on eBay. Who wants another round?'

Kirsten thought of the little boy waiting patiently, having travelled especially to see his favourite football star.

'Excuse me, can anyone tell me where the bathrooms are?' She wanted a moment to catch her breath.

One of the women, who introduced herself as Stacy, offered to show her the way.

As they manoeuvred a path out of the function room, Stacy winked at the doorman and told him they'd be right back.

Outside, Kirsten felt a sense of relief that she could gather her thoughts without loud music thumping.

'He's got his eye on you. Do you know how lucky you are? Thousands of women would kill to be in your shoes right now,' Stacy gushed.

'What do you mean?' Kirsten asked.

'Are you trying to tell me you didn't notice the way Pistol looked at you? He doesn't invite just anyone over to his table, you know.'

Kirsten's heart raced. She couldn't believe her luck. All she had to do now was to work out how to bring up the idea of a clothing line for Cheree Jordan Fashions.

Inside the bathroom, women in tight mini-dresses with bulging cleavages jostled for space in front of an extensive mirror.

'OMG,' a platinum blonde with teased hair declared, 'I just saw Giant Joffie. God, I hope he picks me tonight. They don't call him Giant for nothing.'

A brunette with hair extensions gasped, while reapplying Hollywood tape inside a gold lamé top. Her outfit was complemented by spray-on jeans, which on second glance were leggings with printed pockets and seams, tucked into knee-high stiletto boots.

'Joffie's the best lay I've ever had,' said another.

The brunette looked Kirsten up and down. 'Girl, you are *way* out of your league tonight.'

'Don't mind her,' the blonde said. 'I'm guessing the closest she ever got was screwing the team's water boy. Love your dress.' With that, she was out the door.

'Ignore the pack of bitches,' Stacy whispered. 'You stick with Pete and you'll be taken care of.'

After fixing their make-up, they left the bathroom.

Kirsten excused herself. 'I'll be there in a minute. I just need a quick breath of fresh air.'

'Whatever you do, don't smoke cigarettes. He can't stand the smell.'

Kirsten hurried down the escalator and out the front door, looking for the little boy and his father. He was still standing with his scrapbook in hand, hoping to see his hero.

'Remember me?' she said. 'I'm with Pete Janson inside. You can't actually come into where he is, but I could maybe get him to sign your book if you like.'

The boy's face transformed.

'If you come with me into the foyer, you can have a seat in one of the sofas and I'll take it in and bring it back. Only it might be a little while. He's really busy.'

Kirsten didn't have the heart to tell him his hero was avoiding fans tonight. This little boy deserved better.

'We've waited this long. What do you think, Adam?'

The child nodded, and the trio walked back into the hotel and up the escalators. When it came time to part with his precious scrapbook, Adam hesitated.

'I promise to take really good care of it. How would you like it signed? Specially for you?'

The boy nodded and handed over the book; in exchange, Kirsten gave him her card with her phone number on it. 'If you need to go, just call me and I'll get it straight back to you. OK?'

She hurried back to the function room, feeling pain now with every step as she struggled in the heels. Inside, more people were standing around Janson's table, hanging on his every utterance. Her best chance of talking business was if she could get him in a quiet place for a few minutes.

Thankfully, he stood and ushered her into the same seat. Stacy winked at her.

'What have you got there?' he asked, sliding his arm back around her.

'A little boy outside absolutely idolises you. I was wondering if you'd sign this for him. His name is Adam.'

'Since you asked so nicely,' he said, leaning close enough for her to feel his breath on her face. 'This isn't your kid, is it?'

'No, I mean, I just met him on the way in tonight.'

He signed an illegible squiggle and put the pen on top of the closed book.

'Now, tell me about you.'

Kirsten saw her chance. 'I work for Cheree Jordan, the fashion designer.'

'Who?' He leant in close. The noise in the room seemed to have escalated.

'Cheree Jordan Fashions,' she said loudly. 'Actually, we're looking for a superstar footballer to work with us on a line of clothing. The potential return for this player is enormous.'

Kirsten didn't want to admit that she'd come specifically to target Janson. 'Don't suppose you know anyone who would fit the bill?'

He laughed. 'Who do you have in mind?'

'Someone athletic, successful, a wonderful role model, oh, and handsome.'

She noticed how he crinkled his nose before breaking into a captivating smile. Even his teeth were perfect.

Another round of drinks arrived. 'What sort of money are we talking?'

Kirsten rattled off the potential earnings and he listened intently, occasionally moving even closer to better hear or ask a question. She couldn't help noticing his musk aftershave. After she'd finished the presentation she'd practised all day, another round of drinks appeared.

The footballer took a glass of champagne and handed one to Kirsten.

'It's an attractive proposition. I get lots of offers, but this time I'm definitely interested.' He clinked her glass with his. 'This could be the start of a beautiful relationship.'

She couldn't believe it. Pete Janson was actually talking about doing business with Cheree Jordan Fashions, with her! This had to be the best night of her life. She drank and he toasted to success and they drank again. She pulled out her card and suddenly remembered little Adam in the foyer.

'Almost forgot. The boy needs his book back.'

'Whoa. You can't mention a great business deal then disappear. It's not like you're going to turn into a pumpkin at midnight. My agent's upstairs. He has to sign off on all my deals. We can catch him if you want and give him your proposal.'

Kirsten couldn't believe how easy Janson was to talk to. He was born in a town in Arkansas and spoke kindly of his parents and grandparents. He seemed to share the same family values and said how proud he was of his two daughters.

Janson stood up and put out his enormous hand for her to take. Holding hands, they forged through the crowd, their path slowed by well-wishers squeezing through to high-five, pat him on the back or say, 'Pistol, my man.' One of the women from the bathroom slipped something into his hand. Kirsten presumed it was her phone number. Without missing a beat, Janson tucked it into a much shorter man's shirt pocket and patted his chest. 'Great job today. Here's your tip.'

Kirsten wondered if this was the water boy.

In the foyer, she steered him over to Adam, and Janson stopped to meet the little boy and his father. He even posed for photos, much to Adam's delight. The joy on the child's face was priceless.

'Liam McKenzie's upstairs. If you'd like I can get him to sign this too.' Pete rubbed the boy's hair and promised to return the book very soon.

'We have to go do some business, but we won't be long.'

Kirsten decided this *was* the best night of her life.

They rode the lift to the thirty-second floor, then he led her along a corridor and around the corner. Rows of trays from room service were lined up outside the doors. It looked like an army had been fed. Janson used his key, took off his jacket and told her to chill. He rang his agent, who said he'd be right over, then he propped open the door with the folding lock. Kirsten could barely contain her excitement. She was about to pitch the idea of a clothing range in Janson's name, something her boss had been unable to pull off. She pulled the notes from her bag, straightened her dress and sat on the edge of the chair, careful to show as little leg as possible. Janson disappeared into the bathroom.

A minute later he returned. She glanced up from her notes and gasped. He had removed his pants and had an erection. This had to be some kind of bad joke.

'Oh, you don't understand.' She stood, grabbed her things and headed for the door. 'I didn't come here for that. I'll just wait outside.'

He blocked her path and touched her breasts through her dress. 'No need to play hard to get, honey.'

Panic filled her. 'I want to go,' she stammered. 'I'm sorry, this was not what I intended. I have to leave now.'

Before she could resist, she was on her back on the bed and the weight of him on top of her had forced the air from her lungs. She tried to push him off, but he was too large and strong.

Suddenly pain ripped through her lower body. He grunted and thrusted. The contents of her stomach rushed to her mouth and she wanted to vomit. Just as the room darkened and she was about to pass out, he moaned and rolled off.

Seizing the opportunity, she tumbled off the bed, holding her dress to her waist. She rushed to the door and slammed straight into a human wall. Thank God! Someone had come to help her.

Instinctively, she grabbed him by the arms, like a drowning victim clinging to a lifebuoy.

'Help. Please help me,' she begged in a hysterical voice she hardly recognised as her own.

This giant man pushed her back and placed warm, protective hands on her shoulders.

'What the hell's going on?'

Janson just laughed. 'We all know you don't like the slops but you took your time. Come on, Liam, what's a guy to do?'

Kirsten tried to pull the man to the door. She needed to get away. This man had no idea what Janson was capable of.

Someone else entered the room, this man smaller than the others, then a dark-haired man followed by an even larger

61

African-American man. They must have come to help, thank God.

'Please don't let him touch me again,' she cried.

Janson stood and she heard laughter from behind.

'You don't have to worry about that,' her protector said. 'He's had his turn.'

Without warning, he clutched her around the waist and threw her back on the bed, like a discarded towel. Before she could react, he had rolled her on to her stomach, her face shoved into a pillow. She struggled to breathe. Then more pain tore through her, screams smothered by the pillow. She didn't see the faces of the other men as they took turns raping her.

The phone in her bag rang and she hoped someone would come and save her. The little boy's father knew where she was. Eyes slowly easing to the side, she saw the scrapbook on the side table.

The phone went silent.

8

Outside the Hyde Hotel ballroom, a man in a suit introduced himself as the day's master of ceremonies. Ethan
had stepped to the side to take a call. He had told Anya he
would be in and out during the day, depending on his other
commitments.

'Just let me know if you need any extra audiovisual
equipment.'

The emcee was around six foot two and stocky, with a
noticeably expanded waistline. He handed Anya a clip-on
microphone, which she attached to her jacket lapel. The
battery pack hooked into her skirt waistband.

Ensuring the unit was turned off, Anya thanked him and
took a seat at the back of the function room. The man, whose
name had already slipped her mind, greeted the audience
and explained the day's timetable, repeating the title and
time of each session. The day covered a number of serious
topics, along with 'How to handle an interview', 'Why charities are some of our most important work', and advice on
'Dressing to kill' from a stylist.

Anya noted the irony of a fashion session in a seminar
on conduct. Still jet-lagged, she downed her second coffee,
hoping the caffeine would kick in quickly. After heading
straight to the hotel to check-in, she had had time for a quick
nap and shower before starting work.

She knew this audience would be difficult to connect with.
Young male athletes were not used to sitting and listening

for long periods unless it involved game strategies with their coach.

From the number and distribution of coloured jerseys in the audience, all the teams had sent players to the summit. A larger proportion of gold, purple and green suggested to Anya that they were the colours of the New Jersey Bombers, who were in greater numbers because of their exhibition match against the celebrity All-Stars. A quick scan suggested ten or so players had been chosen from each club. The other audience members could have been administrators, trainers or team psychologists, for all Anya knew. The room was at maximum capacity.

The amount of murmuring, groaning and shifting in seats made her think of high school students being told there was a test at the end of the lesson. Except that these few hundred men had left school and college behind them, and this course was for their benefit.

'Settle down!' A man with *COACH* emblazoned across his jersey stood from behind his front-row seat.

'It won't kill you to listen to what the speakers have to say. They tell me you might learn something useful.'

Amid the mutterings, someone called out, 'How come you don't have to stay, Coach?'

'Because I have real work to do,' he responded, and left via a side door.

Anya took a breath. Without support from men the players respected, the task ahead was made that much more challenging. The least the coach could have done was stayed for the first session, even if he was feigning support for the programme. His life would have to be easier if fewer of his players were arrested and charged with violent offences.

'Our first speaker is a world-renowned pathologist and forensic physician who is going to talk to you about safe sex, an important aspect of sexual behaviour,' the emcee announced. 'Please welcome from Australia, Doctor Anya Crichton.'

A cheer went out within the group and a number of the men hooted like adolescents. She wondered if they were expecting a stereotypical Australian woman – blonde, suntanned and long-legged.

Anya took to the makeshift stage to more cheers and wolf-whistles. Without responding, she plugged in her PowerPoint presentation and pulled up the slide of a pustulating, ulcerated lesion on a barely recognisable penis.

She switched on the microphone.

'What you see here is a result of unsafe sex.'

The contorted faces and grimaces in the first few rows showed the image had the desired effect, until someone further towards the back called out, 'I thought safe sex meant locking the car doors and making sure the handbrake's on?'

Chuckling spread like a wave across the group.

'Or the girl's father doesn't have a shotgun.'

Raucous laughter continued. Anya changed slides and, as the crowd snickered, she identified one of the comedians, who was still being slapped on the back by surrounding admirers.

Tall, broad shoulders, slumped in the chair, one elbow leaning on the shoulder of the player to his right. Wavy blond hair and blue eyes.

'You are?'

'Pistol Pete Janson. At your service.'

'Mr Janson, if you value your career, it's worth taking this lecture seriously. Sexually transmitted infections could prevent you from playing, or worse. And they can also infect your wives and girlfriends.' She paused. 'How many of you think about that after a game?'

One player tentatively raised a hand and was met with a slap to the side of his head by his neighbour.

She had the group's attention again. 'I'm guessing a lot of you get the chance to meet women who are interested in hooking up after a game, especially when you're on the road.'

Shoulders shrugged and heads nodded – some proudly, others sheepishly.

'Did you know that one in four American women has a sexually transmitted infection, and could have multiple infections? That is *one* in *four* women, wherever you go.'

The words hung in the air. They were difficult to ignore.

A voice came from the back. 'Maybe Rocket ought to get checked after last night. She was jail-bait if I've ever seen it.'

'Shut up, man, she was eighteen,' boomed a deep bass.

Janson had a suggestion. 'Maybe you should let the doctor check you out here and now.'

The group laughed again, only more nervously than before. Anya knew she was beginning to get through to some of them.

'How do you know if you've been with one of those women?' Rocket sounded concerned.

She presented a graphic of the female genital organs. 'Symptoms and signs vary according to the type of infection. One of the most common is called chlamydia and it may not cause any symptoms at all. It's actually the main preventable reason for infertility, and one of the reasons why so many more women today are unable to have children than in the past. If it goes untreated, ten to forty percent of infected women will develop painful symptoms of pelvic inflammatory disease. This can damage the fallopian tubes and dramatically increase the chances of having a pregnancy in the tube.' She pointed to the graphic. 'If that happens, it's called an ectopic pregnancy.'

Janson still appeared unimpressed. 'So now you're telling us how dangerous pregnancy is. In case you hadn't noticed, we all have dicks. Some of us, a lot larger than others.' He made a V shape with his hands aimed at his groin.

A few sniggered.

'Hey, Janson, take time out and give the little lady a chance.'

Anya appreciated the attempt at chivalry but it still came with a patronising edge. Seeing women in positions of authority was not something these players were accustomed to.

Over the next hour she discussed syphilis, gonorrhoea, herpes, genital warts, hepatitis A and B and trichomonas, amongst other diseases. The talk covered anal sex as well, and Anya showed slides of severe infections in the throat following oral sex. She explained that the human papilloma virus was associated with almost every case of cervical cancer, the second most common cancer in women.

Judging by the quiet, she wondered whether many had paid this much attention in sexual education courses at school. Much of the information seemed new to the group.

She discussed the main syndromes, including penile discharge, ulcers, groin and scrotal swellings, all with accompanying slides.

'What are you?' someone called out. 'The fun police? You're going to tell us who we can and can't sleep with, when, how and where? This is bull.'

Anya had suspected that some players would resent being told the truth.

'No, that isn't the message at all. Sex is a normal part of life. There are certain inherent risks when you are high profile, though.'

Judging by the numbers of heads nodding, they conceded at least that point.

'Each one of you values your physical health. You train hard, work out, eat carbohydrate loads before games, rehydrate with special electrolyte solutions during every game. You and the team doctors look after you as much as possible. Safe sex is just another way of staying fit and healthy.'

There was silence, which she took as encouragement to continue.

'It's a concern that up to seventy percent of women and a large number of men infected with gonorrhoea or chlamydia can have no symptoms and be totally unaware they're carrying or passing on the infections to sexual partners. You don't have to have symptoms to develop complications either.'

She fielded some questions about condoms and explained, 'They don't guarantee you won't pick up infections, like pubic lice, scabies or even herpes at the base of the penis. But when used properly, condoms are one of the most effective ways of protecting you and your partner from infections, including HIV.'

'Oh man.' Janson shifted in his seat. 'Now you're doing the grim-reaper crap all over again. We all know faggots get HIV and there are no faggots here. Am I right?' He stood and raised both hands above this head.

The crowd let out a resounding 'Yes', which took Anya by surprise.

'See, no faggots here,' said a dark-haired man on the other side of Janson.

Anya looked around the room. No one disagreed.

'HIV doesn't discriminate. And it spreads more easily if certain other genital infections are present. Does it ever occur to you that a woman you have casual sex with could be carrying a potentially fatal infection such as HIV?'

Some of the men shook their heads. Others looked stunned.

An African-American from the front row, wearing a navy shirt and dress trousers, turned to the players.

'What about Magic Johnson? He got it from having sex with lots of women. He was as hetero as they come, and had a wife and unborn baby he could have infected before he found out.'

'Backdoor Benny got it at college,' Janson retorted, 'only he had bets both ways. You tell me you know for sure about Magic?'

Some of the players were either ignorant or in extreme denial about HIV. Anya wondered if homophobia blinded them to the facts.

'Come on.' The man in the front row did not seem fazed. 'During hospital visits I've met haemophiliacs who've had blood transfusions, even drug users who caught HIV. The doctor's right. Unsafe sex is like playing Russian roulette.'

Another hand rose. 'Ma'am, why are men the ones who have to wear condoms? Why don't women protect themselves?'

'That's a good question. Female condoms exist but they aren't as readily available, and cost a lot more than male condoms. The advantage of you men taking precautions is that you can prevent pregnancies as well. You may not be so keen on supporting children you didn't plan for the rest of their lives.'

Mention of money captured everyone's attention.

'And for those of you with wives and girlfriends, think about what you might be bringing home to them if you choose to have other partners and don't use condoms.' She paused to let that sink in.

'There is actually *another* reason for using condoms. In recent years there's been more than a twenty percent increase in head and neck cancers.'

On the screen the slide changed. A tumour deformed what was a woman's tongue. Her eyes were blacked out to maintain anonymity.

'Based on what I've already told you, can anyone suggest why?'

A voice from the back offered, 'I heard the pill causes cancer? You can't blame us for that.'

'No, but as we already discussed, the human papilloma virus is implicated in cervical cancer. It can also cause oral cancers – tongue, mouth, throat and neck. Since oral sex has become more common, it's no surprise we're seeing an increase in those types of cancer.'

The group objected loudly to the notion.

'Come on!'

'This has gotta be crap!'

'Man, that blows, that really sucks!'

Awkward laughter followed.

'One way to prevent it, apart from being vaccinated against the HPV virus, is to always wear condoms for oral sex.'

As she had anticipated, the advice was not well received.

'Now you're telling us we're causing cancer.' A red-haired man who looked barely old enough to be a rookie stood up angrily. 'There's got to be lots of reasons for things like that.' He motioned to the screen. 'Like . . . like smoking, there's more pollution these days, more chemicals in food. Bet there are loads of other causes.'

Others agreed. 'My grandma says there didn't used to be cheese in a can or even the Internet or . . . or cell phones. Maybe any of them's the reason.'

Anya was surprised at how unworldly some of these men were, despite having attended college.

Anya raised her hands.

'I'm not here to judge you, just to give you the most up-to-date information.'

Anya let that sink in, then checked her watch. It was time for a break.

The emcee stepped forward. 'Let's take fifteen. And don't go wandering off. Bathrooms, drinks and snacks are all just outside.'

By the speed with which the ballroom evacuated, Anya would have thought someone had shouted 'fire'.

For the sake of the men's present and future partners, she hoped some of her message had got through. If not, these men's prestige and attraction to women could end up costing them their lives, one way or another.

9

Anya switched off her mike and loaded the study DVD of dramatised sexual assaults into her computer.

Ethan Rye leant on the presentation table, hands in his jeans pockets. 'Please tell me that first slide was computer-generated.'

'Wish I could. You have to remind yourself that's a person, with a family and friends.'

'Speaking of friends, someone's just arrived who is keen to meet you.'

Anya could not wait to meet the woman she would be speaking with next. She left her computer and headed out the first set of double doors. By the coffee table stood Linda Gatby, recognisable from the photo in her textbook.

Taller than Anya had imagined, Linda was wearing a pale blue suit, cream blouse and sensible heels. The colour near her face complemented her blonde hair and pale blue eyes.

She greeted Anya with a hug. 'It is so good to meet you in person. It feels like we've been friends for years!'

The warmth of the assistant district attorney took Anya by surprise. She had always been professional and courteous in correspondence. According to reports, she was often criticised by defence lawyers for being cold. Then again, that was how the media liked to portray powerful women, and Linda was responsible for setting up a separate unit within the New York Police Department to investigate and prosecute sexual crimes.

'Thanks for your kind recommendation,' Anya mustered.

Linda pulled back, still holding Anya by the elbows. 'You have helped me out so many times with your opinions, I didn't hesitate when Catcher asked me to be involved and if I knew you. Besides, how else could I get us in the same city?'

She smiled broadly.

'Catcher?' Anya wondered.

Ethan raised his index finger. 'That would be me.'

'Anything to do with JD Salinger?'

He sounded genuinely impressed. 'Most people think I played baseball.'

He headed for a long table surrounded by players. Presumably this was where the food could be found. A waitress with a tray of hot finger food didn't get close to the table before being relieved of her bounty.

Linda helped herself to a coffee, and Anya opted for tea. They stood apart from the others to speak in private.

'I'm late because an incident took place last night in a nearby hotel. There's reason to believe some of the players here participated in a gang-rape. I'd like your opinion on the exam findings of the victim, a young woman called Kirsten Byrne, when you get a chance.'

Anya looked at the group. 'How is the victim?'

'Pretty traumatised. Problem is, she didn't report it immediately. I only just got the call. Emergency have done a rape kit, but she'd showered first and rubbed her skin raw with some kind of scourer.'

Anya felt for the woman. Wanting to wash off any reminder of the attack was one of the most common reactions to rape. She wondered how much forensic evidence had been destroyed in the process.

Anya glanced around at the group eating, laughing and drinking cans of sugary caffeine drinks as if they were water.

For a moment she understood what the Lilliputians felt like in *Gulliver's Travels*.

Anya knew that members of all the league's teams throughout the country had been sent to this summit. She asked Linda which particular teams were staying at the hotel where the woman claimed she was assaulted.

'The players Kirsten identified came from the New Jersey Bombers.'

Anya glanced around. No one in the room appeared nervous or scared. There was no overt sign that some of them may have just committed a violent crime. She decided to look for scratches on any of their hands or forearms, anything to suggest the victim fought back. Many of them had earphones in and iPods playing. Others spoke incessantly on their phones, while a small number played video games. All in a fifteen-minute break.

Experience and research showed that ten percent of people in groups like these were leaders who initiated aberrant behaviour. An amazing eighty percent, like sheep, followed. That left only ten percent who were strong or capable enough to dissent. They would be the conscientious objectors in the group.

She wondered which personalities here were dominant enough to start trouble and which were strong enough to end it. Anya turned back to Linda and explained that they would run through the video scenarios and she'd ask what the players thought had happened.

'The next session is good timing then. We can run through the DVD scenarios and maybe get some insights into the group's response.'

Anya had sent Linda a copy of the DVD along with the study results when they were published. She was grateful that she could get such an experienced prosecutor's valuable input and insights into the group.

'We could turn the main lights on as soon as each scenario is done. That way you can steer the questions depending on the response we get,' Linda suggested.

'We think alike,' Anya smiled. The more they could see of the players, the more they might learn.

Back inside the ballroom, Anya played the first of the scenarios. It began with a woman at a bar laughing and drinking with a group of men. She was particularly flirtatious with one man, who asked if she'd like to go back to his place. By the way the pair interacted, the attraction was mutual. The man explained that he shared a flat with a male friend.

The girl didn't object, and the pair shared a taxi. The couple began kissing in the back seat. Once at home, they had a couple of drinks and laughs with the flatmate before retreating to the man's bedroom and closing the door.

The sound of a couple making love would have followed the quiet, but the audience began to cheer and whoop. Then, on-screen, the man came out of the bedroom and the flatmate went inside, into the unlit room.

There were more sexual noises, and the sound of some kind of struggle, and then the woman screamed. She hurried out of the room dressed only in a large T-shirt and ran out of the front door.

Anya paused the DVD and turned to the players. 'What just happened?'

There was a prolonged silence.

'You edited out the best bit?' someone shouted.

More quiet, until they realised the question was serious.

One volunteer spoke. 'They went back, had sex, then she left in a hurry. Who knows why. Maybe she sobered up and saw what the men really looked like.'

Anya looked around for someone to explain the problem. Nothing.

'She stole his shirt?' someone else attempted.

The group's response was not a surprise, but was more disturbing given the alleged events of the previous night.

'Can anyone think of a good reason why she ran out the door as if something terrible had just happened?'

Her question was met with more uncomfortable silence.

'What if I told you that she went straight to the Emergency department to report a rape?'

'That's bullshit. She went back to that place willingly,' someone else proclaimed.

From the back of the room came Linda's voice. 'I'm a sex crimes prosecutor and I see many women just like this one.' Linda moved through the aisle between the seats. 'She claims the second man raped her, because she had only consented to sex with the first man.'

'No way.'

'She's lying.'

'She's a slut.'

The group seemed united in its condemnation of the woman. One dark-haired player raised his hand, and Anya gestured for him to speak.

'Hey, she made it pretty clear she was up for it. Look at the way she gave him the come-on and was laughing with both of them. She was up for it and let them both know it.'

Anya was disheartened that no one in the group, or at least the ones who spoke, saw anything wrong with what had happened in that bedroom.

'What if she didn't know it was the second man until after they'd had sex?' Anya prodded.

'Like he said,' a new voice added, 'she let both men know she was up for it, and it was her choice to drink in the first place.'

The consensus still appeared to be that the woman had consented to sex with both men the moment she went back to the apartment. They even blamed her for drinking.

Without further comment, Anya played the next film.

Three men were playing poker and drinking in a house. One said he was too drunk to drive, so the others suggested he sleep on the lounge. They then drank more beer, and laughed together before calling it a night.

The visitor stripped to his boxers and T-shirt and fell asleep on the lounge. He woke up face down, underpants at his ankles, with one of the men naked on top of him. He began to struggle but couldn't throw off the other man. When the man on top of him had finished, the visitor ran out the front door, pulling up his boxers.

The DVD stopped again.

'This man presented to the police that morning. What do you think happened?' Anya paced in front of the players.

'It's pretty obvious. That guy just got raped.'

Without hesitation, there was group agreement.

Linda took over. 'How do you know the sex wasn't consensual?'

'Are you kidding?' the dark-haired man asked. 'No man wants to do that. It's totally unnatural, and it's disgusting. Am I right?' He waved both arms in the air for support, which he received.

Linda moved forward, as if addressing a jury. 'Just like the girl in the first story, he had been drinking. Don't you think by agreeing to go to the men's place he was giving at least one of them the come-on?'

'No way. He never wanted to have sex with them. He just wanted to crash on the sofa.'

The men didn't appear to see any similarity between the two victims.

Anya played the third story. This time, a group were in a nightclub. One couple was dancing on the floor and began kissing. The man ran his hand up the woman's short skirt and suggested they go somewhere where they could be alone. She laughed and took his hand, leading him to the women's bathroom. Inside the cubicle, the kissing became more intense and he removed her panties and undid his fly. Then he turned her around, pushed her head forward and held it down as he penetrated her from behind. She could be heard telling him to stop, arms flailing at his hand and the walls, in what looked like a struggle to get free.

When the man had finished, he did up his trousers and left the cubicle without a word. Another woman walked into the bathroom and found her inside, sitting on the cubicle floor, crying. She told the woman she had just been raped.

'Any comments?' Anya asked.

'What is it with these women crying rape? What the hell did she want from him?' Janson piped up.

'Maybe she was pissed and he just left her there in the toilet. He didn't even say thanks,' a younger-looking man in one of the front rows offered.

An older team mate agreed. 'Yeah, you get girls like that who put it out then want some kind of romance. Maybe he coulda bought her another drink. That would have been a bit more gentlemanly.'

Anya could barely believe her ears. There was nothing you could describe as gentlemanly about the man's behaviour.

'I saw a woman just like this,' Linda announced. 'She agreed to have sex with the man, and openly admitted that, but she only agreed to have vaginal intercourse with him. She had never had anal intercourse before, and thought it was wrong. That's why she objected and asked him to stop. By forcing her, the way you saw, he committed rape. Consent to one sexual act, believe it or not, does not mean consent to every imaginable sex act.'

Anya waited for any new insights.

'Yeah, well, she can't change her mind with her panties around her ankles.'

'That's where you're wrong, I'm afraid. And if you don't listen when a woman says no, you could find yourself charged with a criminal offence, and labelled a sex offender if you're convicted. You can't play for the team if you're in prison.'

'Like that would ever happen. It's her word against ours,' the dark-haired man scoffed.

His choice of words alerted Anya. He deliberately said 'our' not 'my', as if there were safety in numbers when a woman complained about being raped. She caught Linda's eye and could tell the prosecutor had picked up the reference too.

While Linda explained what would happen if they were charged with sexual assault, Anya flicked through her list of players and found the profile she was after. Liam McKenzie had a lot to say, just like Peter Janson.

She wondered where the ten percent of conscientious objectors were in this group, if they actually existed.

IO

Later that afternoon, Anya slipped on her ballet flats, left the hotel and walked north with Ethan. So far, all she knew was that the owners of the New Jersey Bombers wanted to meet her.

Ethan seemed to think the news was positive.

'I've done a lot of work for them over the years and I really think they want to clean up the game, not just pay lip service. I just spoke with Lyle Buffet. Five Bombers' players are being hauled in for questioning over an alleged sexual assault. No one was more upset than him over the allegations that some of his players may have been involved in the reported assault last night.'

Except the victim, Anya thought. She thought of Kirsten scrubbing her skin with a scourer.

Yellow taxis lined the roads and horns blared with almost monotonous frequency. No one on the street seemed to notice. Rain began to sprinkle and they walked a little faster, past tourists who had stopped for photos. As with the noise, it seemed the locals accepted the imposition and stepped around the foreigners without a second glance. Nothing impeded the flow of pedestrians.

For Anya, being outside the hotel was like being allowed to breathe, despite the grey clouds obscuring any trace of sun. The air on her face made her feel alive and helped clear the fog of tiredness. A long walk was just what she needed before a good night's sleep.

The pair strode up Lexington Avenue in comfortable silence. The more north they headed, the more doormen appeared, to open car doors and help residents with shopping.

'I assume it's prestigious to have a doorman here,' Anya mused.

'Did you know there are more doormen in NY than taxidrivers? When elevators became self-service, it was actually made law for buildings to have them, for the safety of tenants and owners. Mind you, none of the doormen I know would ever live in a building that had one.'

'Because they're treated poorly?'

Ethan shoved his hands in the pockets of his leather jacket and smiled. 'Not everyone is appreciative, but doormen know far more about the residents' business than the residents would want them to, or probably realise.'

It made sense. They saw who came and went, who had packages and mail delivered and from whom, and probably knew how much they paid in rent, earned and spent. She glanced sideways at Ethan.

'I imagine you've milked one or two for information in your time.'

The investigator grinned. 'A good source can save weeks of leg-work.'

Eventually they turned into East 72nd Street and stopped outside a high-rise called the Oxford. The building was set back from the street, with its own private plaza complete with European-style stone seats and greenery. The gated entry led them undercover to the foyer of the building. The doorman seemed to know Ethan and bade him good afternoon.

'I could cope with this.' Ethan pressed the button for the forty-fourth floor. 'Indoor pool, health club, basketball court. If I had a spare three million or so.'

Inside the condominium, the white marble hallway and Art Deco columns were stylish but lacked warmth. Anya wondered how difficult it was to keep the floor clean. A secretary showed them inside the palatial dining room with its walnut floor boards and white marble table. Chairs upholstered in white damask suggested young children weren't well catered for in this apartment.

Seated at the marble table and drinking from china demitasses were a man and a woman, while an older gentleman in a Bombers jacket sat at one end, matching cap pulled down over grey wisps of hair.

'Good afternoon, Catcher. And this must be Doctor Crichton.' The man who spoke was in his late forties and dressed in a tailored suit. He had a soft wave in his greying hair; his teeth were glaringly white, and a shiny gold nugget obscured the lower half of his ring finger. He moved across the room and shook Anya's hand.

'I'm Bentley Masterton. Thank you for meeting us at such short notice.'

'This here is Kitty Rowe, one of the youngest and brightest media moguls in this country and a woman with fine taste in football teams.'

The woman stood and touched what looked like an antique pearl choker. It complemented her pink Chanel suit. Blonde hair was swept back off her face, and her make-up was heavier than Anya would have worn but it highlighted her dark brown eyes. Even with stilettos the woman was shorter than Anya.

'Oh, Bentley,' she winked at Ethan. 'You are prone to exaggeration. I'm the second youngest. Welcome to my home away from home,' she said, as if it were a holiday shack. From the dining room, two walls of windows had dramatic city views to the north, west and east. 'Please, take a seat. Can we offer you a drink?'

Anya and Ethan both declined politely and sat down. As soon as Ethan had told Anya about the hastily arranged meeting with the owners of the Bombers, she had gone online to search for information about them. Bentley Masterton was a preacher who had become prominent as a late-night television evangelist. He purportedly had a congregation of ten million people over more than a dozen States. Articles on the man were usually accompanied by photos of him driving expensive cars to do God's work. His church saw wealth as a reward, but was against a system of social welfare. His God seemed to be a different God from the one Anya had learnt about at school. Masterton's father had been a Republican senator until his recent retirement. Blogs were rife with rumours about Bentley's political aspirations and discussion of his charitable works and support for women's shelters. The comments were largely favourable.

Kitty Rowe, on the other hand, had a mother who was a professor of law and a father who ran a media empire. He had a reputation for influencing presidential election outcomes by overtly favouring his preferred candidate in his publications. There was mention of an older brother who worked in Dubai, but he didn't seem to be involved in the family business. Kitty had expanded the empire to involve digital broadcasting and telecommunications and had been photographed a number of times with her controversial father at Bombers football matches. From the number of Internet pictures over the years of him with players, he was a dedicated fan. Given the daughter was in the family business, buying into the club was probably a smart career move.

It did not take a genius to see that a possible political career for Bentley could be greatly enhanced by support from the Rowes.

Masterton held court. 'The New Jersey Bombers were once the pinnacle of this great sport. Our players were admired for their strong Christian values, and their sportsmanship, integrity and dedication to their team, their

84

families and fans. They were the envy of all the other clubs in this league. Our reputation was forged on players who were living legends. Parents right across this country admired them and children aspired to be like them.' The fingers on his nugget hand gnarled into a fist.

Anya was unsure where the one-sided conversation was headed.

'But the Devil has infiltrated our army of believers. Temptation has besmirched our glorious name.'

'Christ, Masterton. We're paying her to work, not listen to you preach.'

The older man, Lyle Buffet, appeared to be the highest authority in the room. A Google search had brought up thousands of articles about his hiring and firing of players, team doctors and management; it seemed he had one of the most hands-on approaches in the game. He clearly expected unquestioning loyalty from his employees and wasn't afraid to speak bluntly to the other two owners of the club.

Kitty Rowe flashed a smile. 'What we're all trying to say is that we want to represent a clean, drug-free team untainted by scandal and sexual impropriety. It's come to the media's attention that there are a number of bad seeds ruining the game for all of us.'

Anya decided to cut to the chase. 'I am aware of the statistics that around twenty-five percent of football players are convicted felons – for crimes involving drug dealing, domestic violence and sexual assault. There appears to be a plethora of steroid, substance and alcohol abuse as well. Like so many other team sports involving men, I believe there is a certain degree of misogyny embedded in the culture.'

The woman stroked her choker with an outstretched middle finger. 'That is one point of view.'

Buffet made a sucking noise as he worked a toothpick around his top teeth. In front of him sat a half-eaten tuna sandwich. 'The bottom line is there's more competition for the attention and dollars of fans today than we've had to face before. Football has always been a national sport. An institution. A religion.'

Buffet glanced in Masterton's direction, but there was no contradiction.

'With all these so-called scandals, families – in particular mothers and therefore their children – are turning their backs on the game. Fewer fans mean fewer backsides on seats and fewer gate takings. That means fewer sponsors. Unless we turn this thing around soon, the club won't survive the next few years.

'That's why we have turned to your particular area of expertise, Doctor Crichton. We want to be the club that leads the way – we want the New Jersey Bombers to be the most family-friendly team in the country.'

Anya knew that if the owners really were sincere, they could attract more women back to the game. In all football codes women had always been the most desirable audience, because they brought their families with them, which ensured long-term, loyal fans. Anya was wondering when the sexual assault allegation was going to be mentioned.

'As you know, I'm here with the league to conduct a series of seminars that involve educating the players about appropriate and inappropriate treatment of women, anger management and education about sexually acquired infections, safe sex and discussions of scenarios in which men and women are vulnerable to assault.' She pulled out three summaries of the course content and handed one to each owner.

Masterton flipped through and paused at a section. 'We do not condone sexual relations outside the sanctity of marriage. I suggest you eliminate this portion —'

'For God's sake, man. Some of our players can barely read and write. Sex education has never been a priority, and you know that as well as the rest of us. They're young, fit and red-blooded. Women hound them. Face it, most of these boys would screw a knot in a piece of wood.' Buffet glanced up at Masterton again. 'Judging by today's reaction, most of what was taught was news to them.'

Anya didn't recall seeing Buffet, but he could have been in the ballroom.

Kitty Rowe took up the brief. 'Catcher, as you heard, a rather delicate situation has arisen today that we would like you and Doctor Crichton to investigate. For the sake of the league and our team, we agree this should remain private until more facts are known. An incident occurred at the Rainier Hotel that allegedly involved five of our most valued players. A young woman has accused them of assault. Of course, we have no idea if there is any veracity to the claim but feel it is in all of our best interests if you could discreetly review the medical evidence, talk to the police – and perhaps the woman – and let us know if you believe there could be a case to answer, or if these players are a legal liability.'

Anya was expecting the incident to be raised but felt uncomfortable giving advice to Linda Gatby *and* the owners. She would have to consider the victim's privacy first.

In Anya's experience, the number of women who voluntarily had sex with a group of sportsmen was very low. Footy chicks, as they were known in Australia, were a particular breed of women, akin to rock groupies, but they did exist. Some didn't even mind being degraded and humiliated. One biography she knew of described how famous soccer players would make naked women hop like bunnies, or crawl around the floor barking, just for laughs. The reality was that there were a very small number of women prepared to do almost anything to say they had slept with someone famous, rich or powerful.

Masterton refilled his coffee. 'We spend a fortune each year preparing for the draft. In his capacity as a private investigator with the league, Catcher assists us in background checks on some of the players we hope to bring to our team. Our handpicked doctors thoroughly assess them for potential susceptibility to injury. What we would like from you, Doctor Crichton, is your professional opinion as to whether these men have committed a serious crime, and the chances of them being brought to trial. We are looking at stricter morals clauses in our contracts with the intention of enforcing them to reduce the escalating costs of defending criminal charges.'

Anya suspected that being female also helped give the public the impression that the owners were committed to finding out whether their players had committed gang-rape. She had a feeling her involvement would not stay secret for long, if the club wanted to set itself apart as family-friendly and respectful of women.

Anya had a lot to think about before she could give them a full answer. How long she wanted to stay in New York was the obvious first question. She told Masterton she would find out what she could in the short-term, providing it did not impinge on the victim's rights. It sounded vague, but she couldn't promise any more at this moment. The trio nodded, accepting that for now.

Anya collected her bag and left. Ethan remained inside for a few minutes, then joined her out by the elevators.

Once they were outside on the street, he asked, 'What did you think of Masterton?'

She dared not say what she really thought about him being a smarmy peddler of his version of religion, but didn't quite stay as diplomatic as she intended. 'I can see him doing well preaching to the converted.'

Ethan laughed and Anya felt a natural warmth between

88

them. For the first time she noticed that he laughed with his eyes as well as his mouth.

'Those three can be intimidating but it helps to know what's at stake. Despite winning the championship, the Bombers are haemorrhaging money and they need to do something radical to save the club. If news gets out that some of the players have been accused of rape, it could send the club into financial ruin.'

Anya didn't know how her role would prevent that if the evidence did suggest the players were guilty, but she didn't say anything.

They waited to cross a busy road.

'What's Buffet's story?' She had read that he was the mastermind behind the team's success, but judging by his physique he had probably never been a player.

'I've known him a long time. He comes across as cantankerous and isn't afraid to bully people, but he's got the best of intentions. He's passionate about the game and knows more about it than just about anyone alive. Hey, we've got some time. I want to show you something.'

He hailed a taxi, and they climbed in.

'The Rockefeller Center, thanks,' Ethan instructed.

He bought two tickets at the booth out front while Anya admired the Metropolitan Museum of Art shop on a corner of the square that resembled the United Nations with all of its flags. 'Let's go,' he said and led the way inside.

'What are we here for?' Anya asked. 'What's this got to do with Buffet?'

'I'm glad you asked,' Ethan said with a cheeky expression. 'First, have a look around.' Large black and white photos adorned the walls, with blue, pink and mauve hues highlighting historical anecdotes and facts. Anya read as they wound their way along. A picture of one of her favourite actors, Gregory Peck, caught her attention. So did two quotes, which were particularly touching.

Unto he who much is given, much shall be required. It was attributed to John D Rockefeller Jr, the man responsible for the whole centre and its artwork collection.

'OK, Rockefeller modified a biblical verse, but the sentiment is what Buffet believes,' Ethan explained. 'He is a descendant of John Jr, and has amassed his own fortune through property development and savvy investments. He may be pretty tight-fisted at times, but he demands no more from his people than he expects from himself.'

Ethan really did respect the old man.

They moved along to see images of the building in construction, and an iconic image of eleven workers with their feet dangling, eating lunch on a girder suspended hundreds of metres above street level. All Anya could think was how the lack of safety equipment compromised their lives. Even so, a letter from the Sheet-Metal Workers' Union was cited: *In this bitter workaday world, especially now, your action stands out as a beacon light to those who earn their livelihood by the sweat of their brow.*

'You would have thought that in the Depression people would have resented Rockefeller with all his wealth. But they worshipped him because he saved the lives of who knows how many by giving them work so they could feed their families. My grandfather was one of those workers, and had nothing but praise for people who used their wealth for good. I think Buffet's a lot like John Jr. When I was struggling, Buffet employed me as part of his dream to help make football a game that provided hope to kids who struggled in early life, through poverty, drug addiction and child abuse or neglect. I don't just do background checks. I help players out where possible and help solve problems they can't manage alone.'

Anya had to admit that the cause was noble, and understood that Buffet was responsible for a large number of jobs, in fact an entire industry, built around his team.

Ethan's history with Buffet also explained his willingness to arrange the hastily convened meeting that had just taken place. She wondered if he would have been so quick if it had been another team within the league. In fact, she wondered whether Ethan's obvious fondness for Buffet, and subsequently the Bombers, would ever present a conflict of interest.

She wandered along a glass beam, designed to mimic the height of the famous girder, and felt giddy looking down, even though it was only an illusion. A photographer offered to take her picture, but she declined. Rockefeller still had had a duty to his employees to ensure their safety and that of the people below who might have been affected by his employees' actions.

She hoped Buffet felt the same way.

Ethan answered a call and his face became solemn. His hair flopped over his eyes as he listened to the caller.

'We have to go.'

'You mean you brought me here and we're not going to go all the way to the top?'

'Don't worry, we'll make it back before you go home. That's a promise. But right now someone is in serious trouble.'

Anya and Ethan arrived at the private gym. Two ambulances and a police car were already outside. A large group of curious onlookers were being kept at bay by a couple of uniformed officers.

Ethan grabbed Anya by the hand and pushed through the crowd. 'Doctor coming through, it's an emergency.' He said something to one of the police officers, Anya didn't hear what, and they were allowed past.

A gym worker opened the door and pointed in the direction of the change rooms. Techno music blared over the sound system, while players sat on equipment or stood around, towels draped over their shoulders. Eerily, no one spoke.

'Players get four hours' exclusive access a day to train at specific private gyms when they're in New York,' Ethan explained as they entered the men's locker room. Inside, a large Caucasian man was being worked on by four paramedics. One had the head, another performed cardiac massage. The other two administered drugs and kept notes.

'Heard someone needed a doctor,' Ethan announced. 'What happened?'

The man at the player's head checked the cardiac monitor, which showed a spike only when his partner compressed and released the patient's sternum. He obscured part of a large tattoo across the man's chest.

'Looks like an OD. We found that by his body.' He gestured towards an empty vial. From the appearance, the markings had been removed. A needle and syringe lay nearby, drops of blood in its tip.

'Is there a chance he's diabetic?' Anya asked, hoping to rule out something reversible. A quick scan of his naked torso failed to show any medical alert tag or bracelet.

Anya recognised him from the ballroom that morning.

'Not according to his friend here.' The paramedic nodded to a red-headed man.

'We're about to give dextrose,' the paramedic announced.

Anya noted it was the same protocol as in Australia. The man temporarily stopped cardiac massage long enough to inject around fifty ml into a prominent vein in the back of the patient's hand. The monitor remained silent.

'What locker was he using?' Ethan wanted to know.

The red-head showed him. 'Is he going to be all right?'

No one could answer that.

Ethan rummaged through the locker contents.

Anya concentrated on the resuscitation attempt. 'What do the pupils look like?'

'Constricted and nonreactive,' the man with the dextrose replied before returning to his tackle box.

If he were hypoglycaemic from an overdose of insulin, the injection of sugar should have made a difference. He could have been in a hyperglycaemic coma, but if he were diabetic there should have been signs before he collapsed. Fixed small pupils suggested opiates. The syringe could have contained heroin, methadone or a similar potent concoction.

'How was he behaving before he collapsed?' she demanded of the friend.

'He had a good workout. After that, I saw him down a couple of bottles of Gatorade and we were joking around.' The man clutched his head with both hands. 'Why isn't he waking up?'

'Did anyone see him collapse? Any detail would help.'

The friend struggled to remain calm. 'He came in here to do a couple of press interviews where it was quieter . . . I wanted an extra towel and he was . . . he was right there on the floor. Not moving.'

Ethan held an empty urine jar with a piece of paper towel. 'There's white powder on the rim. Looks like he used this to dissolve what he injected. My guess is heroin.'

'Administering Narcan,' one of the officers said and there was a pause. Again, the strapping body remained lifeless.

Anya turned to the red-head and looked him in the eye. 'This is really important. Did your friend inject himself with drugs?'

The man's eyes flicked to Ethan and back, as if asking permission to answer. 'No. I mean, he swore he was clean from the moment his wife told him she was pregnant. His boy turned two just last month.'

Ethan slipped something from the locker into his pocket.

More Narcan was administered but with no effect. The paramedics exhausted their protocol before transporting the body to hospital. Nothing short of a miracle would bring this man to life. Even so, the emergency doctors would probably try intra-cardiac adrenalin and other last-ditch procedures so that at least the family would know that everything possible had been done.

Anya thought of a young child losing his father, and a wife about to become a widow. She wondered why.

Twenty-eight-year-old Robert Keller was pronounced dead at 8.45 pm. Anya and Ethan waited at the hospital until the news was confirmed, then headed back to the Hyde Hotel in silence.

In a corner of the bar, Anya placed a bottle of beer and an empty glass on the table for Ethan. She kept the whisky and dry for herself.

'How well did you know him?'

'I met him a few seasons back when there were rumours about his drug taking. He's supposed to have got hooked on prescription painkillers then moved on to heavier stuff.' Ethan took a swig, ignoring the glass. 'He got kicked off his old team and word was he got married and cleaned up his act. The West Coast Sharks only signed him last season. He'd tell anyone who'd listen about that kid of his.' He gulped more beer. 'Guess once an addict . . .'

'Maybe he really was clean, only something caused him to relapse.'

'Your talk today would push anyone over the edge.'

Anya accidentally swallowed the ice with her mouthful, then noticed the lopsided grin.

'Thanks for that five-star review!' She was grateful for Ethan's black humour. The day had been harrowing and his comment released the tension.

The bar had begun to fill with groups of young women, some dressed as if about to appear in an MTV video. Tight dresses that barely obscured underwear, shirts unbuttoned revealing frilly bras, bright red lips and false eyelashes seemed standard attire. They stood around as if waiting for something to happen, many ordering champagne or spirits. None looked older than twenty-five, although it was impossible to tell for certain.

Ethan did not seem to notice. 'Because of Keller's history, the Sharks had him tested on random days each week. It was part of his contract. They were all negative as far as I know, so no one was particularly concerned.' He ran a finger around the rim of the bottle. 'Imagine coming all that way then blowing it for a high.'

'Ironically, being drug-free would have made him more vulnerable to dying from an overdose. He would no longer have tolerance to the drug. It's why so many people die within a couple of hours of leaving prison. Their bodies can't tolerate pure heroin, and one dose is all it can take.'

Having a child was life-changing and made the impossible seem within reach. Thinking of Keller's fatherless son, Anya felt further away from her own child. She checked her watch. Ben would be at school and would not arrive home for a few more hours. She would have to wait to phone.

Ethan finished the beer and ordered another, while Anya chose white wine. She took the opportunity to ask the waitress if there was a function tonight.

The waitress glanced at the groups of young women at the bar. 'They've found out some of the players are staying here and they know the boys are likely to hit the bars after dinner.'

'They're all groupies?'

'Yep.' The waitress wiped the table. 'Get them every time a team's staying here.'

Anya wondered if any of them ever imagined they could be the victim of a violent assault or contract a sexually acquired infection by hooking up with a player.

'There are people who would give everything they had just to be alive, let alone free of illness and pain. And Keller throws his life away like that.' Ethan clicked his fingers.

'Sometimes pain isn't physical,' Anya offered, unsure why Ethan seemed to be taking Keller's death so hard. 'No one really knows what a person goes through.'

Ethan's vulnerability made her want to reach out to him, but she had no idea how. They continued their drinks in silence, Anya watching the women continue to preen until a procession of towering men entered the bar as if they were rock stars. Bar patrons turned and gawked, some of the women squealed and greeted the players by name.

'Do you know the names of the Bombers players who are accused of the assault last night?' Anya asked.

'You already know some of them. For one, Pistol Pete Janson impressed you straight up.'

The cocky wise-cracker from the morning's lectures.

'Is his friend McKenzie on the list?'

'Sure is, as well as a guy who seemed more reasonable. An African-American guy from the front row. Name of Alldridge. It sounds like at least two rookies were in the room but we need to check that out.'

'Hey, Catcher.' A player Anya didn't recognise slapped Ethan on the back.

'I gather you know Doctor Crichton,' he responded.

Recognition showed on the player's face and he hastily withdrew. Another approached and changed course when he saw Anya.

The waitress delivered their second round and whispered to Ethan as she slipped something into his shirt pocket.

'Thanks guys,' he said loudly, removing a row of condoms and holding them up. 'Very funny.'

A cheer went up and Anya felt her face flush. She thought Ethan's face coloured for a moment as well.

The music grew louder and the beat intensified. She could see the attraction for many of the girls. A number of the men were handsome, had muscular physiques and the confidence of movie stars. Drinks flowed and bodies moved closer. A couple of girls began dancing on their own, successfully garnering attention. Pheromones were in abundance.

A smaller, stocky man carrying a beer asked if he could join them. Anya was pleased for the diversion.

'Enjoyed your presentations today,' he managed over the noise. 'Thought I had a handle on all that, but some of what you said blew me away.'

She appreciated the comment, and was reassured that some men in the group had listened.

The man twisted a gold band on his left ring finger. 'Makes me glad I'm married and don't have to worry about any of that stuff.'

'How long?' she asked.

'Seven great years. College sweethearts. We've got two girls, six and four. You wanna see?'

He pulled out his wallet and proudly displayed a picture of the three women in his life, pointing out each one's name. He was clearly devoted.

It was touching to see a so-called gladiator bragging about his family back home. 'They're gorgeous,' she said and meant it.

'I got to thinking about those scenes you showed. You know, if anyone did those things to one of my daughters, I'd wanna kill them.' A cheer rose, and their attention turned to the crowd. 'It suddenly occurred to me that every woman here is someone's daughter. Makes you really think.'

Ethan asked, 'Would you ever let one of your girls date a footballer?'

'Hell no.' The father stood, abandoning his drink. He pulled out an envelope from his back pocket, and another from the other side. 'Took up a collection for Keller's widow. It isn't much, but it's a start.' Ten and fifty dollar notes bulged out of each envelope. He patted Ethan's shoulder. 'I'm gonna turn in. Have a good one. Pleasure to meet you, Doctor, look forward to your next talk.'

After the group's collective response this morning, it was a relief to talk to a player like this. He seemed decent, honest and family oriented. Anya's faith in the supposed ten percent of dissenters, the non-followers, was restored. Her task was to somehow get through to the other ninety percent.

12

With a heavy head, Anya opened the daily papers delivered to her door and read the headlines. Yesterday had been longer and more difficult than she had expected. After leaving the bar, she'd had to wait up for Ben to get back home from school. Now her body was paying the price.

Aspirin dulled her headache and weary muscles, while coffee jump-started the rest. She opted for fruit and muesli from the room service menu. Something healthy should boost her energy levels.

Leading the news was Robert Keller's death from a suspected heart attack following a rigorous workout. A cardiologist commented on the sudden deaths of athletes and possible causes. There was no mention of self-administration of drugs as the cause of death. A 'family source' said that Robert had had flu-like symptoms the week before, while another described the devastation his wife felt at the news. Anya couldn't recall the number of times celebrity deaths were described as 'heart attacks', prior to toxicology results, which took weeks, and by then public interest had waned.

Sharks fans were interviewed, as were other prominent players. Peter Janson was pictured, with a comment about how he and Keller had been close friends since playing in their high school team together. A representative from Nike expressed sadness at the death, and there was a brief mention of the multimillion-dollar deal the company had signed with the star player.

She flicked through for other news and stopped cold at a headline.

Crying rape, the new ticket to instant wealth.

It appeared in the opinion pages. She took a mouthful of hot coffee and read on.

> *Long gone are the days where women married for money and, as the saying goes, they earned every penny. Instead of setting their sights on a gold ring from an older, wealthier man, today's ambitious young women target our famous heroes. Many of these men have fought hard all their lives to achieve what most mere mortals cannot. The latest victims of the cry-rape scam are our elite sportsmen.*
>
> *The plan is simple. The predatory woman dresses up. She may even surgically enhance herself, or change her appearance with wigs or hairpieces. The destination is any party the players attend as part of their promotional duties, usually while they're on the road. The woman flirts with her quarry with blatant disregard for the players' wives or girlfriends back home. Later, they lure the player, or players in some cases, to a hotel room. After entrapping the players into having sex, they immediately cry rape. It's a scam threatening to destroy the fiber of many of our greatest team sports. Football, hockey, basketball and soccer have all fallen victim to it.*
>
> *Publicity is ensured for the woman, who usually employs her own lawyer, and 'negotiations' begin for a settlement. As with all fraudulent schemes, money is the bottom line.*

Anya's hand shook and coffee spilt on the page. She put the cup down on the bedside table and grabbed some tissues from the bathroom to soak up the mess. Lifting the tabloid, some drops splattered onto the white bedlinen. Damn.

She sat on the edge of the bed and wiped her hands before turning her attention back to the article. Who the hell had written this guff? It had to be planted by one of the teams, or their PR people. The byline read *Annabelle Reichman*. It still shocked her that women were often the most derisive and judgemental about victims in sexual assault cases. Gut feeling told her the incident involving Kirsten Byrne was going to feature somewhere in the article.

Out of the 200 reviewed cases of sportsmen accused of rape, only one conviction was recorded. This is lower than conviction rates for the general population. In 199 cases there was not enough evidence to convince a jury that rape had ever taken place. It doesn't take a rocket scientist to realise our players are vulnerable targets for ambitious and unscrupulous women.

Any sensible reader should see that the reasons for those non-conviction stats were far more complex than just false accusations. A traumatised woman had to be extraordinarily strong to go up against a professional team's PR machine, with lawyers, investigators and media digging into her private life. And rape still carried significant social stigma. Anya wondered how Annabelle Reichman justified such distortion of facts.

This completely contradicts the impression the general public are getting about violent, privileged sports stars. Are they paid a huge amount of money for what they do? Yes. But how many workers on Wall Street put their lives on the line every time they go to work? Our footballers are modern-day gladiators who go into war with each and every play. An injury can ruin them for life, so they have to make the most of what they can in their relatively short careers. We cannot begrudge them that. They also perform the extensive behind-the-scenes charity work that is so much a part of being a role model. These altruistic acts are often overlooked or taken for granted, but never by the thousands of children these players inspire and give hope to.

103

In that case, Annabelle Reichman had just argued for members of the armed forces in Iraq and Afghanistan to be paid as much as footballers.

> *A woman who sources confirm targeted Peter Janson for a business deal has claimed he and his friends raped her following a party at the Rainier Hotel this week. Dozens of witnesses saw her flirting with Janson, drinking heavily and cuddling up to him during the evening before boasting that she was going with him to his room. Reliable sources say she has already hired a legal team to represent her. Is that the first thing a genuine victim would do? Did she tell anyone at the party about the so-called attack? No, she quietly left and returned home. It wasn't until the next day that she decided to cry rape. How does a just society allow unsubstantiated claims to be made public before police have even begun an investigation?*
>
> *These women are redefining and diminishing the term 'victim'.*
>
> *It is far too easy to tear down our heroes and role models by crying rape. It is, after all, the new fast-track to fame, money and notoriety. It's time we put a stop to false claims and made the accusers answerable for their lies.*

Anya's teeth ached from clenching her jaw. Annabelle Reichman was the one making the claims public! The injustice and downright misogyny of the article made Anya sick to her stomach.

Her phone's ringtone jolted her back to reality. Linda Gatby was on the line. 'I need to see Kirsten Byrne ASAP, before anyone in the media publishes her name. I'd like you to come with me.'

Anya rubbed the joint connecting her jaw and cheek. 'You need to know that the owners of the Bombers have asked me to investigate the reports to establish whether the complaint has any traction.'

There was a pause on the line. 'I know you'll be professional and only disclose what's in the public domain.'

Anya agreed.

'I've instructed Kirsten not to speak to anyone until we get there. Can you come to my office first? We'll leave from here. I also want to ask Catcher some questions if he's free.'

Anya hurried into the bathroom to change out of her casual clothes. She hoped Kirsten had not yet seen what could be the beginning of a public humiliation in the press.

13

Ethan and Anya arrived at the offices of the special victims' unit within half an hour. Phones rang unanswered, uniformed police stood talking to lawyers or case workers: the few cramped desks were piled high with paperwork. Unlike so many other offices, there was no casual conversation to be heard. They saw Linda Gatby waving to them from the door of a corner office.

'Come in.' She stretched her arms out and hugged Anya like an old friend. 'Thanks for coming. Ethan, do you mind if I talk to Anya privately first?'

She moved some papers and sat on the edge of her desk.

'No problem.' Ethan found a chair outside and began making calls.

'Regarding Kirsten Byrne . . .' Linda put on reading glasses and moved to the leather chair behind her desk, which squeaked as she pulled it in. She opened a file. 'According to the police report, she phoned them at five in the morning and told them she had been raped by four or five footballers at the Rainier Hotel between eleven and midnight.'

'What happened in those few hours before contacting police?' Anya sat forward.

'Apparently she caught a taxi home then locked herself in her apartment, too terrified to call anyone.' She handed across a photograph of a young woman in a hospital gown, revealing her shoulders but hiding her breasts. The skin was abraded in parts, with small streaks of blood in lines.

Anya had seen similar markings before. 'Looks like she showered and scrubbed herself until she bled, probably everywhere she thought the men had touched.'

'That's exactly what happened,' Linda said. 'She continued to use a scourer from the kitchen long after the hot water ran cold.'

Anya knew the problems that could cause for investigators. 'Which means there wasn't much chance of a rape kit providing physical evidence.'

'The uniforms followed procedure and took her to the Emergency department, where a nurse performed a forensic examination, but didn't manage to collect any hairs or semen. I hoped to ask you about the significance of her genital injuries.'

She handed a few more photographs across the desk. Linda was protecting the victim by asking Ethan to wait outside. Kirsten Byrne did not deserve to be violated again by having her photos seen by anyone who wasn't involved in giving a legal or medical opinion. The images showed significant swelling and bruising to her vulval region, and lacerations to her labia major. A rectal tear extended three to four centimetres to her buttock.

'This was a brutal assault, Linda. This tear alone signifies very violent trauma. It's one of the worst I've seen of a surviving victim.'

The prosecutor summarised the alleged assault. 'Kirsten works for a clothing designer and says she was sent to a private party at the hotel to try to meet Pete Janson and pitch a clothing line to him. When he suggested she go upstairs with him to meet his agent, Janson raped her. He had deliberately left the door open and others came in.'

Linda stood up and invited Ethan to join them, and he took the seat by Anya.

'Our victim identified the men in the room as Peter Janson, Liam McKenzie, Clark Garcia and Vince Dorafino, none of whom are strangers to the legal system.' She checked her notes. 'The fifth participant appears to be Lance Alldridge.

'Catcher, do you know much about them?'

He nodded. 'You understand I have to respect confidentiality, but I could give you my personal impressions.'

Linda removed her glasses and nodded.

'Janson is a quarterback with an ego bigger than Texas. He's flashy and tends only to do things if there's something in it for him. McKenzie's the back-up quarterback, huge, arrogant and thinks of himself as a real ladies' man. Alldridge is fairly quiet and I'm surprised he was part of this. Seems like a decent guy. Garcia and Dorafino are rookies trying to fit in and would do anything Janson or McKenzie suggested.'

It sounded like these were boys still in high school.

'Any chance Robert Keller was involved?' Anya asked. Guilt or shame might explain a drug relapse.

'Your OD from last night?' Linda said. 'I already thought of that, but all the alleged attackers play with the Bombers.'

'Did they all supposedly rape the victim?' Ethan asked.

Linda placed her elbows on the desk and her hands under her chin. 'It's one of the problems with these sorts of attacks. After Janson and McKenzie raped her, she said her head was held down, and she didn't see who was behind her. As far as she can recall, she was assaulted by at least four men. She can't identify who did and didn't for sure. Which leaves us with a problem.'

Any defence lawyer would punch holes in the prosecution's case. They could argue all number of things, from mistaken identity to innocence on all of the men's parts. Any doubt as to whether or not every man had raped Kirsten could result in a jury acquitting them all.

'I need to push for a group trial rather than trying them as individuals. That way a jury sees them as the hunting pack they are,' Linda said.

'Can I ask about evidence in the room?' Ethan took out a notebook. 'Did Crime Scene go over the place?'

The prosecutor flicked through the file. 'The lawyers of the accused will find out soon enough. However, I can tell you there was no blood on the bed where Kirsten insists she was attacked.'

Anya found that difficult to believe given the rectal tear she had seen in the photo. 'The rectal injury would have bled a significant amount. In fact, it could bleed on and off for days. When you say on the bed, what exactly did they check for?'

'The police rang the hotel and made sure the rooms weren't cleaned before they got there, but there was nothing on the sheets. No bodily fluids, no hairs, no blood and no semen.' She double-checked the report. 'They did, however, find signs of ejaculate on the floor.'

'And I bet they found semen all over the mattress if they looked under the sheets,' Ethan said. 'It is a hotel bed.'

The thought made Anya uncomfortable. She was going back to sleep in one of those hotel beds tonight. Either the players cleaned the room themselves, or there were problems with Kirsten's story. She was careful not to name the woman in front of Ethan. 'What about the clothes the victim was wearing that night?'

'It's a dress and it does have her blood on it. The lab techs are still working on it.'

'Was she a groupie?' Ethan wanted to know. 'A regular at those parties?'

Linda placed her glasses on the file. 'Are you suggesting a groupie couldn't have been gang-raped?'

'No, of course not,' he said, lifting his hands defensively. 'But if the guys already knew her, or she chased them, you'll have a much harder time proving rape in court. All those events are photographed, and if she's turned up before she'll have little credibility that she went back to the hotel room and didn't expect to have sex.'

As much as Anya hated to admit it, Ethan was right.

But proving to a court that Kirsten had never met any of the footballers before that night would be near on impossible.

14

Ethan returned to the hotel, while Anya accompanied Linda Gatby to the victim's apartment. On the street outside, they had to fight through photographers and reporters. Even though this morning's article had not named Kirsten, reporters had wasted no time in finding out who she was and where she lived.

'I'll get some uniforms down here to keep them out,' Linda snapped. 'This is harassment, and I'll have them charged with stalking if they keep it up.'

The papers had not named Kirsten Byrne, but that was due to editorial policy, not law. An exclusive interview with the 'unnamed victim' in a high-profile case would be a coup, and there was nothing to prevent bloggers and fan sites revealing her identity. The media had historically chosen to protect rape victims by not naming them, but in an age of instant access to information this practice only seemed to pique the public's interest in what victims might have to hide.

In response to their knock on the door of a fourth-floor apartment, an older woman appeared wearing pink rubber gloves and a dark blue apron.

'I know who you are. But is this absolutely necessary to do now?'

'I'm sorry if this is not a good time, but it's important that we speak with Kirsten.'

Linda Gatby handed across her card and walked through the doorway. The apartment felt claustrophobic. Boxes were piled next to a sofa, and clothes were thrown into an open suitcase. With only one internal door, which seemed to lead to the bathroom, Anya assumed the sofa became the bed.

A young woman sat on a cushion on the windowsill, knees pulled up under an oversized shirt. Black leggings covered her legs.

'It's all right, Mom, I need to do this.'

She stood, slowly shuffled across, closed the suitcase and stood in the small area of free floor space. She was clearly still in pain from her injuries.

A small coffee table served as a dining area. Kirsten bent at the knees to clear a pile of books, which included *How to Succeed in Fashion* and *Building a Career in Fashion Design*, and placed them underneath.

She offered her visitors the sofa and sat, tentatively, where the books had been. Mrs Byrne retreated to the nook that was the kitchen.

Linda took out a legal pad and introduced Anya as a leading expert in sexual assault injuries. 'I'm going to ask you to talk to her about the injuries. She may be called on to testify when we go to trial.'

The young woman nodded.

'Are you planning on leaving town?' the lawyer asked.

'I'm taking my daughter home,' Kirsten's mother said. 'This isn't a safe place for a single woman. We tried to tell her that, but —'

'Mom, please. I can speak for myself.' Kirsten addressed Linda. 'I'm going back to Louisville. I can't stay here. Did you see all the people out front? What do they want from me? I didn't do anything wrong but I feel like I'm a prisoner.' She waved an arm in the direction of the window then closed her dark eyes. 'You said it could take months before the case goes to trial.'

Linda's voice softened. 'I did, but it's important that I always know where to contact you. It's early days and I will need to talk to you a number of times leading up to the trial.'

'I'm so scared. What if the men find out where I live?'

Linda sighed. 'I understand you're frightened. What you went through was horrific. But you survived and proved how strong you are. I'll do what I can to make sure you're left alone by those people downstairs.'

The mother used a knife to chip at ice in the freezer section of the fridge. 'We need to leave this hellhole as soon as possible. Your father and I had no idea you'd been living like this.'

Anya wasn't sure what the older woman meant. Was it the size of the apartment, the city, or something she was attacking in the fridge?

'I had a place just like this when I started working at the district attorney's office,' Linda smiled warmly. 'In fact, I think mine was smaller, and the bathroom was shared with the couple down the hall.'

Kirsten looked around. 'I loved this place . . . until the other night. I felt safe here . . . It was supposed to be the beginning of a new life.'

'It still is,' Linda stressed. 'That hasn't changed.'

Mrs Byrne hacked harder at the ice.

Linda clicked her pen. 'We do need to know exactly how you came to be at the Rainier Hotel two nights ago.'

Kirsten's eyes lightened when she talked about her job. 'We were looking at doing a line of clothing involving a high-profile footballer and Cheree thought Janson was a rising star. She wanted to offer him $500,000 plus five percent of net sales.' The young woman leant over and retrieved a file from under the table. 'This is a copy of what I took with me.' She handed it across.

Anya was close enough to see projected sales figures of hundreds of thousands of units in the first month, sketches of sportswear and a chart of the demographics for potential consumers.

Kirsten rubbed her eyes with the palm of one hand. 'I was so stupid to think someone that famous would want to talk business with me.'

She was already blaming herself for what had occurred.

Anya felt for the girl. Physical healing was relatively straightforward. Emotional healing was far more complicated. 'You'd be perfect pitching a project to anyone, famous or otherwise.'

Mrs Byrne threw a solid piece of ice into the sink, startling her daughter. She moved to the sink and wiped her forehead with a gloved hand.

'Damn that woman! She sent my girl off to those . . . those . . . why they're not fit to be called men – even dressed my baby up like a two-bit hooker.'

'Mom. Stop! It wasn't like that.'

'That Jordan woman used you.' The knife followed the ice with a thud. 'And you're the one left with nothing.' She wiped her nose and grabbed her bag. 'I need to get more ammonia and vinegar. Don't open the door to anyone while I'm out.'

Anya suspected the mother felt guilty about not being able to protect her child. Instead of helping, though, her comments sent mixed messages to her daughter, and would to a defence team as well.

Linda Gatby leant forward. 'What a woman wears is her own choice. You have every right to dress the way you want, change your hair, wear make-up and go to parties.' She locked eyes with Kirsten. 'Those men had no right to touch you without your consent. End of story.'

Kirsten buried her face in her hands. 'Part of me knows that, but I can't help wondering if I did something to give Pete Janson the wrong idea. I mean, he was different before we went upstairs and I liked him. I guess it was flattering having a superstar pay me all that attention.' She looked up at both women. 'It was wrong, I know.'

'Janson and his friends are predators. Those sorts of men charm women, trick them, then rape them.' Linda spoke firmly and with the authority of someone who knew a lot about rapists and their behaviours. 'Besides, he's married. He knew exactly what he was doing.'

'That's what I keep telling myself.' Kirsten took a few deep breaths. 'Sorry about Mom. She's still in shock and she's having trouble handling the whole thing. In some way she thinks I'm like damaged goods now. That's why she doesn't want my boyfriend to know.' She lowered her gaze. 'I haven't told him yet, I don't know how to.'

Kirsten was trying to support her mother and protect her boyfriend during her own crisis. She was obviously a strong young woman, and would need to be if she were to endure the legal process of a trial.

'Have either of you been in touch with a counsellor?' Anya asked.

'The hospital gave me a number to call.' Kirsten located her wallet and pulled out a card. 'I'll call them when Mom calms down. But now I lost my job, I don't know how I'll pay for it.'

Anya's phone buzzed. Ethan Rye was on the line. She switched it off and let it go to voicemail. 'You said you *lost* your job?'

Kirsten rubbed her temples. 'Cheree fired me when I got home from the hospital yesterday. She said they were down-sizing and had to cut staff. I was the last to start, so first to go. That's why I have to go home. This week is my last pay cheque. I'm sorry, I don't think it's all sunk in yet.'

Anya wasn't surprised. The physical trauma alone would have exhausted Kirsten's young body, let alone the emotional challenges she now faced.

'There will be some detectives from the special unit I work for coming to see you again, but don't be disturbed. It's important we have all the facts before the men are arrested. If any of them makes any attempt to contact you, let me know immediately, no matter what time of day or night.'

Kirsten nodded.

Linda put the file Kirsten had given her into her leather satchel and looked at Anya. As planned, Anya would ask the medical questions alone.

'I'll be in the coffee shop across the road,' Linda said, and she told Kirsten she would ring later to see how she was doing.

Anya had in her bag a body chart and notepad. 'I know this isn't going to be easy, but I need to go through some of the things that happened that night, once you were upstairs.'

The young woman steeled herself and stared at her hands, as if garnering strength from them.

'I thought we were there to see his agent. God, that sounds so stupid now. I went up to the room and he made a call. I thought he was calling his agent. He closed the door, with the pull-across lock blocking it from closing completely. I was practising the spiel in my head when Pete went to the bathroom. Then he came out, but he didn't have any pants on. I mean nothing, and he had an . . . I mean, it was obvious his penis was erect.'

'How did you react?'

'I just kept saying it was all a mistake. This was just a business proposition. I guess part of me thought it had to be a sick joke.'

Anya could picture the scene. A naïve young woman doing her job, with a man who saw her not as a person but as a sexual toy. Except this man was much larger and stronger, trained to push through any obstacles that got in the way of what he wanted. Kirsten was no match.

'Only he didn't listen. When I said about the business proposition, he said he had one of his own. When he was on top of me, I could barely breathe. He was so heavy and too strong. I tried to push him off. You have to understand. There was nothing I could do. It was like a really bad dream where you can't scream, only it was real.'

Anya offered to get her a glass of water, but Kirsten plainly wanted to continue, and get it over with.

'I went to one of those self-defence classes in high school. But I didn't have a chance to gouge his eyes or hurt him. I was so scared and I just couldn't believe any of it was happening.'

The sound of a siren crescendoing outside made her stop. Kirsten took a few deep breaths as if she were about to dive underwater.

'I heard someone yelling for help, and realised it was me. Another man, they called him Liam, came in.'

Liam McKenzie. Anya doubted this was the first time he and Janson had acted together to rape.

'He walked into the room and I ran to him for help. I grabbed his arm and he asked what was going on. Just then, other men came in. Two of them had dark hair and were drinking. They cheered Janson as if he was some kind of hero. It was like I didn't exist. Then Liam grabbed me by the waist and threw me onto the bed, with my face in the pillow. I tried to scream again, but they were all laughing.' She paused and closed her eyes for a moment. 'I didn't think it could be worse, but he raped me from behind and that hurt so much more.'

Anya had seen the forensic photos. The injury had required stitches, not something usually associated with consensual intercourse of any form.

'I got held down and I think the two other men I hadn't seen before raped me too. I turned my head and saw a black man inside the door and thought he would help me. But then he moved so I couldn't see him and I got raped from behind again.'

Her eyes were now glassy, as if she were detached from her own story. 'It's weird, but to shut out the pain I sort of went outside myself, like I was looking down on what was happening to me.'

Anya had heard this from victims a number of times, as if separating from the experience was necessary for survival.

'I thought they were going to kill me because I'd seen all their faces. Pretty sad that I was grateful when they didn't. After everything they did to me.'

'How did you get away?'

'Someone said there was a party in another room, and by then Pete Janson had gone. When the last one got off me I got dressed as fast as I could and ran out the door.'

The muffled ringing of a phone interrupted. Kirsten dug beneath some clothes to locate it. 'That could be my dad – he said he'd call. Hello?' Suddenly, the blood seemed to drain from her face and she dropped the phone.

Anya moved to catch her in case she fainted. 'Who was it?'

'I don't know, but it was a man.' She was shaking. 'He said he would make sure I never got to lie in court about being raped. He said I wouldn't live long enough to testify.'

15

It was no surprise to Anya that Ethan had discovered Kirsten's identity by the time she had left the apartment and met up with him again. With all the media out the front and people Tweeting the location, it would not have taken the private investigator long to find out.

She just had to be careful she did not disclose confidential information to him as they made some enquiries together on behalf of the Bombers' management.

The guard at the desk glanced at them and took a bite of an oversized sandwich.

Ethan placed an elbow on the desk and leant over. 'Don't mean to interrupt, but we have an appointment to see Cheree Jordan.'

The guard chewed with his mouth open and referred to a printout on his desk. 'Names?'

'Ethan Rye and Doctor Anya Crichton.'

The man looked up at Anya. 'You don't look like a doctor.'

Anya thought that he didn't look like much of a guard, but refrained from commenting.

'Sign here.' They were each given a sheet to sign, and issued with a security pass. 'Through those glass doors and it's the twenty-sixth floor.' The sandwich quickly consumed his attention again.

On the twenty-sixth floor, a middle-aged receptionist seemed equally unimpressed by the visitors.

'Take a seat. I'll tell her you're here. Where are you from again?'

'We're here about the alleged attack on one of her employees.'

The woman didn't bat an eyelid, but picked up her phone, informed Ms Jordan, then collected her bag from the desk. Ignoring a ringing phone, she headed off down another corridor. It seemed nothing stopped lunch in this building.

Twenty minutes later, a heavily made-up Cheree Jordan floated into the foyer in a silk kaftan top, black leggings and chunky high heels.

'So sorry to have kept you, but I don't know what I can say about that nasty business with Kirsten Byrne.'

'I suspect you'll be more help than you might imagine.' Ethan smiled.

She showed them into a conference room, with a glass table, whiteboard and a rack of clothes along one wall. Opposite, a wall-mounted TV played a DVD of the latest Cheree Jordan Collection.

'We don't have a lot of office space, so this doubles up as product storage.' She looked at Anya. 'A size eight, slightly pear-shaped, high-waisted. We could do a lot with those legs of yours.' As her arms moved, a horde of bracelets jingled. 'Skirts are up this year, dowdy is very last decade.'

Anya thought Ethan suppressed a laugh. She dressed for comfort and practicality and didn't appreciate the designer's rudeness. Not that her obvious annoyance stopped the pitch.

'Our latest range would be perfect for you. Silky feminine fabrics especially for working women . . .' She peeled off a black jacket from its hanger and turned it inside out, revealing a mauve jacket with black lining. 'These reversible jackets are so versatile. Absolute genius.'

Ethan interrupted. 'We're investigating the alleged assault on Kirsten Byrne.'

'Terrible business. I should have known that girl was too ambitious for her own good.' She gestured for them both to take a seat and pulled out a BlackBerry, which she placed in front of herself on the table.

'Why do you say that?'

The wrists jingled again. 'Small-town girl with big dreams. That's why I hired her. The fire in the belly, desire to achieve. Only I never imagined she'd be prepared to go to any lengths to further her career.'

Anya glanced at Ethan. 'Do you think she is lying about the assault?'

Cheree pursed her cerise-coloured lips, but her forehead didn't move in response. Botox, Anya guessed. 'Put it this way, I wouldn't put it past her to sleep with someone to further her career.'

The comment surprised Anya. 'She was at the function representing you and your company. Is that correct?'

A message or email seemed to hold Cheree's attention for a moment. 'Yes, I wanted to organise a meeting with Pete Janson about a range of clothing exclusive to our label. We can move over 10,000 units of just about anything we make during an hour of television advertising.' She clicked her fingers. 'People underestimate the power of a home-shopping network.'

And vulnerable people's desperation for quick-fix weight-loss products, exercise machines and useless home products, Anya thought. The pressure to buy instantly was almost unethical.

'So why was Kirsten,' Ethan asked, 'one of your junior staff, trying to set up a business meeting that night?'

A young woman arrived at the door with a tray of mugs and a plunger of coffee. Cheree waved her in. She placed mugs in front of each of them and poured the coffee.

'Do you have any idea how many people block access to football stars? They have managers, agents, minders, coaches, bodyguards and heaven only knows how many other hangers-on trying to prevent anyone talking to them. This is a lucrative business offer, and Pete Janson should have had the opportunity to hear about it first-hand.' She instructed her assistant to stay. The woman adjusted her rimless glasses and joined them.

'So Kirsten went to the party specifically to meet Janson in person and pitch the deal?'

'Yes, but she wasn't supposed to sleep with him, or anyone else. That was never part of her job description.'

The comment took Anya by surprise. It implied that Jordan assumed the sex had been consensual.

Ethan sat back. Anya could not read his expression. 'We have reason to believe she was raped by a number of men that night.'

The assistant's eyes widened. She obviously hadn't heard about the alleged assault.

Ethan continued. 'Was she a football fan?'

The designer scoffed. 'She couldn't tell a football from a snooker ball.'

'Then why send her?'

Cheree checked her phone again. 'This business is about appearance and market research. Janson is known to favour long-haired blondes, so we decided to maximise the chances that he would notice Kirsten in a crowd.'

Anya began to feel uncomfortable. The woman admired ambition and thought nothing of playing on appearances to secure a business deal, yet she seemed shocked that it could lead to sex, consensual or otherwise. She was being disingenuous.

'And the little vixen stole my dress. It's a one-off worth over two thousand dollars.'

A man with a beard stood in the doorway. 'Boss, we need you for a moment on the photo shoot.'

'Excuse me,' Cheree stood. 'I have a business to run. Deborah here can show you out. If that girl doesn't return my dress, I'll sue. Perhaps that's a language she does understand.'

She grabbed her BlackBerry and wafted away, before Anya could explain that the police were examining the dress for forensic evidence. That the woman would be so unsympathetic towards an employee she had sent into the very situation that had resulted in her assault defied belief. Cheree had pimped her own staff member.

On the screen, a tall thin woman walked fiercely down a catwalk.

The assistant removed her glasses, her hands shaking slightly. 'Is that true about Kirsten?'

Anya nodded. 'Do you know her well?'

'She was always polite and kept to herself. She worked hard, didn't go out much. I think she wanted to make her mother and father proud, and she said she had a boyfriend back home.'

'Cheree said Janson likes blondes, but I thought Kirsten had dark hair.' Ethan looked confused.

Deborah stood and led them through the door to the elevators. 'I know Cheree can sound . . . harsh . . . but she really has a great eye for fashion and make-up. Kirsten had one of her makeovers. Everyone here would die to get that much attention from Cheree. Kirsten has nice bone structure and if she lost a few pounds she could be really pretty. Anyway, because she loved her job, Kirsten went along with it.'

Ethan asked her if she had a picture of how Kirsten looked after the makeover.

'There's one on my phone I took before she left that night.' She pulled it from a pinafore pocket and scrolled through the images on the screen to show them.

A woman with a long, slicked-back blonde ponytail posed in a halterneck mini-dress and high heels. She didn't look anything like the woman Anya had seen earlier.

'With lighter hair colour, clip-on extensions and a killer dress, she looked like a whole new person. I barely recognised her. It was like Cinderella, only Cheree was her fairy godmother.'

The question defence lawyers would ask had to be broached. 'Do you think Kirsten went that night to try to seduce Pete Janson?'

Deborah adjusted the frames of her glasses again and led them inside the elevator. She waited until the doors closed.

'She practised her pitch all afternoon and memorised a kind of script Cheree had written in case she got close enough to get his attention. She wanted to get into the party, give him her spiel and get out. I've never seen anyone so nervous. When Cheree told us she had resigned, I couldn't believe it.'

The last comment was news. Kirsten said Cheree had sacked her. 'When did this happen?'

'Cheree told us all this morning. I assumed Kirsten got the deal done and got offered something better. I swear to you, I had no idea about any assault.' As the doors opened, her phone buzzed and she checked the text. 'I'm sorry, I have to go.' She held the doors open for them. 'If you see Kirsten, please send her my love, and if there's anything I can do to help . . .'

Ethan nodded.

In the lobby they placed their passes on the guard's desk. He was nowhere in sight but the crumbs from his lunch were scattered across his computer keyboard. A trolley of boxes stood nearby.

Ethan whistled. 'Expensive taste in champagne. Those boxes are going to Cheree's office. Either she's a big drinker or there's something to celebrate.'

They took the revolving door out to the street.

'She is ruthless,' Anya said. 'She basically prostituted an employee to get to Janson. It's impossible to believe that she dressed Kirsten the way Janson likes and then is shocked that he made it sexual. It's so hypocritical, accuse Kirsten of being ambitious, then sack her and lie to the staff.'

Anya could feel her pulse quicken. Cheree Jordan had no sympathy for Kirsten, no remorse about her involvement, and was now about to have a party.

Ethan hailed a taxi. 'I agree. I think Kirsten was the naïve one, and my gut tells me she went into that party like a lamb to the slaughter. But a defence lawyer will tear her apart. It'll look like entrapment once they're finished with her. And to be honest, a jury might not be too sympathetic to her cause.'

What niggled Anya was Deborah's suggestion that Kirsten had closed the deal with Janson. If that's what they were celebrating upstairs, Kirsten's case just got a lot less credible.

16

From the subway, Anya wandered along 34th Street, glancing in the shop windows, the evening breeze brushing her face. She wanted to see Macy's famed window displays. *Miracle on 34th Street* had been a favourite since she was a child.

She wasn't disappointed. One window contained a stunning black dress on a mannequin, highlighted by a simple silver necklace. Anya held her wrap more firmly and admired the classic style of the outfit. She could picture Audrey Hepburn in it.

She wished there was someone to share this with. With one hand, she touched the cool glass, feeling like the child she wished she could have been – innocent, happy and wrapped in the warmth and safety of family. Her childhood Christmas memories were of an empty place setting, where Miriam would have sat. The stifling heat frayed her mother's nerves after she had sweltered to cook turkey and ham, then she'd receive a call to attend to some sick patient. Anya would be left babysitting Danny, under strict instruction not to unlock the front door to anyone.

One day, she hoped to bring Ben to New York for a wintry Christmas. She could imagine them marvelling at the Christmas tree outside the Rockefeller Center with its lights and decorations, ice-skating in Central Park and dancing on the keyboard in FAO Schwartz together. She wanted him to have happy memories of his childhood, even more so now his parents were divorced.

A gust of wind stirred a discarded piece of paper on the footpath in the direction of Madison Square Garden. No need to check her map: the noise and the sea of people decked out in variations of orange and blue signalled the way.

Ethan had asked her to meet him outside the garden. Despite knowing they were seeing a basketball game at one of the world's most famous venues, she was still taken aback by the chants from an open-top bus filled with supporters parked right out the front. Uniformed police stopped traffic for revellers to cross the road in streams. A brass band added to the festivities.

Anya had to smile. The excitement was infectious. Near the bus, Ethan Rye stood, hands shoved into the pockets of a hooded leather jacket.

'Hey.' He smiled broadly. 'Glad you could make it. Hope you're hungry 'cause they have some of the city's finest upstairs.'

Anya felt her stomach gurgle. She hadn't eaten lunch and now her hunger was catching up with her.

Ethan led her by the elbow towards the entrance. Once under cover, her ears began to ache. The cacophony from the throngs lining up to enter the stadium was almost earsplitting. Bypassing the queues, Ethan led her to a VIP entrance. They made their way up an escalator to the third level and entered the foyer of the Club Bar and Grill.

'This is one of the best places in town,' Ethan said.

Anya studied some of the framed images of ice hockey players, basketballers and even boxers on the purple-padded walls. Above them, sports scores scrolled by in bright red lights. A wood and glass cabinet containing a multitude of silver crystal trophies took prominence. Art Deco wall lighting complemented timber panelling and white linen tablecloths. It had the feel of an intimate, old-fashioned club, but instead of cigar smoke and old men complaining, the smell of warm bread and garlic along with the sound of animated conversations filled the air.

'Gotta love this. You can do business over a great meal and never miss a result.'

The maître d' greeted the pair. 'Welcome back, Mr Rye. Doctor Rosseter phoned to say he's running a few minutes late.'

'Thanks, Frank. We might order anyway.'

'I'll have Bridget see to you immediately.'

He showed them to a table by the wall with a view of the room. 'This is where the celebrities hang out to avoid the masses, along with team managers and some pretty high-powered executives. That guy over there,' he nodded towards a table on the other side of the room, 'the one with the blue sweater round his shoulders, is a high flyer at Nike.'

A man in a Knicks cap and jacket worked his way to their table. He shook hands with Catcher and gave him a hug with his free arm. Anya tried not to stare, but despite the cap pulled low, she recognised the visitor. Leonardo DiCaprio reached across to shake her hand. 'Nice to meet you. Hey, have a great night. And stay in touch, man,' he added, patting Ethan on the shoulder before he moved on.

Not one for being starstruck, Anya nevertheless couldn't help be a little impressed by the company Ethan kept. She wondered what sort of work he had done for celebrities, or whether the contact was merely social. The waitress appeared and smiled broadly as she presented them with menus.

'Would you like pre-dinner drinks?'

'I'll try a glass of one of your Californian dry whites, thanks.'

'And the usual for you, Catcher?'

'Am I that predictable?'

Bridget smiled and explained the menu; the descriptions of each dish made Anya's mouth water. Bridget gave them a few minutes to decide and brushed Ethan's back with her hand as she laid their serviettes in their laps.

A woman's laugh made Anya glance at an adjacent table. She thought she recognised Rosie O'Donnell and had to admit to herself the experience was exciting.

'This place is enormous,' she said, 'and there's a real buzz, even in here.'

'Twenty thousand screaming fans. It never gets old. That's one thing about New Yorkers.' He chomped on a breadstick. 'They're good at supporting their teams. Despite what people say about how isolating it can feel in this city, the people sure do pull together for a good cause like tonight's charity game.'

Anya had heard reports of incredible acts of kindness and unity following the 9/11 terrorist attacks. The images of volunteers pooling together stayed with her. 'How long have you lived here?'

'It's been my base for over ten years now. Before that, I was a bit of a nomad.'

'What's your favourite thing about this city?'

Ethan stared at the lit candle on the table. 'You could never be bored here. So much is always going on, and you can take your pick of sports. Hockey, football, baseball, basketball. I've worked for a number of the teams over the years. One thing about the place, there's never a shortage of the unusual to keep you coming back for more.'

Bridget arrived with the drinks and filled their table glasses with water. 'Are you ready to order?'

Anya went first. 'I'll have the sashimi tuna followed by the roasted Amish chicken breast, please.'

'And I'll start with the crab cake, followed by the sirloin steak.'

'I'll make sure it's medium rare, just the way you like it,' Bridget added, and disappeared.

Anya took a sip of water and had to remind herself this was

work, and that even though they had spent two days together, Ethan was yet to discuss anything personal. The relationship was strictly professional. Still, it intrigued her that he seemed to know a lot of people wherever they went, yet he also dealt easily with strangers, including her. She suspected he was the kind of person everyone knew but no one knew much about. Against her nature, she decided to ask. 'What range of work do sports teams normally want from a private investigator?'

'Anything from keeping tabs on athletes, screening the personal lives of prospective draft candidates, to making sure finances aren't being misappropriated – and of course investigating women who accuse players of assault.' He lifted the napkin from his lap and stood. 'Looks like the other good doctor has arrived.'

A tall gentleman with olive skin and a mop of tight curly hair approached them. His physique suggested he could have been an athlete himself. 'Sorry, buddy, got held up. This must be the famous Doctor Crichton. Pleasure to meet you. I'm Gavin Rosseter.'

'Anya,' she said across the table.

'Hope you started without me.'

Bridget appeared again for his order and quickly returned with a Corona beer.

'Welcome to the good old US of A,' Gavin said. 'I hear you come from Down Under. Great country. I've been once and loved everything about it. Only problem is, it's not on the way to anywhere.'

'Neither's New York if you think about it. I'd say both were pretty good destinations in themselves, wouldn't you?'

Gavin laughed out loud. 'A woman with spirit and wit. We're going to get along just fine.'

The entrées arrived; the smells alone were worth coming here for. Anya savoured the aroma of the orange soy sauce, which complemented the salty tuna perfectly.

Gavin had chosen the white asparagus with shaved truffles, and the scent of musk and nuts made Anya wish she could have ordered that too. Ethan had wiped his plate clean with some sourdough bread almost before the other two had taken their first bite.

'How long have you been a team doctor for the Bombers?' Anya asked Gavin.

'Just over a year. I used to work for the Knicks. I know all the players lined up for tonight's exhibition event. If you like, I can take you to the change rooms and show you around before the game.'

'I'd like that. I'm not that familiar with American basketball or American football and I'm trying to get some insight into the physical challenges football players face, as well as the culture they're part of.'

'It's not dissimilar to your Aussie Rules, which by the way is completely insane. The way the players jump onto the backs and shoulders of other players to catch a ball is crazy.'

'It's called taking a mark.' Anya's father had taken her to more games than she could remember. It wasn't the football she had loved, but the special time shared with her dad.

'That's right. And what about rugby? Your players all tackle each other without helmets or any form of protection whatsoever. Two hundred pounds of muscle running at each other full speed is one mighty collision.'

Ethan sat forward. 'Our game actually evolved from rugby. I think our players are more like blowfish. The padding's partly to make them look more intimidating.'

'How much does padding really compensate for that degree of impact?' Anya asked Gavin.

'It's a good question, but I'm guessing no one would be prepared to give it up for a trial. Irrespective of protective gear, our guys have to be finely tuned and in peak condition. One of my roles is to check them out thoroughly before the draft. The last thing a team wants is a player predisposed to or carrying an injury.'

'How extreme are the physical stresses?'

Before he could answer, Ethan placed his napkin on the table. 'Excuse me, I have to go to the bathroom.'

Gavin's eyes sparked, as if this was his favourite subject. 'These guys are the barely walking wounded after a game. They're our modern-day gladiators and they go into battle every time they step onto the field. It's how they're conditioned. They all live on anti-inflammatories and analgesics. They pop them like Tic-Tacs.'

Likening players to warriors and gladiators appeared to be common. Anya was aware of drug use in almost all athletic arenas, both professional and amateur, despite testing procedures. 'What about steroid abuse? How rife is that among current footballers?'

'Look, I don't condone it in any way. The league, like other sports, has people who use them, but it's estimated at around ten percent or fewer of the players. Strength is important, but so is endurance. The men can lose litres of fluid every game. It's not all that uncommon to have them sitting on the john while I'm in the next cubicle holding bags of fluid to rehydrate them intravenously. Did you know that some of the basketballers go through two dozen bottles of drink during a game? You have to monitor their electrolytes closely.'

Anya reached for the salt and knocked her glass of water, spilling a small amount on the tablecloth. She moved the glass and used Ethan's napkin to soak up the water. Out of the corner of her eye, she noticed Bridget standing with Ethan near the bathroom entrance. Their heads were close and he pulled a wad of money from his wallet, which she slipped into her skirt pocket. If he were paying her for information, this was a public place and not exactly discreet.

Then again, Anya knew so little about Ethan that Bridget could have been his girlfriend, or even his wife.

Gavin continued. 'There's been some interesting research going on into all this. In fact your Garvan Institute found that Human Growth Hormone is more of a placebo than a real benefit. In a double-blind study, players given the placebo improved more in strength, endurance, power and sprint capacity than those given HGH. It's also been shown that players who use steroids have more injuries. The message is getting through, and of course they test for illegal substances.'

Anya had seen another study that suggested otherwise. 'I've read that steroids increase the size of muscle fibres and the number of nuclei in the fibres, which means a user synthesises more protein and makes more muscle, even years after steroid withdrawal. This particular study found that even after steroid withdrawal, users had a competitive edge.'

Ethan slid back into his chair and joined the conversation. 'So an athlete can still be cheating years after taking steroids? How serious can anyone be about catching cheats if footballers are only tested on game day?'

Gavin placed both elbows on the table. 'Very serious. Players are most likely to take stimulants on game day.'

Anya felt the tension between the men and wondered at it.

'How serious can the league be when the World Anti-Doping Agency outlaws fifty stimulants, whereas there are only ten on the league's banned list?'

'To be fair,' argued Gavin, 'the league did begin cracking down on drug use fifteen years before baseball started testing its players.'

Anya had read of the recent scandals involving revered baseballers testing positive for illegal substances. 'Why doesn't the league adopt the same protocols and testing programme as the WADA?' she asked.

Gavin whistled. 'Now that's a whole lot of politics I am happily not involved in.'

'I can answer that,' Ethan said. 'Under league rules, first-time offenders are suspended for up to four games, whereas WADA would impose a two-year ban. The cost of paying a fortune for players who could be out for two years makes the policy more a fiscal than a moral one.'

It was hardly much of a disincentive, Anya thought.

The main courses arrived and Gavin explained the warnings he gave to players.

'I tell the men they're more likely to be out longer with injuries, and I've seen them, from steroid abuse. They get more disc herniations, more knee, elbow, spine, ankle and foot problems. If the muscle grows too quickly, the cartilage may not adapt fast enough, so there's greater stress exerted on ligaments and cartilage. No player wants to increase the risk of rupturing a knee ligament or a disc. It can end a career in the time it takes to hit the ground.'

Anya's roasted chicken breast was exquisite and, judging by their clean plates, Ethan and Gavin had enjoyed their meals as much as she had. They declined dessert and Gavin took Anya downstairs while Ethan attended to some 'business'. She wondered if that meant Bridget.

They moved along the circular grey, windowless corridors, which felt a degree or two colder than the rest of the building. Two security guards recognised Rosseter with the acknowledgement, 'Hello, doc.' Further along, people in grey uniforms with walkie-talkies hovered outside rooms.

They passed a room with *X-Ray* on the door.

'You don't want to take a player out of the game unnecessarily, so doctors can X-ray players here. No CT scanner, obviously, just your basic machine.'

Anya wondered if the cost of the facility was justified. If the player had sufficient pain to warrant an X-ray, surely they weren't capable of playing to their full capacity anyway. Soft-tissue damage could be as debilitating as a fracture but would not show on an X-ray.

'Dressing rooms aren't labelled, to discourage fans from disturbing them. The Rangers and Knicks have separate rooms.' He gestured to two blue doors, one of normal size, the other much bigger. 'The one on the right is for the Knicks basketballers. The Rangers' hockey players need double width for their equipment trolley to get through.'

And, Anya thought, judging from the degree of shoulder padding, just to let players get in and out easily.

'So are their lockers different sizes too?'

'Goalies get wider ones,' Gavin added, studying her. 'You're different from how I imagined.'

Anya felt her face redden. 'What were you expecting?'

'I Googled you. Pathology, rape examinations, victims' rights – well, I mean —'

'You expected someone old and serious, with no sense of humour.'

This time, Gavin's face flushed.

The security guards were forming a line.

'The players are about to enter the stadium. We should probably take our seats.' He placed his hand on Anya's back just as the team's door opened.

They stood aside and a stream of men filed out. Some faces she recognised from television and movies, and others towered high and had the biggest size feet she had ever seen. A few of the Knicks players greeted Gavin on the way past. Seconds later, they heard the roar from the crowd. The excitement in the air was palpable, even though the game was purely for entertainment.

They were seated two rows from the front, mid-court. For a moment Anya felt guilty at taking the seat a dedicated fan would have loved. Gavin seemed right at home and rubbed his hands together as she looked around for Ethan. The stadium was full, and the crowd began banging blow-up beaters, magnifying the volume of noise. Music blared as the teams warmed up, hyping the fans even more. She wondered if she had imagined the smell of bacon.

Ethan appeared, grinning, holding a paper bag. 'Some of our local fare,' he said. 'A knish, a hot dog covered in potato then fried. It's delicious.'

Anya had no idea how Ethan could eat another morsel after their big dinner, but she was beginning to suspect the man had a bottomless stomach. Out of courtesy and curiosity, she bit through the crunchy coating and potato. Ethan was right. It was surprisingly tasty.

The teams were announced and the fans cheered and banged their beaters louder than ever. Long legs and broad shoulders filled the court as players for each team threw balls and hoops.

'Who are you going for?' she asked Gavin.

'The Knicks.'

Ethan booed. 'Go the Globetrotters.'

The exhibition game began and Anya had to admit to being swept up in all the humour. The professional players were not only great athletes, they were skilled entertainers too. She did have to wonder whether the huge salaries and sponsorship deals they attracted were justified, though. They were, after all, throwing a ball, not curing cancer or saving the planet from global warming.

The Globetrotters scored three trick goals in a row, to the crowd's delight. In some ways, the display was vaudevillian. At one point, no one knew where the ball had gone. The referees were as bamboozled as the crowd. Despite the messing around, all the players worked hard to make it look so simple.

Giant screens showed a slow-motion replay. Rock music filled the time-out as women in dance costumes did high-leg kicks while waving pom-poms. Anya took the opportunity to ask Gavin a personal opinion.

'Are footballers more likely to be involved in team sex scandals and domestic violence accusations than basketballers?'

Basketball hadn't seemed to have featured as heavily as other team sports in Anya's previous research.

The sports doctor thought for a moment. 'I guess basketballers tend to be a bit more selfish, and it's not so much about the team for them. It's about their own individual performance. Besides, their faces are on screens, their profile is so much higher, and their sponsorship contracts often have morals clauses in them.'

Ethan offered an alternate version. 'There are fewer felons in basketball than football. Then again, maybe they have better managers and more money to pay people off. Morals clauses don't tend to get invoked for players who are doing well, or are at the top of their game.'

'Basketball players do get into their fair share of trouble,' Gavin said. 'Domestic violence often goes under the public radar, but that can be for lots of reasons. If the wives and girlfriends don't press charges, there's not much anyone can do about it.'

Ethan sounded unimpressed. 'Violence against women should be on the public radar, especially when these guys are being paid a fortune and given everything they want, whenever they want.'

By the chants and cheers from the crowd, these players and celebrities could do no wrong. No wonder so few were ever convicted of domestic violence or rape. Victims weren't just up against the legal system, they were up against the vast number of devotees. Anya was unsure which would be more frightening.

17

With the players doing media and charity events during the morning, Anya was keen to use the few hours off to explore New York. The call from Ethan Rye mentioning an exhibition he wanted to see at the Metropolitan Museum of Art had been welcome. It also gave her the opportunity to find out more about his knowledge of players' off-field behaviour. She suspected he kept a lot of secrets about what he'd seen and heard.

Since their hotel was near Grand Central Terminal, he suggested they take the subway uptown. From the room window she could see that the sun was struggling to make an appearance. People wandered along the streets, some in jackets, others in shirtsleeves. A breeze battered the flags atop an adjacent building. She pulled on jeans, a pale blue shirt and comfortable walking shoes, and carried her black trench coat. In her bag she had a small digital camera, her purse, a scarf and her room key. Ethan was already in the foyer when she left the lift.

'Ready for some culture?' he said with a broad grin. He held in his hand two takeaway coffees. 'Thought you might need this.'

Anya had to admit to being excited at the opportunity to visit places she'd only seen in movies or read about in books. They passed through the foyer of Grand Central to a door leading to the main concourse, sipping their coffees as they walked. True to its name, the building was grand. Its vaulted ceiling with constellations of stars was spectacular. The whole place had a feeling of old-time romantic travel.

'Notice anything different about the constellations?' Ethan asked.

Astronomy was not her strong suit. 'I couldn't even name them. Besides, the constellations in the southern hemisphere don't look the same.'

Ethan stared up, hands in his pockets. 'It's ingenious. The whole thing's backwards. The sky's designed as if you're looking down on it from outside.'

They bought tickets and took the line to 86th Street. Outside, parents were pushing children in prams, accompanied by small dogs. Couples headed for Central Park with backpacks and rugs. They wandered west to 5th Avenue, then south to 82nd Street in a comfortable silence.

The sense of community was evident. A troupe of acrobats in basketball jerseys entertained the crowd who sat on the steps. The buskers combined acrobatics, comedy and a 'no drugs' message. Anya found herself laughing at some of their antics and donated a ten-dollar note to their cause.

Like Australia, America had a relatively short history since colonisation, so the treasures within the Met were more revered than they may have been in Europe. Once past the bag check at the entrance, she couldn't help but smile. The high ceilings, arches and skylight of the great hall made her feel happily insignificant.

'You're like a child at Disneyland,' Ethan grinned.

Up the central staircase, they headed towards nineteenth- and early twentieth-century European paintings and sculptures. Once inside, Anya felt humbled by the magnificence, and number, of Impressionist works. She moved through works by Manet, Cezanne, Pissarro, Renoir, Monet and Degas.

Ethan paused at one of the bronze sculptures. 'I like that Degas takes the glamour out of his ballet models, and the natural poses he chose to capture.'

'She looks as gawky as most teenagers feel.' Anya remembered the awkwardness of those years.

'She has no idea how beautiful she is. It's what makes her even more compelling.'

Anya turned to see his expression, but he had already moved on.

She stopped at Claude Monet's 'The Path through the Irises' and sat on the nearby bench to take in the entire image. She was amazed at how close she felt to being in the garden the painting depicted.

Ethan sat down beside her. 'Monet was supposed to have had nuclear cataracts at this stage, which changed the way he perceived colours. Cataracts absorb more light and desaturate colour, making everything appear more yellow and certain colours muddy.' The painting did have a predominance of yellow, but he had still perfectly captured the purple hues of the irises. 'For him that must have been the cruellest affliction. He described in letters how he saw the world in a fog, and from 1915 his paintings became more abstract. But that could also have been due to his advancing age.' Ethan stood and moved nearer to examine the painting more closely. 'His brush strokes were getting broader at this stage. It's possible that by his mid-seventies, he'd lost some fine hand control, even if his handwriting didn't show it.'

Ethan munched on some nuts from a bag in his jacket pocket.

Anya sat up, surprised at the extent of his knowledge of art.

'What?' He popped another peanut. 'I might have worked a couple of art fraud cases in my time. How about I show you my favourite pieces.'

143

Anya was happy to be led to sculptures by the Frenchman, Jean-Antoine Houdon. 'These guys feel like old friends,' Ethan said.

In one marble bust, the artist had portrayed a young girl, probably five or six, who had the proud look of a child who was beginning to become independent in small ways. She knew that look well, from her own son.

'What are you thinking about?' Ethan asked as she lingered, mesmerised.

She tried to divert the conversation. 'Isn't that supposed to be something women ask men and drive them insane?'

He smiled. 'You didn't answer. Are you missing your son?'

Anya stuck her hands into her jeans pockets. 'If you really want to know, I miss everything about him. I miss his laugh, the cheeky look he gets when he's about to be silly, the dimples on his knuckles still left over from when he was a baby. I even miss watching him sleep.'

In honesty, she missed Ben so much it hurt right now.

'Do you have children?' she asked.

'Me? No. Too selfish.' Somehow, his words didn't sound convincing. 'I think you'd be a fantastic mother.'

Her face reddening, she turned back to the exhibition. 'This sculpture is so full of life and interest. Voltaire, the famous writer, philosopher and civil rights activist.' She thought out loud as she noticed the accompanying description. 'There's a man I'd really like to have met.'

Ethan's eyes seemed to pierce hers, as if he were searching for something.

'You know, he reinvented himself after being imprisoned.'

'Like so many celebrities and sports stars.' Mike Tyson came to mind. Anya focused on the reason for being so far from her child. 'I've been thinking about the five Bombers players. No one is caught speeding the one and only time they exceed the limit. If you do it often enough, eventually you will get caught. Rape is part of a pattern of behaviour. It's not a one-off act. If a man hits a woman once, he'll do it again. If he rapes, he's usually done it before and will again.'

'So I guess once someone's off your Christmas card list, there's no redemption.'

Anya saw his wry grin and wondered if he were baiting her. They meandered their way through a few more galleries, and she paused at Poussin's 'The Rape of the Sabine Women', which depicted the abduction of Sabine women by the Romans, who wanted to make them their wives.

'The Romans didn't have women,' Ethan told her, 'so they took them by force, for the so-called good of their society. What would have happened to any of the soldiers who dissented because they thought abducting women was wrong? Groups, religions, governments, tribes, even families distort morality for their own advantage. Always have and always will.'

'You forgot to mention teams,' she added pointedly. 'On the other hand, they can also nurture a sense of community, and act for the greater good.'

'Or what their leaders manipulate them to believe is the greater good.'

Ethan Rye was sounding more and more like a loner.

'Don't you think people just like to belong sometimes? To find like-minded people they can relate to and trust? You told me on the plane that you agreed with the ethos of football, giving disadvantaged kids hope.'

Anya glanced around the room. An adolescent girl sat on a portable stool and sketched in charcoal. An elderly couple listened to the audio guide as they skirted the room, and a couple in their twenties, both dressed completely in black, seemed more interested in each other than the works of art.

'Belonging can be overrated, and it can be highly destructive. Are you familiar with Milgram's experiment?'

She had read about the famous scientific attempt to explain why ordinary people participated in the heinous crimes that occurred in Nazi Germany. The experiment involved using volunteers in the presence of an authority figure in a white coat. Volunteers were instructed to ask a series of questions of a person in another room, whom they could hear but not see. A wrong answer or no response incurred an electric shock, which increased in intensity each time. Despite the audible screams of pain and protestations by the person in the other room, two-thirds of the volunteers would have continued with the experiment, eventually giving electrical shocks so high as to be lethal. The shocks were simulated, of course, as were the screams, but the volunteers did not know that until after the experiment. The frightening conclusion was that if the authority figure told the volunteers to continue, they did, despite their reservations.

Anya asked, 'Which theory do you subscribe to? That the participants felt powerless to control the outcome, so abrogated responsibility for their part, or that they merely believed that what an expert said had to be right, even if they had doubts?'

'Neither. I think the problem was that they didn't perceive the person getting the shocks to be human. If they eventually did realise that they could have hurt or killed another person, few had the capacity to resist the authority. I'm thinking that happens with gang-rape. Someone initiates it and maybe someone else goes along for the thrill.'

'And the others?'

'They're the unquestioning followers from Milgram's experiment. But I'm betting that some of them felt guilty for not standing up to the authority figures. Our challenge is to find the player who followed the leader that night in the hotel but feels guilty about it. The one who won't pull the lever ever again.'

146

18

Anya headed with Ethan through the tunnel into the stadium and towards the team's bench. The heat contrasted with the cooler temperatures of the last few days. Sun beat down on the playing field and the air was thick with humidity. She peeled off her jacket, regretting the decision to wear trousers.

'Help yourself to a cold drink any time,' Ethan said, as if noticing her discomfort. Alongside the bench was a large tub of ice and bottled energy drinks.

As the Bombers warmed up on the field, spectators continued to fill the seats. Women on the sideline, some clad in bikini tops and shorts, carried signs with the names of players.

Gavin Rosseter arrived looking like one of the team, with his polo shirt and trousers matching the colours of the Bombers uniforms. He acknowledged Anya before talking to one of the players with an intense expression on his face. The man jogged on the spot, then took to the field.

Gavin paced, hands on his hips, studying the players as they did short sprints. An older man with grey hair joined Gavin and they pointed and talked intently. He handed Gavin a piece of paper and appeared to be discussing what was on it. Gavin looked over a number of times to where the opposition was warming up.

Ethan stood with his arms folded, legs wide apart. 'That's Reginald Pope, the senior doctor – he's been around for years and is close, well as close as anyone can get, to Lyle Buffet.

What they're up to is a bit like espionage. The doctors try to analyse the injuries the opposition may have incurred in training.' He pointed across. 'See number twenty-eight? He's favouring that right leg. It isn't so obvious when he walks. Just wait . . . There he goes. See when he runs for the ball?'

Anya nodded. Ethan was right. The difference was subtle, but would be more obvious to a trained eye.

'Could be his hip.' She looked sideways at Ethan. The doctors took notes then spoke to the coach, who wore a microphone headpiece.

'They're tipping Coach Ingram off as to what players are vulnerable and how to capitalise on their injuries.'

Anya was dismayed at the idea of causing more harm to the opposition upon a doctor's advice. It went against all her own ethics, and the first rule of medicine was 'do no harm'. She wondered how Gavin and Pope justified facilitating injuries to opposition players.

As if reading her mind, Ethan said, 'That's what happens when you mix sport, money and medicine. Objectives and roles blur.'

'Who are they playing?' Anya was trying to understand the culture.

'San Diego Chargers. It's meant to be a pre-season practice game. Part of Kitty Rowe and Bentley Masterton's vision for a more family-friendly team. Mothers and their kids get in for free.'

Judging by the near full stadium, the promotion was proving a success. Children waved banners with the Bombers' insignia amidst a sea of green, gold and purple.

The game began. Anya counted twenty-two players on the field, eleven from each side.

Ethan smiled. 'I can give you a quick rundown if it helps. To anyone who hasn't been brought up with the game, it can be tough to follow.'

Anya knew there was an offensive and a defensive team and they took turns, and that touchdowns and goals scored points, but apart from that, the game was a mystery.

'I'm listening.'

The investigator grinned and came to life. He explained the field was a hundred and twenty yards long, a little less in metres, and beyond the goal line was the end line. The ten yards in between was the end zone, which the offence aimed for. If they crossed the goal line with the ball, they scored a touchdown, worth six points. A team with possession had four plays to advance ten yards. If they failed, they lost possession. If they went more than ten yards in a play, they scored four more chances. A goal after scoring a touchdown was worth an extra point, and a field goal scored three points. That covered the very basics, it seemed.

The Chargers kicked off and the Bombers had their defence team on the field. Now the ball was midfield.

'This is a scrimmage, a bit like one of your rugby scrums. The centre flicks it back to the quarterback, then he and the offensive linesmen block the defence from getting to him.'

Anya watched as the ball moved back and the row of team mates ran head on into their marked opponents. She flinched at the crunching sound of men clashing helmets. Clearly, the centre and surrounding players had to block the defence from getting to the quarterback by any possible means. The ball flew a short distance and the catcher leapt in the air, only to be tackled by three other players on the way down.

'Ouch,' Ethan winced. The crowd jeered at the tackle. 'The running back is a bit slow getting up.'

Anya watched Gavin Rosseter run out onto the field with his tackle box. Play was suspended while he assessed the injured man. The coach was yelling into his microphone, shouting names and instructions. A couple of minutes later, Gavin patted the running back on the shoulder and the man stood to cheers and applause from the fans. Anya felt perspiration trickle down under her collar.

Gavin returned to his position on the sideline and wiped his forehead and hands with a towel. The temperature felt as though it had risen a few degrees in the space of ten minutes. The next play saw possession change. The onfield players came off, and the defence team took their place. Across the field, the San Diego Chargers switched benched teams as well. Ethan handed Anya a bottle of cold water. She thanked him and placed it on her forehead. She wondered how the players were coping with all their protective clothing on.

It seemed like a giant game of chess, with strategies for every possible scenario. Minutes later, the first quarter quickly ended, with neither team managing to score.

Instead of the fifteen minutes she had thought it would take, the quarter had taken over thirty minutes. Each time the play stopped, so did the game clock.

The Chargers and the Bombers switched ends following a two-minute break, and Anya watched a player in purple, gold and green begin to stagger. Gavin had seen the same thing, and was already out on the field. He quickly called for support and two other men helped escort the player from the field. Once they arrived at the benches, Gavin called for a stretcher. Just then, the player collapsed to the ground. Anya instinctively moved to help.

'Rocket. Can you hear me?' Gavin tapped on the chest padding. The man moaned incoherently. 'Did anyone see him get hit?'

The team mates shook their heads.

'How was he before the game?'

'Fine, he had breakfast with us and was joking in the locker room.'

'He said something about stomach cramps when we changed ends,' another added.

Gavin and two trainers rolled him so the stretcher could go underneath; it took four large players to carry him back to the locker room.

On the floor inside, Rocket pulled up his knees and moaned louder.

'Can you hear me, buddy?' Gavin unclipped Rocket's chin strap and inched off the tight-fitting helmet. Anya felt for his carotid pulse.

'He's burning up and pulse is at least one-fifty.'

Gavin was obviously thinking the same thing. Heat stroke was life-threatening, and this player was in critical condition.

He called for the trainer as Anya poured the rest of her water over the player's head and neck.

'Quick,' Gavin instructed. 'Get us as many bags of ice as you can. He's really burning up.'

The trainer raced away as Gavin grabbed a blood pressure cuff, which was designed for someone morbidly obese. The man's upper arm was bigger than Anya's thigh. She moved to help.

'BP's only seventy-five.'

Anya knew the player was now at risk of major organ damage, and would quickly die without aggressive intervention.

'Someone get the paramedics.' Gavin grabbed a large gauge cannula and inflated the cuff again. Meanwhile, Anya tried the other arm. The man with the ice appeared; Anya packed two bags between Rocket's thighs and another in the pit of the arm she held. Something, either the cold or the needle Gavin inserted, caused Rocket to scream, sit up and take a swing at them both. Anya reeled back in time to see the needle pull out of his arm and blood gush from the vein. One of the players who matched the man's huge size and weight stepped in and put Rocket in a headlock. Another sat on his legs and pressed on a gauze pad while Gavin inserted another cannula. He quickly withdrew three vials of blood before connecting up a bag of fluids.

'Sorry, doc, he'd never try to hurt you, this isn't like him,' the man at the head said.

Anya yanked up the skin-tight shirt to place more icepacks against Rocket's skin but was hindered by the amount of padding he wore. There were shoulder pads, pads for ribs, neck, thighs, hips and knees, and taped to his forearm was even more padding. She struggled to find skin to come in contact with, so placed another ice pack in the other armpit. Gloves covered his hands, and his socks and shoes were even taped over, presumably to strap his ankles. From what she could tell, there was nowhere apart from his face that could sweat, and even this was encased inside a helmet.

'He's still burning up.' Anya held a bag of ice to his forehead. 'We need to cut all the clothes and padding off.'

The trainer reappeared with scissors and began the task. As any new skin appeared, Anya put ice on top of it.

'Don't you have ice baths?'

'Not till this place gets renovated.'

Gavin continued to squeeze the bag of fluid to make it go faster into Rocket's system. As soon as that neared empty, he switched to a fresh one. The older man from the sideline, Pope, arrived and asked what was going on.

'Looks like heat stroke. He's hypotensive, tachycardic and delirious. Apparently he complained of stomach cramps earlier.'

Pope didn't look concerned. 'I gave him twenty mil of Buscopan and five of Valium after the first quarter. Buffet was aware he had cramping.'

Anya could barely believe what she was hearing. If the player was ill, he should never have been sent back onto the field. And to give him Valium and Buscopan when he could have been dehydrated was not in the best interest of the player's health. Gavin exchanged glances with Anya.

'I'll ride with him in the ambulance,' Pope said, 'and take those bloods with me.'

With one-and-a-half litres of fluid successfully in his veins, Rocket roused enough to ask for a drink. The trainer gave him some sips of ice water and the man who had anchored the patient's massive legs slid sideways onto the floor.

Anya moved to Rosseter's side. 'To diagnose heat stroke, you need to confirm a high temperature. We put bags of ice under his arms . . .'

'And he's got ice in his mouth, so axillary and oral temperatures are out.'

She saw his face drop at the realisation. They'd have to take a rectal temperature, or Rocket faced a barrage of unnecessary tests at the hospital and a questionable diagnosis.

'Then I'll wait outside unless you need me,' Anya said, keen to leave the player with some dignity.

As she closed the door behind her, she heard someone warn, 'You better know what you're doing, Doc. Rocket's not gonna like this one little bit.'

Within minutes the paramedics had loaded Rocket onto a gurney and were running more fluid through his veins. Pope appeared with the vials of blood in his hand, which Anya saw were now labelled.

Once they had gone, she re-entered the locker room.

Gavin's shirt and hair were covered in sweat and he was packing up the contents of his doctor's bag. Blood stained his trousers from where Rocket had pulled out the needle in his arm.

'Thanks for giving me a hand,' he said. 'BP's ninety and his pulse is on the way down.'

The signs were good. Rocket would hopefully survive, if they'd been fast enough to save his kidneys from damage. 'You might want to wash your hands while I get this lot,' she said, bending down.

'Might change my clothes as well.'

Anya closed the bag just as a player came in, cradling his forearm.

'Doc Rosseter? You here?'

Gavin returned, bare-chested, shirt in his hand. 'What happened?' He slipped the polo shirt over his head and pulled it down.

'Got tackled and there was blood.'

Anya could see bone sticking through the skin. The man had a compound fracture of his arm.

Gavin gently began to examine the injury. 'Can you feel me touching your fingers?'

The player nodded.

'Pulses are present and strong. Are you in much pain?'

'A bit.'

Anya imagined a break like that would be extremely painful.

'Did you take anti-inflammatories before the game?'

He nodded again, like a child.

That would explain why he wasn't in too much distress. He already had painkillers in his system when the fracture occurred.

Gavin made a sling and instructed the trainer to take the player to the hospital and wrote down the name of an ortho-paedic specialist who would see him straightaway. Before they had left, there was another urgent call for medical attention on the field.

Anya followed Rosseter, who sprinted out the door. With the frequency of serious injuries, she wondered if any of the team would still be standing after the 'practice' game. Ethan hurried over to her.

'It's Pete Janson. He went down in a tackle, took a hit to the head and hasn't moved since.'

19

The spectators and players waited for a sign. Anything that would indicate Janson was all right. Gavin Rosseter knelt over him, concentrating on his face. Anya wasn't sure if he was testing for breath or trying to communicate with the quarterback.

On the sideline, she stood near enough to the coach to hear Buffet give him orders. 'I don't care if he's damn near dead. You're not carrying him off on a stretcher. It'll demoralise the team and we can't afford that right now.'

'If it's a neck injury, he'll have to be immobilised. I don't see how —'

'Damn it, Ingram! You heard what I said.'

'Yes, sir.' Ingram barely hesitated, barking into his helmet microphone. 'If you can hear me, Janson, get the fuck up. I want you to stand and walk. I won't tell you again.'

The old man hobbled away, having given his orders. He stopped a few metres from Anya.

Anya caught her breath, trying to absorb what had just taken place. The owner was prepared to risk a player's life to maintain team morale in a practice game? This wasn't life and death. It was a sport. The coach was instructing the quarterback to risk serious damage, possibly even paralysis, irrespective of a doctor's instructions.

'Look,' Ethan said suddenly.

Back on the field, Pete Janson pulled himself to his feet, then stood, one arm raised. The crowd erupted in hoots, cheers and applause. Gavin stood with the player, initially holding up two fingers to test his vision, and no doubt asking questions to determine whether he was oriented in time and space. The fact that Janson got up by himself, seemed to dismiss Gavin and held both gloved fists in the air egged the crowd on to make more noise.

Coach Ingram wiped his mouth with an open hand, then readjusted his microphone. 'We've got a game to win.'

Buffet did not watch for long. Instead, he turned his back to the field and stood slightly straighter, as if energised by the crowd's display. 'Doctor Crichton, I know what you're probably thinking. Walk with me. You too, Catcher.'

Ethan gave Anya a look as if to tell her to obey.

Begrudgingly, she followed, fully intending to broach the idea of safety at the first opportunity.

'You're a mother. You have a kid,' Buffet waved a hand, 'who lives with his father.'

Anya knew her credentials had been checked, but was taken aback by this comment. Her personal life was irrelevant to the job requirements. She felt her face redden. This man had no right to bring Ben into this.

Ethan placed his hand on her arm. 'Just wait,' he whispered.

'Your kid's lucky. But these boys out here . . .' He stopped and pointed towards the field. 'Players of this calibre have been mollycoddled most of their lives by everyone from middle school through college. They've been treated better than anyone else and always told they were special. But what would they be doing now without football? Probably jail time, or some dead-end job. Or they could have signed up for a war in a place they couldn't even find on a map. Just so their families can get medical insurance.' He trod slowly, careful to plant each foot on firm ground.

Anya felt a surge of irritation. Buffet was making out he was some kind of saviour.

Play recommenced and the crowd roared at another tackle.

'Everything gets handed to them, sometimes even college degrees they don't deserve. Is it any surprise they think the world revolves around them? I see too many of them waste their God-given talent and betray the team for their own selfish interests. Take Janson. See the way he can turn a stadium of fans?' He clenched one fist. 'That's power – to reach out and change people's lives. Pete has no idea what he's capable of. But I do. And with him in the team, the Bombers far exceeds the sum of individual players.'

Anya wondered if he thought Janson was innocent of raping Kirsten Byrne, or if he was overlooking it for the sake of the team, and his own benefit.

'It's why Kitty, Masterton and I wanted you here today. To see for yourself that this is something so much more than a game of football. Our mission is to elevate this team to its full God-given potential.'

He glanced back at the action. 'I'll do whatever it takes to make that happen.'

At the end of what felt like hours in the heat, Ethan took Anya into the locker room. It was only a few minutes before the end of play and injured players who had been sidelined during the game were already inside nursing their wounds.

'Buffet wants you to know what these boys go through, so here we are. I have to warn you, they're not exactly modest when it comes to their bodies.'

It was no wonder, the way women ogled and fans treated them like gods. 'I've seen the odd naked man in my time,' she said, even if the vast majority of them were dead, and laid out on a steel table.

Even so, as the team filed in and stripped off, she was unsure where to look. The stench of perspiration mixed with liniment was almost overwhelming.

A couple of reporters entered the room, one of them a woman with a dictaphone.

'Yo, ladies in the house,' one of the players said, removing a towel from around his waist and pulling it forwards and back between his legs. 'You wanna piece of this?' he added, as he flicked his penis.

The woman ignored the antics, and instead targeted Pete Janson for the first interview. He didn't bother covering himself with a towel as she asked questions with the recorder near his face. Another player came up behind her, towel in his hand, and acted as though he was humping her.

Anya stepped forward, nodding her head at the male reporter who was talking to a player in the far corner. 'Would you do that to him?'

'Huh?'

The player moved closer to Anya, towering over her in height. She refused to step back.

Gavin appeared. 'Back away from Doctor Crichton, Dorafino, or you might find that thigh muscle needs a lot more investigation before you can play again.'

'I was just having some fun,' he sulked and flicked another player with his towel.

The reporter turned, checking her recorder, blonde hair falling on her shoulders.

'Does that sort of thing happen to you a lot?' Anya asked.

'Hey, it's part of the job. I didn't ask you to come to my rescue or undermine me in front of these guys.'

Anya was surprised by the woman's aggressive tone. 'Pardon?'

The woman placed a hand on her skirted hip. 'Don't give me that. You thought, "Poor little woman being harassed by the big bad men". Well, I know what I'm doing and I've worked damn hard to get here and establish credibility with these players. If you don't have the guts for this, maybe you should leave.'

'That was sexual harassment and physical intimidation.'

'Tell that to someone who cares. If you'll excuse me,' she looked around the room, 'I have a job to do.' The woman moved away and approached another player.

Anya returned to where Ethan was sitting. 'Who is she?'

'Annabelle Reichman. She's got bigger balls than some of these men.'

Anya had seen the name. In the paper. She was the one who had written the vile article on women supposedly crying rape.

She turned to ask if Annabelle had any idea how damaging her opinion piece was, but the woman had already left.

Showers ran and trainers rubbed down muscles. Conversation became amplified as the players disrobed and relaxed. Music bellowed from a sound system someone had in his locker.

A minion collected helmets and padding from each player, picking items from the ground like a mother collecting washing from a teenager's bedroom.

Coach Ingram entered and praised the men for a good hard game. Clearly, they had won, although the room looked and felt like a battle zone.

Ethan checked his phone. 'I'll drop you at the Emergency ward. The nurse who examined your victim just started on duty. You can talk in private and call me when you're finished.'

The investigator might have known Kirsten's name, but he had no need or right to know anything more intimate. She respected him for acknowledging that.

*   *   *

Inside the waiting room, a woman wailed, comforted by a nurse. Anya felt shivers on the back of her neck. From the nurse's presence, Anya suspected the woman had just lost someone close. The rest of the room sat in an eerie silence.

At the triage desk, she asked to see Tina Cincotta.

After fifteen minutes, a nurse with dark hair pulled off her face, stethoscope around her neck and a worn expression appeared, carrying a hospital file. The triage sister pointed to Anya.

'I'm Tina. I understand you wanted to see me about a rape patient. Please come through.'

She headed towards a corridor and invited Anya into an examination room with a bed and a set of stirrups on the floor, ready to be mounted to the bed. Unlike Anya's sexual assault unit, which was designed to be as far from a hospital as possible, this was cold, sterile and smelt like antiseptic.

'Linda Gatby told me you might come by. Please understand that I am treading a thin line here between confidentiality and disclosing information to the police.'

'I understand that.' Anya sat in the chair and the nurse perched on the bed. 'I've been asked to investigate the charges made by Kirsten Byrne against a number of footballers. I'm not working for the defence, but my task is to advise the team's owners if I believe that, based on evidence, a sexual assault took place.'

Tina nodded slowly.

'Assistant DA Linda Gatby has also asked for my professional opinion on the injuries. I've performed hundreds of rape examinations at designated sexual assault units and my particular area of expertise is on wounds and injuries to survivors of assaults.'

'I understand. So what do you want to know?'

A baby cried in the corridor.

'What was Kirsten's emotional state when she arrived that morning?'

The nurse opened the file. 'I remember her because of who she said attacked her.' She scanned her records. 'Her skin was rubbed raw. When she came in, she seemed numb, but was rational, as if she was describing a film she'd seen. There was no emotion in her voice. When I examined her she didn't complain, just stared at the ceiling. That perineal injury was deep, and I had to pad it to stop the bleeding. It must have been painful, but she didn't once complain. There was something so blank about her eyes.'

The pager bleeped and the nurse checked it. 'Have you seen the report?'

Anya had only seen the photos, but Kirsten's mood and responses could not come across in what were clinical notes.

'Just some photographs. From what I saw, the injuries would have caused a significant amount of pain. Did she have a blood alcohol or drug screen?'

The next page on the file gave the answer. Alcohol was present but 0.03. The drug screen was negative. Kirsten had not been drugged or taken drugs and was below the legal limit for alcohol when she presented. She was sober and very aware of what was happening.

'How was her memory?' Anya wanted to know how clear her recollections were, in case she had been drinking and the alcohol had been metabolised in the time between the assault and her presentation to hospital.

'She was lucid and described in detail what happened. I didn't record everything she said, but the policewoman was present. It sounded like a violent and prolonged assault.'

She snapped the file shut. 'Sorry, but I've got to go. I hope that helps you.' She stood and opened the door for Anya.

'Could you do something for me?' the nurse asked. 'Make sure those bastards don't get away with this. I've seen other rape victims of footballers, but not many have the courage to go to the police.'

With that comment, she left the room.

20

Anya could see Jim Horan pacing inside his glass-walled office. She could hear him too. He was speaking into a phone headpiece so loudly that every word was audible.

'I don't care if you think it's a great deal. The offer's not acceptable. How about you double it. Then we'll talk.'

The female assistant knocked on the open door and Horan waved her in. It seemed everyone in New York worked on a weekend.

'Ethan Rye and Doctor Anya Crichton are here to see you.'

He sized them up. 'Not interested.'

Anya exchanged glances with their escort, who shrugged her shoulders. Ethan either didn't hear or ignored what Horan said. He was already inside, settling into a padded chair.

Thrown over a couch were a number of bra and panties sets on hangers.

'You get back to your boss and come up with something that doesn't insult my client.' Horan clicked off his microphone and moved to a chair behind an oversized desk. It seemed he had been addressing the person on the phone, not them.

'I won't bother asking you in.' His tone was sarcastic. 'Whatever this is about, make it fast.' He called after his assistant: 'Hold my calls for three minutes and bring me a Red Bull with aspirin.'

Ethan's relaxed posture showed he was not going to be rushed. 'It's been a while, Jim. How's, what is it now, your third wife?'

The sports manager rolled up his white-sleeved shirt to the elbows. 'You care even less than I do, so let's not waste each other's time. What do you want?'

'To congratulate you on that deal you made for Janson with Cheree Jordan Fashions.'

'That's just a drop in the ocean.' He leant back and clasped both hands behind his head. 'Bigger things are starting to happen for that boy. He has a great future ahead of him. Takes some players four or five years to throw a pass. Took Pete three games. He's the rags to riches tale. Undrafted one minute, one of the game's most valuable the next. Four years later, he's still a dream client.'

'And one of your best investments,' Ethan added.

'Is there any other kind?'

Anya had read Ethan's brief on Jim Horan. He had studied at Notre Dame Law School and was agent and manager for a dozen high-profile footballers along with a handful of rookies. Four of those were out with injuries, another two were suspended for testing positive to banned substances. His current wife seemed to spend money as fast as he could earn it, and his former wives had come from wealthy families and expected to be maintained in a similar style. Anya found it hard to believe that he'd found three women who would marry him – his warmth and appeal matched that of a reptile in a toddler's pool.

'How long had you been working on the clothing deal?'

He rocked back. 'Cheree Jordan. I've been watching her lines for a while. She's one savvy businesswoman. We've been in dialogue for the right vehicle for Pete for some time, and with his recent form, the timing couldn't be better. It'll really boost his profile.'

'And your cachet.' Ethan clasped his hands on his lap. 'Must be difficult, knowing when to time the best deals. Bad timing or unsatisfactory negotiations could really damage a client.'

Anya was unsure if the investigator was angry or trying to provoke the agent. According to Kirsten, and the designer, they had been unable to get through to Janson's management. Otherwise, she wouldn't have needed to go to the hotel that night. Anya wanted to know why Horan was blatantly lying.

The agent's phone rang at that moment and prevented him from responding to Ethan's comment. 'Can't talk long, Terri. Yes, it's a meeting.' He mouthed 'Terri Janson' for their benefit and headed towards the window. Ethan sat forward and scanned the desk's contents.

'This morning I leaked the rumour that you're being courted by multiple cosmetic companies, as the ideal woman, mother and wife. Covergirl already want to meet you.' Horan threw his head back and laughed. 'Things are going better than we imagined.'

As Horan finished the call, the assistant appeared with two cans of drink and a packet of aspirin, and left.

Anya found it odd that despite the threat of rape charges looming over his client, Horan seemed so upbeat.

Ethan reached back and picked up a set of women's underwear. 'Bit small for you, I would have thought.'

Horan leant across and snatched them from him. 'These are for some of my clients from the Lingerie Football Alliance. Victoria's Secret are close to doing a special line for women who like to keep fit.'

Anya had never heard of the alliance.

'Don't suppose you play?' Horan looked her up and down.

Ethan stuck his hands in his pockets. 'Women in lingerie playing American football. It was supposed to be huge but somehow it hasn't got the following some predicted. They dress in these,' he flicked his fingers towards another set on the table, 'in an attempt to prove they're equal, even though they play on a small field, the shoulder pads reveal their breasts and the spectators aren't exactly admiring their ball skills.'

'It's a valid sport,' Horan retorted. 'They're hard-working girls. Who better to promote sport and fitness in the middle of an obesity epidemic?'

Anya found it difficult to believe someone had even come up with the idea, let alone found women to take part or, in Horan's case, exploit. For now, though, she needed to focus on the assault charges.

'Mr Horan, I presume you are aware that Pete Janson and other clients of yours are accused of sexually assaulting a woman at the Rainier Hotel the night of 12 August.'

He popped the aspirin, gulped some sugary caffeine and swallowed. 'Look, if I had a dollar for the number of times women accuse my clients of improper treatment, disrespect, having sex, not having sex . . . Hell, I'd be a lot wealthier than I am now. In fact, a couple of years ago one whacko put Liam McKenzie through hell when she accused him of attacking her with a knife. It was a witch hunt the way the police went after him. But you know what? The judge found he'd acted like a hero and saved her from killing herself.' His hands returned to the back of his head. 'All I can say is thank God for justice in this country.'

Anya made a mental note to look into the case. In her experience, if it was established he'd saved the woman, it didn't make sense that prosecutors pursued the case, knowing how unlikely a successful conviction would have been. Then again, a high-profile conviction could reflect well on a number of careers. Maybe an ambitious prosecutor was prepared to take the risk for the publicity.

Horan continued, as if for Anya's benefit. 'These guys are as famous as movie stars, only with much better bodies. They're recognised everywhere they go and women want to sleep with them, for lots of reasons: fame by association, the thrill of screwing a star, because they have money. Some of them want to catch a husband and don't mind if he's already married. My clients are walking targets for any ambitious, gold-digging or psychologically disturbed woman.'

Ethan mirrored the agent's body language. 'So you're saying it's difficult for them to be seen in public because members of the opposite sex lust after them? I know just the thing that will make sure they go out in public without being harassed or hit on.'

'Are you suggesting bodyguards?'

Ethan winked. 'That's the great thing. It's a lot less expensive than minders. How about this – a style of clothing that is loose, comfortable, looks good on any shape and will guarantee your clients don't get harassed in public?'

He suddenly had Anya's attention as well.

'Go on . . .'

Ethan moved to a whiteboard and began drawing in black. He outlined what looked like a long kaftan. On top of a head he sketched a veil, with a small opening for the eyes.

'In certain Islamic countries, the burqa is worn for those very reasons.'

Anya smiled but Horan didn't seem to see the humour.

'You will find these latest claims are completely unfounded, and my clients have made police statements to prove it. One word against five, would you fancy those odds?'

Anya felt her pulse rev. She could not believe how smug the man was. He would represent anyone, no matter what they did, if it meant making money. And he would turn a blind eye to the next Kirsten Byrne. His protection of the players guaranteed there would be more like her.

'And in case you hadn't heard, your so-called victim has already hired a lawyer. Another case of the green pocket syndrome.' He patted his shirt pocket. 'She's after a payout to keep quiet but we're going to fight this all the way.'

The meeting was over.

Outside, Ethan paced before the elevator. 'The ink on that Jordan–Janson contract is fresh. They didn't even bother to date it before yesterday.'

'Why would he sign a contract with a designer unless it was in his best interest?'

'The asshole's smarter than we gave him credit for,' Ethan said. 'Think about it.' The elevator doors opened and they entered. 'Cheree Jordan sent Kirsten with the proposal, which she left in Janson's hotel room after the assault. Horan's done the deal to further discredit Kirsten's story. The figures on the contract are a lot less than the ones Kirsten showed you.'

'How much difference are you talking?'

'From what I just saw, two hundred grand less and only three percent of sales. My guess is, Horan knows about the rape and is in damage control. And Cheree Jordan knew she had him by the balls and twisted hard. They deserve each other.'

Ethan's version of events made sense. 'So by signing the deal, it looks like they've been in negotiations for a while and makes it seem as if Kirsten went to the party of her own volition. The lesser amount to Janson could mean Kirsten slept with him to get a better deal for her boss.'

'Or acted independently of her boss's wishes to secure the deal. Cheree sacked Kirsten and tells the staff she resigned, or slept with a client to secure the deal – anything to make her look like a manipulative opportunist. Hell, she tried to tell us Kirsten stole the dress.'

It was Kirsten's word against her former employer's. Now Horan was involved, it would look like the deal was in place well before the function at the Rainier Hotel. The case for the prosecution was rapidly falling apart.

21

Ethan's text said he was in a conference room one floor up from the ballroom if Anya needed anything.

She decided to see how he was in person.

Papers were spread across the table around his laptop. If he was using a system to keep track of the documents, it was not immediately evident.

His face unshaven with raccoon-style shadows under his eyes confirmed what she suspected.

'Did you get any sleep at all?' She slid into a chair to his right.

He sat back and clasped his hands behind his head. 'I needed to do some paperwork. It couldn't wait.'

He hadn't been at breakfast, so she assumed he hadn't eaten.

'I'll be right back,' she smiled.

A few minutes later she returned with a cardboard box containing two lattes, giant muffins and croissants filled with ham and cheese.

'I should find more reasons for you to stay longer.' Ethan's face unfolded into a smile, revealing deep dimples in both cheeks. He looked younger when he smiled with his eyes. There was something very endearing about Ethan Rye, and it had taken her by surprise. She was enjoying the time they spent together. More than she wanted to admit.

As he helped himself to a warm croissant, she wondered what other tasks he was responsible for, apart from babysitting Australian doctors.

She picked up a paper with Peter Janson's name on it. His earnings and outgoings were here in detail, including his credit card statements. The amount of information Ethan had access to was extraordinary. She hoped he hadn't checked her financial records. It seemed a gross invasion of privacy.

She held up the printout. 'Does this have something to do with the rape victim?'

He sighed and ran his fingers through his hair. It flopped forward immediately.

'I'm looking for cash withdrawals, regular payments to persons unknown, anything unusual to suggest he paid people off. For example, women he may have assaulted in the past. Cases that didn't make it to court.'

He washed the last bite down with some coffee.

'In that case, maybe you should check Horan's company records.'

'Still working on that. By the way,' he frowned, 'you don't need to know how I got access to these documents because you never saw them.'

'Fine.' She assumed obtaining the information breached a number of privacy laws. Besides, if they were obtained illegally, none of the contents would be admissible in court. It would, though, give Ethan the chance to explore certain potentially useful avenues. If Jim Horan could fight dirty, it was only fair that Kirsten Byrne had someone in her corner too.

The next croissant disappeared from the box.

'The records supplied before the drafts are full of gaps and were done by a contract company. It happens sometimes when Lyle Buffet wants certain players in a hurry. What he doesn't know is that some services only check state prisons, so if an offender is on parole, or has finished serving a sentence, they show up as a negative criminal record.

'Online searches only cover twenty-nine states, so I'm still waiting on word back from three court runners. They have to manually check local courthouses for any other criminal histories for our boys.'

After a couple more mouthfuls, he stopped chewing and checked his watch. 'Don't you have another seminar, the one on drugs, violence and sex?'

'Not for another hour and a half. The business manager wanted to swap times. If you need a hand with anything . . .'

She wanted to help Kirsten Byrne and Linda Gatby in any way possible. And Lyle Buffet and the other owners needed to know who on their team was likely to damage what they were trying to build.

Ethan raised both eyebrows. 'If you really want to stay, you could read through some of these background checks and police reports.' He passed across a highlighter pen. 'You know what we're looking for. Past form, complaints.'

She read about Clark Garcia. The twenty-two-year-old had grown up in Los Angeles and had been in trouble for stealing a car at the age of fifteen. He and a friend had taken a Lincoln for a joyride and been caught with a gun under the passenger seat. Garcia had been driving. His lawyer successfully argued that he was a model student at high school, a star footballer and had been forced by the friend to steal the car.

Six months later Garcia was involved in a break and enter at the school principal's house. It seemed that the principal withdrew all charges, so Garcia would be free to play in the school team.

While at school, he lived with his mother, who worked nights at a 7-Eleven store, while he minded his baby brother and sister. The father died of a heart attack, aged forty-two, when his son was starting high school.

From what she read, Vince Dorafino hadn't fared much better. His mother had left when he was a child. He grew up in foster homes and attended Byzantine High School in North Dakota. He was accused of sexually assaulting a minor, but pleaded guilty to a lesser charge. The judge gave him probation given his sporting abilities and character references from his coach and principal.

The sound of an email dropping into Ethan's inbox interrupted Anya's reading. She looked up curiously.

'This is about Liam McKenzie,' Ethan told her. 'Moved States a number of times, which explains why his criminal record has been tough to trace. He follows a similar pattern to the others. Grew up with his parents, older brother and younger sister.'

He took another sip of coffee and leant back. 'You'll love this. At the age of sixteen, he was arrested for beating a girl-friend who supposedly wanted to break up with him. She suffered black eyes, a bruised cheek and a broken wrist. She later recanted her story and said she bruised her face when she slipped on the sidewalk and hit her head. Police report says no prior episodes.'

The story was very familiar to Anya. Four women were murdered every day through domestic violence in the US alone. And up to four children a day were killed by a family member or partner of a parent. Until society refused to accept any violence towards women and children, then deaths and serious injury would continue to be commonplace.

She had seen many teenagers with low self-esteem and lack of a stable home life who thought love was what a boyfriend said, not how he behaved. They believed beatings were the price of being loved.

Ethan continued. 'On another occasion, he was accused of beating a gay man he claimed had come on to him. Despite the victim having severe head injuries, the judge found that being propositioned by a gay man was provocation and McKenzie had acted in self-defence.'

'That's consistent with the comments he made in the lecture. He wasn't Robinson Crusoe with his homophobic comments but that exoneration might explain why he was so cocky.'

She thought of what Kirsten had said about her assault. For someone so homophobic, McKenzie was the one who had initiated the anal rape.

'This happened in a small town I've never heard of,' Ethan explained. 'Equality in some parts includes everyone except gays, women and anyone with a different viewpoint.'

Anya thought about McKenzie changing states over the last few years. 'He could easily have committed violence against partners in other states. It wouldn't be the first time someone with a violent past moved states and the police had no idea about any prior history.'

For the next half-hour, each read in silence, Ethan on his computer, and Anya trying to sort through the various print-outs splayed around the table.

Ethan slapped the desk. 'Got it!' He rubbed his eyes. 'There's something you don't know. McKenzie and Janson were charged with rape a couple of years back. The victim pulled out the first day of the trial. Rumour had it she was paid off, but there was nothing in either of the boys' records or her financial statements to prove it.'

'Why haven't you told me this? Was all that spiel about a family-friendly team just garbage, when Buffet employs people with histories like that?'

'Hold on a second. It was on the public record, so I didn't need to mention it to Linda Gatby, and it's her job to find out past incidents.'

Anya had thought she and Ethan were working, to a

certain extent, together. 'It doesn't explain why you kept it from me.'

Ethan breathed out. 'It made more sense for you to go over the medical information about Kirsten Byrne without any prior knowledge of charges against the players, which were withdrawn anyway. That's why they weren't in your dossiers. It's one of the reasons I wanted you here. You're unbiased and could actually be objective. Besides, these men are supposed to be innocent until proven guilty, right? I'm guessing Linda didn't tell you because she wanted your objective opinion on Kirsten as well.'

Begrudgingly, she had to admit Ethan had a point.

'So if you already knew about the complaints, what did you just *get*?'

'I've been trying to track the woman down.' He rubbed both hands together. 'We just got her address. I think we should see how she's doing.'

Anya suddenly felt uncomfortable about finding the private address of a woman who did not want to be found. If she had been raped, this would be another form of violation.

'Isn't there anyone else?'

'I don't see many other options.'

Anya closed her eyes. If these men had a prior history that would have a bearing in Kirsten's case, she felt an obligation to investigate that, even though it would be painful for the woman involved. It might just save another woman from going through the same thing.

There had to be a reason the woman had refused to testify. She wondered if Jim Horan had had anything to do with it.

Ethan slid a newspaper clipping over.

Charges of rape against star quarterbacks Pistol Pete Janson and Liam McKenzie were dropped by the DA this morning. The two players say they have been vindicated and want to get

174

on with their lives and the noble game of football. Their accuser,
a stripper from Queens, refused to testify, leaving the DA with
no alternative but to drop the charges. Speculation is rising
that the woman sought a significant payout from the accused,
which sources close to the players say amounted to extortion.

Anya did not need to read more. The fact the article mentioned the word 'stripper' explained enough.

22

Ethan drove to Brooklyn and parked outside a playground with swings and climbing equipment. A mixture of black, white and Hispanic children played together, while others preferred to stay close to their mothers.

Ethan checked a photo. 'That's Darla Pinkus.'

He pointed to a thin woman pushing a little girl on the swing. The child squealed, 'Higher, Mama.'

Anya watched for a few minutes, familiar with the simple joy of swinging, which for a child was akin to flying. Ben used to beg to be pushed harder to soar as high as possible. She remembered the same feeling, as though there were no constraints or limits.

Darla complied, but there was no excitement in her voice, no encouraging her daughter on to greater heights. She looked almost mechanical, as if her mind was elsewhere. Even with a hooded sweatshirt and baggy pants, hair plaited, she was an attractive woman, with a large bustline and narrow hips.

Ethan took a step forward and Anya touched his elbow.

'I'd like to talk to her first.'

He shrugged. 'Fair call. I'll be right here if you need me.'

Anya grinned, reached into her bag and pulled out some tourist guides. 'If you sit on a bench reading, you're less likely to raise suspicion in a kids' playground.'

Even though Ethan was well aware of surveillance techniques, he cheerfully took the brochures without a word and duly sat at a nearby bench.

The wind picked up and Anya shoved her hands into her trouser pockets. 'You can swing really high.'

Darla didn't seem to notice Anya addressing her daughter, she was lost in her own thoughts.

'Mind if I sit here?' Anya asked.

'Uh huh. Bet I can go higher than you. You want to see?'

'I know you can, I have a little boy back home and he swings just like you.'

Darla looked across.

'Why didn't you bring him to play?' The child slowed herself by bending her knees on the way up.

'He lives a long way away, in a place called Australia.'

'That's where kangaroos come from. Mommy showed me in a book.'

Anya smiled. 'It sure is. Your mum is pretty clever.'

Darla let go, stepped back and lit a cigarette, careful to shield the match from the wind. 'I've always wanted to go to Australia. Are the beaches as pretty as people say?'

'Better. South of Sydney is a place called the Sapphire Coast. It's called that because the water is such a beautiful blue. Just like sparkling jewels.'

'There are lots of dangerous things there, Lilly,' Darla said, 'like poisonous spiders, snakes, and they say wild dogs can snatch a baby with their teeth.'

Lilly's big brown eyes widened further. 'Did a dog take your boy?'

Anya laughed. 'No. It's really safe in the city where I live. I came here to work for a few weeks, but he has to stay home and go to school. Actually, he's not much older than you.'

Darla took a drag and exhaled away from where her daughter sat.

'I couldn't leave my kid. I mean, going to work is hard enough.' She glanced around the playground. Two boys played on small horses wobbling on spring bases while their mothers sat nearby with prams, chatting away to each other. A father encouraged a set of identical twins down the slide.

'Actually, if you help me, I could get back home sooner.'

Darla clutched the front of her top, as if doing so added warmth. 'I don't see how —'

'I'm a forensic doctor and I'm investigating a possible assault on a woman by several football players. I think you may know some of them.'

The woman stubbed out her cigarette and grabbed her daughter's hand. 'Honey, we have to go.'

Lilly jumped to the ground, broke loose and ran off towards the slide.

Darla stood, hand on her forehead. 'Haven't you people done enough? What more can you do to us? You got me fired, made me sound like a cheap whore in all the papers.' Her eyes flared. 'I almost lost my daughter because of what you did to me.'

'I'm sorry, I didn't explain properly,' Anya stressed, raising both hands with open palms. 'I don't work for the players and all I would like is to talk to you about what happened. I read the hospital report and believe you were raped that night in the club. You deserve to be heard.'

'Yeah, well, too little too late. Lilly!'

The little girl was chasing the twins around the slide, and the three were giggling and squealing.

'Please hear me out. I've come a long way to see you.'

Darla stopped and looked Anya up and down. 'You really from Australia?'

'Usually my accent gives it away.' Anya pulled out her passport as identification.

Darla tapped a foot on the ground and lit another ciga-rette. 'We can talk back at my place.'

The child slipped her hand into Anya's on the way back. Darla turned to look over at Ethan.

'Is he with you?'

'My minder, you could say. Without him I'd drive on the wrong side of the road and spend all my time getting lost. Do you mind if he talks to you as well? He's working with me, too.'

Anya signalled for him to come along and Darla did not object.

They walked a couple of blocks to an apartment building. Graffiti covered the ground floor walls and elevator doors. A sign indicated the lift was out of order. Three flights of stairs later, they reached number 316. A woman across the hall opened her chained door and peered through the narrow gap before closing it again.

Darla fiddled with two sets of locks and then whispered, 'Her son was killed in Iraq a year ago. She's lost her marbles and spends all day waiting for him.'

Once inside, she instructed Lilly to take off her coat, which she hung behind the door, and untied her shoelaces. The little girl disappeared into a side room. 'Don't forget to wash your hands.'

'I know,' came the predictable response.

Darla opened the window. Thumping from upstairs echoed through the apartment. 'The woman above us minds kids for money. Luckily, the ceiling hasn't collapsed yet.' She grabbed a pair of sheets and some clothes from the lounge and placed them in what Anya presumed was the bedroom. 'Have a seat and I'll put some coffee on. Sorry about the mess. There's nowhere to hang washing, and I can't afford anything bigger.'

Anya and Ethan sat. On a noticeboard were photos of Lilly at various ages. The sparkling eyes were the one constant in each image. No photos of a man, or partner. Despite the minimal space, the place was clean and homely. A basket of toys in one corner kept the floor free of obstacles. The little girl skipped back into the room and presented her hands to her mother for inspection.

'Good girl. How about a peanut butter and jelly sandwich?'

The child nodded and sat herself on the floor by the coffee table, tucking her slippered feet underneath her.

'How do you have your coffee?'

'Any way it comes, thanks.'

'I only have half and half milk,' Darla said, placing three mugs on the small table in front of them. Anya preferred low-fat milk, and said so.

Lilly's sandwich didn't last long before the crusts were separated from the bread and abandoned.

'I want you to go and play in our bedroom while Mama has a talk to the grown-ups.'

Lilly trotted off compliantly.

'You're a great mother,' Anya commented. 'She's a real credit to you.'

Ethan seemed happy to let the women develop a rapport.

Darla sat down at the coffee table as her daughter had. She wiped a long piece of hair from her eyes.

'It isn't easy sometimes, but I try. The last two years have been the toughest.' She moved the plate to the side. 'What do you want from me?'

Anya tried to ease into details of the assaults. 'We want to know exactly what happened that night you were attacked at the Gold Banner Club.'

'I was a stripper there. Hell, I knew I had a good body, so I took my clothes off for money. I used to be a dancer so I knew how to move, and the money was great when you're a single mother.' She looked towards the window. 'Not much else a girl without an education can do. Lilly's father took off a month after she was born.' She turned her attention back to her visitors. 'Don't get me wrong. I never had sex with the clients and I've never taken money for sex. A girlfriend told me that Rudy, the manager, had a strict no-touching policy, which is why I agreed to work there. That was part of the act. The guys

181

paid more for you to take more off, and dance more, hoping they had a chance with you, which of course they never did. I only ever stripped down to a thong, and you see more than that at the beach. One girl was paying for her college tuition by stripping. She told me I should sit the high school diploma, and I would have if things had turned out differently.'

'Where did the dancing take place?' Ethan obviously wanted to know the layout of the club.

'There was the general area downstairs, where guys would pay to see you strip around a pole, then there were the private rooms upstairs, for VIPs.'

'Did the high cover charge attract a specific clientele?'

'I guess, but the drinks were how Rudy really stung the customers. Our job was to get them to buy us drinks before we stripped, making them feel like it was some kind of date. Only, like I said, there was no touching.'

'I read that the club was a hangout for movie stars and prominent athletes,' said Ethan. 'Were they ever seen by the public, or did they get ushered in a back way?'

Darla tucked her legs beneath her and held her chipped mug with both hands. 'Rudy wanted them to be seen. Said it was good for business. And word got out pretty quickly whenever someone big was in the club. So they'd enter through the main doors, wave at the crowd, then Rudy'd take them upstairs to the VIP rooms and give them free drinks all night. They could go through a thousand bucks' worth of champagne. Rudy was cheap, so he had to be making money out of the deal.' She lowered her gaze. 'He was always doing coke, but I never asked questions.'

Ethan explained, 'Rudy had a name for dealing long before he got into clubs. It makes sense that's how he made real money. The club was how he avoided paying taxes on it.'

'I swear I wasn't into drugs. I never touched the stuff. Look, some players had their favourite girls, but still, there was no touching, even in the VIP rooms. We usually had one of the bouncers outside the door in case of trouble. All we ever had to do was call out if a client got out of line.'

Anya asked gently. 'What happened that night? When things went wrong.'

Darla stared down at her drink. 'I was dancing, I'd taken off all my clothes except my thong when one of the players, McKenzie, grabbed me from behind and tried to dance with me. I told him to let go or I'd call the bouncer, but he shoved me to the couch and covered my mouth with his hand. I could hardly breathe. Janson was laughing and cheering as McKenzie held me down and raped me. Then Janson took over.'

'Did you know who they were at the time?'

'They were regulars, all the girls knew them, but this was after some big game they'd won and they were all really drunk, much worse than usual.' She shuddered.

'Liam McKenzie started it. That asshole thinks he can get away with anything. And he sure as hell got away with raping me. So did Pete Janson.'

Darla retreated to the bedroom and came back with a box. Inside were handwritten notes, newspaper clippings and a wad of letters.

'The police didn't care. I was just a stripper, so I had to be asking for it.'

She handed over a couple of envelopes with her name on them. Neither had return addresses.

Ethan read one, Anya took the other. She felt a chill at the first line. *Die you dirty slut. Rot in hell. You will pay for what you did to two of America's favourite sons. We know where you live.*

Anya could hardly believe the venom of complete strangers thousands of miles away, judging by the postmark. It was like the letters her father had received after news of Miriam's

183

disappearance appeared in the papers. It took only a few days for sympathy towards the family to be replaced with hatred and accusations of satanic rituals, child abuse and other sick theories as to what had happened to their precious Miriam. Had Anya not been cleaning the shed out years later and found the stash of hate mail, she may never have known the extent of the ongoing trauma compounding the family's grief.

Luckily Danny, who had been born after Miriam disappeared, had been sheltered from the ugly accusations, although not from the hurt of false hope. Every year on the anniversary of Miriam's disappearance, some crank contacted them saying they knew what had happened to her. Everything from where she was buried, to where she lived now with her own family.

The letter in her hand typified the vile treatment victims of incomprehensible crimes often received. Rather than deal with the realities of the crime, it was easier for people to blame the victim.

'You got death threats and the police didn't care?' Anya felt incensed.

'Why would they?' Darla searched for something in the box. 'I wasn't anyone important.'

'This letter looks like it was written by a woman.' Ethan's brow furrowed. 'There's a lot of ranting about family values, then this: *Those men are honourable. They put their lives on the line every time they play football. They are valuable members of this society, and have beautiful wives and families. You are the refuse of the world, and don't deserve to live.* Don't suppose any of these moral crusaders mentioned the fact that their married pillars of society betrayed those beautiful wives and children when they went voluntarily to a strip club, broke curfew and breached their own contracts.'

'You don't get it. These guys are untouchable. They might as well be gods with the big money they make, and all their sponsors. They're famous, so I had to be lying, trying to bring them down. I was a money-grubbing whore no one cared about.'

Upstairs, a new round of stomping caused a small amount of paint to float from the ceiling to the floor. The noise alone would have driven Anya to live somewhere else.

'Do you have any idea who made the threats?' she asked.

Darla turned the box's contents out on to the coffee table. 'Take your pick. Some are postmarked from Minnesota, others from Nevada and California. A lot are local. In case you're wondering, someone put my previous address on the Internet.' She pushed aside a faded envelope with her finger-tips, as though she could hardly bear to touch it. 'This one was the worst. It says my bastard child would be kidnapped and killed for my sins if I continued to claim I was raped. It was put under my door the day we were supposed to go to court.'

Suddenly it became completely clear why Darla had refused to testify against her attackers.

'I grabbed Lilly and what we could carry and left. We stayed in a shelter for a couple of nights. That's how we ended up here.'

A frantic series of knocks interrupted. Darla padded down the corridor and opened the apartment door, safety chain still in place.

'No, Mrs B, I haven't seen him. You know wars can take a real long time . . . Promise, I'll let you know if I see him.'

She closed the door and returned to her visitors, pulling an errant strand of hair from her face. 'Look, I did what I had to to protect my child. At least I live in the real world, unlike poor Mrs B. Her kid isn't ever coming home, only she doesn't get that. I'm sorry, but if you're trying to nail McKenzie and Janson, it's too late for what they did to me.'

Ethan pointed to the correspondence. 'Do you mind if we borrow these to help us with our investigation?'

'Take what you want. I only kept it to remember why I tried to fight them in the first place. I don't care if I never see any of it again.'

Anya collected the papers and put them back inside the box and closed the lid. Ethan rose and thanked her for everything. Box in one hand, Anya wrote her name and number on the back of a receipt she had pulled from her purse.

'If you need to talk, or think of anything that could help us, I'll be around for at least a few more days.'

'How'd you find me anyway?'

Ethan handed her his card. 'It's my job to find people, and keep their secrets. Don't mean to pry, but if you're looking for work, I might know somewhere – nice place where people treat you with respect.'

'Thanks. I appreciate that. Finding decent work isn't easy when you've been labelled a whore on television and in all the papers.'

Anya smiled at Ethan as they followed the corridor to the stairwell.

'What?'

'Finding her work isn't exactly part of the job, is it?'

'The way I see it, the men who raped her made money out of all the publicity. So much for a system of justice. They didn't just rape that woman, they screwed up her entire life. And I'm thinking it's no coincidence she gets a death threat against her daughter the day the case was going to trial.'

'Just like the one made against Kirsten Byrne.'

It was unlikely to be a fan. A lot was at stake if Janson and McKenzie were convicted; the men, their families, their agents, the Bombers and the league itself all had a lot to lose.

She wondered who had made the threat and how far they would have been prepared to go to make sure the woman didn't testify.

23

Back at the hotel, Anya sat on her bed with a Cosmopolitan cocktail from room service. She pored over online articles about the trial involving McKenzie and Janson. Headlines read like advertising slogans. *PISTOL PETE AND THE STRIPPER.*

The wording in each screamed of bias. The media angle seemed to be consistent. Mention 'stripper' in every headline, then list the successes of Janson and McKenzie, quote anonymous sources to defame Darla's character, and show a blurred photo of a pole dancer. Others chose to showcase photos of the men with their children, with wives denouncing the story as lies, and as an attempt to extort money and ruin the good names of their husbands. One magazine mentioned the fact that Janson and his wife had agreed to marriage counselling.

The same issue boasted a feature on actresses who appeared naked in films. One starlet declared she only took her clothes off if it was 'essential to the integrity of the story', while in another rag talked about routinely walking around her house naked. No one suggested that actresses who disrobed on stage or film were immoral, were prostituting themselves or prepared to have sex with crew members. No reporter implied that they were asking to be raped. The double standards and imbalance of power galled Anya.

In many ways, Darla was right. The job she had stripping was safer than many other situations. She had security outside the door, and there were rules that were supposed to be adhered to. On the other hand, any woman meeting a man in a bar and going home with him was potentially at risk of harm. But that wouldn't have been big news. The mention of stripping seemed, in the readers' minds, to be synonymous with prostitution and 'moral turpitude', as one reverend publicly declared.

There was almost no mention of the fact that these men were married, yet they regularly attended strip clubs.

The coach was quoted as saying, 'These guys are warriors. They train hard all week and put themselves on the line every time they play. Who could blame them for letting off steam every now and then? Boys will be boys.'

Anya could imagine the reporters lapping it all up. Of course the woman was a liar, another article declared. Remember Adam and Eve? From the beginning of history, man had had to put up with temptresses. Such articles would have been laughable, if not for the damage they did to Darla Pinkus. The woman's version of what had happened was credible, and by going to the police and giving a statement she had embarked on a real David versus Goliath battle. Funny how no one viewed it that way in the media.

Anya finished her drink and licked the taste of cranberry juice from her lips. She turned to the last two unread letters from Darla's box of clippings. One was pretty much like the others; the second was handwritten, neat and easy to read.

I'm sorry to hear about what happened to you, but you have to stop what you're doing. You don't understand who and what you are up against. They will destroy you.

For your own sake, you have to drop the case.

Anya breathed out. Her first thought was that this was another letter trying to frighten Darla into leaving the players alone. Then something about the letter caught her attention.

You don't know me, but I know you. I was you and am you.

This isn't easy to say, but I was raped and hurt very badly by one of the men who attacked you.

I know you are hurting but you're just making things worse. Stop now before it's too late.

You can't win against him. He's too strong.

I am sorry you have to hear this, but it's the truth.

The letter was unsigned.

24

Terri Janson answered the door in white skinny jeans, high heels and an off-the-shoulder top. Her long platinum-blonde hair had a slight wave. The heart-shaped face was pretty but not what Anya considered beautiful. She looked like a number of famous faces Anya could never quite tell apart.

'Come in,' Terri said, almost theatrically. Her toenails matched the shade on her fingers. Inside the apartment, she proudly showed off a view of Central Park. 'We needed two homes since we're both spending more time here for work. I thought Pete could stay here instead of at the hotel but that's not allowed, apparently.'

She sounded irritated.

'It's hard to explain to the kids why Daddy's in town but not able to be with us.'

'Your work sounds demanding.' Anya decided to change the focus from Pete to Terri. Ethan had mentioned she modelled at car shows, which was where she had met her husband.

She seemed happier to talk about that. 'I'm exploring some exciting business opportunities with cosmetic companies. I'm even considering my own line of children's clothes, something affordable but fabulous. Little girls love a bit of bling as much as their moms.'

Anya could only imagine. The apartment was furnished simply, with a giant TV mounted on the wall, speakers in each corner, and a black leather lounge in front of a zebra-patterned rug. A neon Budweiser sign hung on the adjacent wall. There were no bookshelves, magazines or clutter in sight.

'Can I get you anything?'

'Coffee would be great,' Ethan answered, and Anya agreed.

'Nanny?' she called. 'Coffee for our guests.'

Two little girls came running into the room, both wearing identical rose-patterned dresses with a sequined sash around the waist. Each had their hair in two high ponytails, with sparkly clips keeping wisps off their faces. Both girls had round cheeks and their mother's eyes.

Terri stroked the tops of the girls' heads. 'This is Liesl and Emma.' The smaller child carried a baby doll.

'Hi, I'm Anya, and this is my friend Ethan.' Anya knelt down and pointed to the doll. 'Who is this?'

'Kim. She special.'

Liesl flicked her sister's head. 'Emma is only three and always sleeps with her.'

'And how old are you?' Anya smiled.

Liesl held up five fingers.

'You're almost grown up.'

Liesl giggled and covered her mouth with her hands.

Terri disappeared and returned with a tray of pastries. A young woman, presumably the nanny, carried another tray of cups, saucers and a coffee pot.

'Thank you, Nanny, you can take the children to the park while we talk.'

The young woman placed the tray on the sideboard and took the children by the hands. 'We'll get your cardigans, little ones.'

The accent was French. Terri poured the coffees and offered them all a seat. She sank into the lounge and crossed her legs.

'Mr Buffet rang to say you were coming and asked me to help where I can. This business at that party the other night is outrageous. Our lawyer says we should sue that woman for defamation for all the trouble she's causing. What do y'all want me to do? I could do interviews to let everyone know Pete didn't touch her.'

Ethan began. 'First, a bit of background on you and Pete would help us. How long have you been married?'

'Six years. We met when he was starting college. It was love at first sight. For both of us.'

'Would you say you have a good marriage?'

Terri's mouth kept a smile, but the rest of her face seemed to freeze. She took a moment before speaking. 'Well, life is busy with the children, his work and mine, but we're very happy, if that's what you're getting at.'

'I suppose what Ethan's asking,' Anya tried, 'is how well Pete treats you. Have you two ever had any difficulties?'

Terri recrossed her legs and hugged the top knee with both hands.

'That's a personal question.' She flicked her hair and raised her chin. 'We are as much in love as the day we met. What couple doesn't have —'

'Terri, has Pete ever been violent to you? Or the girls?'

She was quickly on her feet. 'This is ridiculous. I don't know who you've been talking to —'

Ethan remained seated and placed his coffee cup back on the tray. 'We know there have been at least two incidents in which the police were called by neighbours.'

Looking down, she dismissed him. 'They were just lovers' tiffs and the neighbours completely misunderstood. It was all my fault. Pete came home tired, and said something about an attractive reporter and I became jealous. It was petty and I shouldn't have said anything, but Pete was angry that I even imagined he could be unfaithful. He went to leave and I stood in his way. All he did was move me to the side, then slammed the door. The neighbour must have heard that and called the police.'

She twisted the diamond on her ring finger. 'The second time, I don't even remember what it was about. I dropped a saucepan and burnt my hand. Pete helped me, but the neighbours misunderstood again. I guess they see how big he is and just assume he's violent.'

'Unfortunately,' Anya said, 'footballers are trained for violence. Sometimes they can bring their work home.'

'Well, Pete isn't like that.' Terri returned to the lounge. 'He told me all about that woman who accused them of rape. He's right. She has to be mentally disturbed. He feels sorry for her, but this woman is threatening my family. What are you and Mr Buffet doing about it?'

Ethan glanced at Anya. 'What exactly did Pete tell you?'

'That she's a crazed fan who followed him to his room, where she slept with the others and later cried rape. She isn't the first, you know. It started in high school, the moment his star began to shine.'

She disappeared into another room and returned with her own large box, the contents of which she upturned onto the rug.

'This is just a small example of what we have to deal with.'

Anya bent forward and picked up an envelope. Inside were nude photos of a woman, along with her address and phone number.

'Some of them are obscene, what these women say they will do for Pete. There are DVDs as well, with some fans talking to Pete as they touch themselves. And these are the ones I intercept and protect him from. Fan letters, they call them. I call them filth. We get hundreds every week, from women all around the country. Some are teenagers, others are in their fifties. Others tell him to leave me, say I'm being unfaithful behind his back. This is the trash we have to deal with.'

She bent down and began returning items to the box. 'Pete is no angel, but I know for sure he would never have to force himself on a woman. There are enough willing to throw themselves at him everywhere he goes.'

25

Anya wondered why Terri Janson kept photos and letters propositioning her own husband. Maybe it was to make her feel more secure, knowing he had married her, not one of them. She suspected Terri had been abused by her husband, but there was nothing anyone could do unless it occurred in public, or Terri decided to make a complaint. From what Anya had learnt from Kirsten and Darla, Pete Janson was a dangerous man who had complete disregard for the women he raped. He treated them like objects provided for his enter-tainment, then discarded them as soon as he had finished.

She pictured the two young girls dressed in matching outfits, growing up with a man who assaulted women with impunity. She only hoped Terri could protect them from witnessing the violence or being victim to it themselves.

On the way back to the hotel Anya stopped at a deli on Lexington and bought her favourite comfort food. In the hotel room she slowly demolished the giant piece of cheese-cake, savouring the thick, creamy texture. Her peace was interrupted by a knock on the door.

The clock by the bed glowed 10.30 pm. She wiped her mouth and checked the peephole.

Ethan Rye stood, hands on hips. She opened the door.

'I need you downstairs. It's an emergency.' Seeing the anxiety in his face, she grabbed her room key and bag from the bedside table and slipped on her shoes. Yoga pants and a sweatshirt would have to do.

Ethan was already holding the lift when she arrived. 'What's going on and what sort of emergency?'

A Japanese couple entered as the doors closed and he remained silent.

Eleven floors down, he pulled her by her elbow along the corridor and around a corner. A large man stood outside one of the rooms, continuing to knock. 'Catcher, he still ain't answering.'

'Vince. You're sure he's in there?'

'Man, I heard him go inside about an hour ago.' He bent down for Ethan's benefit but his whispers were like that of a child. 'I think he had company, but I heard her go. Then his wife came up, only he didn't answer.' Ethan dialled a number, and they could hear the phone ring inside the room. The large man frowned more. 'He don't go nowhere without that, it's got all his numbers.'

And all the incriminating evidence about his illicit liaisons, Anya thought. 'He's probably in the shower,' she said, adding under her breath, 'washing off the smell of another woman.' She couldn't see the immediate need to panic. Vince's loyalty seemed over the top, particularly since it meant helping a friend betray his wife. The sexual health lecture obviously hadn't affected their behaviour.

'My room's next door and I'd hear if the shower was on, ma'am.'

It occurred to Anya that the man must be Vince Dorafino. One of the five accused of raping Kirsten. It struck her not only how loyal but how polite he appeared.

Ethan looked around and pulled out a keycard. 'Don't ask,' he urged and opened the door. There was no security lock in place. They entered and saw the unmade bed, pillows discarded on the floor of the suite, along with a set of men's clothes. Out of the corner of her eye, Anya saw Janson wedged in the wardrobe, hanging by a belt attached to the hanging rail. His face was swollen, deathly pale with blue lips; his arms hung limply by his side.

He was naked apart from a condom.

She reached for a carotid pulse in his thick neck. The head and hands were cold. Pete Janson had been dead for a while.

Ethan called 911 for an ambulance.

He locked eyes with Anya and seemed to accept there would be no need to attempt resuscitation. Quickly, he slipped the security lock across the door. Anya stepped back and examined the room, looking for anything that might seem out of place. Three trays of empty plates sat on the desk. Using her phone, she photographed the position of the body and the layout of the room. Paramedics were bound to disturb the scene. The fact that a woman had been here made the death potentially suspicious. Without disturbing anything, she checked the bathroom and found containers of unnamed white pills. They would have to be collected by the police for analysis and comparison with toxicology results from the post-mortem.

Ethan stood staring at the body. 'Someone's got to tell Buffet.'

Anya would have thought the wife and family were more of a priority. Suddenly, someone began pounding on the door. 'What the hell's going on in there?'

Ethan looked to the ceiling. 'Someone must have called Horan. He's going to be pretty pissed at losing a meal ticket.'

He opened the door and was pushed back by the agent. He saw the body immediately.

'For God's sake, do something!' He rushed to remove the belt, and Ethan wrestled him back. 'It's too late, I'm sorry. Police and an ambulance are on their way.'

Horan's face contorted as he pulled free of the hold and ran into the bathroom. It sounded as though he was throwing up in there. The paramedics, one male, one female, arrived in time to hear the toilet flush.

'Someone's going to have to do crowd control out there. The corridor's full.' The male paramedic looked at the body. 'Is that Pete Janson, the footballer?'

Anya confirmed it.

'We'd better go through the protocol,' he said. 'If only for the family's sake.'

Ethan was on the phone to hotel security asking them to clear the corridor and make a service elevator available for the gurney. The mention of media packs and negative publicity for the hotel seemed to achieve his goal.

With gloved hands, the paramedics went to undo the ligature around Janson's neck. 'We need to keep that,' Anya instructed. 'It could be evidence.'

The female officer raised an eyebrow.

'I'm a forensic physician.'

'What are you, psychic?' She had braces on her teeth and a slight lisp. 'You usually come later.'

'I'm staying upstairs and heard there was an emergency.'

Ethan knocked on the bathroom door and Horan appeared, wiping his face with a wet cloth. Anya thought that he had probably put his fingerprints all over the bathroom. So much for maintaining the scene for police.

The female paramedic shook her head as the four of them lowered the massive body to the floor. Horan's help comprised moving the clothes out of their path.

As the ECG leads were attached to Janson's chest, Anya scanned his body for bruises or any defence injuries to suggest he had struggled. A blackish purpura on his left bicep caught her attention.

'He got that in the game,' Ethan commented. 'I saw it in the locker room. Thing is, he seemed to have learnt something from your lecture. At least he was wearing a condom.'

The woman with the braces smiled. 'So much for

protection.' She was at Janson's head with a breathing mask over his large jaw and nose.

The male officer checked the machine. 'He's in asystole. We could shock him in case it's fine V-Fib.' He placed two gel pads on the chest and charged the defibrillator. 'Move clear,' he said, and the other three moved back while he shocked Janson. 'This guy is – was – a legend. One of the best players I've ever seen.' He studied the monitor. 'Still asystole.'

Anya kept quiet. She could hear a commotion in the corridor outside.

'Increased the joule count. Clear.' The body bucked but the ECG remained a flat line as they repeated the process.

'I need to see my husband!' came a voice from outside the door.

Horan moved to the door and opened it. Janson's wife caught sight of her husband's lifeless body and screamed. Horan clutched her to his chest, stopping her from interfering with the work of the paramedics. She collapsed onto the floor in tears. Horan sank with her and held her tightly.

Two uniformed police arrived.

Anya and Ethan stepped outside to speak quietly with them. Coach Ingram and a number of the players were already outside being kept at a distance by hotel security.

Ingram shouted, 'Rye. What the hell is going on?' Ethan signalled for the coach to be allowed closer. He thudded along, adjusting his cap. 'If he's that sick, why aren't they on their way to hospital already? Where the hell is Rosseter?'

The older police officer had a notebook out. His name badge read *Bilson*. 'Sir, please let's start with some facts.'

Ethan explained why there was nothing Rosseter or anyone else could have done, making sure no one further down the corridor could hear.

'You mean Pistol Pete Janson?' Bilson removed his cap. 'I met him once, he was real nice to my boy.'

It was clear how effective the team's PR machine had been. If it hadn't given Janson such a clean-cut image, Kirsten Byrne might have been more wary that night at the Rainier Hotel.

Coach Ingram slumped against the wall. 'Does his wife know?'

'She's inside with his agent right now.'

'For the record,' Ethan stressed, 'as far as anyone else is concerned, he's in a critical condition after a collapse. No need for the media wolves to find out until we've talked to Buffet. I trust, officers, you can keep this from leaking out until Pete's family can be told. He's got parents, brothers and sisters, as well as his kids. The last thing you want is for them to hear it on the news or from some damn reporter.'

The representatives of the NYPD nodded. 'We can arrange an escort to hospital.' Bilson called for the hotel manager, who was waiting with the other players. 'We need a plan to get Janson out so nobody sees him.'

'Of course, we'll do anything possible to help, officer. The staff and hotel facilities are at your disposal.'

Bilson sneered, 'Hotel staff leak like a sieve. The fewer people involved the better, especially since the press would pay anything for a story or photos. We don't want that. You got that?'

'Yes, officer. Leave it to me,' the manager said.

A second ambulance crew arrived, along with two more police officers and a pair of detectives. Keeping this a secret had to be impossible, Anya thought.

Within minutes the group had devised a plan. A head-scarf and a hat appeared, and the corridor was cleared of onlookers. The hotel manager lay on the second gurney, scarf and hat hiding his face, his body covered with a sheet to his chin. He was to be taken out the front door to the first ambulance. The second ambulance, which would be parked at the loading dock in the underground carpark, would carry Janson, still being worked on by the paramedics. Ethan phoned Gavin Rosseter and instructed him to meet the ambulance at the hospital.

With the plan under way, Ethan and Anya were no longer needed. 'One of us will need to talk to you and get statements,' Bilson said. 'Where will you be after we check out the room?'

'At the bar downstairs,' Ethan answered for both of them. 'That sounds reasonable.'

Anya opted to go to her room first to change. Around the corner from Janson's room a large crowd had gathered, kept at bay by hotel security. As they pushed through, Anya tripped on someone's foot, falling heavily to the floor. The contents of her bag spilt everywhere. Someone helped her up, and Ethan gathered up her things. She had hurt her wrist, and perhaps her dignity, but was otherwise fine.

Ethan fussed over her until they were back upstairs at her room. She invited him inside because she suspected he did not want to be alone. That reaction was not surprising. It wasn't every day a civilian found the body of someone he knew, strung up and naked in a hotel room. Ethan's calm resolve during the last half-hour was admirable. She respected the way he had done everything possible to minimise damage and scandal for the family and, by default, everyone associated with the team. She was surprised, though, that even in what was most likely his death, people were protecting Pete Janson.

She threw her bag on the bed and Ethan turned on the television, flicking through every news channel he could find. She grabbed fresh clothes and closed the door of the bathroom. Inside, she washed her hands, filled the bath, added some soap and dropped in her yoga pants and top. Death had a smell that clung to clothing. After she had taken a shower she offered Ethan a chance to wash up, which he seemed grateful for.

A news break caught her attention. A newsreader with perfect hair announced, 'In breaking news, we have uncon-firmed reports that Pete Janson, the New Jersey Bombers' star quarterback, has been rushed to hospital after appar-ently collapsing at his hotel tonight. There is no word yet from the hospital or a spokesman for the Bombers. We will, of course, keep you updated as news comes to light.'

Ethan caught the last few moments. 'We couldn't keep a lid on it for long, but they'll be outside our rooms any minute. We'd better go.'

26

They sat on bar stools around a small drinks table. Ethan had a Scotch and soda, while Anya opted for mineral water. She did not want to be alcohol-affected when they spoke to the police.

Gavin Rosseter had notified them. Janson was pronounced dead on arrival.

'I can't believe he's gone.' Ethan stared at his glass. 'When you saw him on the field, he was so . . . fit and healthy. Just like Keller.'

In death, he was like Keller. Both died alone, with people nearby they could have called. Then again, each was engaging in a high-risk behaviour. She thought about the drugs that were in the unlabelled containers in Janson's bathroom.

Anya asked, 'Do you think it was an accident?'

'I can't imagine anyone being able to hold him down and strangle him. You saw the size of the guy.'

'Unless he was drugged. We don't know who the woman in the room was and the timing's pretty coincidental, don't you think?'

Ethan took a gulp. 'You would have needed horse tranquillisers. That guy could down two bottles of Scotch with a case of beer chasers.'

Anya could imagine, given his weight and mass. But why elite athletes drank to excess always amazed her. It countered so much of their training and fitness. 'Labwork will tell us what was near the sink and in his system.'

Ethan ran his finger around the rim of his glass. 'Do you think he killed himself?'

Anya could not ignore the possibility of suicide, but there was something else to consider.

'It could have been an accident. Auto-erotic asphyxia would explain him being naked, but in the cases I've seen, there is usually paraphernalia about, like pornography within reach, and they usually have some kind of release mechanism connected up if they're alone. If it's with a partner, it's erotic asphyxia. The one asphyxiated is totally dependent on the person they're with to release the noose in time.'

'That's a lot of trust.'

Bilson and his colleague appeared and Ethan waved them over. The bartender immediately suggested they could talk more privately in the restaurant section next door. Presumably, the presence of two uniforms unsettled some of the patrons. They moved to a table with white linen, set for the following night's dinner.

'This shouldn't take long,' Officer Bilson said. 'This here is Eduardo Rodriguez,' he indicated his partner. 'The detectives took the wife to the hospital. She was pretty hysterical.'

He took a breath and exhaled with a slight wheeze. He had a ruddy complexion and broken capillaries over his nose and cheeks. 'I'm afraid your friend didn't make it. Obviously, we're considering the possibility of suicide. Did Janson suffer from depression?'

Anya was slightly surprised. 'What about auto-erotic asphyxiation?'

Rodriguez's eyes widened. 'Which is?'

Anya couldn't believe she had to explain this to a police officer, but she obliged. 'The people who practise it seem to think that by cutting off the blood supply to the brain during climax, the lack of oxygen gives them a heightened sexual experience. The idea is to rig a mechanism by which they can release the ligature before blacking out. Unfortunately, sometimes they black out before they can release it. It's very high risk and thought to be the cause of a number of male teenage deaths that are deemed suicide.'

The young officer gave her a look of doubt. 'And you know this because?'

'I'm a forensic pathologist and sexual assault expert.'

'Oh.' Rodriguez rubbed a pimple on his chin. 'How long do these characters strangle themselves for?'

'Some people do it apparently from beginning to orgasm and after, while others report the lack of oxygen gives them a euphoric feeling, so strangle themselves at the beginning of arousal then release the tie, then tighten it again at the peak of orgasm. They think the rush of oxygenated blood to the brain is what enhances the whole sense of pleasure.'

She paused as the barman brought them all water and asked them to call if they needed anything.

'I saw a fellow years back,' Bilson recalled, 'a pharmaceutical salesmen, I think he was. He died with a tie around his neck, only he was dressed like a woman. Skirt, panties, fishnets, the whole lot. Pathologist back then said it was an accidental death caused by misadventure. That's what they called it.'

Anya spoke more softly. 'Exactly. People who commit suicide expect their body to be found and they're not usually naked or dressed in a way they wouldn't want to be seen by loved ones. Besides, with all the pills in his bathroom, Janson didn't need to hang himself.' She sipped on her water.

Ethan spoke next. 'There's often a note with suicides. We didn't see evidence of one.'

Bilson pulled a handkerchief from his pocket and sneezed into it. 'These days people can text or email suicide notes. We'll see if he had a computer. There weren't any pills when we went over the scene.'

Anya shot him a confused look. 'There were two unlabelled vials of tablets. They were by the bathroom sink.' She remembered Jim Horan going in there and throwing up. He couldn't have missed them. Something clicked. 'Horan could have flushed them down the toilet.'

'The man who was comforting the wife. Who's he officially?'

Ethan clenched his jaw. 'A lawyer turned agent; the worst kind. He could have been protecting his client's reputation.'

'Were they close?' Rodriguez asked.

'About as close as a cobra and mongoose can get. Janson's reputation meant money to Horan. Surely the elephant in the room is the condom. Bit odd, don't you think, for someone to pop on a condom just to kill himself? Even Janson would have known that a pair of trousers had more dignity.'

'Maybe once he was naked,' the younger officer suggested, 'he got natural . . . urges.'

Bilson coughed and his partner went quiet.

Ethan curled his lip. 'Most men I know don't use protection to raise their own flagpole, even after one of the good doctor's lectures.'

'Were there any calls to or from his room, or his phone?' Anya asked.

'I'll check,' Bilson said. 'You said these people rig a mechanism to get themselves out of it. What would we be looking for?'

Anya thought of a number of cases she had performed post-mortems on. Some were teenage boys who probably thought they had tied slipknots in the scarf. Others used plastic bags to cover their faces and kept a knife nearby to cut loose when they climaxed. Another method was to use a mud bath. Apparently, the weight of the mud compressed the chest and made breathing difficult.

'It can be anything from a bow, like how kids tie shoe-laces, to something more complicated, like a hook attached to another string that can release the tie. Really experienced men can carry little kits with tools and hooks in them.'

A number of the players filtered through to the bar. The barman must have closed it for their exclusive use.

'We better go talk to some more players before they drown their sorrows,' Bilson said, hauling himself from the chair.

'We'll have another look at the room later. It's sealed so no one will interfere with it for now. Thanks for your time. If we have any other questions . . .'

Ethan pulled out a card. 'I'm assisting Doctor Crichton, so you can reach either of us on this number.'

The officers moved towards the bar, which was strangely quiet.

'See the older cop's badge?' Ethan finished his drink. 'It's a dupe.'

'Do you mean a fake?' Anya felt the heat rise in her face. 'Please don't tell me I just said all that to a journalist in disguise.'

He slid out of the booth. 'No, he's the real thing. It's just some of the older cops use fake badges. He probably comes from a family of police and the badge is handed down to each generation. The dupes are slightly smaller. The real one's gonna be locked in a safe somewhere.'

Anya raised her eyebrows, wondering why he mentioned it.

'Just wanted you to know I'm still paying attention. Let's have another look at that room before NYPD's finest get there. Are you with me?'

Anya didn't hesitate.

27

With the players downstairs and a uniform outside Janson's door, Ethan let himself into the room two doors down, which belonged to another team member. The officer barely acknowledged them.

Once inside, Ethan removed two pairs of latex gloves from his pocket. Anya wondered if he always carried spare gloves, or whether it was something he did while working with footballers.

'Don't think I ever want to get inside your head,' Anya quipped.

'After the lesson you gave us tonight, I was thinking the same thing about you.'

Ethan removed a skeleton key and unlocked the interconnecting door, then the one connecting Dorafino's and Janson's rooms.

After fifteen minutes of silent searching they hadn't found anything that helped answer their questions.

Ethan checked the messages using the room phone. Terri had called twice, the first time saying she was on her way over to talk about the questions Ethan and Anya had been asking. The second one was angrier, reminding him that she'd left two messages on his cell and was in no mood to be messed around.

However, Vince had heard her leave, without entering the room, which ruled her out of direct involvement in the death. That left the 'company' Dorafino had mentioned.

Anya checked the wardrobe and looked for any holes that might have been made inside. She looked behind a print above the bedhead. If he'd done this regularly, it was possible he made holes where no one else would find them. The paint was intact.

'These places are made of concrete for fire safety reasons.' Ethan looked behind the dresser and under the bed. 'He would have needed a drill to make a dent in any of it.'

'And no one saw anything like a small toolkit.'

'Just as no one saw the pills in the bathroom.' Anya moved inside, careful not to disturb anything. Horan had made a mess of the place, with towels strewn all over.

'Is it worth looking inside the S-bend?' Ethan asked.

'They would have dissolved by now anyway, and I have the image on my phone. Toxicology will find out whatever he had in his system.'

'Glad you said that. Plumbing is not one of my specialties.'

Inside the bin in the bathroom, Ethan found a number of pieces of paper, some with phone numbers on them. He photographed each with his phone.

Just then Anya thought she heard someone in the corridor. She froze, her pulse racing. How would they explain to the police what they were doing? Ethan held a finger over his lips and quietly removed his gloves. She did the same and tried to think up an excuse for being in the room again. Would they believe a lost contact lens? It sounded ridiculous even to her. She hoped Ethan was a much better liar.

Two male voices became louder before they heard the sound of an electronic key in a door but it was the door to the adjoining room.

Ethan stepped quickly and quietly from the bathroom and returned with two glasses. Anya thought he was joking, but he held the glass to his left ear, against the wall, frowning in concentration. Anya did the same with her right ear. The muffled conversation suddenly became a lot clearer.

'What the hell are we going to do now? The police are already asking questions. Pete was supposed to fix everything.'

'Man up! We're not going to *do* anything. We stick to exactly what we said in the police statements. That is it!'

'What if I can't remember exactly —'

Something thumped the wall. Anya started, and the glass slipped from her hand. It hit her shoulder, then bounced forward into her left hand, narrowly missing the wall. She breathed a sigh of relief.

'Do you realise what's at stake? If we stick together, the police have got nothing. I got rid of any evidence, so we're good if we all keep to the plan.'

There was a pause and the same voice spoke again, this time more calmly. 'How about you treat it like the playbook and that way you'll memorise it.'

'Do you even care? Pete is *dead*.'

'Of course I do. But you sleep with dogs long enough you get eaten by fleas. Right now we'd better get back downstairs before anyone misses us. Get changed into something you can talk to the press in, and get it together!'

The door clunked and the voices faded.

Anya breathed out and felt perspiration on the back of her neck.

'Let's go,' Ethan said. 'If there was anything else here, chances are Horan or the wife took it. We'd better go back to the bar and prove who was in that room.' They reversed their entry path and Ethan made sure to lock the adjoining doors.

They headed for the lift and as they rounded the corner, came face to face with Buffet. Anya felt guilty about what they had just done.

'Knew if you were worth your salt you would have gone back to that room,' Buffet said, puffing on his pipe. 'We need to talk.'

If he were aware of the no-smoking signs, he didn't care. Nor did the policeman guarding Janson's room.

They headed to the lifts in silence, and rode to the thirty-third floor where they entered a set of double doors that led to a suite. Anya began to feel nervous. Buffet wasn't about to thank them for finding Janson, not when the media had found out so soon afterwards.

Inside, Kitty Rowe, in a mauve tailored suit and silk scarf spoke on the phone at a work desk, a notepad in front of her full of scribblings. She glanced up but barely acknowledged them. At the dining table, three men with shirts and ties sat answering phones, while two others talked at the same time. The suite also contained a long lounge and separate armchairs. A giant flat-screen TV resembled a monitoring station, with multiple images onscreen at the one time, all of news stations and ESPN.

Bentley Masterton stood alone at the bar.

Buffet pointed to the seats. 'Sit down.' It was an order, not a gesture of hospitality.

They each sat in separate chairs.

'We need to put a lid on this thing before it goes any further. You two were brought into our team to help clean up our game, improve our public image. Fan numbers are falling, which means sponsorship and income are plummeting. Unless we do something, this team will be defunct within two seasons.' He moved to the bar and unscrewed a bottle of Scotch. He took two swigs straight from the bottle.

'Do you have any idea how much of my life has been spent building the Bombers? The name, the reputation? I made it what it is today. And because of Janson, it's all in jeopardy.'

Something caught his eye on the screen and he picked up the remote from the coffee table. A female reporter stood outside the hospital. The other images faded and this one was enlarged.

'Tonight New Jersey Bombers fans, and fans around the country, are mourning the loss of one of football's finest players. Pete Janson has died after an apparent heart attack in his hotel room this evening. Desperate efforts by paramedics to revive him were unsuccessful. The hospital has issued a statement saying that Pete Janson was pronounced dead at 11.15 pm this evening.'

The reporter became mute as a montage of Janson images filled the screen.

'Rosseter had the good sense to describe it as a heart attack. That should buy us a few days.'

'My network will run a special on the great charity work Janson was part of and offer it to the others as a simulcast,' Kitty said.

Masterton chimed in, 'Did he actually do any charity work?'

'That's the good news. He was always first out for a photo op with a crippled kid or homeless black person, anything that would get him a headline. We've already put together some footage that's previewing,' she checked her watch, 'in seven minutes. We'll run it on the half-hour overnight and through the morning. We're also getting anyone who met the guy in passing to say how great he was, yada, yada, yada and how he inspired them to change their lives.'

There was no hint of grief or sadness in the room. It was as if an election campaign was in full swing and Janson was running for an important office. Anya couldn't believe the man who allegedly raped a young woman a few nights ago was being held up as a saint.

In death, almost everyone was stripped bare of all pretence, their public face inevitably unmasked. In contrast, these people were creating a special death mask for Janson.

'On your instruction, the grieving widow is refusing interviews. We'll line up an exclusive once we hear from Oprah and Barbara Walters. Ellen might even throw her hat in the ring. Those two young daughters are gold.'

'Have you contacted the Vatican for a statement?' Anya muttered under her breath. She wanted nothing to do with a PR campaign for a sex offender and moved forward in her chair, ready to stand up and leave.

'Doctor Crichton,' Buffet said, 'we brought you here to help us assess the liability some of our players presented, and educate them in sexual health. I speak for all of us when I say you've been following our brief.' He stopped and, as if on cue, the minions in the room finished their conversations and quietly filed outside.

The three owners, Ethan and Anya remained.

'What happened in that hotel room, and what's the autopsy going to reveal?'

Anya was unsure what Buffet wanted from her, and hoped it wasn't more of the good spin campaign.

'Autopsy will approximate time of death, which had to be at most an hour before we found him. Initial assumption is that he died of asphyxiation from a belt pulled tightly around his neck, which was tied to the wardrobe. He was naked apart from a condom on his penis.'

'You think he did himself in?'

'The odd thing is that he could have stood up if he wanted to and was able. The rail was a lot shorter than he was.'

'So you're thinking murder?' Buffet certainly did not mince words.

'The only way would have been if he were drugged, and it would take an incredibly strong person, or people, to stage it. It took four of us just to get his body down.'

Buffet puffed on his pipe.

'Any of the players could have done it. Janson didn't

exactly go out of his way to be popular. If we think about suspects, half the women he met could qualify, along with his wife and any of the players whose wives he slept with.'

Ethan placed his hands on his thighs. 'There's another couple of possibilities. That Janson was engaged in a dangerous sex act that went too far, or the woman he most likely had sex with before his death was involved.'

'What kind of sex ends up with a dead footballer?' Masterton sounded outraged. 'What sort of organisation are you running? *She* was supposed to teach these boys all about safe sex. Now what sort of message does that send to the younger fans?' He threw both hands in the air.

'A responsible message,' Anya replied. 'One in four Americans now has a sexually transmitted infection, and if your players go around having unsafe sex, they can infect any number of women, not to mention their own wives and girlfriends. And what about unwanted pregnancies? A tribe of single mothers with illegitimate children suing for paternity and child support would tarnish the team even more. Judging by their collective ignorance, I'd say sex education was way overdue for these pampered men, who have the maturity of pre-pubescent boys.' She knew she should stop speaking and leave with dignity, but if they were concerned about money and public image, they had to hear the complete truth.

'AIDS is not something from the past, it's on the rise and an infected player risks infecting other team members as well if he gets an injury and isn't even aware he's infected with the virus. How much litigation and scandal would that open you up to?'

'Don't take that tone with me, young lady. For all we know, Janson learnt this "sex act" in your so-called lecture.'

Anya stood to leave, her anger boiling over. Before she could speak, Ethan interjected.

'I attended the doctor's talk and it was the height of professionalism. Many of the players, including married ones, told me how much they'd learnt and how they wished they'd been given that information years ago.'

Masterton guffawed like a child. 'We can see why you're defending her.'

'Settle down, Bentley,' Buffet scolded. 'Janson was no choirboy and you knew that when we signed him. We asked Doctor Crichton to investigate the sexual assault complaint made against a number of our players, including Janson.' He turned to Anya. 'Does the Byrne woman have a case?'

Anya glared at the evangelist. 'I believe it's strong. The physical injuries are consistent with her story of gang-rape.'

'This just gets better and better.' Masterton's hands were in the air as though he was indeed praising the Lord. 'Who the hell screened the players for good character? When I bought into this organisation, you assured me there would be no more sex scandals after that court case fell through. My congregation will not tolerate me being associated with something so —'

'Oh do hush up,' Kitty said. 'You only care what's made public. I'm sure Doctor Crichton here is wanting to get to the truth.' She stroked the silk scarf around her neck as though it were a cat.

Buffet took command. 'Find out the truth, Doctor Crichton, so Janson's family can be told before anyone else learns it. If any of my other players are involved in his death, we need to know. I'm doubling your fee because the matter is so pressing. Now, please excuse us while we get back to work.'

Anya stood, trying to comprehend what had just taken place. Ethan opened the door and followed her out.

'They loved you,' he said with a grin.

'You think that went well?' Anya asked incredulously.

'Hell yeah. They've just given you – which means us – a free hand in finding out what happened tonight.'

She wasn't sure she wanted to be involved at all. 'Yes, but at what price?'

'I saw the way you were in that room with Janson's body. You were in your element. And come on, you have to admit, you want to know as much as I do. The first thing we need to do is confirm whose those voices were in the room next to Janson's just now.' He extended a hand. 'Are you with me?'

For Kirsten Byrne, Darla Pinkus and any of the other women these men had assaulted, she would do what she could. The pair shook on it.

28

There they were. The only photos on the cell phone. Pete Janson, blue and lifeless, in all his naked glory. Certain outlets would pay a fortune to publish them. And Lyle Buffet would pay more to keep them hidden. It wasn't difficult to imagine Bentley Masterton's feigned disgust at the images either. There was a fortune sitting right here.

Anya Crichton was proving too smart for her own good. She needed to be monitored. A loose cannon, not the foreign token she was supposed to be, damn it. There were other ways to clean up the league.

The cable connected the phone to the laptop. Step one. Download the photos and keep the originals. Crichton would never suspect they had been copied. If she realised the phone was missing, there would be a good few hours for her to panic. It wouldn't hurt to keep her rattled.

She'd have the device back soon enough and be loath to let it out of her reach again. Even better.

The second step was more time consuming. The spy software took much longer uploading. From now on, no matter where she was, it was possible to hear everything the clever doctor said and heard.

Switching it off was fruitless.

The phone was now a listening device, even when it was switched off. It was amazing that something so innocuous could be a veritable wealth of ongoing information. The software made the job so much easier.

Everything Anya Crichton discovered about Kirsten Byrne and the five players, and whatever she learnt about Janson and Keller's deaths, would be recorded.

The chances of her putting it together were remote, but this was insurance and the stakes were higher than the naïve doctor would ever comprehend.

The final step: activate the GPS tracking device on the phone. Task complete.

Now, Anya Crichton would never be out of sight or earshot.

Back in her room, Anya kicked off her shoes and climbed onto the bed. It was almost time to ring Ben. Reaching inside her bag for her phone, she removed her wallet, tissues and a muesli bar, but there was no trace of the phone. She checked in the pockets and compartments – twice. The phone wasn't there.

Where was it? Damn. This was the phone she used to call home using Skype. More importantly, it contained the photos of Janson hanging in the wardrobe. It had to be here. Tipping out the contents, she rummaged again, with no luck. She could feel her heart pounding faster in her chest. She searched under the bed and pulled off the covers. She ran to the bathroom but all she found were her toiletries. She wanted to throw up. This could not be happening. If those pictures got out, it would devastate Janson's family and have serious legal repercussions for her. The thought was too horrible. It had to be somewhere. She tore the sheets off the bed and felt every inch of them for the phone. Nothing. God, where was it?

She mentally retraced her steps from the time they'd found Janson's lifeless body. The last time she had it in her hand was in Janson's hotel room. She rubbed her elbow, remembering the trip in the corridor.

It must have fallen out when she dropped the bag. She rushed downstairs and scoured the corridor. Someone had to have picked it up, but there was no record of it having been handed in at reception.

Whoever had the phone may not yet know what was in their possession. Either that, or someone had stolen her phone. She didn't know which was more disturbing. By now, her clothes were sticky with perspiration from panic.

The events of the night played like a horror movie in her mind. She checked under the bed, pillows, chairs and cushions for the umpteenth time before giving up the search, short of breath and riddled with guilt. Ethan and Buffet would find out soon enough. She dialled home from the phone in her room.

Ben answered straightaway, as if waiting for her call.

'Hi, Mum.'

'Hi, sweetie, how was your day?'

'Good.' The word always ended with an upward inflexion as if it were a question. That made her smile, despite the ongoing sick feeling about the phone.

'What was good about it?'

'I got a sticker for being a good reader, and being helpful. And I played soccer at lunchtime and kicked a goal.'

Anya had seen her son play soccer, which at his age consisted of a pack of boys all running together in the same direction.

'That's great. Your dad must be teaching you well. Did you bring any notes home from school?'

Despite being so far away, she wanted to be involved in the day-to-day workings of his life.

'There's a fête in a few weeks and we'll have rides on the oval, and fairy floss and games and . . . I can't remember what else but there's other stuff.' He giggled, which was what he usually did when he forgot something in the middle of a story.

She laughed with him.

'Will you come? Pleeeeeeaaase?'

Anya scratched the base of her throat.

'I'll do my best, but you have to let me know when it is.' Hopefully it would be after she arrived back home.

'Mum, I really miss you.'

She closed her eyes. 'Me too, sweetie. I miss you so much.'

'I think Dad does too.'

Ever the matchmaker. Sometimes she thought Ben was a little old man stuck in a child's body.

'He wants to say hello. Here he is.' As if as an afterthought, he added, 'Bye Mum, love you.' She heard him call out, 'Dad, Mum wants to talk to you.'

He was definitely an old soul in a child's body.

Martin came on the line. 'Hey, Annie, how's it going in the Big Bad Apple?'

'Well, since I've been here two footballers have died, so I'm obviously doing wonders for their health.'

'I was joking when I told you to knock them dead,' he said. 'I didn't mean it literally.'

An awkward silence followed.

'Want to talk about it?'

'Not right now. How's Ben going at school?'

'He's doing well, talks about you more at bedtime, wanting to know where you are on the map and when you're coming back.'

'Hopefully soon. I'll be home as soon as I can.'

'I did some checking on the Internet and the Australian dollar's looking better. Ben and I could meet you in Los Angeles and maybe we could go to Disneyland or do a cruise. You and Ben could share rooms if you like, and I can be in a separate one. Kind of like a family holiday for our son.'

Anya sat up straighter, not knowing what to say. Ben would love having both his parents together, and a break was a great idea. She just wasn't sure how Martin's girlfriend would take to the concept.

'What about Nita?'

'She knows how important you are to Ben and wants what's best for him.'

Anya wanted to buy time to think about it. She and Martin had been getting along recently, but a holiday was something else. Ben could easily get the wrong idea about them.

'Let's see how the next few days go and I'll let you know.' She thought of the lost phone. She could be fired by the morning.

'Fair enough . . . Oh hey, I've been offered a part-time job tutoring nurses at the local university campus. I can start next semester.'

'Congratulations, that's wonderful news.' She meant it.

'There's one more thing, Annie, look after yourself. OK?' He lowered his voice. 'We both miss you.'

Her stomach clenched as she hung up the phone.

The knock on the door woke her at eight. Having fallen asleep in her clothes, she stumbled to the door, trying to recall if she had ordered breakfast.

'Sorry.' Ethan was showered and shaved. 'I waited till I thought you'd be up.'

The phone. She had to tell him.

'Ethan, there's something you need to know.'

'You lost your phone?'

She blinked slowly as he held it in his hand.

'How did you —?' She felt a sudden elation.

'Got a call from reception last night. Someone handed it in and since mine was the number called most often, they phoned me on it.'

Anya let out a heavy sigh of relief. She could have hugged Ethan.

'What about the photos?'

'All there, intact. As far as I know, they're not on the Internet and no papers have called for a comment.'

'I can't believe I lost it.'

'Anyway, just wanted to get it back before you worried.'

Too late, she thought, having pulled apart her room searching. The relief at it being found by someone honest, and handed in to a smart receptionist, more than made up for it, though.

'Hey, since you're awake now, do you mind if I come in for a minute?'

Anya wanted a hot shower and something to eat. The inside of her mouth felt like she'd been chewing newspaper in her sleep.

'It won't take long.' Ethan didn't seem to notice her reluctance to invite him in, or didn't care. He entered the room, laptop in hand.

'We know Dorafino had the room next door to Janson, but it didn't sound like his voice we heard last night.'

He downloaded a video clip from YouTube. 'I found some interviews with the players and wanted to run them by you. I know these guys but they all sound alike to me. I'm better with faces.'

It seemed to Anya that the two men they had heard talking were not concerned with Janson's death so much as what would happen to them after the night in the Rainier Hotel. Unless there had been another incident that required them to make police statements not long before Janson died. Based on the combined past history, that was not beyond all possibility.

Ethan turned to his laptop and checked the YouTube interviews, starting with McKenzie appearing on ESPN.

He paused the clip, then replayed it. Anya leant over his shoulder to watch the screen.

'That's it. The dominant voice,' Anya said.

Ethan agreed. McKenzie had told the other man to shut up and stick to the police statements. Once they confirmed the other player's identity, they would access the actual statements and see how they compared.

Next clip was of Vince Dorafino claiming he was the world's greatest tight end, while showing off his backside with a dance. His voice was more nasal and the cadence was more varied than the second voice in the room.

They agreed he was not the man.

A search for Lance Alldridge followed. Ethan had trouble locating a clip of the man described as a BFG, in reference to Roald Dahl's story of a big, friendly giant. But for someone so friendly, Alldridge had a distinct tendency to keep quiet in the presence of a microphone. Eventually, an interview was located. His deep, rich tones excluded him. He was the player in Anya's first lecture who had tried to explain to Janson that HIV was not exclusive to gay men. He did not sit with the others, or dress like them, but he was still allegedly part of the rape that night.

That left Clark Garcia. During a statement from inside a locker room, the rookie struggled to sound articulate. He uttered phrases like 'one hundred and ten percent', 'big effort' and 'hard hits'. Anya estimated his IQ as below average. He could have had trouble remembering plays, and what he was told to say in his police statement. That left a potential weak link in the four remaining suspects.

Comparing the size of the men on the videos to their interviewers, it was easy to see how any of them could have overpowered a woman like Kirsten Byrne.

'What now?' Anya asked Ethan, who tapped his pen on the desk.

He closed his laptop. 'You've got two hours before you meet with the medical examiner.'

Anya stretched her back and glanced at the dishevelled state of her room. Ethan was polite enough not to comment.

'What bothers me is that Kirsten's injuries would have bled significantly, even in the room. But no blood was found on the sheets or towels.'

'You're right. It's the part of the story that makes no sense. None of these guys knows how to clean shit from a shoe, let alone clean bloodstained bed linen.'

Blood was difficult to remove, especially from white hotel sheets.

It was possible Kirsten had the wrong room.

Or had she been raped somewhere else? But what reason would she have for lying? They needed to find out.

29

Twenty minutes later they headed for the Rainier Hotel. Ethan had explained that, as was customary, the organisation that had hosted the event on the night of the rape had provided their celebrity guests with rooms to freshen up, rest in, or stay overnight if they preferred. They could entertain guests privately upstairs after being seen and photographed downstairs. Janson had no doubt told his wife he was at a work function. He may even have gone home to their apartment in the early hours of the morning, after the alleged rape, and woken up in his own bed.

'Just follow my lead,' Ethan instructed.

At reception, he put his arm around Anya's waist.

'My fiancée and I were huge fans of Pete Janson, and we never got to meet him in person.' He pulled her closer. 'It sure would mean a lot to us if we could maybe just see somewhere he's been. Didn't he stay here?'

The check-in staff member smiled showing perfect teeth. 'We did have the pleasure of his company, and we're all shocked by his passing.'

'We can't believe it. It's just so tragic.' He turned to Anya. 'We might even have the wedding here, honey, what do you think? It's where Pete came to a party.'

Anya felt strange that she was playing along, but she wanted to see the room, to make sure it was as Kirsten had described, and make sure there was nothing the police might have missed. 'Could we?' She rested her head on his shoulder.

'It's an unusual request,' the woman behind the desk said, 'but what happened to Mr Janson has touched us all. Let me see what I can do.'

Some fast clicking at her keyboard gave them an answer.

'You're in luck.' She waved for a porter. 'Could you please accompany this lovely couple to room 3210? They would like to see it before they book their wedding.' She handed them a brochure about the hotel facilities and a card with the name of the hotel's wedding planner.

Inside the room, the porter opened the curtains, showed them how the television worked, gave them a tour of the bathroom and then stood by the door. Ethan still had his arm around Anya, but let go to hand the man five dollars. 'Do you mind if we have a moment to make our decision?'

The porter stepped outside. Ethan checked under the bed while Anya examined the wall behind the paintings.

'If he was into auto-erotic asphyxia, he might have practised it here. No screw marks anywhere.'

Ethan lifted the sheets and checked the bed. 'Nothing. I guess it was a long shot.'

The porter knocked on the door.

Anya straightened her skirt and Ethan moved to her side. He opened the door and replaced his arm around her waist.

'We love it,' the groom-to-be announced, and kissed Anya on the cheek.

When she stiffened, he just squeezed her tighter.

The porter seemed unimpressed. On the way back to the elevator, they passed a cleaning trolley, left idle while a maid was in a room with the door open and the television blaring. It would be easy to steal sheets from the trolley, although disposing of the bloodstained ones would be slightly more difficult.

Anya had a thought.

'Can we check the mailroom? You know, to see if we can get wedding gifts delivered to the hotel.'

Ethan looked at her with eyebrows raised.

The porter pressed the button for the conference level and told them it was on their right. They exited, and he went back to the ground floor.

Anya had to admit the charade had been amusing, but Ethan had overplayed the affection part. She had always been a stickler for rules and doing the right thing. Whether it was a new place, the lack of constraints in her job description, or Ethan's influence, it didn't matter. He obviously knew how to lie his way into any place. Watching him in action was fascinating. But now she had him guessing.

She rang the bell to the mailroom and an elderly man opened the top of a stable door. Dressed in a brown short-sleeved shirt and trousers, he looked as if the effort of answering the bell had taken all his energy.

This time she did the talking. 'My good friend says he posted a package to my sister from here the other day and she rang me to say it hadn't arrived. I was wondering if you could check your records to make sure it was sent.'

The gentleman lifted a cardboard concertina file that looked like something from the 1960s. The cardboard dividers were browned, aged and flaking at the edges.

'Do you know what date he says it was s'posed to go?'

'Early on Friday the thirteenth, I think.' It would be the earliest mail after the night's assault. 'McKenzie is the name.'

He grunted, closed the box and collected another, in even worse condition, from beneath the desk. Flicking through the files, he located a pink receipt.

'Where does your friend live?'

Anya looked at Ethan, who obliged by reciting McKenzie's home address. The man grunted again. 'Nope. That ain't where it got sent.'

'Maybe you remember,' the investigator tried. 'It was for Liam McKenzie, you know, from the New Jersey Bombers. He swears he sent it home – earlier – to my sister.'

The old man rubbed his chin and looked up to the right. 'Now you mention it, I do recall something.'

Ethan reached into his pocket and pulled out a twenty dollar bill.

The man looked around, snatched it and slipped it into his trouser pocket.

'Got to work the next mornin' and there was these plastic bags inside the door and an envelope with enough money to send the package and then some.' He wiped his nose with the back of his hand. 'I boxed the bags up and sent them on their way.'

'Are you sure they got sent?'

'Yessir. Did it myself.'

Ethan swivelled the pink paper and saw the weight: 4.5 lbs. He wrote down the address.

'Thanks for your help. I'll tell Liam. He probably had a big night the night before, if you know what I mean.'

The old man chuckled. 'Him and me both.'

As Ethan left, the stable door was closed again.

Less than half an hour later, they were inside Starbucks with a latte each and copies of the five police statements regarding Thursday 12 August that they'd already sourced. What struck them both was the similarity between sentences, down to use of the same words and phrases. Either each player had a savant's memory, or they had written the equivalent of a playbook about what went on in the room that night with Kirsten.

They reeked of collusion, but defence lawyers could use them as five witnesses with the same true version.

Pete Janson described how a woman who gave her name as Kirsten flirted with him in the bar and they shared a few drinks. He then asked her to his hotel room to party with some friends. She eagerly agreed and at her request he even signed an autograph in a boy's scrapbook, met the child in the lobby then got Liam McKenzie to sign his scrapbook later, before returning it to the boy after Kirsten had left it behind.

I do recall her mentioning that she worked for a fashion designer, but she seemed more interested in having sex with me. I am a Christian family man, but admit that I have human failings. I strive each day to be closer to Jesus. I fell prey to temptation that night in my room and at her insistence I had sexual intercourse with the woman I believe to be Kirsten Byrne. We had both been drinking earlier in the bar as many people will be able to confirm. I did not use a condom, and she did not ask me to. At no time did the woman tell me she did not want to have sex, or say that she was being hurt. In fact, she moaned with enjoyment while having sex with me. After that, Liam McKenzie entered the room followed by Lance Alldridge, Vince Dorafino and Clark Garcia.

Kirsten ran over to Liam McKenzie and embraced him. She was naked at the time. She then led Liam back to the bed, where they proceeded to have sexual relations. After that, I believe she asked to have sex with the other men in the room.

I cannot say what happened after that as I went into the shower in order to go home. When I came out, Kirsten had gone. I went home to my family.

The first I knew of her complaint was when the police asked me to come to the station. It was then that I discovered Kirsten Byrne claimed we had raped her. This was not the case, as my team mates can verify.

I believe the events to have occurred exactly as I have described. This is a true statement of what occurred on the night of August 12 of this year.

Truth was subjective, Anya thought, but proving the statements were lies was a whole new ball game. Now Janson was not around to be cross-examined, his statement would stand. Even in death he was still able to hurt Kirsten Byrne.

30

Anya arrived at the Manhattan Medical Examiner's office on First Avenue. Like so many other government institutions, the building was decades old and could have done with a facelift. Inside was worse. The mortuary, autopsy rooms, toxicology and histology labs, along with X-ray and photography facilities, were crammed into a few small floors.

The glamour, open space and proliferation of high-tech wizardry portrayed on some television dramas could not have been further from the reality.

Doctor Gail Lee was expecting Anya. Ethan had other business to attend to, and she was glad for the small amount of personal space. This trip had made her realise how much time she usually spent alone. Surprisingly, though, Ethan was proving better company and far less intrusive than most people she met.

Doctor Lee was in the midst of watering a brown-tipped fern on the filing cabinet in her office. When Anya knocked, she was wiping some water off a file beside the plant. Doctor Lee lowered her round, red-rimmed glasses and smiled warmly.

'Anya Crichton, how long has it been?'

'Four, maybe five years since the symposium. You presented sudden cardiac death, if I remember.'

Doctor Lee smiled. 'We had a fascinating discussion about familial cardiomyopathy.'

The senior medical examiner had written countless articles on the pathology of sudden death and irregular heart rhythms.

She finished wiping the file. 'Welcome to my neck of the woods.'

Her hair was still black but with a few grey hairs scattered through. What used to be waist length was now cut in a short bob with a straight fringe. The style reminded Anya of the character Edna in *The Incredibles*.

'Please, take a seat.'

Anya looked around the cramped office and gathered from what she saw that Gail was a hoarder. Files, preserved specimens in glass, journals and papers covered every surface. The plant probably never stood a chance so close to the air conditioning, which was spewing air colder than necessary for comfort. A computer in the corner was the only obvious piece of technology.

'Thanks. I've been investigating the veracity of a sexual assault claim against Peter Janson and some of his team mates. That's why I was around when Janson's body was discovered.'

Gail dug through a pile and pulled out the police report.

'I agree time of death was within an hour of when you found him. Lividity was beginning to form in his legs, suggesting he'd died in that semi-upright position. Of course, toxicology will take a few weeks, or even longer given our backlog.'

In many ways, that would suit Janson's family and the Bombers' management. By then, media speculation about the death would have died down and the lasting memory in many people's minds would be of the heart attack, as described by Gavin Rosseter.

'I'm still waiting on the medical history from his family doctor. All I have is a health summary by the team doctor. Are you aware if he suffered from either depression or epilepsy?'

Anya sat forward. 'Not that I know of.' For the pathologist to ask that question, something had to be wrong on gross examination of the brain.

'Do you think cause of death was something other than asphyxia?'

The woman handed over a number of photographs. 'What do you make of the gross findings on the brain?'

Anya studied the images. A shiny light brown layer of what looked like scar tissue lay on the surface of the frontal lobe of the brain.

'He had a head injury at a game the other day but got up and kept playing, and was apparently fine after that.' There was the possibility of a bleed between the lining of the brain and the skull, known as an extradural haemorrhage. Sufferers could be lucid and conscious after a head injury then deteriorate as the bleed increased in size and put pressure on the brain.

'What about an extradural?'

'Nothing to suggest it.' She pulled out a series of photographs with similar images. 'This one is of a boxer who fought for twenty years, then killed himself at the age of thirty-seven. Compare this to that of a seventy-five-year-old dementia patient.' She pointed to one that looked almost identical. 'Janson's lies somewhere in between.'

'His doesn't appear to be from an acute injury, like the one he sustained the other day. It looks more like a scar than a haematoma.'

'That's my thinking. The sort of scar that happens when the head is used as some kind of battering ram or punching bag – again and again.'

Anya sat back in amazement. 'But he was only twenty-seven, and I've seen the helmets. They're padded with foam and inflatable sections customised to the shape of the player's head. There's no chance of it slipping either. Those helmets move with the skull and, I would have thought, absorb a lot of force.'

235

'I did a literature search and it seems what I found in Pete Janson – although we do have to wait until the brain is fixed and dissected – is that he had CTE.'

Anya had heard of chronic traumatic encephalopathy. The first cases had been reported in former boxers, of whom it was thought twenty percent would develop it. Recent data suggested that percentage was, in fact, much higher. If what Gail said about Peter Janson's brain was true, the repeated trauma from his sport would have caused irreversible brain damage. She thought back to the game and the number of audible collisions in each play during the short period she had been on the sideline.

Gail said, 'I'd be keen to know if he suffered personality changes – extreme aggression, loss of inhibition, forgetfulness and intractable depression. The former players who have been studied each committed suicide. With the degree of damage to Janson's cortex, I can't exclude it.'

'He was accused of raping a woman last week. She apparently went to discuss a business proposal and he assumed she was there for sex. He went to the bathroom and returned naked from the waist down.'

Gail tapped a pencil on the desk. 'Sounds like disinhibition from frontal lobe destruction.'

'Or a sign of overt aggression. It's difficult to know if that was new or part of his personality in the first place. These men are trained to be brutal and don't necessarily understand how to switch that off.'

'That is disturbing.' Gail shook her head. 'Any signs of depression since he was accused of rape? Surely that would have affected his career prospects and had a significant impact on his family. Shame, embarrassment, remorse.'

Anya doubted that. 'Janson seemed pretty cocky and was apparently with another woman in his room just before his death. We have no idea at this stage who that woman was, although we assume it wasn't his wife.'

'Living with a cat is far less trouble,' Gail muttered. 'It always amazes me how people with fame and success manage to complicate their lives.'

'He has been accused of rape before. I suspect the sexual aggression has been going on a long time.'

'In relative terms, so might the brain damage.'

Gail made a good point. Anya appreciated that complete examination of the brain tissue would take more than a couple of weeks. First, the entire organ would have to be fixed in formaldehyde then dissected into shavings smaller than a hair in thickness. Special immunological stains were used to reveal the presence of abnormal proteins. What Gail would be looking for was tau protein in the absence of beta-amyloid – the indicator for CTE. Patients with Alzheimer's characteristically had distinctive patterns of the two different proteins. Beta-amyloid correlated with the earlier stages of brain deterioration. As the disease progressed, tau protein became more prevalent and was thought to cause severe and permanent damage to brain cells.

This had raised the question of how many patients treated in Alzheimer's facilities were the victims of head trauma, possibly from contact sports earlier in life. Unfortunately, the answer would only ever be found at post-mortem.

Because Janson's brain showed such similarities to that of a boxer or an elderly dementia patient, the diagnosis of CTE was a strong possibility.

Gail removed her glasses, revealing a pressure mark at the bridge of her nose. 'I want to run a test for ApoE4 which, as you know, appears to predispose certain people to trauma-related brain injury.'

Anya was familiar with the apoprotein. Studies had shown that patients who tested positive for the gene component released more tau protein into the cerebrospinal fluid following a head injury than people who tested negative. That meant more permanent damage was likely in the positive patient. Potentially, parents might demand the right to know if their children were predisposed to brain damage before they commenced contact sports. It would be a legal minefield.

'That's a good idea. You'll know a lot more if you identify tau protein in the absence of beta-amyloid in Janson's brain. CTE may not have been the direct cause of death, but it could have been a contributing factor.'

The air conditioner clunked and the room became even colder. Anya pulled on her cardigan. 'What do you think about auto-erotic asphyxia?'

The red glasses were back in position. 'That's tricky because it appears the scene was disturbed without being photographed.'

'Actually, I took some shots on my phone before the body was interfered with.' Anya lifted her bag onto her lap. 'Force of habit. They may not be great quality, but they give the layout of the room and position of the body.' Again, she was grateful the device had been returned.

'If you don't mind, just email them. That way they'll be on file. Our online security is as good as it gets.'

Anya put the bag back at her feet.

'Was there any history of his practising it, or any sexual paraphernalia, pornography, bondage equipment at the scene?'

'No. But he was naked, wearing a condom.'

Gail steepled her fingers together. 'That is highly suggestive.'

The doctor's phone rang but she ignored it. She readjusted her glasses as she read the file. 'If he were a regular practitioner, I would have expected him to use something to protect his neck from bruising by the belt. Particularly, as I keep being reminded, because he was in the public eye.'

Anya had to agree. The bodies she had seen sometimes presented with a towel or cloth around the neck beneath the ligature to prevent bruising.

'Suicide is still a possibility,' Gail said. 'Either way, it's such a waste of life. The condom is curious, but could have been part of some bizarre sexual ritual.'

Anya thought suicide was a long shot. Janson had children and a wife to live for, and he seemed to revel in the adulation and privileges fame and money brought.

'He seemed to have a rapacious sexual appetite, not that he was unique in terms of celebrities or sportsmen. But there is the issue of that woman in his room before he died.'

The pathologist scanned her desk a number of times. 'There were no signs of a fight, and three hundred pounds would be difficult to choke while he was conscious. The blood alcohol level was 0.05, not enough to render him incapacitated. As I mentioned, bloods have been sent off for tox screening so we'll know more then. Homicide isn't high on my agenda, but I have been proven wrong before.'

Gail pulled at one of her small silver earrings. 'He had a significant number of gastric erosions, my guess is from taking ibuprofen or the equivalent. From what I can gather, athletes pop them like jellybeans. There is something else of interest, but unrelated to the specific cause of death.'

She located an image of the top half of Janson's face. 'Two and a half inches behind the hairline is scarring. There's no loss of hair, so the procedure was probably elective and I assume cosmetic, although it's something I'm not familiar with.' She held X-rays of the head – front and profile – up to the ceiling lights.

'This man seems to have had work done to his frontal bone – again, not documented in the medical history I was given.'

Anya tried to work out why anyone would need to shave back the bone beneath his forehead. Unless, she thought, he had illegally used growth hormone and developed visable side effects like thickening of the skull and jaw. If it had begun to change his appearance, the doping agencies could become suspicious. So his enablers could have organised a cosmetic surgeon to make the effects less obvious, completely disregarding the dangers to his health of continuing to use the illegal drugs.

She sat back, horrified at the possibility. It was the only logical explanation.

Despite having little sympathy for the way Janson behaved, he was, she suspected, partly a victim of his handlers and the insatiable push to win.

'Were there any identifiable signs of anabolic steroid abuse? Any scars, scabs, abscesses from possible injection sites?'

Gail referred to her notes. 'As you would anticipate, his physique was very muscular and he had large hands, feet and a prominent jaw, but not out of place in a person his size. There was a torn bicep muscle on the left, but nothing else you would expect, like acne or testicular atrophy. The heart was enlarged and hypertrophied, but not out of the ordinary for an athlete.'

So far, Anya thought, nothing stood out, although anecdotally players who used steroids ruptured muscles more easily than non-users. There was nothing tangible to confirm he had taken them.

Gail continued. 'There was some scar tissue present in the upper outer quadrants of both buttocks, but the team doctor had prescribed vitamin B injections for fatigue, apparently.'

She scowled. 'What athlete isn't going to be fatigued with all the weightlifting and training he would have done? Not to mention being slammed at great speed into other massive objects.'

Anya knew that blood tests after death were unlikely to be of help in any diagnosis of illegal steroid use. Janson wasn't about to pee into a cup.

'I contacted a friend who's a neuropathologist and he agrees it looks like another case of CTE. I told him about your interest in the case. He's got time to meet you today up until two o'clock if you'd like.' She wrote down his contact details. 'His office is in the building next door.'

She pushed back her chair and stood. 'Of course, I won't know for certain about CTE until I look at the brain histology and stains. I'll leave you to decide how much you tell the family for now.' She checked her watch and grabbed her coat. 'I'm sorry, I'd love to take you to lunch, but I have a meeting with the mayor. An Islamic Moroccan tourist was killed in a hit and run, and the international media are suggesting it was racially motivated.'

As she left, Anya considered what she had just learnt. The game Peter Janson loved could have left him with brain damage, particularly to the frontal part of his brain. There were also additional effects of illegal steroids.

Lyle Buffet wanted his players to go in like warriors, tackle hard and push their bodies to their absolute physical limits. She had to wonder cynically whether minor brain damage made players easier to manipulate. The downside was frontal lobe injury could make these men more violent, more prone to depression and drug addiction, aggressive and sexually uninhibited. Like Victor Frankenstein, the game's powerbrokers produced their own monsters and set them loose onto the world. Nigel Everett had told the senate committee that it wasn't the fault of the bad apples, but was the barrel that remained toxic. It was sounding more and more like he was right.

She wondered what role, if any, Gavin Rosseter and the other team doctor had in the steroid cover-up, and how much they played a part in creating unstoppable men who were likely to harm themselves or others.

If this news got out, not only would the reputations of Pete Janson and the Bombers be irrevocably damaged, but the entire league, worth eight billion dollars, would be in serious trouble. People had been murdered for a lot less.

31

After a quick call, Doctor Harrison Leske met Anya in the foyer of the Medical Sciences Building. The Canadian neuropathologist was easy to spot. Over the phone, he described himself as of average height, thin and with Harry Potter glasses, although he wanted to make it clear his glasses preceded the boy wizard's popularity.

In person, Leske looked exactly like the Harry Potter from the movies, only older and without the Hogwarts uniform.

'Please, call me Harrison. I was thrilled to get Gail's call about your visit. Do you mind if we talk on the move? Columbia University has agreed to let my team monitor impact to helmets during practice.'

Anya was grateful for any time he could offer at such short notice. 'I'm not too familiar with CTE.'

He picked up a backpack and a briefcase. 'No one is, which is why this research is so important. If you have the time, you're more than welcome to come along. That way I can show you some of the data so far.'

If Anya were going to mention the possibility of Janson having CTE to the owners of his team, she needed to ensure she had all the facts straight. The more she knew, the better. 'I'd appreciate that.'

They walked to a parking station facing First Avenue as students, professionals and tourists all hurried to wherever they were going. Leske unlocked a blue Prius and placed his bags on the back seat. Anya automatically headed to the left-hand side.

'Unless you'd like to drive . . .' he offered with a grin.

Anya blushed. 'Force of habit.'

She sat in the passenger seat, still feeling awkward. At home, this was where the steering wheel would be. As they headed north, large drops of rain beaded on the windscreen.

'The shower should pass,' he said, stopping at a set of lights. 'Even if it were snowing, practice would still be on.'

The thought of standing in the rain for the afternoon didn't have much appeal, but if games were played in almost any conditions, there wasn't really a choice. Thankfully, as Harrison had predicted, the sun reappeared just as they arrived at 218th Street.

'Welcome to the Bronx,' he said, seeming to enjoy being a tour guide. He turned into Baker Stadium and used a pass to access the parking.

After talking to a security guard, they headed towards the arena and were met on the field by a man who was enormous even by league standards. He had to be six foot seven or eight and was broader than any of the players she had seen so far. As he walked, his right hip rocked upward and the knee refused to bend. The depth of his voice was inversely proportional to his height.

The neuropathologist introduced him as Roman Bronstein.

'Doctor Crichton is visiting from Australia and is interested in learning more about CTE while she's here.'

'Nice to have you with us. The more people who help get the word out, the better.'

Thankfully, Doctor Leske had not mentioned Pete Janson's death as the trigger for her interest.

They headed towards a table full of equipment on the sideline, monitors and computers protected by a makeshift tarpaulin.

'That knee playing up?' Leske sounded genuinely concerned.

'Not one of its better days.' Bronstein gave it a rub. 'That's what I get for all those years of prednisone injections just to get onto the field.'

The former player now had a fused knee, with minimal movement. The more Anya learnt about the medicine associated with professional sports, the more disillusioned she became with the doctors who worked in the field. Sucking trauma-related fluid from a knee joint then replacing it with powerful anti-inflammatory injections should never have been a routine treatment. No wonder this man's knee was permanently damaged. She wondered if the players would consent to the treatments if they fully understood what would happen long-term. Then again, the money they were paid in their relatively short careers could set them up for life.

It wasn't difficult to imagine professional athletes choosing successful careers, adulation, money and sponsorships over conservative medical treatments and shortened careers.

Two younger men adjusted wires attached to helmets. They were probably student research assistants. One flicked the hair from his eyes, which she assumed was his version of hello. The other looked up then returned to checking something on his computer.

Roman let out a rich, hearty chuckle. 'Don't say much, but they do come cheap.'

Harrison explained that Roman had started a foundation following the suicide of one of his former team mates. At post-mortem the friend was found to have had CTE.

'We had never heard of it and no one imagined that all those times we got mild concussion were dangerous. If it was bad, we'd get scanned, go home and be back at practice the next day. A lot of the time we just played on. A couple of times I couldn't remember what happened in the rest of the game. The body was working but the brain wasn't. Looking back, it's scary to have lost chunks of time.'

The sound of cleats on cement caught their attention.

'The Lions are in the house,' Roman announced.

Players straggled onto the field, all in padding. The research assistants handed helmets to two players and assisted with doing them up.

'We're monitoring the amount of force that impacts have on the heads of each man on the field. There are six sensors inside every helmet. Using a system called HITS, we can measure the force and location of every blow to the head.'

From what she had seen, plays didn't last long and teams were pulled off and substituted with changes of possession. She was curious to see how many impacts there were to each head. Presumably not that many.

Under the tarpaulin, Leske studied the monitors. 'With each collision, we can map the spike and determine which positions encounter more head trauma, and who has the most significant force of trauma. So far, linemen seem to incur the most blows.'

Anya considered the amount of protective gear. 'What about the effectiveness of the helmets? A lot of science has gone into making them absorb more force than they would have years ago.'

'True,' Leske said. 'They are custom-sized. You have to put it in context. One player weighing, say, three hundred pounds sprints towards another, say, two-eighty, who is running at full force from the opposite direction.' He arced his fists together to represent the players. 'It's a true head-on collision with massive impact. No helmet can offset that much force.'

Bronstein added, 'Headgear was designed to help, but that just led to a more aggressive approach to butting heads and striking.'

And therefore, more dangerous play, with a false sense of safety. An image of bulls running at each other and clashing horns came into Anya's mind.

The players warmed up, running around the field. Meanwhile, trainers set up equipment for drills and other exercises.

'They'll start with the blocking dummies, then move on to the sleds.' Roman pointed to rows of blue foam cylinders attached to metal bases shaped like a sled. 'That's where they work on using their hips to maximise power and drive through the opponent. After that, they'll do game plays.'

The coach began yelling and trainers picked up foam shields as players ran at them. Anya noticed some had their heads down more than others as they made contact. The time passed quickly as they watched the university students throw themselves at makeshift barriers and push with all of their strength. What surprised Anya was the speed of many of the large young men.

'Keep an eye on number sixteen,' Leske said. 'He just got a 95 g to the front of his head.'

Anya scanned the field. A trainer stood with a hand on one player's shoulder, talking quietly before they both returned to their previous activities.

'Are you measuring g-force?' It was something she associated with space and air travel.

'Imagine a car hitting a wall at twenty-five miles per hour. The driver isn't wearing a seatbelt and his head hits the windscreen. The force of that impact would be around 100 g.'

The concept was horrifying. 'The boy in the number sixteen jersey just had the equivalent of a head injury in a car accident and he got up and kept practising? How can that happen?'

Leske knitted his eyebrows. 'Exactly. If he continues to function, it is considered a sub-concussive insult. What is significant is the cumulative effect of these incidents. If we continue to monitor him, we could easily find that even a glancing blow from an elbow could be enough to give him a serious concussion.'

Anya could not believe how casual the players and coaches were about head injuries. 'Why doesn't he just come off?'

Roman folded his arms. 'It's hard for someone outside the game to understand, but it's what you do. If you can stand up and walk, even with a broken arm, you're okay to play. You owe it to your team mates, coach and the fans. It's like a war zone. Unless you are severely injured and incapable of playing, you have to keep fighting, no matter how many bruises you get.'

And keep taking it 'for the team', she thought. The difference here was that this was practice for a game. And bruises don't normally cause permanent brain damage or spinal cord injuries. She wondered how keen the players' mothers would be if they appreciated the dangers involved.

A crunch of helmets echoed through the stadium, catching all of their attention. Anya winced again.

'That's 84 g to the top of seventy-six's head,' Leske confirmed, 'and a 78 g to player eighteen.'

Roman qualified, 'I'm not saying that's right, but it is the most violent sport in the world. To keep going back on the field, players are conditioned from an early age to push their way through any obstacle, be that an opponent, pain or even a broken bone.

'On the basis of some of our figures, we estimate that some linemen can be hit over a thousand times a season, counting practice and games. Over a career, that could be extremely debilitating. We used to think depression and alcohol and substance abuse after retirement were associated with loss of income, status and celebrity. These men are often untrained for any other job. Football's been all they have known since they were kids. But our data suggests the game itself could be causing the depression, mood disorders and high-risk behaviour even after they stop playing.'

It made so much sense. Robert Keller's drug overdose could have been related to more than an addiction to pain killers after an injury, even if the post-mortem didn't show CTE. If he had lived, he could have been faced with severe dementia from an early age. With thousands of footballers playing in the league each year, the potential public health issue was enormous, and very costly in terms of medical care and loss of function and quality of life. She thought of Keller's widow and young child.

Anya accepted the game was brutal, but she couldn't think of any other legalised sport apart from boxing in which participants risked so much every time they took part. Even Roman Bronstein made the field sound like a war zone, but these were not soldiers fighting for their countries. If this sort of thing happened to animals, the public outcry would be deafening.

This game was played in schools, by children with brains that had not yet fully developed. Anya stood in silence as she digested the information and thought about the possibility of her own son wanting to play a contact sport.

Frontal lobe damage affected a person's ability to make considered decisions, and lowered inhibition. If Peter Janson had endured fewer brain injuries, perhaps he would not have been as violent off the field. And perhaps Kirsten Byrne might not have suffered as a result. Robert Keller might still be alive to be a father to his child.

'You wouldn't do this to crash dummies,' Anya said eventually. 'You already know these collisions are harmful. In any other research, anything near these negative outcomes would mean ending the entire study.'

Leske took off the Harry Potter glasses and cleaned the lenses with a handkerchief. 'Over a century ago, there was a move to ban football in Ivy League schools because it was thought to be a game of barbarism that was corrupting educational institutions. The movement came close to succeeding.'

'And look at it today,' Roman said. 'It's a massive industry that doesn't count the money spent on medical bills for injuries. If we're to stop the carnage to our boys, we'd better have some pretty convincing results to show the league.'

Leske took note of another collision. 'Our findings will be controversial enough once they're published. Doctors who treat the players are employed by the teams, so there is a conflict of interest right from the start.' He looked out at the field.

'There are a lot of people with vested interests in football and its ongoing success. No one in my lifetime is likely to thank us for this research. We have to protect our players in spite of the game, if we are to save the league.'

32

Anya arrived back at the hotel and found Ethan sitting in the lobby with his laptop, munching on a box of Cracker Jacks.

'Glad you're back, because we've got work to do.'

She wondered what he imagined she had spent the entire day doing. All she wanted now was to sit and have a coffee before she did another thing. Ethan clearly had other plans.

He closed his computer, shoved it into a bag and stood up, brushing the crumbs from his trousers. 'We've got a meeting in the bar. And good news, it's happy hour.'

'One drink and I'm likely to be under the table.'

'That I would pay to see.'

Either the investigator had had a restful day, or he had found what he had been looking for. With a bit of luck, she could sit quietly with whomever it was they were meeting. After that, the evening was free so she could take a long bath and grab an early night.

They trekked around to the bar, which was full of business suits. They secured a spot in the corner, with a bench seat, coffee table and square leather chairs. She wondered how many they were expecting. Ethan grabbed four menus from a nearby table.

Just about every snack on it had appeal. 'They don't do knish here, I checked the other night,' she admitted.

He smiled warmly and nudged her shoulder. 'We'll turn you into a real New Yorker before you go.'

Two Bombers players, dressed in jeans and buttoned shirts, sauntered around the corner and nodded in Ethan's direction. One of them was Vince Dorafino.

'Clark, Vince, I believe you know Doctor Crichton.' Quiet music played in the background, which at least made conversation easy to hear.

'Yeah, sorry about jokin' with you the other day,' Dorafino said.

What he'd done was neither clever nor funny, but Anya said nothing, more curious to know what Ethan had uncovered. She was uncomfortable enough sitting opposite two of the men who had in all probability raped Kirsten Byrne, although she tried not to show it. When the men sat down, Ethan moved a little closer to her.

'As you may know, we have been asked by league administrators and your bosses to look into the incident at the Rainier Hotel the other night. Hey, before we start, would you like something to eat? It's on me.'

The men nodded sheepishly and straddled the square leather seats. Ethan handed them each a menu. Garcia looked at it; Dorafino knew what he wanted.

'I'll have nachos and a beer.'

'Sounds good,' Garcia agreed. 'Same for me.'

Ethan signalled a waitress who took their orders. Anya ordered fries with aioli, and a lemon, lime and bitters to drink, while Ethan settled for a beer. It was the first time she had seen him refuse the opportunity to eat.

'Guys, we're sorry about what happened to Pete and know how hard this is, but we want to hear your versions of what happened that night. So far no one's given you a chance to tell your side of the story.'

They looked at each other, neither volunteering to go first. Eventually, Garcia spoke. 'We said it all in the police statements.'

Dorafino sat straighter. 'Our lawyers told us not to talk to anyone about that night. We said everything in our police statements.'

'We know that, but those things are so formal, we wanted to hear your story, in your own words. We just want to hear it for ourselves, then Mr Buffet and the others will know we've done our job.'

Mention of Buffet seemed to make a difference. Garcia rubbed his hands down his jeans. 'There isn't much to tell. There was a party in Janson's room and someone said a woman was doing half the team. The door was open, so we went in and she was humping McKenzie. After he finished, she invited us to have sex with her.'

Anya was intrigued by the sudden change in his language from casual to more formal.

'I asked if she was okay with it, and she agreed. She even appeared to be enjoying the sex and asked for more.'

The waitress arrived with the drinks, much to Garcia's relief. He drank half of his in a couple of mouthfuls.

'I read your statement, and that's exactly what it says.' Ethan took a swig of his beer. 'Did you have to write them yourselves?'

Garcia's eyes darted to his team mate then to Ethan.

'Sorry, that was a dumb-ass question. Of course you wrote them. They're typed and signed by you. What I meant was, did anyone suggest what to say in your statements?'

'No,' they said in unison.

'In your words, Vince, what did you see and hear that night?'

'Like Clark said, we were drinking downstairs then went up to our corridor. Pete was having one of his parties and the door was open. This woman was humping McKenzie then invited us to have sex too. Group sex isn't against the law, you know.'

The hairs on Anya's arms prickled. It was the same line Brett Dengate had used to justify his friends raping Hannah on their wedding night. Only she got the distinct impression these men had rehearsed their lines in advance.

'I know. Guess it happens a fair bit with all these women trying to sleep with you.'

Both men grinned like children. They had begun to relax.

'What happened then, Vince?'

'Like I said, this woman was humping McKenzie and invited —'

'No, I mean, did she talk to you, did she tell you her name, give you her number? You can tell me, was she a looker?'

Dorafino hesitated. 'We didn't talk much, if you know what I mean.'

'You forgot to mention in your statement if the lights in the room were on or off.'

Dorafino looked at Garcia. 'I don't remember. On I think. Yeah, they were on.'

Garcia nodded.

'I was a bit confused by the order of things you described, and Pete Janson isn't here to help us out. When did Alldridge have sex with her? Before or after you?'

'He came in last and he wanted her all to himself. Even stopped some other guys from coming in. Once he stepped up to the plate, we were out of there. He likes his privacy, if you know what I mean.'

Anya tried to hide her discomfort at hearing the men speak so casually about the episode.

'Did the scar across her face put you off?' Ethan tried. 'Beauty is only skin deep, but,' he whistled, 'it's still pretty nasty.'

'Who looks at the mantel while you're stoking the fire, right?' Dorafino's attempt at humour failed.

'So she asked you to have sex with her, but you didn't look at her face?'

'Like we said,' Garcia repeated, 'she invited us to have sex.'

Ethan reached into his bag and pulled out the police statements. 'There's one thing in here I don't understand.' He groped around for something else in his bag. 'Sorry, but I left my reading glasses upstairs.' He handed the papers across. Dorafino took one look and switched his with Garcia.

The men had memorised the same statement. Anya realised what Ethan was doing.

'You've each got your own?'

The men nodded. Garcia ran his hands down his jeans, twice.

'Vince, in your second paragraph, can you just go over the first sentence.' Dorafino read from the page. *'On the night of 12 August I was in my room having drinks when —'*

'Thanks, I wanted to make sure the date was correct. Clark, there was a bit of yours that I wanted to double-check what you meant. A fancy lawyer could make you sound like you were contradicting yourself. It's in the second last sentence.'

The player sat, looking at the paper then back at Ethan. 'It's all pretty clear. I don't know what your problem is.' He put the copy on the table. 'Man, you're supposed to be helping us, not asking us bullshit questions. We're outta here.'

He stood and Dorafino followed.

'Before you go,' Ethan said, 'please take this. If you can remember anything about that night that could help us, please call me straightaway.'

He wrote on the back of his card. 'This is my private address.' He moved to hand the card across to Garcia.

Anya intercepted it. 'Your writing is worse than a doctor's,' she jibed.

The player took the card from her and examined it. 'I can read it fine. And sorry about losing it just then, we're all a bit rocked by what happened to Pete.'

'No sweat, appreciate you coming.'

They left the bar.

Ethan leant back against the headrest.

'Clark Garcia can't read a word.'

'That was clever, writing nonsensical letters and numbers on the card.'

'We now have two identical handwritten statements, one of which is supposed to have been composed, reread and signed by a college graduate who is completely illiterate.'

33

The second time the phone rang, Anya exhaled heavily, drew in a breath and was tempted to hide under the warm water. Instead, she climbed out of the bath and wrapped herself in a towel.

'Quick, turn on the TV,' Ethan said through the phone. 'Go to CBS.'

'I was getting ready for bed, can't this wait?'

'By tomorrow this will be all over the media. You need to see this now.'

Unenthusiastically, she pressed the power button on the remote and located the channel. 'Now what?'

'It's about to come on. An interview with Terri Janson, the grieving widow. Jim Horan did the deal.'

It seemed very quick for a wife to appear in any media so close to the death of her husband. Anya immediately thought of the two little girls and the impact losing their father would have. No doubt the agent was thinking of them too, and the emotional interview Terri could deliver. Tears and pathos were what the gossipmongers and voyeurs wanted to see.

An ad for mouthwash finished and a woman behind a desk announced an exclusive interview revealing the shocking truth behind Pete Janson's death.

'The popular quarterback for the New Jersey Bombers was found in his New York hotel room this week hanging from a rail in the closet. The police are conducting an extensive investigation as mystery shrouds Janson's final moments.

Was it homicide? Was it suicide? Terri Janson believes she knows the truth. Please be aware, this story contains graphic sexual references.'

A montage of Janson playing football, as a child and a teenager, with disabled children and cancer sufferers, and on his wedding day filled the screen, accompanied by orchestral music. A voice-over gave a brief biography concluding with his marriage to Terri and the arrival of their two daughters.

It resembled a political campaign – for a saint.

The scene then faded to the white couch, with the attractive widow heavily made up, her platinum-blonde hair done in a loose bun.

A box of tissues was visible by her side.

'Terri Janson, thank you so much for joining us.' The interviewer leant forward and touched her subject's hand. 'I understand this is an extremely difficult time for you. Let's start with how the children are coping.'

'They're what's keeping me going. Pete called them his little princesses, and they adored him. He would be so proud of how brave they're being.' She dabbed her eye with the padding of a finger with false nails.

'What have you told them?' the interviewer asked.

'That their daddy's an angel in heaven, and he can see us but we can't see him any more.'

For Anya, the image of Janson's body was anything but angelic.

The reporter continued with the puff piece, asking what Terri loved about her husband, how proud his family was of him.

Anya tightened the towel as the air conditioner chilled the air.

'Ethan, is there any point to watching this? I'd really like to catch up on sleep.'

'Hang in there, a contact told me she's about to drop a bombshell. One the owners are not going to be happy about.'

She hoped it was worth getting out of the bath for. This was the first time she had relaxed and unwound since getting on the plane, and the idea of an early night was too tempting to resist.

'Terri . . .' The female reporter spoke with a considered, level tone; it sounded as staged as the whole interview. 'Do you think your husband committed suicide?'

The camera zoomed in on her face. 'There is no way he would ever kill himself. I know that for a fact.'

'How can you be so sure? I mean, he was hanging by the neck, with his own belt.'

Terri clutched a tissue and dabbed her eyes again. The pause couldn't have been planned better for dramatic effect.

'I know, but it isn't what people think.'

'What do you think happened that night in the hotel room?'

'He said how lonely he got whenever he was away from me, and how much he missed sleeping in bed together when he was forced to stay in hotels with the team for weeks on end, as he was for this summit in New York. We were all here but unable to live like a family in that time. That hurt him.'

Ethan was still on the line. 'Wait for it . . .'

Anya's heart rate accelerated. Was the wife going to out her husband for being an unfaithful wife basher who raped women for entertainment?

The camera panned back, first a little, then more. 'You see, to keep our marriage interesting, we used to, well, be very active sexually and would try different things. One of those things was what some people call erotic asphyxia.'

Anya sat on the edge of her bed in disbelief, the phone still near her ear. A grieving widow was talking on national television about a sexual fetish she and her husband shared.

'She's going to tell the world he died of extreme masturbation.' Ethan sounded as shocked as Anya felt.

Without any concept of privacy, Terri Janson proceeded to show a series of silk scarves, handcuffs with blue feathers covering the cuffs and other bondage paraphernalia.

'Convenient how she's chosen to omit details like the other woman who was in the room before he died and the fact that he was wearing a condom.'

'Maybe he was a clean freak and didn't want to make a mess.'

Anya laughed.

'Any luck finding out who the woman in the room was?'

'None so far. Still working on accessing CCTV footage. Police got the files first but I'm hoping to get a lead on them.'

In the background, the widow carefully explained each piece to the interviewer, just managing to stay short of a complete re-enactment, while the reporter manhandled it all for the camera.

'Why would she do this?' Anya muttered. She thought of the impact it would have on the children. 'She *wants* the world to know he didn't kill himself?'

'Insurance policy for one.' Ethan crunched in her ear. She could hear him devouring what sounded like another pack of nuts, despite having finished dinner only an hour ago.

It wouldn't be the first time a family had argued accidental death during a high-risk sexual activity in order to claim the insurance from a policy that exempted suicide. But it could also be for religious reasons. Some faiths still considered it a mortal sin, and refused to allow the victim to be buried in consecrated ground.

'That sort of intimacy demands a phenomenal amount of trust,' the journalist said, the camera capturing her penetrating gaze.

'And I was the only person he trusted to have sex with that way. We talked about how dangerous it was to do alone and he promised me. He promised me,' the camera managed a close-up, 'he would never do that alone.'

'Just like he promised to be faithful in his wedding vows,' the voice down the phone quipped.

'Is she suggesting someone murdered Janson? The toxicology reports aren't even back.'

The journalist leant forward in her seat. 'Terri, what do you think happened that night in the hotel?'

'I talked to him earlier in the night and Pete said he had a headache and was going to lie down for while.'

'Was that unusual?'

'Pete never got headaches.' The widow bit her lip and looked to the side, the camera lapping up every second of her struggle to remain composed. 'He got a hit in the head during the game the other day and kept playing. He wasn't himself after that.' The tears erupted and she asked the interviewer if they could take a break.

Anya had to admit, the interview was compelling viewing. In less than half an hour, Terri Janson had admitted to a sexual perversion, negating any responsibility her husband had for infidelity in that hotel room, and placing liability for his behaviour – and subsequent death – at the hands of the coach, doctors and team owners. It could not have been better scripted.

Ethan answered a call on his mobile phone, before returning to Anya.

'You've got to hand it to her. She just garnered the nation's support to sue the Bombers for wrongful death. We'd better get some sleep. Tomorrow could be a long one.'

Anya put the phone down and thought about what she had just watched. The public airing of such intimate details was mindboggling. When her sister had disappeared, Anya's family was pressured to do media and public appeals. Her mother and father did, but they kept Anya away from the cameras as much as they could. Unfortunately that only increased interest in her, and helped to feed rumours that she had been involved in Miriam's disappearance.

She felt for Janson's daughters who were now thrust into an unforgiving spotlight. Children at their school would now know about their father's sexual proclivities. And kids were capable of being far more cruel than adults. She had learnt that the hard way.

The whole interview seemed contrived and unnatural. She thought of Jim Horan's comments about getting Terri a deal with a cosmetics company. Maybe this was nothing more than self-promotion in a world that needed something ever more shocking to capture its imagination and attention.

Anya dried off, pulled on fresh pyjamas from the suitcase and climbed onto the bed. The tiredness suddenly felt over-whelming as she lay, mind running over the last few days. So much had happened since she had boarded the plane. She checked the clock. Ben was still at school back home, but she could not stay awake the extra few hours to talk with him. It was better to call in the morning, her time.

The phone rang and she wondered what Ethan had forgotten.

'Buffet here,' the gruff voice announced. 'There's an urgent meeting in my suite in ten minutes. Be there.'

34

Anya arrived at the suite and wrapped her damp hair in a clip before ringing the doorbell.

A man she had not met but who had been there the night of Janson's death answered and invited her in. Inside, on a couch sat Kitty Rowe in jeans, an ice-blue sweater and heeled ankle boots. Bentley Masterton sat beside her, biting his thumbnail, his jacket and tie thrown over the back of the couch.

Buffet growled orders down the room phone. Gavin Rosseter sat at the dining table, reading papers and high-lighting information with a neon yellow pen. His right knee jiggled beneath the table. Doctor Reginald Pope stood opposite, absent-mindedly drumming his fingers on the conference-sized table. Gavin glanced up as if irritated by Pope's habit, but did not speak. He offered Anya a seat next to him.

The tension in the room was palpable. It seemed that everyone was waiting for Buffet to speak. Ethan was notably absent.

At the other end of the table, next to Coach Ingram, sat two men with identical short haircuts. They had to be lawyers, judging by their dark suits. In the centre was a platter of sandwiches, and another coffee machine had been placed in the suite. This looked like being a long night.

Anya checked she had her copy of the autopsy report and the results from one of the genetic tests Gail Lee had emailed late that afternoon.

Buffet slammed down the receiver and hobbled over to an empty chair, choosing to stand behind it. The other two owners stayed on the couch, still able to watch the proceedings.

'Did you all see that farce of a puff piece tonight with Janson's widow?'

All heads nodded.

'Well,' one of the lawyers began, 'no one's been served so there's time to publicly discredit her story.'

Masterton stood and poured himself a Scotch from the bar. 'She has dragged all of our good names into the gutter with her disgusting display of sex toys and sordid intimate details. Why, Pete Janson committing suicide is bad enough, but this whole other business is a complete abomination.'

Anya found it bizarre that a religious leader would be more condemning of masturbation than gang-rape. Masterton ran women's shelters for victims of domestic violence but seemed oblivious to his own players' violence against women.

Kitty Rowe cupped a glass of white wine in her hands. 'The piece was totally choreographed. The woman was too well rehearsed; everything from the head tilts to the fluttering eyelash extensions. It had the mark of a savvy manager and a seasoned production team.'

'Well that cuts out Jim Horan,' Buffet said. 'The man's a complete buffoon.'

'I agree this was out of his league,' Kitty Rowe began. 'As a professional courtesy, the producer called before the show aired and said Max O'Connor is now managing Terri Janson.'

Rosseter leant closer to Anya. 'O'Connor's a real ambulance chaser. He grabs the "miracle survivor", the "against the odds" victims, and turns them into national celebrities. He's so quick on the scene of a disaster, you'd think he set the whole thing up.'

264

Anya remembered Terri Janson talking to Horan by phone in his office; it had sounded as though he had a deal for her. This manager must have promised a lot more, and quickly. She thought of the way Horan consoled Terri after seeing Janson's body.

'Horan's trying to sell a book proposal on Janson, the scandalous sex and drugs exposé,' Kitty Rowe added, with sarcasm.

Instead of flushing the drugs down the toilet in the hotel room, Horan had probably kept them for his own commercial ends.

Masterton paced, drink in hand. 'We're supposed to represent family values. The Janson woman and Horan will ruin that. How do we stop them perverting everything we stand for? We have a lot of people depending on this team for their jobs. Our office employees, advertisers, kids at risk who hand out the programmes. Without this club, all of those people will be without work. God-fearing Christians who give us their all.'

Buffet banged his fist on the table. 'Settle down, Bentley. We all know you're responsible for many of our employees and volunteers, but we need to focus.'

He glanced around the room. 'First we need to find out if Janson's wife has a case for wrongful death. Pope? Where do we stand medico-legally?'

The older doctor swept some thinning hair away from his ear. 'Doctor Rosseter conducted a neurological exam and found he was oriented, alert and fully functioning. He denied having a headache and was keen to play on. Rosseter has documented what took place and the results of the neuro questionnaire as recommended by the league.'

Rosseter nodded.

'May I ask,' Anya tried to be as diplomatic as possible, 'did Janson lose consciousness, even for a few seconds, when he was hit?' She could suddenly feel the heat of Buffet's glare. 'It is the first question a defence lawyer will ask.' Particularly, she thought, given that no one on the sideline saw him move until Gavin was at his side.

Rosseter answered, eyes still fixed to his paperwork. 'I don't believe so. The players who were on the field claim he remained conscious the whole time.'

'Good,' one of the lawyers commented, taking notes.

'The medical examiner is going to want to know Janson's movements between the time he was hit and his death,' she added. The air in the room felt thicker and even less congenial.

Coach Ingram appeared drawn and tired. 'That's easy. These boys are timetabled. Janson showered with the team after the game on Sunday, then they all had dinner at the hotel. He was his usual smart-ass self and ate everything like normal. He met his curfew at 11 pm. At seven the following morning he had breakfast with the other players and he ate fried eggs, bacon, sausages, hash browns, toast and a wheatgerm smoothie. I know because I sat with him to talk plays. At 9 am he had a photo shoot with the team and then attended the children's hospital to meet kids with cancer.'

He glanced at Buffet and the lawyers.

'I'm told the pictures are up on the team website. At noon he had lunch with six of the team in a disadvantaged school, where he then played with some of the kids before attending practice that afternoon. He performed well and that night attended a party with sports journalists at Chelsea Piers.'

Every minute of Janson's day was documented. It almost sounded like a prison routine.

It was even more apparent to Anya how little time these men spent with friends outside the team, and how insulated they were. As Terri Janson implied, they did spend more time with each other than with their families. Between coaches, managers, owners, trainers and doctors, these men were like children herded everywhere and not allowed independent time.

They were to all intents and purposes isolated from the real world, which explained a lot of the adolescent and anti-social behaviour. It also gave them a sense of invincibility. She wondered how many of the players actually paid a bill, knew how to operate a washing machine or could even balance a chequebook.

'Did he show any signs of headache, or have trouble with co-ordination, speech, memory? Anything that could have suggested the head injury was affecting him?'

Ingram was adamant, and a little too defensive. 'I would have known if one of my players, let alone our top quarterback, was less than a hundred percent.' His tired eyes glared at Anya. 'You don't know these men. I live with them 24/7 and know them better than my own sons. I would have known if anything was wrong.'

Gavin Rosseter added, 'I do the rounds at night. These guys always ask for painkillers, and sometimes sedatives to help them sleep. It's usually when they mention every minor ache and twinge. Janson didn't want anything. Said he had no trouble sleeping. He would have been the first to complain if he didn't feel right. He was a bit of a hypochondriac like that, paranoid that something minor could affect his career.'

And yet, Anya thought, he didn't think that raping women, beating his wife or casual sex with fans would damage his career, despite having a morals clause built into his contract.

'How many concussions did he actually suffer? There's a cumulative effect the lawyers will home straight in on.'

Pope rolled his eyes. 'This is football. Players take hits all the time. If we documented every thump and bruise, there'd be no time to treat the serious injuries.'

Anya resisted the temptation to explain the seriousness of concussion to the experienced physician, demeaning him in front of the others, but she took note of his opinion.

'So there's no complete medical record that's kept for the span of a player's career?'

Rosseter seemed to understand her point. 'Medical reports are kept confidential and, in practice, incidents aren't always recorded, or deemed significant enough by the team doctor. A bad record can affect how players are traded or bought in the draft.'

Anya could not believe what she was hearing. Buffet demanded unconditional loyalty from his players, yet treated them like possessions, to be traded or discarded at the first sign of wear and tear.

'These men aren't used cars, to be sold on once they're no longer functioning at their best.' Yet again she felt the barbarism of the game, but this time it had nothing to do with the behaviour of players. She looked around the table at those responsible.

'We can't be blamed for that if everyone else does the same thing,' Buffet announced. 'Let's move on.'

'I'm sorry, but you can't. The lawyers will push that point because of the severe damage to Janson's brain.' She told the room what she knew about CTE and the preliminary results she had discussed with Doctor Gail Lee. She went on to explain the symptoms: depression, aggression, substance abuse, forgetfulness and eventual dementia, and mentioned the study that Roman Bronstein and Harrison Leske were conducting at Columbia University.

Pope came to life. 'Those symptoms just described half the country's population.'

He glanced around, as if expecting a laugh. No one was amused. 'And as for CTE, some cases have been shown in boxers, but there is no evidence that footballers are prone to it. For all we know, it could be something that happens in athletes who already have a mental illness, or as a consequence of substance abuse combined with even mild trauma.'

Anya tried not to sound patronising. 'There is actually a genetic link that predisposes certain people to more severe damage from head injuries. My guess is that Terri Janson will argue her husband should have been tested. It's a bit like checking a boy doesn't have haemophilia before he plays a contact sport.'

The lawyers feverishly took notes.

'Pete Janson's blood was tested at the autopsy. They're waiting for the result of the ApoE4 allele,' Anya added.

There was a prolonged silence.

Anya continued. 'The thing is, if this sport was car racing and even one or two deaths had occurred, there'd be a revision of safety procedures and standards that would have to be accepted by all competitors.'

Masterton approached the table. 'Well this is the great game of football. Do we have to listen to this self-righteous nonsense from someone under our employ? Heck, she isn't even one of us. The way she's talking, you'd think she put Terri Janson up to this whole interview business.' He stood behind Anya. 'Did you?'

Gavin Rosseter placed his hand on Anya's arm, in support, rather than to silence her, she assumed.

Buffet thumped the table. 'Bentley, shut the hell up! We need to know what we're dealing with. And the press are going to eat this stuff up.'

Kitty Rowe stood. 'Not necessarily. To routinely test players would infringe their civil liberties. I can haul out no end of experts who would say we did Janson a favour by not testing him for that gene. Without us he wouldn't have had a successful football career or the means to support his family so well. That test would have taken all his fame and success away. We racked our conscience to come to that decision, but we put our players' families first.'

'I like the way you think.' Masterton seemed to have forgotten his angst and moral indignation.

'If Terri Janson wants a trial by media, we'll give her one.' She refilled her wine glass.

One of the lawyers spoke. 'We're already looking into her private life and suspect she was having affairs.'

Buffet looked weary. 'You do what you have to.' He patted the lawyer nearest him. 'While you're all here, it's come to my attention that at least one of the players in the alleged incident at the Rainier Hotel lied in his police statement. I'm therefore invoking the morals clause in his contract. He will be traded, or fired immediately. Little shit had the hide to push for a bigger salary to keep quiet on Janson's affairs and off-field antics.'

Rosseter and Ingram looked up.

'I will not be blackmailed. As of today, Clark Garcia is finished.'

The meeting was at an end for Anya. As she and Rosseter left, she asked about the neurological questionnaire the doctors used to assess players with head injuries.

'The Neurotrauma Functional Assessment.'

Anya was unfamiliar with it. 'Do the local emergency departments use it?'

'It's issued by the league, specially designed by one of its own board members.'

The neuro questionnaire was, therefore, not an objective medical assessment.

Gavin Rosseter may have inadvertently contributed to Janson's death. The team was in significant legal trouble.

35

Ethan was short of breath when he arrived at Anya's table. He didn't wait to sit down. 'You know Roman Bronstein?'

Anya swallowed a mouthful of eggs and looked up from her computer.

'He's funding the head injury study. Why?'

He slid into the seat opposite and lowered his voice. 'Word is, his home just got raided.'

She put her fork down on the plate. 'What for?'

'Illegal performance-enhancing drugs. He's been charged with supplying.'

It didn't make sense for him to be risking players' health by dealing in steroids while also trying to get a better deal for them by funding concussion research.

'What evidence do the police have?'

'That's the thing.' Ethan helped himself to a piece of toast on a spare plate. 'They acted on an anonymous tip-off they received late last night.'

Anya took a sip of warm coffee. 'He seemed really passionate about developing protocols to save lives and prevent future disabilities. Why would he supply players with dangerous drugs on the side?'

Ethan smeared honey on the toast. 'Maybe that's how he gets the money. Kind of like the Robin Hood of footballers' health.'

Anya watched him devour the toast and follow it with a pastry. 'Don't be shy, help yourself.' She had never met a man who ate so much, so often and managed to stay so trim. The man was a metabolic machine.

The waitress brought the coffee pot over and offered to fill Ethan's cup before cheekily requesting his room number. Anya could have sworn the waitress was flirting. The investigator definitely had a certain charm.

'You said there was an anonymous call to police, after Columbia's training session last night?'

She wondered about the timing. The research was just getting definitive results and could change the way players were assessed and whether or not they were permitted back on the field. That would be bad news for all sorts of people.

'That's what my source says. Did any of the players approach him?'

'He was there when we arrived but the players hadn't taken to the field.' She and Leske stayed until practice had finished, but Bronstein excused himself about half an hour earlier. 'He mentioned picking up his daughter from dance class. He didn't have any contact with the players. The only ones who did were two research assistants and they're employed by neuropathology.'

'I might just check out the daughter's dance class. If he can't run his business . . .'

'He can't fund the research and the study will fail.' She pushed her plate away and told him what had occurred at last night's meeting and how she had explained about the research they were doing on CTE. 'Incidentally, where were you while Masterton was having his conniptions?'

'I was following up a lead on the woman who was in the hotel room before Janson "checked out". Seems Dorafino didn't see her or know her name.'

'Any other leads?'

'Nothing concrete.' Another piece of toast disappeared from the plate.

'I need to talk to Harrison Leske.'

'Just let me grab some breakfast and I'll come with you.'

Anya noticed a couple opposite them kissing passionately across the table. The shiny gold bands on each of their fingers suggested newlyweds. With all the infidelity she'd heard about over the last few days, she hoped they were actually married to each other.

Ethan headed back to the buffet. Anya continued to read over her notes from the preceding night. Testing for the ApoE4 allele would be outlawed if Buffet and Rowe had their way. She thought he and Pope were being short-sighted if they could not see how much of an issue this would become, if not now, then in the very near future.

Ethan returned with a yoghurt, banana, apple and bowl of cereal. 'I've just come from a meeting with Buffet.' He spoke quietly. 'More damage control about Janson. But something doesn't sit right. The woman hasn't come forward, so she's got something to hide. Look at all the mistresses who come forward for their fifteen minutes of fame and financial gain. Either this woman is loaded or she needs the affair, if it was one, to stay secret.'

Although, from the way women threw themselves at the players, it could have literally been anyone off the street. Maybe he was alive when she left and she hadn't registered his death – unlikely given the media frenzy, but not impossible.

She checked her phone for messages and placed it on the table where she could see it. That way there was no risk of losing it again.

Something else had been bothering her. 'Don't you think it's a little coincidental that within a few days Robert Keller and Pete Janson are dead? They both just signed significant sponsorship deals, albeit with different companies.'

'Maybe someone wants to ruin the league's reputation. They weren't in the same team, so it can't be a Bombers vendetta. I agree it's odd, but these guys are risk-takers. They're away from home and do stupid things.'

The way members of the team acted, they were capable of destroying themselves. No need for anyone outside to do it for them.

'Hate to say it,' he chomped on the apple, 'but we need to find out where Kirsten Byrne was when Janson died.'

'She's in police protection. Linda Gatby organised it the day we saw her, after she started getting death threats.'

'Sorry, I didn't know. Guess that cuts her from the equation. The lawyer Jim Horan told us she'd hired had nothing to do with Janson and his friends. She's suing Cheree Jordan for wrongful dismissal.'

So much for that vile journalist suggesting Kirsten was merely an opportunistic whore. Anya remembered reading the papers that day, after Keller's death. Pete Janson was quoted in an interview.

'Janson and Keller were friends in high school. Didn't Terri tell us that the accusations of abuse started back in high school, when he began to star?'

'I can check if they were involved in anything illegal from that far back. Have to admit, I stopped looking after we found Darla.'

Anya realised it sounded ridiculous. The deaths probably were unrelated. High-risk behaviours performed often enough led to accidental deaths.

She watched Ethan combine the yoghurt and muesli, stirring the sloppy concoction.

'What do you think the chances are of successfully suing Buffet for wrongful death?' He managed through a mouthful.

'Terri's lawyers will probably argue that a reasonable person in the football business would have known about the specific risk of head injuries to people who tested positive for Apoloprotein E4. They could have a point, that is if Janson does prove positive.'

Ethan put down his spoon and pushed the bowl to the side.

'Then you'll get players claiming discrimination if they're prevented from playing by the team. We have to accept there are inherent risks in everything. That's what life is. If we only allow people who have the good genes to play, where does it all end?'

Ethan's top lip curled, as if disgusted by the concept. 'Next thing, we'll be testing infants for all the potential genes. If they have those . . .' he clicked his fingers twice, '. . . fibres. What are their names? The ones that show you'll be either a sprinter or long-distance runner?'

'Fast and slow twitch muscle fibres.'

He clicked his fingers again. 'They're the ones. Where will it all lead? We're talking eugenics, and it's just the beginning.'

Anya noticed Ethan's hands were shaking as he reached for his coffee cup.

'Let's back up,' she said quietly. 'We're not talking about people who want to create the perfect society, or a superior race. No one's suggesting embryonic testing to help parents select which ones they'll keep, based on whether or not they have the build for an athlete, a supermodel, a genius IQ or a brain that is more resistant to head injuries.'

A family of six passed by the table. The last two children straggled, looking at the food on every table they passed.

A waitress refilled their water glasses and Anya hesitated before explaining, 'What could be debated is whether the test should be offered to kids in school who suffer concussion in sport. That way the parents would be more able to make an informed decision about whether they want that child to continue playing a contact sport. If a child tests positive for a genetic component that can make the brain damage from head injuries much more severe, don't you think the parents deserve to know? Or would you prefer to condemn that child to a far greater risk of early dementia and chronic traumatic encephalopathy?'

Ethan took a few deep breaths. 'You're right. I'm sorry I got so heated.' He smiled. 'I can just see Buffet's face when he found out about a potential lawsuit.'

Anya smiled. 'I'd say it's lucky he didn't burst a blood vessel.'

Ethan sat back.

'I've got more news on McKenzie. The night after raping Darla at the strip club, he visited the mailman at his hotel, just like he did after Kirsten. Guessing he got rid of his clothes that time.'

If he were posting items with potentially incriminating evidence on them, they had to be at his home. If the women consented to sex, he wouldn't have had to hide anything. There was no doubt in Anya's mind: Liam McKenzie was a repeat rapist.

'So Linda Gatby needs to organise a search warrant for his place.'

'That's the trick. McKenzie doesn't mail them to his own home. He sends them to his dear old mother.'

Anya wondered what his mother would make of blood-stained sheets, and whether or not she even opened the packages, or kept them until his next visit.

'So, fancy a road trip to New Jersey?'

Anya drained the last drop of coffee from her cup. 'Are you sure we're not going to spook her by dropping in before the police can search the place?'

'If she knows we're working for Lyle Buffet, she'll think we're trying to exonerate Liam. Besides, you learn more when you surprise people.'

36

Something else had been bothering Anya. 'Ethan, can I ask you something?'

A black limousine waited outside the hotel. A number of men in black suits congregated and joked with porters. The smell of cooking meat wafted from a kebab seller on the corner. When he saw the investigator, the limousine driver donned his cap and stamped out his cigarette.

At the curb, taxis lined up and tourists clambered in almost as quickly as others climbed out. As Anya stood watching, a fire engine turned the corner, its siren blasting. A flash of flame in the passenger window caught her eye. One of the firefighters was lighting a cigar as the unit raced to its next emergency. She wondered if the irony was lost on him.

'No rush, buddy,' Ethan reassured the driver and turned to Anya. 'Sure. If I can I'll answer it.'

'What if we're being used to make it look like the league and team owners are doing the right thing?' Anya was still troubled by the timing of Bronstein's arrest.

'It's a reasonable question. The only way to answer is to say that I trust Lyle Buffet. The other two, I don't know for certain. They have their own reasons for being involved in the game. Masterton uses the team to employ people from his church. The kids who hand out programmes at games are juvenile offenders who are being rehabilitated in a programme initiated by Masterton. The club allocates funds each year to pay them. Church members take care of cleaning and maintaining the grounds, and the club seems happy to have them doing the work. Kitty Rowe spends her life trying to get her father's attention, but Lyle has always been honest and upfront with me. He lives for the game. I'd like to give him the benefit of the doubt.'

'Let's hope they don't try to bury any information we find that could help Kirsten's case.'

'I won't let that happen,' Ethan assured her.

Inside the limousine, Anya phoned Harrison Leske but the call went to voicemail. She left a message asking him to call her.

Yawning, she stretched her legs in the back seat; she sank back into the leather seats, exhausted.

'You should rest on the way. It could be a while, especially if there's congestion.'

Normally, Anya would have argued that she was fine, but as the car turned into the Lincoln Tunnel to cross the Hudson River, traffic slowed and she gave in to the tiredness and closed her eyes. Her sleep pattern was still in a different time zone. Images of her smiling son appeared in her mind as she faded into the liminal state between sleep and wakefulness.

In the background she could faintly hear Ethan tapping on the keys of his laptop. The sun warming her window nudged her further into somnolence.

When she woke, they were driving through tree-lined streets. She sat up and licked her dry lips. 'Where are we?'

'New Jersey. We're not far from Plainfield.'

She checked her watch; she had been asleep for just over an hour.

Ethan reached into his bag and pulled out a fresh bottle of water. 'The air con tends to dry you out.'

She unscrewed the lid with a nod of thanks and looked at the two-storey houses set back from the road, with green grass in abundance. 'Please don't tell me I snored.'

He smiled and the skin around his eyes crinkled. 'No, but you do talk in your sleep.'

Anya felt her heart gallop and blood rush to her cheeks.

Ethan smiled even more warmly. 'You said my name.'

Anya face flushed. 'Oh. I didn't. Did I?' What had she said? She tried to read his face.

'No, but you must have thought about me, otherwise you wouldn't have blushed like that.'

She crossed her arms and looked out the window, embarrassed that he had caught her out.

Knowing he had done a background check on her before the league employed her, she felt vulnerable knowing Ethan knew personal details about her when she knew very little about him.

'Where do you actually live?' she asked. He stayed at the hotel but supposedly came from New York.

'Here and there. I crash at a friend's place some of the time. She's a wildlife photographer and is usually away with her boyfriend on some exotic safari.'

He leant forward and pressed the button to close the glass partition between driver and passengers. She assumed it rendered their conversation private.

'Can I ask you something?'

Suddenly Anya felt even more self-conscious.

'How can you stand dealing with other people's loss and pain when you went through your own? I mean, with your sister's disappearance.'

It was no surprise he knew about Miriam. It still made the news every few years, particularly when Anya was involved in a prominent case.

'That can't have been easy. Nor can it be easy living without knowing what happened to her.'

Anya sipped the water and looked out the window. 'It's

hardest on my parents. They divorced. Mum still sets a place at the table every night for Miriam. It's been more than thirty years . . .' There was little else to say. Miriam was taken by someone at a football game and hadn't been seen since.

He rubbed his chin. 'I'm sorry. No one should have to go through that. I'm trying to work out why you do what you do.'

'It's not complicated. Families deserve closure. They deserve to know what happened to someone they loved. If I can help in any way, it makes my job worthwhile. And it beats sitting around all day brooding.'

'I could try and look into it, off the record.'

Anya appreciated the offer, but they had employed private investigators before and discovered nothing.

She deflected the conversation. 'My turn. I have a personal question for you.'

'Is this truth or dare?' He snapped the laptop shut.

She would not be put off. 'Why did you become so riled when I mentioned the gene testing for players?'

It was his turn to look out the window. 'It's a civil rights issue I happen to feel strongly about. I'm also in favour of free speech and the constitutional right to remain silent.'

Anya stared at him. 'Do I need to do a background search on you?'

He looked at her, then down at his lap. 'I don't want anyone else to know, and frankly I can't believe I'm even telling you, but my father died from Huntington's disease.'

She took a silent breath. It was a devastating condition caused by a defective gene, which led to progressive loss of brain function. There was little anyone could do to prevent the loss of muscle co-ordination that eventually led to trouble swallowing and speaking. Even more difficult was the emotional changes and eventual dementia a person suffered. With the dominant gene, Ethan had a fifty percent chance of developing the disease. There was no cure.

'I'm sorry.' She locked gazes with him. 'Have you been tested?'

'It's a no-win situation. You either have the test and know you're dying, or hope there's a fifty percent chance you won't get it.'

There was another option. 'What if you are free of the gene? You wouldn't have to live your life under that massive cloud of uncertainty.'

The car slowed and turned into Forest Avenue.

'No one knows what's around the corner. At least this way I have hope, just like your mother. I don't think I could live without that.'

He lowered the glass partition. 'Is this the address I gave you?'

'Yes, Mr Rye, this is the McKenzies' house. I just called as you asked, and they are home.'

The pair were greeted at the door by a middle-aged woman, with larger than average cherry lips and thick, well-cut hair. She wore black pants and a matching long-sleeved top with wide white cuffs on the end of bell-bottom sleeves. The outfit disguised the woman's apple shape. A long silver chain around her neck completed the outfit.

'You have a beautiful home,' Anya commented, entering the lower storey and admiring the polished wooden floors. 'Have you lived here long?'

'Four years this November. Our son bought it for us, after he won his first college trophy.'

By the pride in her voice, anyone would have thought her son had single-handedly won every game for the team.

'He's a wonderful son, and such a good boy. A mother couldn't ask for better,' she added.

'The family couldn't be any prouder.' The father entered the room and shook their hands. His hand was large, coarse and callused. He was, or had been, accustomed to physical work.

From the foyer to the living area, framed photos of Liam adorned every available surface. In one photo he looked younger, and was with two other children, a boy and a girl. Ethan homed in on that one.

'How many children do you have?'

The father's chest deflated. 'Three, only we lost our eldest son a couple of years ago. Our daughter still lives in Minnesota, with my sister. We're taking care of her son while she finishes high school.'

So, Anya thought, the daughter either dropped out, or had the baby while still at school. But that didn't explain the paucity of photos. Sometimes grief leads people to rid their homes of constant reminders of their lost one, but she found it difficult to believe that a mother would remove almost all images of her late child and her living daughter. Liam seemed to be a favourite, even at home.

'When did he first show an aptitude for football?' Ethan enquired.

The father beamed. 'From the age of three that boy could kick a ball, catch, and run fast. He'd win all his races at school, then in middle school he tried out for football. Pretty soon he was playing up a couple of years. And that was before he really grew. The coach had him marked as special right from the start. Why, he was the first one in our family to go past high school. Then he got seen by some scouts and before we knew it he was being offered college scholarships. And not just any, Ivy League scholarships. I come from a long line of men who work hard – mechanics, labourers, we're good with our hands. Liam turned that skill into a dream job.'

'Gamma!' A toddler ran into the room and threw himself around his grandmother's leg. Mrs McKenzie patted the top of his head and told him to go back on the verandah and draw something on the blackboard. By the looks of his dirt-stained hands and knees, that wasn't what he'd been doing. Judging by the smell, he'd soiled his nappy as well. He was at the stage where he wanted to be independent but had yet to be toilet-trained. Anya wouldn't have let her son play outside alone at such a young age.

'Ooeee, Pearl, what've you been feeding that boy? Why, it makes a man's eyes water.'

Mrs McKenzie pursed her lips. 'That'd be the meatloaf. The one you had two plates of. Jonah, we're going to change that diaper right this minute.' She took the child's hand and turned to her husband. 'Vernon, would you like to offer our visitors a drink? There's homemade lemonade on a tray in the kitchen.'

The trio left Ethan and Anya alone for a moment. 'The eldest son was killed when a drug deal went wrong,' Ethan said quietly. 'He'd been in trouble with the police for years, even served a couple of years for assaults and burglary. I gather the parents put all their energies into Liam and the eldest son missed out.'

Mr McKenzie returned with a tray of drinks and placed them on the coffee table. Anya collected her glass and asked if she could help the grandmother. To be honest, she enjoyed being around children and thought giving Ethan a chance to talk to the father alone might be productive.

Jonah waddled with a giant grin into the corridor.

'Can I see where you play outside?'

Two big brown eyes looked up and he waved his hand for her to follow. 'They're a handful,' Anya said as Mrs McKenzie appeared from the room.

'I'm getting too old for all this.' The grandmother looked weary.

'If you like, I'll take him outside and see if I can wear him out. Then maybe he'll have a sleep and give you a break.'

Outside, Jonah ran for a ball and kicked it on the second attempt. Anya walked over and kicked it back, much to the little boy's delight. Mrs McKenzie followed.

'You must really miss Liam when he's away.'

'He's a good boy, he looks so much smaller on the television. He sends me things every week, and I send back homemade cookies. They're his favourites, since before he could even walk. He says they make him think of home.'

'Does he send you presents every week?'

Anya had been wondering how to broach the subject of the parcels, but the mother had brought it up, as if she were proud of her son's attention to her.

'Oh, not what some would call presents, but I enjoy getting them. Sometimes he sends his washing. I know this sounds old-fashioned, but I love doing it for him, and he says it's like smelling home when he gets his things back. He gets terrible nosebleeds since when he was a kid, so sometimes his sheets are dirty. I wash them in ice cold water and they're as good as new.'

The sheets were incriminating but only circumstantial evidence. Once washed, it would be impossible to prove they were the same ones used that night in the hotel.

Jonah chased the ball down, stopped and ran at it again, this time falling over as he extended his leg. Without a hint of tears, he jumped up, stared the ball down and made contact with his foot again. This time the ball rolled straight to Anya.

'Good kick!' she praised, and turned around to hear his grandmother applauding.

'Just like your Uncle Liam,' Grandma smiled. 'You keep practising and you'll be just like him.' She picked up the hose and began watering the rose bushes. The hose leaked from the nozzle, leaving puddles down on the ground where she stood. She didn't seem to notice.

Anya kicked the ball back to Jonah and moved closer to the roses.

'The team owners have asked us to look into the accusations of sexual assault made against your son and a number of his team mates.'

The older woman scratched her shoulder and sighed. 'That woman's just another of those gold-diggers after my boy. They chase him across the country and make no bones about what they're after. The way they throw themselves at him! Why, it's shameless. He's red-blooded and you can't expect him to resist all temptation. The good Lord knows how hard he's worked to get where he is and he deserves to have some fun. But these women don't want fun. They're out to bring him down. Get whatever they can out of him, however they can. Did you know that woman from Connecticut tried to blackmail Liam to withdraw assault charges? Now you tell me, what sort of woman cries about being attacked then demands money?'

Jonah ran around, kicking the ball into the fence before reclaiming it and taking aim at his new-found partner. Anya trapped the ball and pushed it back in his direction.

She recalled the agent mentioning the case and that it was decided Liam had, in fact, saved the woman's life.

'Did you know her personally?'

'We met her once, I think. Liam liked her to start with, he was always on the phone or texting her. The woman was clearly obsessed with him. And when he broke things off, she went crazy with a knife. If Liam hadn't stepped in to stop her, who knows what she would have done to herself?'

Mrs McKenzie made a good point. Assault victims did not normally demand money in return for dropping charges. If criminal charges failed, then a woman might seek compensation through the civil court – not necessarily for the money, but for acknowledgement that the man, or men, had hurt her. From what she knew, this assault case was unusual from the beginning. Perhaps McKenzie was a target for disturbed women. Film and television actors sometimes had to take out restraining orders against overzealous fans.

Jonah ran, chasing the ball into the bush near the fence where his grandmother had just been. After squatting down, he manoeuvred the ball out with his hand and pushed it away.

'No! Jonah!' Mrs McKenzie yelled.

The little boy slipped in the muddy puddle left by the hose. His hands and trousers were mud-streaked.

She switched off the tap, stomped over to her grandson and, after grabbing his hand, smacked him on the backside a good number of times. 'You've dirtied your good clean clothes again! What have I told you about playing near mud?' She slapped him once more.

The little boy started to shriek; despite the padding of a nappy, the whacks probably hurt. Anya wanted the grandmother to stop. 'I'll take him in and clean him up if you like.'

Mrs McKenzie stopped smacking and composed herself, wiping the curls from her forehead with the back of one hand. 'He's always getting into trouble, just like his mother.' She grabbed the crying toddler by the hand and marched him towards the back door, where she began to strip him of shoes, socks, trousers and shirt.

'If you want to help,' she said to Anya, 'you can clear my son of the false charges against him and stop that woman blackmailing him for money. You know she has already got herself a lawyer.'

As she slid open the door and pushed the now silent boy inside, Anya heard her say, 'I'm getting too old for all this.'

37

Walking out to the limousine, Anya described what had happened in the backyard.

'I was hit as a kid, can't say I never deserved it either,' countered Ethan.

'That's not the point.' Anya had been disturbed by the scene she had just witnessed. It was easy to understand the frustration of having a child get mud all over his clothes, but that was what kids did. They explored and played and sometimes got dirty in the process. It was true that the previous generation had a different style of parenting, but even so, Mrs McKenzie's behaviour bothered her.

'She lost control. I thought she was going to hose him down with cold water to teach him a lesson. And that was with me, someone who is investigating her son's case, standing there watching. You'd think she would have been on her best behaviour. What would have happened if I hadn't been there?'

The driver opened the door and Ethan slid in beside her.

'You're assuming she controlled herself in front of you. If that's the case, she wouldn't have hit him in the first place, instead she would have kept up the nice grandma facade while you were present. If that's the worst she ever does, it hardly constitutes child abuse. The father let slip something about the daughter trying to get clean. That boy was probably born a crack addict. If you ask me, the kid's lucky to have his grandparents caring for him. He looked well fed, the place was clean, and did you see the pile of books in the basket behind the sofa?'

Anya had managed to miss that. Ethan had a point. Children that age didn't read books themselves. It usually took an adult to pique their interest. She had to admit the boy seemed friendly and went enthusiastically to his grandmother in the living room. As soon as they noticed the smell in his nappy, he was cleaned and changed. A far cry from children left in their own excrement while parents had their next hit. Jonah did look well fed, and the toys in the backyard were in good condition. Someone could have caught Anya on a bad day when she was first a mother. It could not have been easy to find yourself responsible for your toddler grandchild, with all the time and energy demands that responsibility entailed.

If Liam McKenzie hadn't used drugs or been involved in gangs, it made some sense that the parents doted on him. She wondered what came first, favouring the sport-star child to the detriment of the others, or giving him special attention after the others had proven themselves to be disappointments. Either way, the family had its fair share of dysfunction.

'So what about the mother's claim that our stabbing victim tried to extort more than $25,000?'

'Like I say, there are many sides to the story. Our football star, the alleged victim, and the lawyers for both sides. Somewhere in there the truth has to be hiding. It's just up to us to find out where it is.'

When they returned to New York, Anya chose to take the train to Connecticut, given it was apparently quicker than going by road. Ethan had a meeting with Lyle Buffet and representatives from the league's legal advisers. She appreciated the opportunity to have some quiet time to herself and read the file Ethan had been faxed by one of his many court contacts. From the station, she took a taxi.

If, like so many other women, Alison Walker refused to speak, the trip would be wasted. But Anya wanted to know what had really happened that night Liam was judged to have saved her life. The taxi rolled past rows of identical white weatherboard houses, each made slightly individual by a garden and the colour of the car in the drive.

Children's bikes littered the lawns, as if they'd been dropped in the race to get inside. Ben had just learnt to ride a two-wheeler. She could picture him riding up and down these quiet streets. The taxi pulled up short of the corner. Anya paid the driver and asked him to wait long enough to see if anyone was home. He touched the peak of his Yankees cap. 'Sure thing, ma'am.'

A blue Pontiac swung into the empty drive and out stepped a large woman dressed in a collared shirt and jeans, which were pulled a little too tight at the waist.

'Excuse me,' Anya called as she walked up the driveway. 'Could you please tell me if Alison Walker lives here?'

'Depends on who's asking.' The woman opened the boot, which contained bags of groceries.

Anya stepped forward and offered her card. The woman glanced at it. 'I could print them on any computer.'

Taken aback, Anya explained, 'I'm a forensic physician from Australia. The only other ID I have with me is my passport.'

'So you cut up dead people.' The woman turned to the groceries. 'What's that got to do with Alison?'

'I specialise now in seeing survivors of sexual assault and domestic violence. I came a long way and was hoping to talk to Alison. If it isn't convenient, I can come back.'

The woman placed a hand on one very rounded hip and scanned Anya from head to toe. 'Who sent you?'

'I'm investigating cases involving Liam McKenzie.'

The woman grabbed two bags and slammed the boot. 'Well, she don't give interviews, and if you're a friend of his, you're trespassing. Get off my property right now or I'll call the police.' She headed for the door, jeans swishing at the thighs with each step.

'I'm not his friend. I'm looking at women McKenzie may have assaulted over the last few years.'

The woman slowed, then stopped at the doorstep and half turned.

'No one else believed us, why should you?'

Anya stepped closer. 'On the way here I read the original police report and saw the photos. I don't believe Alison hurt herself that night.'

The woman turned around fully. 'Mother Teresa you ain't. What's in it for you?'

'It's my job, and the reason I'm here is because I don't have loyalty to any of the teams or players. I guess that makes me unbiased. And I don't believe in paying off witnesses before they testify.'

The woman stopped and watched a cable van drive past.

'Are you trying to tell me you would turn down thousands of dollars if it was thrown at you? If you were poor and needed the money?'

'If I accepted a bribe, I'd risk losing my registration.'

The woman scoffed and unlocked the screen door.

Anya tried once more. 'I need to work to support my family.'

'Girl, you don't just come from another country, you're from another planet! Ain't too many people who'd turn down thousands of dollars.'

Anya half smiled and shrugged.

The woman's frown softened. 'I've been nagging my sister to talk to someone apart from me. Someone professional.'

She looked at her visitor for a few more seconds. 'I'm Bethany.'

Anya waved to the taxi driver, who eased away from the curb. She reached out and took one of the grocery bags. As Bethany fiddled with two sets of locks, Anya noticed a camera mounted on one corner of the roof. A quick glance around revealed it was the only house with that sort of security.

Inside, Bethany threw the keys on a hall table.

'Ali, we got ourselves a visitor.'

It took Anya's eyes a few moments to adjust to the dimmers. Bethany led the way to the small but neat kitchen and placed the groceries on the bench. She yanked back a set of curtains, almost pulling them from their hooks. Light flooded the room.

'She must have heard us talking and closed everything in this place. God made light so we don't have to sit in the dark.'

She took the bag from Anya and began removing boxes of biscuits, pasta and cereal, which were quickly dispatched to cupboards. 'Alison! I said we got a visitor.' A number of TV dinners from the second bag were placed in the freezer section of the old Westinghouse. 'Now, how 'bout I make some lunch. Then I gotta get back to work.'

Bethany was obviously a woman in charge and organised, particularly given she did the food shopping in her lunch break.

A frail young woman, who stood about five foot two inches, appeared in the doorway, long hair and fringe hiding much of her face. She leant against the open door, like a shy child nervous about meeting a stranger.

'What did you open them up for?' she asked in her sister's direction.

'People gotta see inside their own house.' She filled a kettle and placed it on the gas stove. 'I gotta go back to work, but I can stay for a bit.'

The woman slowly entered the room and sat at one end of the laminated kitchen table, facing away from the window.

'Does the light hurt your eyes?' Anya asked.

'Ain't nothing wrong with the eyes the good Lord gave her.' Bethany began searching kitchen drawers and cupboards. 'Where in tarnation did you hide the knife this time?'

Without a word, Alison got up and reached into a cupboard. Inside an oblong casserole dish was a chopping knife.

Anya watched her shuffle back to the table and sit, hands cupping her throat. For a moment the scars on her face were just visible.

Her heart went out to this woman. The reason for closing the curtains was more than likely to avoid being seen clearly. Hiding the knives in a new place after her sister left the house was far from normal safety procedure, even if there had been children in the house. This appeared to be a terrified and traumatised woman. Nothing like the image the press had painted of a gold-digger who had targeted an innocent footballer.

'I wanted to ask you about Liam McKenzie.'

Ali pulled her robe tighter, revealing a fine tremor in the process.

'It's OK,' Bethany said, chopping vegetables and dropping them into a saucepan. 'She ain't got nothing to do with him.'

'And I'm not with the police either. I'm a physician and I treat women who've been hurt by men.'

Bethany wiped her hands on a towel and left the room, returning with a folder.

'This is what that man done and got away with.'

Anya opened it to look at the contents, sensitive to the sister, who turned her face further away.

An envelope contained a head shot of a young woman, carefully groomed, with perfect hair and make-up and a striking smile. The eyes sparkled into the camera. Ali had been very attractive.

'One of them Hollywood agents wanted her to do ads, she was so pretty.' Bethany continued chopping. 'No wonder McKenzie wouldn't leave her alone. I warned her about men like him with their money and smooth talk, but what does a big sister know?'

Anya turned to the next image and took a silent breath. This time the face was unrecognisable: eyelids so swollen they were closed; blackened cheeks. The next shot showed an eye forced open, revealing a haematoma on the lateral aspect consistent with a fractured cheek. The next picture closed in on the lips; both upper and lower had splits up to three centimetres and sutured. With such a profuse blood supply, lips healed quickly without intervention. These wounds had to be more than superficial, or no one would have bothered with the stitches.

'I took them ones the first time he hit her. All promises and roses, saying he don't know what come over him, and how it was never gonna happen again. The judge said the pictures couldn't be shown 'cause they were . . . What's that word? Where heaven forbid a jury could think bad things about McKenzie?'

'Prejudicial?'

Bethany pointed the knife in the direction of the table. 'That's it. Prejudicial. Judge said 'cause there was no police report, anyone could have hit her. Them fancy lawyers tried to say she got herself beat up so she'd make more money out of the case.' The chopping became more aggressive.

Anya turned to the small woman at the table. 'What sort of boyfriend was he, in the beginning?'

Ali stared into space, and for a moment her eyes shone. 'A real gentleman. Kind, considerate, and real loving. I met him at a party, only I'd never heard of Liam McKenzie. I'd never even been to a game. He asked me out and wouldn't take no for an answer. The next day flowers arrived, all romantic and expensive.'

Bethany added, 'I warned her not to let that turn her head. A man who has to buy love ain't worth lovin'.'

Ali sighed. 'I thought he was handsome and he had the kind of eyes that laugh. Next week, he called all through the day just to ask where I was, what I was doin'. It sure felt romantic.'

Anya had seen the signs many times. What many women thought was flattering and caring was in fact the beginnings of a relationship in which the man sought control of every aspect of his girlfriend or wife's life – where she was, who she was with, day and night. Pretty soon, he'd be the only one she spent time with and she'd be cut off from family and friends; then he had even more control, which was exactly what he wanted. The pattern of behaviour was all too predictable. As his power over her grew, her self-esteem lessened. The cycle of abuse had begun.

'He'd text me at least a dozen times a day asking what I was doing, saying he was thinking about me.' A small smile unfolded, but out of her sister's line of vision.

'In the beginning, we were real happy. I was working and he was playing well. I even learnt about football and went to a couple of matches, but I couldn't bear to watch him get hit or smashed into.'

Anya had read about a back injury that had sidelined McKenzie for four matches. She was trying to work out the timing of that in the relationship. 'Did he injure his back at some stage?'

'Yeah, tore some muscles. He couldn't cope with being home and he was worried that he might not play again. Even when he went back on the field, he had a lot of pain and that lasted for months.'

Bethany interjected, 'Ali gave up her job and moved in to care for him, and is he grateful? Hell no. The *big* man blamed her for everything. Tell her, Ali, tell her how nasty he could get.'

The younger sister's eyes dulled. 'I'd cook him food and if it wasn't what he wanted, he'd tip it in the trash and I'd have to cook something else. He would fly into these rages and I didn't know what I'd done to upset him. If he'd had more than one drink or painkillers, he would just get out of control.'

It sounded as if Ali was finding excuses for her then boyfriend's behaviour.

'Is that when the violence began?'

She slowly nodded, as if ashamed. 'The first few times he said he didn't mean to. He would always be so sorry and promise to make it up to me. I still loved him.'

'Did you see anyone who could have helped you?'

'I tried talking to his coach about taking some pressure off, but that got him so angry. I heard him come home and slam the door so I hid in the hall closet. He started yelling at me for interfering, looking in rooms and slamming doors, then I heard him open a beer . . . then another one . . . I hid in the closet until he fell asleep.'

The kettle whistled and Bethany wiped her hands before pouring three cups of instant black coffee and placing them on the table. She went back for a carton of milk, one spoon and a chipped sugar bowl.

Anya removed the file containing the pictures following the knife incident from her bag.

'Did the violence get worse before that night?'

'He was good when he started playing again. Then I saw a picture of him in the papers with another woman, having breakfast at some hotel. They were kissing.' She touched her mouth with one hand as she spoke. 'I thought I loved him and he loved me.' She clutched the cup again. 'Next time he came around, I told him it was over.'

Bethany sat down next to Anya. 'I talked her into staying with me. He kept phoning up saying the picture was a set-up and she couldn't leave him. I thought as long as she was here, she'd be safe.'

Ethan had said infidelity was a cause of domestic violence in some of the players' relationships. He was wrong. Infidelity wasn't the cause. Being caught out enraged the unfaithful partner and upset the other one. In this case, only one became violent.

Alison remained silent as Anya took out the photographs from the hospital.

'It's time to talk about it,' the older sister finally said. 'The good Lord knows we can't keep going on like this.'

For the first time Anya could see a definite family resemblance in the women's expressions. One had a fuller face, but the brown eyes were so similar. They both looked like women whose spirit had been broken. Anya could only imagine what they had been through.

Still, Ali remained quiet.

'I was at work that night at the nursing home. I wasn't gone more than ten minutes . . .' Bethany's eyes welled with tears, which she dabbed with the back of her hand.

Alison reached across for her sister's hand. 'I've never told you, but I'm glad you weren't here that night. He was out of control and there's nothin' you could have done. Nothin' I said could stop him.' She concentrated on the cup in her other hand. 'I've gone over everything I said and did that night so many times. I even blamed myself for making him lose his temper. I would have forgiven him but he didn't even give me a chance.'

Anya knew from the images that what came next was a horrific fight, one the diminutive woman was lucky to have survived.

'I told him to leave and he did – for a while. Then he knocked on the door and asked if we could talk. He was all calm and gentle, telling me he loved me.' She shook her head again, as if she'd done wrong. 'So I let him in.'

Tears fell down Alison's cheeks, her pain still alarmingly raw.

Anya glanced at the hallway, where the attack had taken place.

'As soon as I opened the door and turned around he grabbed me by the hair and slammed my head into the wall. It sounded like an explosion, and I saw blood on the paint. I didn't know it was mine until he turned me around and started punching me in the face.' Her voice remained calm. 'I cried and begged him to stop, but he kept telling me he'd teach me never to leave him. He was gonna make sure no man ever looked at me again. That's when he went to the kitchen and got the knife.'

Bethany almost apologised, her voice husky. 'I used to keep it in the drawer. He would have seen it there when he came for dinner.'

Ali continued, matter of factly, 'He raped me. When he was done, he said no one else would want me without eyes or lips. He reckoned that would make me want to kill myself, he didn't even need to do it for me. I tried to fight, I really did, but he was too strong.'

Anya felt her stomach clench. No matter how many stories of violence she heard, the depravity of a man who claimed to love his partner, yet committed such atrocities, still horrified her. The incisions on the lids were anything but random. Liam McKenzie had tried to cut out Alison's eyes.

It made perfect sense that she hid the knife in a different place each day.

'After he cut my face, he grabbed my wrists and cut them too.'

297

Even in a rage, he had had the capacity to think clearly enough to make it look as if Alison had attempted to kill herself. This was a calculated act that had taken place metres from where they were sitting. Being in the same house had to be a constant reminder.

Bethany thumped the table. 'Then he called 911 and said Ali had tried to kill herself. Then he called me.' Bethany stood and moved to the kitchen bench, her back to them. 'When the paramedics arrived, he acted like the concerned boyfriend, and told me Ali needed help. She'd tried to kill herself and he wrestled the knife from her. That's how he explained being covered in her blood.'

'Have you had any contact with him since?' Anya asked. 'If he was so supposedly concerned about you?'

Bethany blew her nose. 'Oh, that takes the cake. Someone rang here the next day and said they was his lawyer. He said he knew how many medical bills we got and said we could get Ali all the care she needed, and more. I asked what he was talkin' about and he said Liam wanted to help, even if his presence would upset her. He wanted to pay us $25,000 and sign some piece of paper saying we ain't never gonna talk to no one about it again.'

'What did you tell him?'

Bethany's hands went back on her hips.

'I told him where he could stick his money. Ali was on a breathing machine in intensive care.' She turned around and pointed at the corridor. 'Blood was still on the wall from what he'd done. The next day, I got reporters on the doorstep and people saying we were trying to get money out of McKenzie. The dang lawyer went and told them we wouldn't take Liam's generous offer and how it would have got her cared for in a facility designed for people who were dangerous to themselves. Like Ali wasn't right in the head. They said us turning it down proved we were trying to blackmail him into giving us millions. Then all the neighbours started believing what they read. That he'd tried to break up with Ali and she'd threatened to hurt herself with a knife. My sister is supposed to have wrestled with him and cut her eyes and lips during the struggle, then her wrists. All them bruises are supposed to be from him restraining a crazy woman. Hell, he even had the judge believing he was some kind of a hero who deserved an award for helping a fellow citizen and protecting the neighbourhood!

'In this country, money buys anything. Anything but us.'

38

Later, Anya met up with Ethan in his makeshift office on the conference level while he reviewed copies of the hotel's surveillance. He paused while she filled him in about her meeting with Alison and Bethany.

He listened intently before commenting, 'McKenzie's not going to crack and break ranks with the others. He's too self-assured, and clearly used to manipulating the legal system. My money would be on him making the threats against Darla Pinkus's daughter and Kirsten Byrne.'

Without phone records tying him to the threats, or a confession, he was never likely to be charged with threatening witnesses.

Anya considered Alldridge the odd one of the group. He hadn't associated with the others at the seminar and had remained quiet through her remaining sessions. On face value, the only thing they had in common was football.

'What about Lance Alldridge? Have you spoken to him yet?'

Ethan leant back in his chair. 'Since that first day, he's had a lawyer by his side the whole time. Even follows him to the john. Word is, Lance goes out alone at night, supposedly to see a woman, but no one else in the team has seen her yet.'

Alldridge could have been protecting her from the other players, or was distancing himself from them after Kirsten's assault. That meant he could be the weak link they were looking for.

'What do you know about his background?'

'Not much.' Ethan picked at a bagel. 'He flies beneath the radar. Always turns up on time for practice, does every charity obligation, has never been in trouble before.'

'What about past girlfriends or wives?'

'He's had some gorgeous girlfriends but nothing long-term, it seems. I met one, she was a TV anchor, and there was never any rumour about scandal or violence.'

Maybe he was the big friendly giant when he wasn't taking part in gang-rape. 'So why would he participate in Kirsten's assault?'

'That's the million-dollar question,' Ethan replied. 'He's eating tonight at a restaurant on West 56th Street. I've booked a table for two at the same place, Zeppi's. It's close to Carnegie Hall, and a popular spot for celebrity spotting, I'm told.'

'Is that an invitation?' she asked, suddenly feeling peckish.

'If you fancy French food and fine conversation.'

She answered with another question. 'Meet you downstairs in thirty?'

Anya quickly freshened up and changed into a midnight-blue dress. Despite the dinner being for work, she was still going out to a fashionable place in New York and wanted to feel feminine. The dress was more fitted than she normally wore but, with a nude-coloured pair of heels, she had to admit to being happy with her appearance. She decided to wear her hair down for a change.

In the lobby, Ethan grinned. 'You look . . . well . . . I mean . . .'

'Thank you,' she said with a smile.

Unlike Lance Alldridge, Ethan and Anya did not want to be seen tonight. They were shown to the table the investigator had requested, out of direct vision from the player's seat. The maître d' assured them Lance would face the street. With 6 pm reservations, Alldridge was probably catching a show or movie afterwards.

A woman at the door offered to read Anya her tarot cards. The only way a psychic would gain credibility with her was if she predicted who Lance Alldridge and his friends would assault next. Or successfully locate her missing sister.

Ethan glanced around the room at each corner and the ceiling.

'You do that everywhere we go,' Anya said as they were escorted to their table.

'What?' He actually sounded self-conscious.

'First thing you do is look around the entire room. I assume you're checking for exits.'

He raised both eyebrows. 'Actually, that is what I do.'

Anya smiled as he pushed her chair in behind her. 'Must be a man habit.'

He took his own seat. 'More of a survival tactic, in case of a fire, bomb scare or other reason to evacuate a crowded place. My father was a firefighter.' Ethan glanced around, this time more slowly. 'He would have loved this place. He always dreamed of visiting Paris, and now there's a touch of it in midtown.'

The tin ceilings, wood panelling and mellow lighting gave the place a European feel, completed by the Art Nouveau posters and drawings on the walls. French accordion music played quietly over the speakers. As they perused the menu, tables began to fill.

Anya had to remind herself they were here for work, not pleasure.

'Is your mother still alive?'

Ethan continued reading. 'No, she died of breast cancer years ago.'

303

Getting any personal information from this man was like pulling a tooth.

Ten minutes later, the African-American footballer escorted his lady friend to their table.

Lance Alldridge had good taste. Not only in his sartorial choice of charcoal suit and open-necked shirt, but the woman with him turned heads. She looked elegant, but not in the Hollywood way. Striking was the term Anya would have chosen. Tall, with auburn hair tumbling below her shoulders. Ethan leant sideways, napkin in hand, to have a better look.

She walked confidently in killer stilettos that showcased perfectly toned calf muscles. No hint of either shyness or attention-seeking. The emerald dress hugged small breasts and an even smaller waist, flattering without exposing much apart from her willowy alabaster arms.

Glancing the arm of a passing drinks waiter, she apologised without any apparent sense of embarrassment. This was a woman with class and self-assurance.

'She could be looking for media attention, or otherwise trying to boost her profile,' Ethan suggested. 'The best and fastest way is to be caught in a romantic clinch with someone more famous.

'I've seen her before,' Ethan added. 'Just can't think where. She's not your regular groupie.'

Without taking notice of anyone else in the room, Lance pulled out the chair for his date then took his seat, sliding the chair back to accommodate his large form, bumping the diner behind him. A quick apology, shaking of hands and promise of an autograph later, then he turned his attention back to his female companion. The minor commotion had attracted the attention of other patrons and a photographer who had followed them in off the street. Within minutes, Lance had done his public duty, posed for snaps with and without his date, and signed anything from serviettes to a chef's hat.

It didn't take long for Anya to see the attraction of Lance's girlfriend for him. She was animated and had the kind of eyes that glimmered when she spoke. In the background, Piaf sang 'Je Ne Regrette Rien'.

After ordering the grilled chicken paillard with mustard sauce and French beans, Ethan ordered wine. Anya opted for the steak to boost her iron levels, with side orders of greens and potato gratin.

A table of six clinked champagne glasses as they toasted an elderly gentleman in their party. The waiter brought a cake with one candle as the group sang 'Happy Birthday'. Alldridge's auburn-haired friend listened to and applauded the song. She had long fingers, which she continually used to emphasise parts of her conversation. Notably absent were any flashes from diamond rings. A gold filigree bracelet adorning her right wrist was the sum total of jewellery on display. Again, this woman was unusual.

The body language across the table was relaxed. She was the more tactile of the two, frequently reaching forward to touch his hand or arm. Lance sat back in the chair and seemed to speak less often, but still seemed to be fully engaged in their conversation.

Drinks arrived, the mains soon after, cooked to perfection. Anya watched the couple share entrées and main meals, each selecting a portion from the other's plate without fuss or encouragement. That single act was their most telling sign of intimacy. The woman stood and placed her serviette on the back of her chair. The two shared a laugh as Lance quickly swapped his empty plate for her half-finished course.

Meandering her way past tables on her way to the bath-room, she had the contented look of a woman in requited love. Anya saw she'd left her purse and phone at the table.

It seemed unusual to miss an opportunity to touch up make-up when press photographers could snap a picture at any time. She, like Ethan, was intrigued by this woman.

Something towards the door caught her attention. The maître d' acted as if he was ejecting someone just inside the front door, but the close contact and quiet conversation between the men signalled a pre-existing relationship.

'See that?' Ethan said. 'The maître d' pocketed a bribe before security ejected that press photographer. Info about celebrities doesn't come cheap.'

At least one person on staff had just taken payment for information about their patrons. As Anya was fast learning, celebrity was an industry in itself.

She ate the last of the steak, mopping up every morsel. In the woman's absence, Lance signed a couple more autographs between finishing his meal and waving for the bill.

After paying in cash, he pulled his phone out of his jacket pocket and either texted or checked messages.

'Those smart phones are a nightmare,' Ethan complained. 'You never know if someone's making a call, checking sports results or playing a game. The only good thing is the amount of information stored on them if you ever have to borrow one during a case.'

Anya gave him a sideways glance, wondering how many laws he broke in the course of an investigation.

The woman returned and Lance stood, all smiles, thanking the staff on their way out. Ethan swiftly moved to the door, pausing by the maître d', a twenty-dollar bill in reserve.

'Don't suppose you know who the glamorous woman in the green dress is?'

'I'm told, sir, she's a violin virtuoso with the New York Philharmonic. They're performing tonight.'

By the expression on Ethan's face, he hadn't expected the footballer to be dating a prominent classical musician. Lance kept very different company from his colleagues. This girl-friend could have some insights into his off-field behaviour. Or maybe she didn't know about his penchant for gang-rape. Anya was concerned she could be at risk of being sexually assaulted.

'Do you know what's playing?' Ethan rallied.

'Rachmaninov. It's a sellout, but I can arrange tickets if you're interested.'

Nothing like entrepeneurs in New York, Anya thought. If a dollar was to be made, guaranteed someone down the chain would make at least two.

'I'm more of a sports fan.' He patted the man's back. 'Thanks anyways. But where are they performing, in case I change my mind?'

'Avery Fisher Hall at the Lincoln Centre.'

Ethan thanked him for a lovely evening. Outside, paparazzi photographed the couple, flashes catching the face of other patrons. The woman shielded her face as the doorman held open a taxi door.

Ethan made sure he secured the next taxi for the short drive, the twenty-dollar note now back in his pocket. The couple was easy to spot near the entrance to the concert hall. The woman reached up to kiss Alldridge on his cheek, before handing him a ticket and heading towards the stage entrance.

Once out of the cab, Anya and Ethan followed from a distance. Lance entered the foyer and bought a drink at the bar. Instead of going inside the actual hall when the doors opened, Lance checked his phone and headed back out to hail a taxi.

Ethan grabbed Anya's hand. Another taxi pulled up to the curb. He quickly opened the door to usher out its occupants.

By the time the elderly man had paid the driver and assisted his wife safely onto the sidewalk, the taxi Lance was in had turned the corner and was out of sight.

'He went inside as if he was going to listen to the performance. Next thing, he's out and gone.' Ethan ran his hands through his hair.

'Maybe he felt ill and headed back to the hotel.'

'There's only one way to find out,' he said. 'Wait until the show's over and see if he slips back in.'

They headed for the centrepiece of the Lincoln Centre, a yellow lit fountain. Tourists surrounded it like moths to a flame, sparking a flurry of flash photographs. The smell of chlorine reminded Anya of days spent as a child at the local swimming pool. Something about the sound of running water was calming. She wondered where Alldridge had gone. The concert would have been a thrill to see; then again, maybe he was only pretending to like music to get to the girl, just as Pete Janson had pretended to be interested in Kirsten's business proposal.

'You can go back to the hotel if you like,' Ethan offered.

The night was fresh and being outside felt better than being inside a stuffy hotel room.

'We haven't had dessert yet.'

Ethan kept an eye out. 'Maybe he's gone to get flowers and is coming right back.'

On the street, a mobile vendor sold ice creams. Anya bought two while Ethan watched the entrance to the Avery Fisher Hall.

They enjoyed the ice cream in silence and strolled despite the humidity.

Eventually, Anya spoke. 'The waitress before we saw the basketball game. Why did you give her extra money?'

Ethan did a double take. 'Wow. Where did that come from? Why? Are you jealous?'

'Hardly. So do you tip every waitress wads of cash?'

He licked ice cream from above his top lip. 'She's an old friend. Husband walked out and left her with two little kids. I help out sometimes when I can, and she pays me back whenever she can.' He looked sideways. 'And in case you're wondering, there are no strings attached.'

'OK.' She felt a little foolish. 'Did you mean it when you mentioned the job to Darla Pinkus?'

'She's got an interview with the Dream Foundation next week. It's associated with Madison Square Garden and does a lot with kids. She can take her daughter on the job most days.'

At the museum, this man had told her that belonging was overrated, yet he acted like family to people he barely knew. She couldn't work him out.

An hour and a half of conversation quickly passed, and then a taxi pulled up and Lance Alldridge climbed out. Anya and Ethan turned their faces to each other, to avoid being seen. They need not have bothered. Lance seemed intent on one thing: getting back inside the auditorium before the performance finished.

They headed back to the street. 'The night wasn't a total loss. He's met with a woman he doesn't want his team mates to meet, then left her for somewhere he doesn't want her to know about.'

Ethan gave a self-satisfied smile.

'We just got our leverage. Alldridge is our weakest link.'

39

Ethan headed back to the conference room and opened the door with the key the hotel had provided. Anya ordered coffees from room service and two Cosmopolitans for nightcaps. Neither of them wanted to be seen in the bar or to deal with any of the players they might run into there.

They sat through footage of people entering and leaving the hotel elevators.

'Was this before or after Janson died?' Anya asked.

'By the number of people, you'd think it was after, but there were a lot of women prowling that corridor. It could have been any one of them going into his room.'

He sat forward in his chair. Janson, arm in arm with a smaller woman, entered the frame. His formidable size obscured her face from the camera.

'Damn.' Ethan ran his hand through his hair. 'It's impossible to identify her.'

'Can you at least see what she's wearing?'

'New York's unofficial all-weather uniform: black dress and heels, sunglasses and scarf, only it's around her hair. Doesn't exactly narrow it down.'

Anya had yet to tell him of an email she had received during the taxi ride back. By now, the widow and her lawyers would know.

'I just got a call. Janson was positive for the ApoE4 gene component. He was at greater risk from head injuries than someone without it. The wrongful death suit could set a precedent that could have a big impact on football.' The pun was unintended.

Anya had to admit to leaning on the side of knowledge rather than civil liberties. If she had the opportunity to discover what sports placed her son at greater risk, she would want to keep him safe by knowing what activities to avoid. Surely every parent deserved that. Civil libertarians often didn't consider a parent's right to protect their children.

She let the information sink in.

'Don't underestimate the league. It will throw everything it can at the case, to prevent a precedent being set in the courts. If it loses, the issue will be tied up for years. I suspect Terri Janson will settle before too long.'

The head-injury research was going nowhere without funding, and any results, no matter how legitimate, would be tainted since Roman Bronstein had been formally arrested for drug dealing.

Ethan didn't seem too concerned. 'Having to deal with this rape case is going to be a bigger problem. Five Bombers players involved doesn't look good. And the team could end up with a huge hole in their offence.'

Anya could not believe what she was hearing. Ethan sounded most concerned about the skill deficit left if the rapists were excluded from play.

'They'll be out because of the morals clause anyway, given what we've found out so far about McKenzie and Dorafino,' Anya said. 'Garcia is already benched, and we know Lance Alldridge has something to hide.'

Ethan rubbed his forehead.

'If the case goes ahead,' Anya continued, 'Janson will become a martyr to those who demand genetic testing by high schools and colleges before letting kids play sports. His lawyers will want to preserve his reputation for tributes.

They'll deflect blame to the other four. And that's the good news for Kirsten.'

Ethan disagreed. 'That venomous piece that maligned her is only the start. The strategy defence lawyers use is deny, deny, then denounce. They'll go at Kirsten with every resource possible, and what they don't know they'll make up. Hell, a team of guys like me is already back in her home town digging up any bit of dirt they can find.' He rubbed his index finger and thumb together. 'People who want to be quoted will have more than enough incentive to come forward.'

Anya felt as if she had been hit with a fist to the chest. She thought Ethan believed the same things as she did. Now she had no idea what to think. The way he was speaking, Kirsten would be better off staying silent and avoiding a trial. The men would be free to rape again, but at least the team's offence would still be strong.

He wheeled the chair to his computer. 'Look at some of these. A court case will only make this worse.'

Anya tentatively read some of what was on the screen. It was a blog discussing the accusations made by Kirsten against the five players. So far, there were eight thousand comments on this site alone.

Why would they bother with a whore like her when they could have anyone they wanted? She's a fucking liar.

Kirsten Byrne should burn in hell. She's willingly slept with all those men and now lies about it. She doesn't deserve to live.

Let the fans show her what justice means. Anyone have her address?

I'd die to sleep with any of them. She ought to be grateful.

313

The skank is only after money. Where do I donate to the defence fund?

She killed Pete Janson. He died because of the stress brought on by her bullshit accusations.

Anya could not read any more. Without knowing any of the facts, these anonymous people were threatening and libelling Kirsten. She could not see one entry offering support.

'That blog was started by a female fan. One page has 200,000 fans supporting the boys. It's only been up a couple of days. The public is already passing judgement, and most everyone blames the victim. She needs police protection now more than ever. If you think Darla got a hard time, that was nothing compared with what Kirsten will face.'

She sat silently, attempting to understand the degree of hatred towards an innocent victim. 'Do you really believe that Kirsten shutting up and disappearing is the right thing to do?'

Ethan pulled the hair back off his forehead.

'What's right and best aren't necessarily the same thing.'

'So that's it then. You stop investigating Alldridge, even though you know Garcia recited his statement and can't possibly have written it.'

'I didn't say that.' He advanced the tape. 'Dorafino says he never saw the woman's face. I wondered if he was lying but . . .' He leant forward again. 'Why would she be wearing a scarf and sunglasses inside?'

The drinks arrived and Anya thought about it. 'She wasn't only avoiding being identified by players or people in the hotel, she was avoiding the cameras.'

'Given that CCTV recordings are on a loop and are wiped if no incident requiring review takes place . . .'

'Our mystery woman may have known something could go wrong in that room.'

This was the first real evidence suggesting that Pete Janson could have been murdered, or died during sex with this woman.

The next tape showed a crowd milling in the corridor on Janson's floor. The larger figures, including the Bombers' coach, stood out. The woman in the black dress was not clearly visible in any of the frames. She could have been in the group, but the images weren't clear enough to differentiate individual features. Despite the advancements of the digital age, closed circuit television was far from high definition.

Anya finished her nightcap. She had to go back to her room, check her emails and formalise a report for the owners of the Bombers. It would state that she believed there was compelling physical evidence to support Kirsten Byrne's claims, and that, based on past history of at least some of the players, in her opinion and experience there was a high probabilty they would continue to commit violent acts against women.

'I've got some paperwork to do in my room.'

She grabbed her bag and headed for the door.

'Meant to tell you, you were right.' Ethan's eyes didn't leave the screen. 'Apparently there was an incident at Janson and Keller's old high school. They were both involved. One of their former team mates recalled something being hushed up but didn't know what had happened. Looks like it never made the papers or went to court.'

She turned around. 'You think their deaths weren't a coincidence?'

'We won't know until I go there and check it out.'

40

Back in her room, Anya checked the emails. Her secretary was coping fine back home and, in her usual motherly fashion, urged her to stay as long as she needed, or wanted. Some more requests for expert opinions followed, all of which could wait until she returned. She replied to the senders and agreed to consult on the cases. No point turning down work; the nature of freelancing meant she didn't know when it would be offered next.

With her official seminar commitments finished, the report was all she needed to complete.

As for Janson, a legal case on wrongful death would attract opinions from every neurological, psychiatric, genetic and ethics expert in the nation, given the possibility of suicide and CTE. Raising the issue had been enough in her brief by the Bombers' management.

She could be home in a few short days.

But the footage of the woman with Janson troubled her. Who was she and how could she have killed Janson? If he had been drugged, a woman that size would have had no chance of positioning him in the wardrobe. He had to have been a willing participant in the sexual act. Chances were, she'd hidden her identity because she was someone who could be recognised. Maybe she was a wife or girlfriend of one of the other players.

It wouldn't be the first time the team code had been broken with someone else's partner. That would give her man motive to kill Janson – if he found out.

317

Then again, Pete had hurt a number of women through his sexual behaviour and seemed to have been adept at making enemies. Terri Janson put on a good act, but Anya suspected there was a calculating callousness about her. Maybe that was just a learnt behaviour from having lived through Janson's off-field antics for so long.

The court case involving Darla Pinkus had fallen through, but Terri had still endured the public knowledge that her husband had been a regular at a strip club and had had sex with one of the women there and that he'd admitted to having intercourse with Kirsten Byrne in his police statement.

Terri had two girls to protect. Janson dying before charges were laid against him for raping Kirsten Byrne was, in some ways, a better outcome for the family.

She wondered if it was Terri Janson under the sunglasses and scarf. Wives weren't supposed to be in the hotel rooms and it would be simple for the coach to access surveillance tapes if necessary. Dorafino could have heard her leaving and assumed it was another woman.

The connection between Robert Keller and Janson played on her mind, too. It seemed they had been involved in something at high school but it had been kept quiet. Their deaths were too close in timing, in the same city, and Anya didn't believe in coincidences.

She decided to write the reports in the morning and then share her suspicions with Ethan after she had finished.

As she undressed for bed, her thoughts turned to the investigator she had spent such an intense amount of time with. Despite his allegiance to Buffet, he had remained professional, following up on leads even if they might discredit Bombers players.

Without ever meeting Kirsten Byrne he had respected her claims enough to prove Garcia had lied about his statement.

And organising a job interview for Darla Pinkus went way beyond Ethan's job description.

He seemed like an ethical, principled man, even though she sometimes found him difficult to read. And she still didn't know very much about him. But she did know she liked his company and she was starting to admit that she found him attractive.

She climbed into bed, closed her eyes and wondered how she would feel saying goodbye to him.

She awoke at 9 am. The room was still in darkness. She checked her phone. No calls or messages. Ethan would normally have called by now. Nothing on the room phone either. She wondered what he was up to.

After breakfast, she went for a walk before sitting down to write the reports that would send her home.

She was absorbed in her work all day and barely had time to think how odd it was that she hadn't heard from Ethan. She was just stretching her cramped shoulders when she heard her phone beep, letting her know she had a message. She smiled when she read it, then went into the bathroom to shower.

In the evening, Anya met Ethan in the lobby. He was smiling broadly, dimples on full show.

'Thanks for coming —'

'Catcher! Yo.'

They turned to see Clark Garcia storming his way towards them. Ethan stepped in front of Anya.

'You lying bastard. You set us up.' He clenched a fist and shook it in the investigator's face. 'We thought you were on our team, but you and your bitch here just couldn't mind your own business. You had to stick your noses in.'

'Clark, I know you're upset, but you don't want to get into any more trouble.' The concierge near them quietly summoned security.

'Hell, what more can they do to me? I'm out of the team, can't afford no lawyer now, and it looks like I'm going to prison. Man, I got nothing to lose.'

Two security men arrived and approached from either side. Garcia saw them and began to back away. 'You better watch your back, man. You're gonna pay for what you've done.' He turned and left the hotel.

After asking if they were all right, the staff moved away.

'Let's get out of here,' Ethan said. 'We have something to do on the way.'

The taxi stopped at the Rockefeller Center.

'Told you we'd come back.' He acted as if nothing had happened in the hotel. 'You'll be going home soon and I didn't want you to miss this.'

They rode the elevator to the top and headed out to the viewing decks. The breeze was like a catharsis, blowing away the week's events.

The view of the city as the sun began to set could only be described as spectacular. For the first time since arriving, Anya was orientated to the layout of the city. To the north, upper Manhattan surrounded the vast area of Central Park. To the west and northwest, the Hudson River twinkled against the orange horizon. They moved to view the south and southeast as the gust picked up.

Ethan looked over her shoulder to point to the Empire State and Chrysler buildings. From there she located Grand Central Station and their hotel, and to the west she could see the lights of Times Square. He showed her Ellis Island, and told her that this was where the von Trapp family, on whom the *The Sound of Music* was based, arrived in 1938; how at last count there were 1,848,570 cars registered in NYC, give or take the 15 or so that had crashed in the last few minutes.

He put a coin into viewing binoculars and peered in. 'Are you looking forward to going home?'

'I can't wait to see Ben, but I have enjoyed working here, meeting Linda Gatby and catching up with Gail Lee. It's been a whole new experience learning about football too.'

He stepped aside so she could get a better view, and she felt his breath on the back of her neck. She began to shiver. She turned her head and her cheek brushed against his. He didn't pull away.

'What if Terri Janson was the woman with Pete?' she asked quietly.

'You keep pulling things way out of left field.' He considered it for a moment. 'It's a possibility.'

The breath again.

'I finished the reports. So I guess my work is done.'

'What if you have more to do?'

She looked up and his lips met hers. She closed her eyes and kissed him back, her body in a sensory cacophony.

He turned and held her face in his hands. Her heart pumped faster and every fibre tingled with his touch. Suddenly her thoughts raced. What were they doing? She was heading back home and he had made it clear he didn't want any attachments, with the possibility of Huntington's disease in his future.

Carefully, she eased away.

'If I offended you,' he managed, 'or acted inappropriately —'

'I'm not sorry.' She shrugged her shoulders and smiled.

Half of her said she was crazy, the other half wanted more of Ethan.

'What happens now?' He moved forward and stroked her hair, awakening feelings she hadn't let surface for years. Her veins heated up again.

She honestly had no idea. Ben had been her priority for so long.

The ringtone disturbed them. Ethan waited before answering.

'Thanks. We'll be right there.' He took her hand in both of his and kissed it.

'Sorry, but we have to go. Lance just started dinner with some of the team and if he disappears again I really need to find out what he's doing. I know he's hiding something; a gambling problem, a hooker fetish, I'm not sure what because he leaves no money trail. I have to catch him in the act, so to speak. It's the only other way I can think of to help Kirsten's case.'

'Well, let's go.' Anya assumed she was included.

'You should head back to the hotel.'

'I'm coming for the ride.'

The taxi ride to the restaurant where Alldridge was dining passed in silence. Outside, they met a middle-aged man wearing a dark sweater, jeans and a frayed cap. Ethan introduced him merely as one of his support team who had been tailing Lance since he left the hotel. The man handed over the keys to a blue Toyota Corolla and headed off on foot.

'This time we won't miss the cab,' Ethan quipped.

They sat in the front seats and watched the restaurant for any sign of Alldridge. It was as if the last hour had never happened.

Other members of the Bombers ventured out in a pack but Lance apparently remained inside. A few minutes later, he came out and hailed a taxi.

Ethan started the engine and pulled into the traffic. By now, it was dark and the city had begun its other life.

They followed him to West 52nd Street where he exited the taxi, crossed the road and walked to the next block. 'Stay in the car, get in the driver's seat just in case of trouble.'

'What are you expecting?' Anya was suddenly afraid for Ethan. 'What's going on?'

'I'm just saying lock the doors. If anyone approaches the car, drive around the block. You can drive, can't you?'

'Yes,' she said indignantly. 'Where are you going?'

'I already told you. To find out Lance's secret.'

Anya hated being treated like a child. How did kissing her give him the right to push her around and treat her like a helpless infant? She wasn't sure what made her madder: the fact that they had kissed or the fact they had stopped.

Anya watched Ethan keep in the shadows as he followed Alldridge. She peered ahead to see where Alldridge might be going and saw him approaching a club. Suddenly, certain anomalies seemed to fall into place. The club was called Vlada, and judging by the number of men and lack of women entering, she could tell it was a gay bar. Something that had been nagging at her finally made sense.

It was possible that only four of the five men in the room had sex with Kirsten Byrne, yet all five had admitted to it. Dorafino and Clark said Alldridge wanted Kirsten to himself and stopped others coming into the room. He could have been protecting her and, to keep face with the others, claimed he had sex with her too.

Being gay could explain why he didn't rape her, but he obviously didn't want anyone to know. What didn't make sense was why he would admit to having sex with Kirsten at the risk of being charged with something he did not do. Something that could get him a jail sentence and destroy his career.

She turned her attention to Ethan once Alldridge had entered the bar. A large man parked a car, got out and headed straight for the investigator. Without warning, he slammed Ethan into the front of the next building. They disappeared into the shadows, then Ethan spun back into view and was hit in the side of the head. He buckled over and another hit sent him to the ground. The large man landed a kick in his kidney and he arched, just as another blow smashed into the side of his head.

As Anya fumbled for the ignition key, she hit the accelerator, causing the car to skid towards them. She shone the headlights at them and honked the horn loudly. Before the attacker sprinted off, she heard him call out, as if as an afterthought, 'Dirty pervert, you sick fucking bastard.'

That was when she saw the balaclava covering his face.

Slamming on the brakes, Anya opened the door and ran to Ethan. He was unconscious but breathing.

By now, some men had filed out of the club and offered to help. One phoned 911 as Anya tried to examine Ethan. Blood poured from his head wound. His pulse was thready. He could have been bleeding internally.

'You're going to be fine,' she repeated, hoping that if she said it enough, it would be true.

41

Anya sat in the waiting room, silently praying Ethan would be all right. The surgeon had confirmed he had a fractured skull and a perinephric haematoma from being kicked in the head and kidney while on the ground. At the moment he was being ventilated to reduce intracranial pressure and assess whether or not the kidney needed to be removed.

His condition remained critical.

She sat with her face in her hands, which were blood-stained from where she had touched his face and head after the beating. Two uniformed police arrived and spoke quietly with the nurse. They headed over to her and sat, caps in hand. One carried a brown bag containing Ethan's watch, wallet and keys.

'Excuse me, ma'am, can we have a talk to you about your friend?'

Anya looked up. 'His name is Ethan Rye.'

'Can you tell us what happened?'

She took a deep breath in. 'He's a private investigator and he followed someone to that club.'

The officers looked at each other. 'Vlada?'

Anya nodded as she remembered its name. 'He didn't have time to go in before he was attacked by that man.'

'Can you describe him?' one asked, taking notes.

She strained to remember any tiny detail that would help. 'He looked like a football player, massive. He had dark clothing and a balaclava on his head, I think.'

'Do you know who may have wanted to hurt Mr Rye?'

She thought back to earlier in the evening. 'A sacked player from the Bombers, Clark Garcia, threatened Ethan earlier in the hotel. He said Ethan would pay for what he had done. The concierge and security men witnessed it.'

'Ma'am, is your friend gay?'

Anya looked up. 'What? No.'

'Are you sure? He was outside a gay club, and we have reason to consider this a hate crime. We have a number of witnesses who heard the attacker call Mr Rye a pervert.'

Anya shook her head. 'No, you've got it wrong. He was there for work, following someone. This had to be Garcia. He would have called out to try and shift blame from himself.'

'Ma'am, did anyone know where you two were headed this evening?'

She thought about it. They had had no idea where Lance Alldridge was headed. 'No.'

Their point was obvious. How would Garcia have known where Ethan was going to be at that moment?

She could not accept that he had been attacked for being near a gay club. It was too convenient a coincidence for Garcia.

Anya looked up then and saw Lyle Buffet walking slowly down the corridor.

'Officers, might I have a word with Doctor Crichton?'

Without taking his name, they stood and asked if they could get Anya anything.

'She could use a hot coffee,' the old man said. 'Looks to me like she's in shock.'

'Yes, Mr Buffet, we'll see what we can do.' They handed him the brown bag. 'You should take this for now.' The two headed for the tearoom. They clearly knew the way.

'Are you all right?' He sat down next to her. 'They called me because I'm recorded as Catcher's next of kin.'

She tilted her head, wondering if she'd heard properly.

'I never had a son, or any children for that matter. My wife wasn't able to. Anyway, Catcher has been like the son I always wanted. I'll get him the best medical care money can buy, I promise you that.'

They sat in silence for a while.

'Where's your wife?' Anya asked.

'She died of a stroke ten years ago now. She was a football widow all her married life. Since then, the Bombers have taken up all my time. Sometimes I wish I'd let her know how much . . . Well, you can't change the past.'

'It sounds like she was very tolerant and patient.'

The old man half smiled. 'More than any man deserved. In fact, something tells me you two would have got on. You see, up until you arrived, my wife and Catcher were the only ones who ever told me what I needed – rather than wanted – to hear.'

A nurse came out and asked if one of them would like to sit with Ethan.

Anya looked at the old man with a new respect. 'You go.'

'I'd like that, but make sure you get some sleep. I'll call you if he wakes or there's a change.' He handed her Ethan's possessions. 'He would want you to look after these.' Surprised, she helped him to his feet. The owner's strength seemed to be failing him at this moment.

'One more thing, Doctor. Thank you for being there for him. I know you made a difference.'

Anya hoped so, for Ethan's sake.

She returned to the hotel feeling numb and trying to comprehend the last few hours. In her room, she showered and dressed in her yoga pants in case she was called out in a hurry.

Ethan's personal belongings lay on the bed. She opened the wallet and lifted his room key, trying to work out how

327

anyone had found him outside the club. They had to have been followed.

She headed down the corridor and let herself into Ethan's room. Inside was a mountain of paperwork. On the desk sat a portable printer. Stick-on notes covered each pile, with a title or place name. She looked at the pile labelled *Clark Garcia*.

There were summaries of his previous employment history, what teams he had played for, and his criminal record, which hardly came as a shock. Being illiterate must have been difficult to mask at high school and college, yet being a footballer protected him from the usual academic scrutiny. There were photocopies of letters describing his poor attendance and justifications from the Dean and football coaches as to why he should be permitted to complete the course. A flurry of B grades followed. Garcia had cheated his way through college, with help from the influential.

A file on Janson sat underneath. She sat back on the bed and began to read. Janson attended Lincoln High School in Chatham, Tennessee, and had a C grade average. There was a scant medical record comprising vaccinations and the occasional X-ray. No mention of concussions. His parents would probably recollect better, she thought.

A single page report mentioned an incident in high school. A young woman had reportedly been sexually assaulted under the school bleachers. Charges were never laid.

A pile of DVDs sat in a box, with dates from the last week. By their position next to the desk, Ethan may not have seen them yet. They were CCTV footage from the night Pete Janson died. Anya switched on the television and inserted a DVD into the player. It was of the lobby. People came and went, and she saw the ambulance officers and police head for the lifts, accompanied by a staff member.

She watched people come out of the lift but couldn't see anyone with a black dress and scarf. Then she saw her, sitting in the lobby working on a laptop. From the camera angle, and with her head down, all she could see was the scarf covering her hair.

Half an hour passed before the woman in the chair closed the computer and headed for the reception desk. It was difficult to see any view of her face. Replaying the tape made no difference. The woman was still anonymous. Only this time, she handed over a phone to the desk clerk.

Anya wondered why anyone would find a phone, then work for a while on a computer before handing it in.

Why hadn't the woman given the phone to the concierge straightaway? Anya pulled her mobile from her bag and checked the outgoing calls. Nothing apart from ones she had made. Then she looked at the time on the tape and it was after she had checked with reception about whether her phone had been handed in. The desk clerk wasn't the same one she had spoken to. Obviously, the clerk she had spoken to hadn't passed on her query, which was why Ethan had been called. So there was a possibility this was her phone being handed in. What had this woman done to it?

The footage was a dead end, but the high school incident needed exploring. There had to be a connection between Keller's death and Janson's. It suddenly occurred to her that Ethan had planned to visit Lincoln High.

Maybe someone didn't want him going and preferred him out of the way. She pushed the thought from her mind. It was most likely that Clark Garcia had bashed Ethan. He had threatened him and had motivation for the attack.

The question that plagued her was how he'd known where they were going to be.

42

The following morning, Anya woke, neck aching and head throbbing. She had spent hours going over the paperwork and CCTV footage in Ethan's room. She checked her phone: no messages from Lyle Buffet.

The only thing to do was shower and dress; by 7.30 am, she was back in the intensive care ward. Lyle was still at Ethan's bedside in a recliner chair, covered in a blue hospital-issue rug.

The old man seemed to have aged overnight. He woke when she entered and looked relieved to see her. Outside the private room, the day's routine had begun with floor polishers and cleaners fussing around beds and machines.

She noticed immediately that Ethan had been weaned off the ventilator, a good sign.

'Nurse said he's beginning to stir. Doctors say he needs to stay in hospital to keep an eye on that haematoma. Any change for the worse, and he'll lose that kidney. If he does as he's told, he might just get away with keeping it.'

'That's positive news.' She felt a cascade of relief.

He had not mentioned Ethan's brain function.

'Why don't you sit with him while I take a break?' He rose and passed Anya. She patted his arm gently and took the seat by the bed.

Half an hour later, Ethan's eyelids flickered before staying open long enough to snatch glances of the room. Eventually, he managed to smile at her through his bruised and swollen face.

'Sight for sore eyes,' he mumbled.

He knew who she was, another good sign. She squeezed his hand and he drifted off again. His body needed time and all its energy to heal.

Buffet stood hunched in the doorway, watching.

'Can we talk?'

Anya assumed it was about Ethan's condition.

They walked into the waiting room and sat down on the lounge.

'There's no easy way to tell you this. Masterton and Kitty no longer want Catch working for the Bombers.'

Anya felt her blood pressure soar. 'You're firing him?'

Buffet looked even more weary. 'I have no intention of firing him, but Masterton made it pretty clear he didn't want Catcher – or you – being involved with the team's business any further. I've never seen him so angry.'

Anya could barely believe the old man. 'Angry about what? That some of his precious players are rapists, or is he worried his church will be sullied? Sacking Ethan won't change that.'

Buffet sank into the cushion at his back. 'Masterton doesn't care if he's shooting the messenger. He has Kitty's support. I'm wondering if I have the energy to fight them.'

Anya could see that this was an ending for Buffet. His partners were uniting against him and the decisions he had made.

'You have to understand that Janson was worth a lot of money to a number of people and his reputation was everything. Masterton, for all his faults, manages to do some good in the community. He feels a scandal like the one involving the Byrne woman could damage his charitable causes. Profits made from the team finances some of those ventures, like shelters for women and children. He helps underprivileged kids and gives work to people who most need it.'

Anya was not concerned for herself, but Ethan deserved better. He had life-threatening injuries as a result of his connection with the team. If it wasn't for the owners' direction, he would never have been following Lance Alldridge. And discovering Garcia's inability to read was part of what he had been asked to do – investigate Kirsten Byrne's claims. Now the team owners were disavowing themselves of him. She immediately thought of Cheree Jordan firing Kirsten.

'Masterton isn't saving anyone but himself. He makes money on the backs of players who rape women and get away with it, but that's supposed to be okay because he funds a shelter or two to make up for it. Talk about turning the other cheek when it suits him.'

'The game is changing and I'm getting too old to take on new ways.' Buffet's face became more drawn as he stared into the distance. 'This head injury of Janson's. I ordered him to continue playing, as I have with so many other boys over the years. That's something I have to live with.'

He was alarming her. 'What are you really saying?'

There was an awkward silence and Anya wondered if he had heard her. After a few moments more, he spoke.

'I'm thinking of selling my stake in the team before the season starts.'

That was it? No further explanation? The game meant everything to this man and he was potentially walking away from it.

Anya tried to digest what had just occurred. Ethan may have lost his job, she was heading back home and Buffet may no longer be involved with the Bombers. Ethan would be devastated when he found out.

Still stunned, she left Buffet on the lounge and headed back to Ethan's bedside. A nurse checked the monitors and intravenous fluid lines.

'You can make yourself coffee in the kitchen. I can come and get you if he wakes up. Sedation could knock him out for a while, and the seats in there are a lot more comfortable.'

The offer was tempting. She grabbed her laptop and handbag. Lyle Buffet had gone.

The nurse was right. The blue walls were welcoming and the lounge was much kinder to her back than the intensive care chairs.

On the coffee table lay the day's papers.

She flicked through, barely registering the headlines. Sports coverage focused on Sunday's pre-season exhibition game between the All-Stars and the Bombers. Capacity crowds were expected at the stadium.

The second, a tabloid, was full of celebrity gossip and seemingly defamatory articles. Then she saw it. A photo of her with something splattered on her jacket and chin, with the caption: *The woman brought in to clean up our football league, Doctor Anya Crichton.*

She looked again. The picture was taken outside the court with Hannah, the day her case settled. The stains on her jacket and face were eggs.

Not averse to controversy, the so-called international expert on sexual assault has a reputation as a tough, unyielding man-hater. In a time when mothers are revered in society, this is one woman who could not even keep custody of her own child. Many are left wondering why.

Yet this crusader for women's rights has an agenda. She did not come to clean up our prized league, she came to destroy it.

Anya felt her pulse gallop and her breath tighten. The bile continued.

At the insistence of Lyle Buffet, co-owner of the Bombers, she has spent valuable league money trying to dig up dirt on any of the players supposedly involved in a group sex incident. Team owners questioned her idea of informing players on health issues when she openly promoted promiscuity, oral and other types of sex.

Bentley Masterton, respected preacher and philanthropist, said he was disgusted that this foreigner was permitted to besmirch the good names of so many heroes of the game. He agreed that group sex was not acceptable but conceded that consenting adults had the legal right to have sexual relations in private.

In an exclusive interview, Masterton revealed that each of the players involved had expressed remorse and were now working through the issues with their families – only one was not so fortunate.

'I believe that Pete Janson committed suicide as direct result of Doctor Crichton's involvement,' Masterton disclosed. It is understood she had been to his home and made accusations against him in the presence of his two young daughters.

Anya put the paper down, hands shaking. She felt the anger seethe through her every pore. Two photos of Kirsten Byrne also appeared, showing her before and after Cheree Jordan's makeover. An acrid taste rose to Anya's mouth.

Last night, this supposed paragon of virtue was involved in a brawl outside a well-known gay NY nightclub with her new buddy, 'companion' to Lyle Buffet, Ethan 'Catcher' Rye. It appears Rye began by showing Crichton the view from the Rockefeller Center, then the pair moved on to some of the city's less salubrious sites.

God, how did anyone else know where they had been earlier that evening? It would have been difficult to follow them from taxis to the car in peak hour, and the street had been quiet as they waited for Lance Alldridge.

Suddenly Buffet's losing interest in his beloved game made sense. He had already seen the papers and the implication that he was an old gay man with a young male lover. It also suggested she was a lesbian in some pathetic attempt to justify the accusation of man-hater and unfit mother. It said more about the reporter than about her, but most readers wouldn't see that.

She needed to see what else had been written.

Something terrible must have happened to Anya Crichton as a child to spread such bile about men wherever she goes. Supposedly a victim advocate, Crichton fails to accept that any of the women who accuse sports stars of rape could be lying. As every man knows, it's easy for any woman to accuse a man of sexual assault.

The rest she scanned until the final paragraph.

In the few days she has been in our country, two of our most valued role models and players have died under tragic circumstances. Inside sources say that the heinous accusations she was inciting did irreparable harm to players and put unnecessary stress on them and their families. Perhaps Robert Keller fell victim to the pressure as well. So much for cleaning up the game.

True fans will be glad to see the back of Anya Crichton.

The author's name stood out like fangs. Annabelle Reichman.

But how had she found out about last night? Ethan could not have told her – he had no reason to.

Anya shook the contents of her bag onto the table. It seemed crazy, but maybe someone slipped something inside,

336

like a tracking device. She turned off her phone but it stayed lit for longer than normal, and she opened the back and took out the battery. Nothing seemed out of place. Ethan's phone received the same treatment but its light shut down as soon as it was turned off.

Anya searched blogs about tracking devices on her computer. One couldn't have been in the car because they'd only picked up the car after they'd been to the Rockefeller Center.

Think!

What if the Corolla had been followed from the restaurant? Was Clark Garcia involved in some way with Annabelle? Or was Ethan's attacker another player who set Garcia up?

Anya continued to search the Internet.

When she found the answer, she sat still in disbelief. A site sold software that enabled someone at a distant location to listen in to every conversation a phone owner had. One of the signs was a phone continuing to stay lit after shutting it off.

What sort of sick mind devised the software, and why was it so readily available? Reading on, it became clear that any of these programs could turn almost any phone into a listening device. More disturbing, it functioned whether the phone was switched off or not. The phone constantly transmitted and acted as a GPS tracking device.

A few minutes later she confirmed her phone had been tampered with. It was acting as a portable bugging device. She felt nauseated. Someone had been listening to every conversation that she had thought had been in confidence. The loving chats with Ben, discussions with Martin, and every word she and Ethan spoke. Nothing they had said – or done – was private.

It would explain how Ethan's attacker found him last night. All they had to do was track the damn phone.

But if they were tracking her phone, were they after her instead?

Someone had put the software on the phone. It had to be the woman in the black dress and sunglasses that she'd seen with the phone on the CCTV footage.

Whoever did it had fed stories to Annabelle Reichman. With confidential information, the reporter had then accessed Bentley Masterton for an exclusive interview. Was the mystery woman actually Annabelle? But her articles seemed so supportive of the players. Anya tried to recall what the prickly journalist looked like from her brief meeting with her in the locker room. She remembered blonde hair, but she couldn't confidently identify the woman from the footage as Annabelle Reichman.

Following the website instructions, Anya located the source of the software on her phone. Her first thought was to delete the data and reload the factory settings, but then it would be obvious she had found it. Instead, if she left the phone by Ethan's bedside, whoever placed it there would assume she was still at the hospital.

Anya grabbed her bag and headed for the airport.

43

Anya arrived at the high school too late. Classes had finished for the day. A summer storm was in full swing. From a pay phone, she rang Linda Gatby's number. The prosecutor was still in the office.

'It's Anya here. I'm in Chatham, Tennessee.'

'Are you all right? I saw what that Reichman woman wrote, and heard about Ethan. Is there anything I can do?'

'Not right now, but thank you. I'm looking into a possible connection between Peter Janson and Robert Keller. Ethan was investigating it and I have a feeling he was beaten to stop him coming here, to where they both went to high school.'

'Anya, what you're doing is crazy then. Let the police handle it.' She could hear the anxiety in Linda's voice.

'It's ok. I found a listening device in my phone and left it at the hospital. No one knows I'm here but you. If I don't check back with you in a few hours, send out the troops. This may be important for Kirsten's case.'

Before Linda could argue, Anya said she had to go and hung up.

The droplets of rain on the door multiplied as they raced downwards, joining forces on the way. Wind gusted through the phonebox, sending a chill through her. She pulled a pashmina from her bag and draped it over her head. The main street had a post office, diner and bar, as well as a supermarket and specialty shops.

Thinking about the small community she had grown up in, Anya recalled that it was the postmistress who had always known everyone's business. She hoped it was the same here.

The door jingled when she entered.

'Storm's gonna get mighty fierce before it passes.' The older woman barely glanced up from her crossword. Glasses hung around her neck on a purple plastic chain. 'Is there something I can help you with?'

There was no one else behind the desk, and no one in line.

'I know this is a little odd, but I was wondering if you could help me with an enquiry.'

'Don't s'pose you can think of an eight-letter word for "unsettled". It starts with an R and second last letter is an S.'

'Restless?' Anya suggested.

The woman filled in the squares. 'Been looking at that for the last hour. Restless. I'll be damned.' The woman sized her up and down, this time with the benefit of the glasses. 'You're not from around here?'

'No, I'm actually trying to find out about something that happened several years ago at the high school. As far as I know, it involved two students named Peter Janson and Robert Keller.'

'Why, are you a reporter?'

Anya shook her wet hair. 'No, a physician, actually.'

The woman closed the newspaper. 'Terrible business that, it was like those three were cursed. I remember they were such sweet boys and such talented athletes. The Jansons moved especially from Arkansas for their son's career.'

'Three?' Anya wondered if they were talking about the same case.

'Poor Nelson Short, rest his soul, was the first to go. Was a time when he, Pete and Robbie were inseparable. Whole town would turn out to see them play.'

Anya listened. Three team mates were all dead.

'That's terrible. When did Nelson pass away?'

The woman looked to the corner. 'Years ago now. He's long gone, don't think he was more than eighteen at the time.' She leant over the counter to speak more privately. 'I blame the girl. She was a handful to her parents, as if they didn't have enough to worry about. From what I hear, she started it by flirting with another boy, knowing Nelson would get jealous. The lug couldn't control his temper. Next thing, Nelson took a punch, hit the ground and that was it. Police said his skull must have been thinner than normal, or it must have been a freak punch.'

'At eighteen? That's a terrible loss.' Anya tried to sound sympathetic, given this woman had praised the three. 'Who hit him?' This could have been the incident involving Keller and Janson.

'Some boy from the next county. He spent some time in jail and who knows where he is now.'

Rain pelted against the roof and shop front. 'You might want to sit out the storm in here.'

Anya got the impression the post office was never particularly busy.

'What about the girl?' she asked.

'She's long gone now, was too good for this town. Her mother still lives on Holy Oak, couple of blocks back, one over.' The woman seemed to stretch her memory as she pointed directions. 'Lisa. That was her name. Lisa Fowler. Some say she did it on purpose because of a rumour someone started.'

'What sort of rumour?'

'Some say Pete, Robbie and Nelson were horsing around with her sister. Others say the girl lured them to the bleachers one night.' She opened the paper at the crossword and searched for more clues.

'May I borrow your phone book?' Anya asked.

The woman flopped the thin publication onto the desk. It was attached via a thick cord. 'That storm's already turned nasty. What's an eight-letter word for determination, starts with a T, ends in Y?'

Anya wrote down the address for Fowler, and the Short family just in case.

'Thank you so much, ma'am, and try "tenacity",' she added before jingling the door on her way out.

The rain had set into a heavy fall.

She ran across the road to the diner, sidestepping puddles on the way. An older woman waited tables.

'What can I get you?' she asked. It was too early for the evening rush, and too late for lunch.

Anya chose a seat at the counter and took a menu from her.

'You look like you could do with something to warm you up.'

'Coffee would be great, and a piece of your chocolate cake, thanks.'

'Where you from?' The woman reached beneath the counter and pulled out a mug, which was then filled with warm coffee.

From under a cake lid, she produced a slice that could have fed four people.

'Australia.'

'Saw a show about the Barrier Reef on the Discovery Channel. Most beautiful place I've ever seen.'

Anya was impressed and felt more at ease. The speakers played Frank Sinatra. 'Music keeps the teenagers out,' the woman said proudly.

It was hardly surprising. 'Have you lived here long?'

'Only thirty years.'

Anya decided to ask the woman while no one else was in the diner. 'I don't suppose you remember about ten years

342

ago, a supposed incident involving three high school boys. Pete Janson, Robert Keller and Nelson Short?'

The woman nodded. 'I know you shouldn't speak ill of the dead. People around here seem to think those boys are heroes.' She leant on the counter. 'These are the same ones who still call the Civil War an act of northern aggression.'

The comment was a little offputting and suggested inherent parochialism. The locals probably wouldn't appreciate a foreigner asking too many questions. She decided to find out as much as possible from the waitress.

'What do you think happened?'

'I think they took advantage of that poor girl under the bleachers, knowing they would get away with it. Funny how fate catches up.'

Anya sipped her coffee, enjoying its warmth. Another customer entered and the waitress busied herself wiping the counter.

After the cake, and a second coffee, Anya walked over to the till to pay. 'Don't suppose you remember the name of that girl?'

'Sure do, it was young Patsy Fowler. Still lives with her mother. They look after each other now.'

Anya rang the doorbell and a woman in her sixties opened the door, slightly stooped. Her hands were distorted from arthritis.

'Can I help you?'

'Hello, Mrs Fowler, I was wondering if it was possible to speak with Patsy.'

'Who's asking?'

Definitely not a friendly start. 'My name is Anya. May I come in?'

'You're not from round here, are you?'

343

'No, New York,' she tried.

The woman's expression relaxed. 'My daughter Lisa works there. Do you know her?'

'She told me about Patsy,' Anya lied.

'You might as well come on in. She's tidying her room. Patsy, you got a visitor,' she called and sat on the sofa. The television in the room was loud but was left at that volume.

An overweight figure with a large grin entered the room.

'Yes, Momma?'

Patsy was wearing high-waisted jeans with a checked shirt neatly tucked in, hair in ponytails. She had the facial features associated with Down syndrome.

'Did Lisa tell you she's got the brains of an eight-year-old? Sometimes she forgets to tell people that.'

Anya's heart sank. Janson, Keller and the Short boy could not have had consensual sex with Patsy. She was mentally disabled and incapable of giving consent. Nor was someone with the mind of a child capable of luring them somewhere to have sex.

'Hi, Patsy, I'm Anya.'

'Hello. You wanna see my room?'

Anya smiled. 'I'd love to.'

This was the girl the three men had raped. She would have been unable to testify against them, but that did not mean they should have got away with it.

If Patsy's sister, Lisa, had been going out with Short, one of the attackers, and had instigated a fight, it was feasible that she had been hoping he would be hurt.

The bedroom was pink, with images of unicorns and fairies on the walls.

'You draw really well,' Anya commented, before meeting every one of a shelf of soft toys by name.

A noticeboard had multiple postcards of New York. 'My big sister lives there,' Patsy boasted.

'Do you have any pictures of her?'

Patsy reached under her pillow. 'These are special,' she put her finger to her lips. 'Secret special.'

The small album held pictures of two little girls, one obviously Patsy.

Anya flipped the pages, admiring the younger sister in every shot. Patsy giggled and covered her mouth with both hands.

Two photos on the last page stood out. Lisa had dark hair, but the face was familiar. Now she was blonde.

Anya was staring at a picture of Annabelle Reichman.

44

Immediately after leaving the Fowler home, Anya found a motel for the night. She phoned Linda Gatby and had to leave a message on her cellphone about Annabelle Reichman and her sister's assault by Janson, Keller and Short and her suspicion that Annabelle had tampered with her phone and was the mystery woman with Pete Janson.

Returning to the hospital the following evening, she arrived to find Ethan being discharged under strict instructions to avoid any strenuous activity and to rest for three more weeks. The kidney haematoma had not increased in size but could still cause problems. Instead of resting, he insisted on trying to speak to Lance Alldridge before tomorrow's charity game.

Anya called Linda Gatby from a hospital pay phone and left another message. Anya debated whether to tell Ethan about Annabelle Reichman, but seeing how ill he looked, she decided to hold back for now. He was determined enough to see Alldridge, despite being ordered to rest. Any more stress and he could lose a kidney, or worse. Anya was still trying to work out what Annabelle's involvement was. And if she was honest with herself, she had a niggling doubt about where Ethan's true loyalties lay. She was desperate to talk to Linda.

In Anya's short absence, Clark Garcia had been arrested for the assault on Ethan. The police had found blood on his shoes and trousers when they'd gone to interview him. He had requested immunity in exchange for testifying against the other four involved in the attack on Kirsten Byrne. He claimed someone had rung him anonymously to tell him where Ethan was throughout the evening.

Ethan said the police planned to arrest Alldridge and McKenzie after the game. After that, there would be no chance to speak with Alldridge in private.

Ethan refused to allow Anya to confront Alldridge alone, despite the fact he was supposed to be resting. They decided that in the morning, Anya would pretend to have surveillance photos of Alldridge in her bag, in case he needed convincing.

Ethan arrived at the Hyde Hotel in a limousine to collect Anya. Together they headed for Lance's friend's home.

The auburn-haired woman answered the door to her apartment wearing a silk gown, her eyes bloodshot and with dry tear-streaks down her cheeks. She looked up and saw Ethan's bruised face. 'What —?'

'It's vital we see Lance,' he urged, 'before the game.'

'This isn't a good time.'

Anya stepped forward. 'We know he didn't rape Kirsten.'

The woman's expression altered. Her puffy eyes widened. 'Thank God.' She looked around outside before ushering them in. 'I can't talk sense into him. He's going to be arrested in a few hours because he won't tell them —'

'We know,' Ethan said. 'We want to stop him from making a terrible mistake.' Ethan looked pale and weak, and had to be in a fair amount of pain – not that he showed it.

She grabbed his good hand, as if thanking him, and led them to a room off the corridor. From the doorway they could see a music stand and violin lying on its case.

'I can't get through to him. It's like he's given up.'

Anya touched her shoulder. 'Please understand, we need to speak with him privately. If you don't hear what we say, you can't be subpoenaed to repeat it.'

The woman nodded and clutched her robe at the chest. 'Please just help him. He's a good man and could never have done this. Believe me. He's the type of man a woman knows she's safe with. I love him like he's my brother. I know he's innocent.'

They waited until she had disappeared. Inside the room, Alldridge sat at an upright piano, tapping the same note. He turned when he saw them but barely reacted. He was already dressed in a suit and tie, almost as though in preparation for when the police came to arrest him later in the day.

Anya reached for the envelope in her bag and Ethan wasted no time.

'You didn't rape Kirsten, did you?'

He ignored them.

Ethan stood firm. 'Listen to me, Lance. You don't have to be charged with anything. Four men assaulted her, and we know who they are. You're not one of them. I think you led them to believe you raped her after they'd finished and left the room. Tell me I'm wrong.'

The tapping on the key stopped. The piano stool grated on the wooden floor as he stood up. 'Get out. Or I'll throw you out. Both of you.'

Ethan cautiously stepped between the large man and Anya.

'You've known me a long time,' he said. 'I'm here to help you, even if you're not smart enough to know it. I saw you at the Vlada club. It wasn't your first time either. We have photos that prove it was you.' He gestured towards the envelope in Anya's hand.

The enormous shoulders slumped and Lance sank back onto the stool.

'How much do you want?'

Anya put the empty envelope back in her bag. There were no photos, of course, but Alldridge wasn't to know that.

349

A clock ticked on the wall as if counting the time left. Ethan took a breath.

'We don't want your money, you idiot. We want to stop you making the biggest mistake of your life.'

The large man looked up, confused. Despite his size, his brown eyes had the vulnerability of a child about to be punished.

Ethan pulled across a wooden chair and sat facing him. 'We don't want you to ruin your life by going to prison for something you didn't do.'

He closed the lid on the piano. 'You don't get it,' he said. 'Either of you.'

Anya tried. 'It makes no sense to confess to a crime you didn't commit and face a jail sentence just to protect team mates. These men are not even your friends.'

Alldridge buried his face in his hands. 'You don't understand. No one does. Catcher, who the hell do you think beat on you?'

Ethan held his ribs and coughed. 'I know it was Garcia.'

'And word's out you were near a gay bar. You saw what the papers said about that. Made out you were some sicko.'

Alldridge turned the stool towards the window and stared out. His tone was even and controlled. 'Players don't just dislike gays, they beat the shit out of them. And McKenzie even got away with it by saying this one guy came on to him. Man, players call us faggots and boast how they'd have no problem being violent to any man who propositioned them. So how do you think the locker room will be? Seriously. Do you think I'll ever play again if I come out and admit the truth? I'll have more chance of being killed on the field than anyone else out there. These guys would rather have drug dealers, rapists and wife beaters in their team than someone like me.'

'Your career will be over if you go to prison,' Anya argued. 'You'll be labelled a sex offender for the rest of your life.'

He turned to look at her. 'And the public will forget about it, just like they forget about everything else guys like Janson and McKenzie have done. Prison time didn't stop Mike Tyson making a comeback. And Hollywood turns out to support Roman Polanski after he admits to having sex with a thirteen-year-old girl.

'The public has a short memory for everything but someone being gay. Celebrities can bash their wives and girlfriends and what happens to their careers? Nothing. But what happened to Rupert Everett when he came out? That was it for him as far as lead roles were concerned. What's the cruellest rumour about a successful man? Being unfaithful, sleeping with prostitutes, bashing women? No, accusing him of being gay.'

Anya still could not believe that a man would choose to go to prison for a crime he did not commit rather than admit who he really was. But what he said about the public perception of celebrities was undeniable. Still, he did not help Kirsten the night of her attack. He could have called the police and made a stand against his violent colleagues. He chose not to.

'You heard what they said about those movies you showed us. No normal man would ever want to have anal sex, so that had to be rape.'

Anya's frustration built. 'And yet these men are the first to anally rape women. Lance, this is so wrong. They have a warped view of men, women and sex. They don't represent the majority of people.'

'That's where you're wrong. They are the average people. All you have to do is look at the fans.'

Anya refused to accept that. 'If you expose McKenzie for what he is, you would be gaining the respect of a huge movement opposed to violence against women. You could become a spokesperson, a role model, and you would be doing the right thing.'

'Maybe in your world, but not this one. Women fans are the first to blame the victim. Look at the way Kirsten Byrne is being treated. Women are behind a lot of it, so don't tell me I'd be a hero to them.'

Ethan held the hair out of his eyes. 'It doesn't take away your skill. Everyone knows you're one of the best ambassadors for the game. No one can deny that.'

'Maybe. But what if I have a bad day? What's the crowd going to say? If I get injured and don't get up, I'm limp-wristed and a girl. I'll be the number one target for every opposition player for behind-the-play attacks. And I'm black. How many black gays can you name?'

'I get it. Homophobia is rampant, but it's wrong. Things are starting to change. Hiding can't be the answer.'

Alldridge shook his head. 'It's the only answer. All I need to do is show remorse, say I've learnt the error of my ways and all will be forgiven. You can't say you've realised being gay was a mistake and be forgiven. Once you're tainted, that's it. Do you think I like living like this? I hate the deception and lies, but that's just the way it is.

'I have to do what is right for me and my family. I can't take back what happened to that girl, but I can try in my own way to make it up to her.'

'But you're not responsible.'

'It doesn't feel that way.' He thumped his chest, with tears in his eyes. 'I knew what they were doing was wrong and I didn't stop it. It made me sick to see them hurting her like that, and she isn't the first.'

He put one hand on the window and lowered his forehead to the glass. 'I got scared for her and for me. The mood turned so fast in that room. Four against one if I tried to stop them. I figured I'd stop any more than that from coming in. That way we both might make it out in one piece.'

'I get you're feeling guilty, I get that.' Ethan tried to move between him and the window. 'But you don't have to take the blame for raping her.'

Alldridge checked his watch. 'I've got to go. My lawyer says I'll be arrested after the game. I can't be late or they'll think I've absconded.'

Anya had a sinking feeling. None of this was right. McKenzie probably would get away with doing minimal time and then resume his career – if his lawyers didn't manage to get him off. Chances were a jury would acquit him even with damaging evidence. As much as it galled her to admit it, Alldridge was absolutely right.

His friend knocked on the door. She was dressed in jeans, a teal-coloured blouse and carried a jacket.

'The car's outside. It's time to go.'

'How long have you known him?' Anya asked her.

'He's been my best friend since college. My boyfriend doesn't mind us hanging out together when we're both in New York.'

Lance walked towards the door and turned back. 'Catcher, Doc, I appreciate you trying to help me, honestly. You're all right. But this is something I have to do. Hey, you never know. With a little luck, God may be on the good guys' side today.'

45

Anya and Ethan arrived at the game with tickets Lyle
Buffet had left them. From their seats they could see the
old man on the sideline, barking into the coach's ear.

Anya wished there was something she could do to stop
Alldridge from ruining his life and to testify for Kirsten
Byrne instead. Anything she or Ethan said to the police was
hearsay. Lack of his DNA at the scene meant little, considering none of the others had left DNA apart from Janson
and McKenzie, and theirs was on the carpet, and the others
had incriminated Alldridge in their statements. She racked
her brain to think of a way of saving his privacy and ensuring
he didn't go to prison for something he hadn't done.

Excusing herself, she called a lawyer she knew in Sydney
on her reprogrammed mobile phone. Usually an ency-
clopedia of ways to manipulate the legal system, he drew
a blank. Either Alldridge informed on his team mates or
accepted he was complicit when the crime was committed,
and that he continued to act as an accessory. The only option
seemed to be a plea bargain, which would be in the lawyers'
minds anyway.

Buffet had told Ethan that Liam McKenzie's mother had
already given an interview denouncing Kirsten Byrne as
an extortionist trying to ruin her family. The press might
just lap it up. The notion of the loving family destroyed
by a heartless blackmailer had pathos and injustice, not to
mention money, sex and scandal.

Anya returned with a bottle of water for Ethan. He needed to stay hydrated and was looking more pale.

'Thanks. How did you go with your lawyer friend?'

She flopped into the chair, feeling defeated. 'Laws are different from country to country, state to state, but we've already thought of everything he could come up with.' But she'd at least finally got hold of Linda Gatby and was able to relay to her the information about Annabelle Reichman. Linda was going to do some quick checking.

Their attention turned to the game, which was about to start. The Bombers took to the field and would make the first play. Anya quickly picked out Liam McKenzie, who pumped his fists to the crowd. He had been in trouble so often with the law and had always come out unscathed. He acted as if he'd already been tried and acquitted. She wondered if he appreciated how damning Kirsten's testimony might be.

'Now he's dead, they'll blame it all on Janson. They'll say Pete was the ringleader, the bully, they were intimidated by him, they thought she consented because she didn't complain or scream.' Ethan turned to her. 'They're going to get away with it and McKenzie will be free to rape and bash women and anyone he thinks is gay. Any time he likes.' He held his ribs again and let out a small cough.

Anya's gut feeling was that the investigator was right. Kirsten Byrne was about to be dragged through the media and have every aspect of her life upturned, and all for nothing.

Rock music blared through the stadium, hyping up an already charged crowd of ninety thousand. The pair sat in silence and watched Lyle Buffet wave at the coach, giving orders about every aspect of the day's plays. Buffet's empire was crumbling, but he wasn't giving up on a single game. Anya spotted Gavin Rosseter on the sideline, along with Reginald Pope, the senior doctor.

The game started with the Bombers' centre snapping the ball back to the quarterback, who passed it on to a running back. Five yards later he was stopped by three of the opposition's defence. On the third play, Alldridge blocked a player and the two exchanged words. As they separated, the crowd cheered. After the fourth play, possession changed hands and the teams swapped over. Anya found the stop-start nature of the game frustrating, but was beginning to appreciate the strategy component.

The cheerleaders performed as music blasted again.

The following play, a Bombers player intercepted the pass and ran twenty yards, much to the crowd's excitement. The Bomber paid for his trouble with a heavy tackle and took a few moments to get back to his feet. The medical team stayed put. He seemed to be all right.

Teams changed over again, and McKenzie strutted back onto the field. The centre passed the ball back and it was quickly offloaded to a running back who unsuccessfully attempted to charge through the defence. Anya wondered at anyone running at full speed into a wall of men. She could see why concussions were so prevalent in the game. There seemed to be no regard for self-preservation.

The next play, McKenzie threw the ball straight into the arms of a player who had broken through the defence's ranks. He sprinted into the end zone, and the crowd erupted again as the player did a cartwheel and danced for the spectators.

'Touchdown,' Ethan said unenthusiastically. He sat forward. 'Look. Behind the play. McKenzie's down.'

She wondered if this was a ruse, to feign injury and avoid being arrested today. Anya watched Rosseter and Pope run onto the field. McKenzie lay on the ground on his back with a trainer fussing over him. Rosseter leant over his face and seemed to be speaking. The quarterback didn't appear to respond. Then she saw his legs move.

'He's conscious now,' she said, 'but it looks like he was knocked out.'

'Let's see if they follow their own protocol or instead want McKenzie to be the crowd's poster boy today.'

Buffet stood shouting at the coach as Rosseter and the trainer helped McKenzie to his feet. He was pushing the doctor away.

Rosseter seemed to argue with Pope, who grabbed him by the elbow as they walked back to the sideline.

McKenzie rubbed the back of his neck, before waving to the crowd.

Ethan excused himself. 'I need to go to the bathroom.'

'Are you all right?'

'Just tired, and the headache's back. Besides, that little show would make anyone want to throw up.'

The assault had taken more out of him than he was prepared to admit. She wished there was something more she could do to help him. She had never felt so useless. His head injuries could accelerate the Huntington's disease he feared so much.

The rest of the on-field exchanges passed in a blur until half-time. Anya's mind whirled, and she thought more about Annabelle Reichman. It had to be more than just coincidence that she reported on a sport that involved interviewing her sister's rapists. If it was revenge she was after, a decade was a long time to wait when she lived just streets away from them back in high school. So why would she put herself through that . . .

Before he returned, Anya placed a note on Ethan's seat under her water bottle.

Gone to get you a knish. Back soon.

She grabbed her bag and headed straight to the locker room.

Security stopped her at the door. 'No one's allowed inside. Mr Masterton's orders.'

She paced. 'I have to see one of the players. It's an emergency.'

The two men on the door stood legs apart, arms folded. 'Sorry, ma'am. You could be the President but we still wouldn't be able to let you in.'

One of the men turned away and spoke into his earpiece, then seemed surprised when the door opened and Rosseter appeared with his duffle bag. His face was red, and the veins in his neck were distended.

'I just got fired,' he said through a clenched jaw, throwing his bag on the ground. 'Anya, you saw it. McKenzie took a solid hit. He was knocked out, but says he's fine, so he's being sent back out there.'

He paced, hands on his hips. 'I wanted to pull him off but Pope's overruled my decision. Pope doesn't care about the players, it's all about what the owners want – winning.'

Anya was surprised that Rosseter had not seen any of this coming. She was relieved he was ethical enough to stand up to Pope and his employers. She grabbed the opportunity to clear up a couple of things.

'Was Pope behind Janson's frontal lobe bone surgery to remove signs of growth hormone abuse?'

Gavin nodded. 'I only heard about it later.' He paused. 'McKenzie's being arrested after the game. Along with Alldridge. They want this to be a good game, for maximum press coverage. Players don't matter to Masterton at all.'

'So he and Pope risk McKenzie's life and future by sending him back out. I know he's a thug but no one deserves to be treated like that. And he's going along with it. He can't wait to get back out there and return the favour to the guy who tackled him.'

Only on the football field was that sort of violence acceptable.

Rosseter stopped. 'What are you doing here anyway?'

'I wanted to see Dorafino. There's something I need to know but these goons won't let me in.'

'Well, it looks like I just left my keys inside.' He patted his pockets and raised an eyebrow. 'What is it you want me to ask?'

'Was Janson having an affair with a female reporter? I'll fill you in later, but I need to know.'

He disappeared back inside and returned jangling his keys.

'Vince says he bragged about Annabelle Reichman. Apparently she was in earlier.'

46

It all fell into place. Annabelle Reichman was almost surely in the hotel room with Janson before he died. Therefore, she had to be the woman in the black dress who had put the spying software on Anya's phone. And Robert Keller had given an interview to a reporter just before he died. Odds were it was Reichman. All she had to do was supply him the drugs; a former addict would have had trouble resisting, especially when they came from a beautiful woman. She didn't even have to administer them herself.

Janson had set himself up. Perhaps it was the offer of erotic asphyxia, only she didn't respond to his need to have the belt around his neck released.

What bothered Anya was why Reichman had waited so long to harm Janson and Keller, and how she had managed to get Garcia to assault Ethan.

She rang Linda Gatby and told her that Reichman had already been in the Bombers' dressing room. After hanging up, she tried Ethan. No answer. She ran to the All-Stars' locker room and approached their security.

'Is there a blonde-haired female reporter inside? It's an emergency.'

'No, ma'am, she left a while ago.' She asked the guard where the press room was and headed upstairs to the booth overlooking the field. Outside, she demanded to see Reichman. After a couple of minutes, the reporter came out.

'This had better be good. I'm working.'

'It is,' Anya said. 'I know you were behind Ethan Rye being almost beaten to death.'

The woman's face hardened. 'You're completely insane. I heard Clark Garcia is responsible. In fact, I reported it.'

'I found your little present on my phone. You've been illegally tapping my conversations from the moment Janson died. We know you were in the room with him,' Anya bluffed.

'It proves nothing. I was doing an interview. And I did not sleep with him. It wasn't my fault if his sick sexual habits got him killed.'

She was there, and she probably watched him die.

'And, you'll find that I don't actually own any spy phone software. That belongs to someone else. I've had enough of this. You've got nothing.'

Anya blocked her path. 'Did you know Peter Janson and Robert Keller went to high school together?'

'God,' the reporter threw back her head and sneered. 'You're so pathetic. I wrote a piece about Keller where Janson talked about how they met. Like I said, you've got nothing.'

She waited for Anya to move before stepping to the side. Anya mirrored the action, again, blocking her way.

'It's quite sad, don't you think? Two boys whose lives were cut short so early. Bit of a coincidence?'

'You're like a stupid toy that needs the batteries taken out. For the last time, each one killed himself. Everyone knows it. Pete and Robert were risk-takers. Only each one went too far and paid the price.' She looked around. 'If you don't get out of my way, I'll call security and have you thrown out. Once I finish the follow-up piece, you and your ridiculous theories will be an even bigger joke.' She shoved forward, knocking Anya's shoulder.

'I know you went out with Nelson Short,' Anya raised her voice, 'and started the fight that killed him.'

Annabelle spun on her heel and dragged the hair back from her forehead, this time looking around for anyone who may have heard. She moved closer. 'You must be desperate. That could have been anyone from high school, besides, teenage boys and testosterone just add up to trouble. Ask anyone.'

'I did. I asked Patsy. She has a lovely room, photo albums and postcards. She likes to talk about you, and the past.'

Reichman's eyes filled with rage. Anya stepped back, hands extended, half expecting to be hit.

'I can understand how angry you must have been when they raped her. They committed one of the worst crimes possible.'

Reichman's hands began to shake and she pushed back against the outside wall. Her anger seemed no longer directed at Anya.

'I spent years trying to forget what those bastards did to her. I moved to New York and thought they'd get what was coming to them eventually, just like Nelson. Only they never suffered. Things just kept getting better and better for them – more money, fame and fans. People idolised them. They were never going to pay for hurting Patsy.' She wiped her nose with the back of her hand. 'So when I got the chance, I gave fate a helping hand.'

Annabelle looked up. 'You know the worst part? Janson didn't even remember my sister's name. Not even when he was choking to death. The bastard and his friends raped her and he couldn't even remember. He deserved what he got.'

'So you killed him,' Anya said softly.

'No, he killed himself. By his own sick games. He even bragged to me about his fetish and asked me to play. For some reason I thought it would be satisfying having him trust me with his life then slowly watch it drain away as he realised who I was. But he blacked out before he could suffer.'

'We know you were in the hotel room with him, and the police will find out about your sister. You had motive and opportunity.'

'He did it to himself. Like I said, you've got nothing.'

'What about Robert Keller?'

Ethan appeared just then, behind Annabelle.

'What can I say? He was a drug user and couldn't resist temptation. At least he remembered Patsy. I wasn't even there when he injected himself. You can't tie me to his death. I'm just a reporter they happen to trust.'

'Actually, that was one of your mistakes,' Ethan cut in. 'Because you weren't there when he injected the drugs, you were unable to take the plastic bag that contained the heroin. We've found a set of prints, and I think when we take your fingerprints, we'll have a match.'

Anya remembered him taking something from Keller's locker and putting it in his pocket. Ethan had quickly grasped the situation.

Reichman remained defiant. 'You can't charge me with anything.'

'Wrong again,' said a new voice. 'Second-degree homicide and supplying illicit drugs are just for starters.' Linda Gatby was accompanied by two police officers.

'Why write those filthy articles blaming the victims, when your own sister had been one?' Anya demanded.

The reporter's eyes flared. 'Those women were never victims. They chose to be with those players and they deserved everything they got. Patsy had *no* choice. They attacked her and she didn't even know what they did to her. Those boys have everything they ever wanted and didn't truly deserve any of it. I wanted to take it from them when they couldn't fight back. Just like they did to my sister.'

They escorted Reichman to the ground's security centre.

'I want Masterton,' she screamed. 'Get Bentley Masterton *now* or I'll tell the police everything.'

Anya moved towards Ethan. 'How did you know about Annabelle Reichman?'

'Linda phoned me on her way here, assuming I knew about what you'd found out about Annabelle. Why didn't you tell me? Do we have a problem with trust?'

'No,' Anya replied quickly. 'It's only now that I fully appreciate how damaged Annabelle is. Her thoughts about the other victims are so twisted. She really meant everything she wrote.'

Suddenly, Ethan had become pale.

'Are you all right?'

He was sweating.

'Can we go back and sit down?' he asked.

Anya put her arm around his waist and helped him to some empty seats nearby.

From the roar of the crowd, they became aware of a commotion on the ground. A stretcher was being carried onto the field.

'Who is it?' Anya asked one of the crowd behind them.

'Liam McKenzie. He got kneed in the head when he was on the ground and he hasn't moved.'

For Pope to allow a stretcher, the injury had to be undeniable. The doctor was beside McKenzie, shaking his head and talking into a handset.

Coach Ingram clutched his head with both hands. The commentator announced they had just received word that McKenzie had suffered what appeared to be a neck injury and was unable to feel his arms or legs. He repeated the words for even more dramatic affect.

Ethan sardonically groaned, 'Oh, no.'

'Do you think Annabelle Reichman had anything to do with what just happened to McKenzie?'

He shook his head. 'I thought about what Lance said about the good guys winning today. At the beginning of the game he got in an altercation with the opposition, words were exchanged, and after that McKenzie started getting some heavy tackles.'

'So?'

'What would make footballers target a single player?'

Anya was puzzled for a moment, then it made sense. 'You think Lance said something to the opposition. You think he told them McKenzie was gay, knowing what they'd do to him on the field. And because Pope kept him playing even with a head injury, he was more at risk.'

'Live by the sword, as they say.'

They left the game and headed back to the hotel.

That evening, news of Alldridge's arrest and McKenzie's quadriplegia filled the news.

47

Anya arrived at Lyle Buffet's penthouse in a deep violet dress she had bought specially for the occasion. Inside, she was greeted with a hug by Lyle and then by the other guest, Linda Gatby.

Ethan sat in a lounge chair, pillow behind his back. She bent over and kissed his cheek before he had a chance to get up. He was still pale but at least Lyle would order him to rest, and maybe he would actually listen.

'Thank you for coming,' Lyle said. 'That's the most colour Catch's had in his cheeks since being in hospital.'

'Who wants to eat?' Lyle showed them to an oak table. The lights of the city sparkled all around. They were served a sumptuous banquet of quail, fish, caviar and Peking duck.

Anya sincerely hoped this wasn't their host announcing his retirement. Instead, he sprang out of his chair to answer the door again as dinner came to an end. Anya and Linda talked about cases, while Ethan's face gave nothing away but a self-satisfied smirk.

As dessert appeared, Bentley Masterton entered the room, accompanied by Kitty Rowe. Anya assumed the best part of the evening was over.

Bentley was obviously taken aback by her presence but, ever the showman, smiled and greeted them all like long-lost friends. Kitty made no attempt to hide her distaste at their presence.

'I thought we were finalising our business,' she said.

'We are,' said Lyle. 'So let's get this over with. The sale of the Bombers.'

Anya glared at Ethan. She didn't feel she should be present but he would not meet her gaze. He seemed to be avoiding it. Linda was clearly nonplussed by events and continued to select morsels of dessert for her plate. 'Don't mind me,' she said, picking up a handmade chocolate truffle.

Anya felt like Alice at the Mad Hatter's tea party.

'We brought contracts,' Bentley said.

Lyle put up his hand. 'No need. I've made a couple of changes.'

Bentley and Kitty shifted in their seats.

'Now, you, Bentley, will hand over your share of the Bombers to me, which will leave Kitty with one-third, for which I am prepared to make her a generous offer.'

The media mogul's mouth opened and Bentley guffawed. 'Hand over? You mean you'll sell to me, you crazy old man. Remember, I'm doing you a favour by buying you out.'

'Yes, of course,' Lyle nodded, 'but I've had an assessment of the club's worth and I'm afraid it's worse than we anticipated.'

'We all know the club's been haemorrhaging money, despite being last year's champions.' Ethan now joined the conversation.

'No wonder with these sex scandals,' Bentley retorted. 'You wouldn't invoke the morals clauses in the contracts, you pay the price.'

'Actually, we have paid a heavy price,' Ethan continued, 'but not for that.'

Linda Gatby wiped her mouth with her napkin. 'Fascinating when you get talking to people, the things you learn. In a global financial crisis, lots of people are suffering. But not everyone.'

'For God's sake, will someone get to the point,' Kitty demanded, gulping half a glass of wine in one mouthful.

Linda clasped her hands together. 'I had a fascinating conversation with Annabelle Reichman, whom I believe you know, Bentley.'

He scratched the side of his neck. 'Of course I know who she is. I've been briefed all about her.'

'She certainly knows you, Bentley. Actually, she claims you ordered Garcia to bash Ethan outside the Vlada club.'

Bentley scoffed, 'That's ridiculous. How would I possibly have known where he was? And I had no reason to.'

Linda was toying with her prey. 'That is true. But you believed you did at the time. You thought Ethan was investigating your financial involvement in the Bombers.'

It looked like Bentley's blood pressure had suddenly plummeted. He was more gaunt than Ethan. As far as Anya was concerned, dinner had just got far more entertaining.

'Do you recommend the torte?' she asked Linda, who reached across to place a piece on Anya's plate.

Lyle seemed to find his appetite at the same time.

'Now, where was I? That's right. Bentley.'

'How can you take the word of an insane criminal over mine? I've never been so insulted.'

'Stick around,' Lyle said. 'You ain't seen nothing yet.' He pulled out a file and Linda passed it on to Ethan.

'These are the financial statements, along with copies of pay slips to club employees like the At Risk Children. Actually, there were no pay slips because the children aren't paid, are they, Bentley?'

That neck seemed to be aggravating him. He wouldn't stop scratching. Kitty remained silent.

'Which was a problem when it came to them doing you favours. The two you asked to plant drugs on Roman Bronstein lacked a work ethic and snorted the stuff themselves. They replaced it with talc and other household powders. Seems they didn't have a lot of faith in your paydays, so took it in kind.'

Anya was thrilled. The head trauma research was back on, and Bentley was open to civil and criminal action. He might even end up funding the research, thanks to his own stupidity.

Annabelle Reichman had downloaded the software onto Anya's phone, but she said someone else owned it. That's how Bentley had found out about Roman Bronstein. He had listened to her conversation with him and Harrison Leske.

The club's financial problems made sense. Bentley had to have been milking money from the club from the moment he had bought into it. His church employees would have paid every invoice submitted without question, and despite charging the club thousands each time the stadium was cleaned, the staff employed by his company would have received a small portion of that amount. The rest he pocketed. That type of fraud was easy if he employed the staff. He was defrauding his own club. The gold nugget ring suddenly seemed even more obscene, Anya thought.

'You should eat something,' Linda said. 'You look a little peaky. I should probably mention that while you've been here, the police have executed search warrants on both of your homes.'

Kitty Rowe stood and left immediately. Bentley followed suit.

Lyle laughed and the mood became infectious.

'How did you find out about Masterton?' Anya wanted to know.

Linda replied, 'Annabelle Reichman wanted the charges dropped. In exchange, she would hand us Bentley. She used his own spyware on his phone as insurance in case anything went wrong. He thought he was using her to spy on Anya.'

Ethan explained further. 'A forensic accountant doublechecked the financial records and confirmed the embezzlement. Explains why the Bombers were losing so much more money than some of the other teams.'

Anya asked what would happen to Reichman. 'She'll be charged with supplying drugs to Keller, but we really can't prove she killed Janson. Negligent homicide is unlikely to stick, and what jury would blame her?'

So Lyle would get his club back and Ethan would be employed by the Bombers again. Plus Linda had a high-profile scalp to her name.

'How's Kirsten Byrne doing?' Anya wanted to know.

'Surprisingly well. She has decided to testify, and Lyle has kindly offered to pay all her legal fees – including the wrongful dismissal case and for any counselling she may need. Now she has choices and it's a good way to empower her after what she went through. I think she'll be okay.'

Anya noticed the old man had turned a deep shade of crimson. In a way, she was sad to leave these people she admired and respected.

Lyle Buffet walked around the table and handed her an envelope. 'This is a bonus for you and your family.'

She opened it. Inside were two first-class tickets to LA for Martin and Ben, and a week at Disneyland followed by a cruise, two cabins included.

'How did you know?'

'The reporter had transcripts of your phone conversations,' Lyle said. 'I took the liberty of giving your son the family holiday he seems to want so much.'

Anya didn't know what to say. Ethan remained silent.

She checked the dates on the tickets. Ben and Martin were already on their way.

48

The next afternoon, Anya headed down to the lobby with her bags. She was still smiling over the email she'd just received from a very different Hannah back in Sydney. In it Hannah had described her new boyfriend from church and how well he treated her. She went on to explain that through the therapy she had undertaken following the rape she had learnt how a man should treat her. Love was a behaviour, not just something spoken. Up until now she'd had no idea what being loved really meant or felt like. She had thanked Anya for bringing out the truth, as it had given her a better life than she otherwise would have had.

Anya felt excited about Hannah's new life, and was reminded again why she had chosen this profession. She had always wanted to help bring closure, and make a positive difference. Emails like this made it all worthwhile.

As she checked out, she noticed Ethan sitting quietly on a nearby lounge chair.

She walked over to him.

'You forgot something,' he said, pulling himself to his feet. He pulled out a tourist brochure and unfolded a map-sized panorama of the observation deck at the top of the Rockefeller Center. On one side was the daylight view; flipping it over showed the night vista.

She smiled. 'Thank you.' She reached over to hug him, careful not to squash his ribs or hurt him. His face was still bruised, but he brushed his cheek against hers and kissed it, lingering for a moment.

'If you come back, I'll think about having that genetic test,' he whispered.

She let go and breathed out. 'How's Lyle doing?'

'He's talking to the league about studies on head injuries. Pope retired this morning and Rosseter's back on the payroll. Seems you made an impression on him too.

'Buffet's decided to settle with Terri Janson and is changing the team line-up. There are a lot of great guys on that team. Good, honest men who deserve to be ambassadors for the game. He's decided to reward them and get rid of the bad apples.'

Anya checked her watch. She had just enough time to get to the airport.

'I have to go.'

'I know.'

'Take care,' she said. 'You know my email.'

'And phone number, address, and tax file number. Do you want me to go on?'

She couldn't help grinning. 'Look after yourself,' she said. 'And keep up the hope.'

He stroked her hair for a moment.

She kissed his cheek and headed for the airport before she changed her mind.